Critical acclaim for Chrissie Manby

'Lots and lots of uncomplicated fun'
Heat

'Manby's novels are made for holidays'
Glamour

'Nothing short of brilliant'
Marie Claire

'This sassy and addictive read will make you laugh – a lot!'
Closer

'Funny and inventive'
Company

'A gloriously delicious read! . . . Packed with warm characters and hilarious situations'
handwrittengirl.com

'Hilarious . . . I loved it. Six stars, hurrah!'
Daily Mail

'I just couldn't put it down'
www.chicklitreviewsandnews.com

'Destined to keep you up until the small hours'
Daily Mirror

Also by Chrissie Manby

About the author

Chrissie Manby is the author of twenty romantic comedy novels and a guide for aspiring writers, *Writing for Love*. She was nominated for the Melissa Nathan Award for Comedy Romance in 2011 for *Getting Over Mr Right*.
Raised in Gloucester, Chrissie now lives in London.

You can follow her on Twitter @chrissiemanby or visit her website to find out more: www.chrissiemanby.com.

a Wedding at Christmas

Chrissie Manby

First published in Great Britain in 2015 by Hodder & Stoughton
An Hachette UK company

3

A CIP catalogue record for this title is available from the British Library

Paperback ISBN 978 1 473 61538 0
Ebook ISBN 978 1 473 61537 3

Typeset in Sabon MT by Palimpsest Book Production Limited, Falkirk, Stirlingshire

Printed and bound by Clays Ltd, St Ives plc

Hodder & Stoughton policy is to use papers that are natural, renewable and recyclable products and made from wood grown in sustainable forests. The logging and manufacturing processes are expected to conform to the environmental regulations of the country of origin.

Hodder & Stoughton Ltd
Carmelite House
50 Victoria Embankment
London EC4Y 0DZ

www.hodder.co.uk

To Astrea Mair Neema Maki-Thomas

THE BENSON

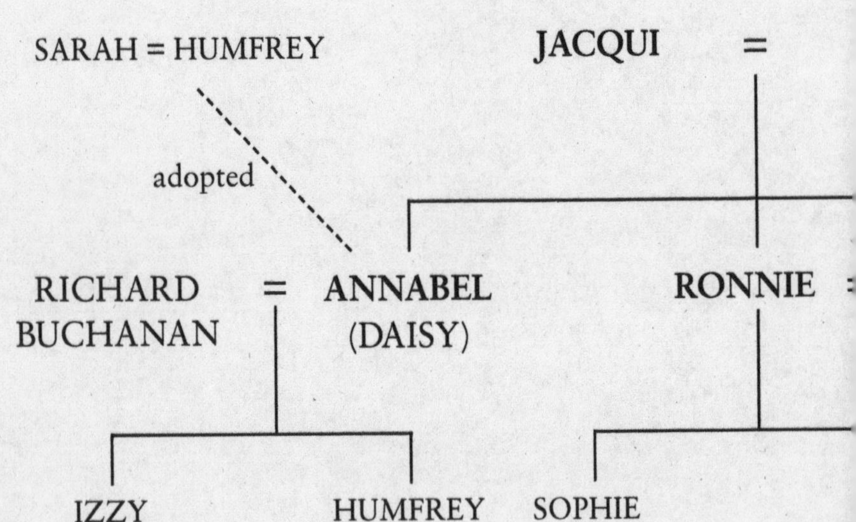

SARAH = HUMFREY
adopted
JACQUI =
RICHARD BUCHANAN = ANNABEL (DAISY)
RONNIE =
IZZY
HUMFREY
SOPHIE

FAMILY TREE

MARK EDWARDS

CHELSEA ----- ADAM BAXTER ≠ CLAIRE (D.)

LILY

JACK

Chapter One

Chelsea

The engagement is announced between Adam, elder son of Mr and Mrs Graham Baxter of Richmond, Surrey, and Chelsea, youngest daughter of Mr and Mrs David Benson of Coventry, West Midlands.

Chelsea Benson smoothed one of the five copies of *The Times* she'd bought that morning out on the kitchen table and read the announcement again. And again. A whole month after Adam's proposal, Chelsea still couldn't quite believe it had happened. To her! To Chelsea Benson! The girl everyone thought would be single for ever (actually, that's not what Chelsea's friends and family thought at all but Chelsea had done a very good job of projecting her own worst insecurities onto them).

Chelsea polished her engagement ring – a simple but deeply tasteful diamond solitaire set in a platinum band – on her jumper and carefully folded the newspaper shut. She looked around the kitchen of the South London home she now shared with Adam and his seven-year-old daughter Lily with a feeling of deep contentment. Pinned to the door of the fridge, by a magnet in the shape of the cruise liner on which they'd taken their summer holiday, was Lily's drawing of their little family-to-be. In the picture, Chelsea's hair was yellow rather than its actual chestnut brown and Adam was slightly cross-eyed and scary-looking, but Chelsea loved it all the same.

The alarm sounded on Chelsea's iPhone. Three o'clock. It was time to think about heading out to do the school run. How the idea of it made Chelsea smile. This was her life now. From perpetually disappointed singleton to yummy mummy wannabe in the space of twelve months. She very much enjoyed rocking up at the primary school gates to wait for Lily to run out. That moment when Lily spotted Chelsea among the waiting adults and beamed at her was always magical. Even the moments when Lily came out of class with a furious frown because she'd been made to do Maths when she wanted to do Art or English were still magical for Chelsea. It was hard to believe it was only just over a year since Lily and Adam had come into her life. In another year's time she would be Adam's wife and Lily's stepmother. For now she was the blissful fiancée.

Lily was one of the first out of school that afternoon. She was bursting with news as she ran across the playground.

'Persephone Harwood Clark's mummy said you and Daddy were in the newspaper!'

'It's true. We were.'

Chelsea explained the engagement announcement. She had been delighted when Adam suggested they put the news out in the old-fashioned way.

'I've told everybody we're having a really big engagement party,' Lily said brightly. 'And then we're going to have a big wedding and you're going to be the most beautiful bride and I'm going to be the most beautiful bridesmaid. And Daddy will wear a suit and I'm going to get a new dress. And I'm going to have a different new dress for the engagement party,' she finished breathlessly. 'Isn't that right?'

'Any excuse for a new dress is all right by me,' said Chelsea.

Lily put her little hand in Chelsea's as they headed for the gate. Having that tiny paw tucked into hers was the loveliest feeling in the whole wide world, thought Chelsea.

Chapter Two

The Benson-Edwards Family

As it happened, Chelsea and Adam had not planned to have an engagement party at all but everyone else in the family was determined to celebrate in style. Chelsea's older sister, Ronnie Benson-Edwards, insisted on having the bash at her house in Coventry. Ronnie's semi wasn't the most glamorous of locations – the kitchen was a work in progress, despite the fact that Ronnie's husband Mark was a professional kitchen fitter – but it was convenient. The party was going to be held over Sunday lunch, which meant that Adam's relatives, who mostly lived in the South East, were easily able to travel up to the West Midlands for the day. It also meant that Chelsea's elderly grandfather, Bill – known to the family as Granddad Bill – would not have to go far at all. Chelsea's mother and father, Jacqui and Dave, could simply bring him round the block in his wheelchair. It was very important to Chelsea and Adam that the eighty-seven-year-old family patriarch be there.

At the other end of the age spectrum, Chelsea's seven-year-old nephew Jack took the party planning very seriously. Chelsea was Jack's favourite aunt and, as far as he was concerned, he knew exactly what she would want.

On the Saturday before the celebration, Jack accompanied his mother to an enormous cash-and-carry on the outskirts of town to help her buy everything a professional party hostess needed. Ronnie had a card for the cash-and-carry courtesy of her boss at the funeral parlour where she worked part time. Her boss bought tea, coffee and paper handkerchiefs there in bulk. That afternoon, Ronnie also bought tea, coffee and paper handkerchiefs in bulk (Granddad Bill might make one of his tear-jerking speeches). She also bought white paper tablecloths embellished in gold with 'Congratulations on your engagement' and paper napkins and laminated cardboard serve-ware to match. She bought fifty plastic champagne goblets, another fifty plastic pint glasses and enough Twiglets and cheesy Wotsits to feed an army.

There were going to be around forty guests. It was the largest gathering Ronnie's house had ever seen but she and Mark had already worked out how everybody was going to be accommodated. If it was warm and sunny – which wasn't a complete impossibility on the last weekend of September – they would have a barbecue and people would sit outside. Easy. Ronnie and Mark would be borrowing deck chairs and foldable picnic tables from everyone on the cul-de-sac where they lived. If it wasn't sunny, they would still have a barbecue – Mark would just have to stand outside with an umbrella while he watched the sausages – but the guests would be seated inside. If they opened the folding doors between the lounge and the dining room, they could get at least twenty deckchairs around the walls. A further ten could squish into the sofa and armchairs. Six on dining chairs. Children on the floor. No problem.

As he trailed behind Ronnie and her loaded shopping trolley Jack asked, 'Is there going to be a special children's table?'

Ronnie told him there probably should be, even though Jack and Lily were the only children likely to sit at it. Jack's cousin Humfrey was too small at less than a year old. His teenage sister Sophie and cousin Izzy, who were best friends as well as cousins, were almost adults.

'Then we should get this,' Jack said, pointing out a *Doctor Who* table set. 'And this.' Another table set. This one had a *Frozen* theme. 'We can do half the table Doctor Who and half the table Elsa.'

'Excellent idea,' said Ronnie. 'Lily will be pleased.'

The ready-made table sets went into the trolley.

'And these?' suggested Jack.

Ronnie allowed him to add two big bags of mini Mars bars to the growing pile of naughty snacks.

'Perhaps we could open one of them tonight,' Jack added casually. 'To give us energy for tomorrow.'

'Oh, all right then,' said Ronnie. 'You've twisted my arm.'

The day of the party dawned bright and sunny. The forecast was looking good. Ronnie was very relieved about that when she saw the state of the deckchairs her neighbour Cathy Next Door had dragged out of her shed. Kind as it was of Cathy to offer her assistance – she was a very good friend – Ronnie wouldn't have wanted those filthy things inside and on her carpet.

Ronnie and her immediate family started preparations at eight in the morning. Sophie vacuumed and Jack dusted. Jack loved to get his hands on the feather duster and Ronnie made the most of his enthusiasm, knowing that within a couple of years, she'd have a very hard time persuading him that housework could be fun.

Ronnie's mother Jacqui and father Dave arrived with Granddad Bill at around nine. Bill was soon parked in front of the television with Fishy the ancient family cat on his lap.

'Fishy's actually older than Granddad Bill in cat years,' Jack liked to point out.

Down in the garden, Dave and Ronnie's husband Mark assembled tables and deckchairs. Sophie and Jack covered the tables with the white and gold paper cloths, using bulldog clips to keep them from flying off if the wind picked up. In the kitchen Jacqui helped Ronnie butter around eighty bread rolls. Sophie joined them and started to cut cheese and pineapple into cubes. Jack assembled the traditional tasty duo on cocktail sticks (without managing to spear himself, for once). Later, Jack impaled more than a hundred cocktail sausages, again without mishap unless you count the five he dropped on the floor.

'Three-second rule!' declared Ronnie, quickly picking them up and blowing off the dust. She popped one into her mouth.

Sophie tipped dozens of bags of crisps into the big bowls Jacqui had brought from her house for the purpose. Jacqui took the plastic seals off three huge bottles of ketchup. Dave and Mark filled an old tin bathtub with ice for the white wine and beer. Cathy Next Door had provided the bathtub. It was amazing what that woman had in her shed.

While the children put out the snack food and folded napkins, Jacqui and Ronnie finally turned their attention to the engagement cake.

It was a triumph, that cake. Jacqui had spent every evening for the past two weeks making tiny pink sugar flowers. She'd taken a day course in sugar-icing sculpture the previous year. Meanwhile Ronnie had made the base – a classic fruitcake – and covered it with plain white royal icing in preparation for Jacqui's floral flourish. With a shaking hand, Jacqui wrote a message of congratulations to her youngest daughter and her future son-in-law in gold sugar gel. She kept having to stop to steady herself. It took a full fifteen minutes to ice just seven words.

'It's beautiful, Mum,' said Ronnie, when the last of the flowers was in place.

'Do you think so?'

'I do. It looks like something you'd get in a shop.'

'It's *really* good, Grandma,' said Sophie. 'I think this is the best cake you've ever made.'

Jacqui made a lot of cakes. Earlier that year she'd made a chocolate sponge decorated to look like a Dalek for Jack. Ronnie's birthday cake was in the shape of a handbag. Jacqui had made a three-layer lemon cake iced with gold stars to celebrate Sophie's impressive GCSE results.

'Auntie Chelsea is going to love it,' Sophie decreed.

'What do you think, Jack?' Jacqui asked her grandson.

'Hmmm. It hasn't got any people on it,' said Jack. 'Isn't it supposed to have people on it?'

'That's for a wedding cake. This is for an engagement,' Jacqui explained.

But she was still persuaded to have two of Jack's treasured *Doctor Who* figurines planted in one of the sugar flowerbeds and everyone agreed they were the perfect finishing touch. One was supposed to be Matt Smith. The other one was a Dalek.

'Ha!' Jack laughed. 'Auntie Chelsea is a Dalek!'

'I'm sure she'll be really pleased with that,' said Sophie.

At half past eleven, the guests of honour, Chelsea, Adam and Lily, pulled up in Ronnie's driveway. Jack raced to open the door to them and, as he did so, three golden helium-filled 'Congratulations' balloons escaped into the Indian summer sky.

The party had begun.

Chapter Three

Everybody

Everyone that Chelsea and Adam loved was going to be at that party. Chelsea's parents, Ronnie's gang and eighty-seven-year-old Granddad Bill were there from the start, of course. Adam's parents were driving up from their home in Richmond. His sister Julie and her family came from Hertfordshire. Adam's little brother Tim travelled from nearby Birmingham, where he was studying Sports Science at the university. Meanwhile, Chelsea's eldest sister Annabel came from her home near Warwick with her husband Richard and children, seventeen-year-old daughter Izzy and Baby Humfrey. Though Annabel was Chelsea's big sister, she had grown up apart from the Benson family, having been given up for adoption as a baby. Only a year and a half had passed since Annabel had tracked down Jacqui and Dave, who were her birth parents, but in that time, she had become an important part of her younger sisters' lives.

There were friends too. Cathy Next Door was there, of course, pointing out which were her deckchairs to anyone who was interested (and to plenty of people who weren't). Ronnie had invited several of her neighbours who had all got to know Chelsea over the years. There was a girl from school that Chelsea hadn't seen in a decade.

Lily loved the children's table, which was, according

to Jack's plan, very much half his and half hers. Ronnie had even gone to the trouble of making some special cakes for the children, who probably wouldn't like the grown-up engagement cake, with its richly fruited base (and dash of brandy). Jack's cakes sported *Doctor Who* pictures on rice-paper discs. Lily's were all about *Frozen*.

'Though I think I'm growing out of *Frozen* now,' Lily confided to Sophie and Izzy, when they joined the smaller children for a while. 'Please don't tell Auntie Ronnie. I don't want her to be upset,' she added as an afterthought.

As the guests arrived, Chelsea and Adam made the rounds, introducing each other to people they had not yet met. Adam already had Cathy Next Door's approval. She offered him an arm wrestle, as she had done at Ronnie and Mark's wedding reception, almost a year earlier.

'I'm afraid I haven't had time to train,' said Adam diplomatically.

'Come on,' said Cathy. 'We'll put a tenner on it. Best of three.'

Chelsea intervened. 'I don't want my fiancé to have a broken wrist when we walk up the aisle.'

'Is Cathy Next Door always so scary?' Adam asked Mark once Cathy was out of the way.

'She was even worse before her sex change,' said Mark.

'She never had a sex change,' Ronnie interrupted. 'Mark Benson-Edwards, stop spreading rumours and put the sausages on.'

While the sausages browned on the barbecue, Mark's generosity with the wine and beer soon had most people nicely relaxed.

Jack and Lily were in charge of taking people's coats

and making sure that Fishy the cat stayed out of the bedroom where they were being stored. Fishy had a penchant for nest building and a keen eye for quality fabric. She'd once made a bed out of Chelsea's one and only Chanel jacket. The last thing Ronnie wanted was for Fishy to get her claws into the real Burberry mac belonging to Adam's sister.

Meanwhile Sophie was in charge of music.

'But none of that emo rubbish,' Ronnie had told her.

'I'll play something from the *olden days* instead,' said Sophie, sticking on the best of Take That.

With everybody taking their roles seriously, the party was going smoothly. However Jacqui could not relax until Adam's parents arrived. She and Dave would be meeting them for the first time and Jacqui had an idea that they would be very grand since their son was so well mannered and had been to a private school. Chelsea had not quelled Jacqui's fears when she described the Baxters' beautiful home near Richmond Park and Ronnie subsequently Googled the street and revealed that there wasn't a house on that road worth less than three million pounds. The Baxters might as well have lived on another planet.

'No curtseying,' Ronnie warned her mother, when Mr and Mrs Baxter's car pulled into the cul-de-sac at last. 'Oh wow!' she continued to tease. 'They've only got a Rolls Royce and a chauffeur!'

Of course Adam's parents did not have a chauffeur or a Rolls Royce but Ronnie's joke helped to distract Jacqui just a little so that she wasn't completely obsequious when she opened the door to them.

'We're so glad to be here,' said Sally Baxter. 'We've heard so much about you all. From Adam and from Lily.'

'It's great to meet you at last,' agreed Graham Baxter, Adam's dad.

Chelsea bounded down the hallway to meet her future in-laws. Sally and Graham's delight at seeing Chelsea was obvious and Jacqui began to relax.

'It's great that you could make it,' Jacqui said to Adam's mum. 'Did you have much traffic?'

'It's always quite heavy coming out of London.' Sally rolled her eyes. 'But we wouldn't have missed this for the world. Can you believe it? Our children are getting wed.'

Sally Baxter took Jacqui's arm and gave her a friendly squeeze.

'So, you and I have got plenty to talk about. Chelsea makes Adam so happy and I can understand why, now I see what a wonderful family brought her up. How kind of her sister to open her home to us all.'

Jacqui beamed with pride. She accompanied the Baxters into the back garden in search of Dave so they could be introduced to him too. They found him by the barbecue and on his third bottle of Spitfire. Just as Jacqui was about to call him over (so that Sally Baxter wouldn't get barbecue smoke on her lovely dress), Dave let out an enormous belch.

Jacqui momentarily wondered if she could pretend that Cathy Next Door's husband was Chelsea's father instead. Cathy was married to a monosyllabic postman called Scott.

But when Dave finally noticed that the honoured guests had arrived, everything went remarkably well. The three bottles of Spitfire had broken through Dave's inhibitions – he was normally quite shy – and he complimented Sally's dress. Then Jack, sent over by Ronnie, brought the Baxters two plastic flutes of champagne without spilling a drop and asked them, 'How do you do?' They were instantly charmed.

'You must be Jack,' said Sally. 'Lily has told us all about you.'

'What did she say?' Jack asked, instantly suspicious.

'I didn't say anything!' Lily announced, coming to reclaim her grandmother. 'This is *my* grandma, Jack.' She wound herself around Sally's legs possessively.

'Well, this is *mine*,' said Jack, claiming Jacqui by putting his own arm around her.

'Yes, but I'm going to be sharing your grandma when Daddy and Chelsea get married.'

Sally and Jacqui shared a smile at their grandchildren's antics. They were going to get along very well indeed.

'The Baxters are lovely people,' Jacqui later confided to Annabel, her eldest. 'I'm very glad that Chelsea's going to have nice in-laws. It's so important. One of the best things about being married to Dave was Bill. Especially when Chelsea and Ronnie were small. I don't know what we would have done without him.'

As the party progressed, Granddad Bill was wheeled out into the garden and parked beneath an awning (also borrowed from Cathy Next Door) for shade. Jack was under strict instructions not to try to make the old man play the Dalek in one of his interminable *Doctor Who* games, though with Lily to show off to, Jack wasn't as determined to bother Granddad Bill as usual.

The weather stayed good. The September sun soon burned the few clouds that had dotted the sky first thing in the morning away. Mark was in his element in charge of the barbecue, though Ronnie would not let him wear his favourite apron, which was decorated with a cartoon of a curvaceous naked female body. She wouldn't even let him wear the apron with the naked torso of Michelangelo's *David* on it either. That was a gift from Cathy Next Door.

'I don't care if it is a classical sculpture, you can't wear a picture of a penis at my sister's engagement party.'

Jack and Lily were very helpful, circulating with bowls of crisps and taking plates of food to some of the older members of the party, who were less able to get up and down. Jack prepared a huge plate of food for Granddad Bill, arranging a sausage and two jammy dodgers to create a smiley face.

'That's proper good, that is,' said Granddad Bill.

'It's you, in food,' Jack explained. 'And here's another bottle of Spitfire from Dad.'

'I've won the bloody lottery,' said Bill.

'Don't say "bloody"!' said Jack, not-so-secretly gleeful at having got away with saying it himself.

At about three o'clock in the afternoon, Jacqui went to find her husband so that he could preside over the official part of the day's proceedings. She hoped Dave wasn't too drunk. They'd discussed the plan several times in the run-up to the party and getting tipsy wouldn't help. Jacqui really didn't want Dave to make a show of the Benson family in front of the Baxters.

Thank goodness, Dave was merely *quite* drunk.

'Jacqui says I've got to make a speech,' he said, standing up and swaying a little with a bottle of Spitfire still in his hand.

Chelsea covered her eyes in comedy horror.

'I thought I wouldn't have to do anything until the wedding reception but what *her indoors* says goes. You need to remember that from now on, Adam. Don't try and argue with a Benson woman. It just isn't worth it.'

'Dave,' Jacqui sighed. 'You're showing me up.'

'Sorry, my darling. Anyway, I haven't prepared anything and, as you all know, I'm a man of few words, so this is going to be short. Chelsea . . .' Dave raised his glass towards his youngest daughter. 'I remember the day you were born. The football was on the telly. I wanted to call you Coventry City FC.'

Everybody laughed.

'But your mother got her way, as usual, though I've never lived it down with my mates at the pub.'

There were a few jeers from the back. Chelsea had not been named for the football team. Jacqui had just liked the sound of the word.

Dave continued. 'Chelsea, you were a beautiful baby and you've grown into a beautiful woman. Not just beautiful but loving and kind. And very successful too. We don't tell you often enough how proud we were when you went to university to learn how to speak French and how proud you've continued to make us since. We're not in the least bit surprised that Adam wants to marry you. You're a girl of many qualities. Though she can't cook, mate.' Dave addressed his future son-in-law directly. 'But you probably know that by now.'

Another wave of laughter rippled around the garden.

'Anyway, I could go on but then I'd have nothing left to say next September, on your real big day. So I'm just going to ask you all to raise your glasses in a toast to Chelsea and Adam. Adam and Chelsea! Congratulations to you both.'

'Congratulations!' Jack and Lily shouted loudest as they clinked their glasses of Coke together.

'Hip hip hooray!' cried Annabel.

'And now I think it's time for the cake,' said Dave.

'Mmmm, cake,' said Jack, doing his best impression of Homer Simpson for Lily's amusement.

There were gasps of admiration as the cake was brought out of its hiding place in the shed. It had been put in there so that Chelsea and Adam wouldn't see it and Fishy the cat wouldn't sit on it.

'I put Doctor Who on there!' said Jack to anybody who would listen. 'And the Dalek. The Dalek is Auntie Chelsea.'

'That's beautiful,' said Sally Baxter to Jacqui. 'You've really got a talent for cake-making.'

Jacqui was pleased. 'Thank you but Ronnie baked the actual cake. It's a fruitcake. I'm no good at them. I just did the icing and the flowers.'

'Whoever did what, it's amazing,' said Sally. 'I would never have the patience for all that sugar art.'

Ronnie placed the cake in the middle of the buffet table and stood back so that photographs could be taken.

'Will you put that picture on Facebook, Sophie?' she asked as her daughter took a snap.

'Everything's got to be on Facebook these days,' said Cathy Next Door to Annabel's husband Richard. 'Personally, I stay off it. I don't want everyone knowing what I'm doing all day and all night. It's a government plot and people are sleepwalking into it. They're gathering information on us all the time and one day they're going to use it against us.'

'I expect they are,' said Richard amiably.

'That's why I'm keeping my sunglasses on today. Everyone's taking photographs and I don't want to be identifiable when they go online.'

'Bloody good idea,' Richard nodded. 'They'll have some sort of recognition system that can work out exactly where we're standing, using the garden foliage to pinpoint the terrain. They could have a sniper here in half an hour. Assuming they haven't already been following you since breakfast.'

Cathy Next Door looked at Richard askance, as though she guessed he might not be entirely serious. That was confirmed when Richard went ahead and took pictures of the cake and the party guests that Annabel would later load to her Facebook account and share with Ronnie and Jacqui.

Once Facebook had been satisfied, Adam and Chelsea stepped forward to do their bit. They posed for more photographs, then Ronnie handed them a cake slice. It was a new knife, which she had bought specially for the occasion. Silver-plated with a fake ivory handle.

'Thank you, Mum and Ronnie,' Chelsea said. 'This cake is so beautiful.'

'It seems a shame to cut it,' Adam agreed.

'But you must!' said Jacqui. 'We all want to taste it!'

Jack and Lily squabbled over the first slice. In the end, Chelsea cut the slice in two and stuck Doctor Who on one bit and the Dalek on the other. No prizes for guessing who had the Doctor. And in any case, both children quickly discovered that Ronnie was right. Neither one of them really liked fruitcake. They merely picked at the icing. The adults, however, all agreed that the cake tasted even better than it looked. Jacqui was delighted.

Chapter Four

Granddad Bill

It was a wonderful day. The only thing missing – the only thing that stopped the engagement party from being a quintessential Benson family occasion – was that Granddad Bill didn't try to sing / belch a tribute to his granddaughter and her fiancé. The party was so busy and so much fun that the lack of singing went pretty much unnoticed but later everyone would say that, of course, it was the first sign. Of course they should have been worried that Bill merely sat on a corner of the patio, nursing one bottle of Spitfire all afternoon, and not even touching the sausages that were his favourite food. Yes, in retrospect, there was obviously something awry. How had they failed to notice?

At around five o'clock, Ronnie was in the kitchen, putting the kettle on for the twentieth time that afternoon when Jacqui took her by the arm and pulled her into the hallway for a private conversation.

'Ronnie.'

'What's wrong, Mum?' She could tell from Jacqui's face that it wasn't good news.

'Will you keep everybody outside for a while, love? It's Granddad Bill.'

Bill had been brought indoors about an hour earlier after announcing that he was too hot, even under Cathy Next Door's tattered old awning.

'What's wrong with him?' Ronnie asked.

'We don't know. He's having a bit of a turn. We've called the ambulance. They'll be here any minute. But you're not to worry. Your dad and I have got it all under control. We mustn't let this spoil Chelsea's party. You know Bill wouldn't want that. You just go back out into the garden and carry on as though nothing has happened.'

But there was no chance that Bill's sudden turn wouldn't spoil Chelsea's party now that Ronnie knew about it. Ronnie never was the calmest of people under pressure and upon hearing the news that an ambulance had been called, she instantly freaked out. Jack, who had the ears of a bat when it came to anything that might be described as excitement – good or bad – was soon in the hallway too. Lily followed him. Seeing Ronnie in a state, the two children panicked. Jacqui's attempt to broker Bill's quiet exit from the party had completely failed.

Ronnie insisted on seeing her grandfather. Bill was slumped in his chair. Dave was trying to persuade him to take a sip of water. Ronnie threw herself onto her knees in front of the old man and took his hands.

'Don't go, Granddad Bill. Don't go! Not now!'

'Ronnie, love. Give him some space,' Jacqui pleaded. 'He's too hot.' But Ronnie stayed with her head on the old man's knees, crying and begging him to stay.

'He isn't going anywhere,' Jacqui insisted. 'Ronnie, please.'

Chelsea joined her sister, mother and father at Bill's side. 'Granddad.' Chelsea took his hand. 'Stay with us.'

The ambulance, thankfully, did come quickly and the paramedics worked so calmly, that everyone else (except Ronnie) remained relatively calm as well. Blood pressure and vital signs were taken. One of the paramedics assured Jacqui and Dave that Bill was going to make it but that they would take him to the hospital just in case. Jacqui and Dave followed close behind in their car. Dave was much too drunk to drive but Jacqui had stayed off the alcohol all day because she wanted to impress Sally Baxter. Impressing Sally Baxter was the least of Jacqui's worries now.

Of course the atmosphere at the party changed after that. Even Annabel's bon viveur husband Richard turned down a beer in favour of a cup of tea. Adam's family wished Chelsea's grandfather a swift recovery, then set off towards their respective homes. Annabel and her family remained for a little while. They sat in the garden, making stilted small talk while they waited for news from A and E.

When Jacqui called to say that Granddad Bill was stable but would be staying on a ward for the night, everybody heaved a sigh of relief. Anything else would have been too awful. A terrible omen for poor Chelsea's upcoming marriage.

'Well,' said Richard, accepting the beer he had been refusing for the past two hours. 'That's great news. Let's have a toast. To Granddad Bill.'

'Granddad Bill,' the last of the party guests mumbled.

'And, of course, to Chelsea and Adam. Congratulations to you both. Marriage is a wonderful thing. It certainly changed my life for the better.'

'Good job you said that,' said Annabel, giving her husband a poke.

Adam wrapped his arm around Chelsea and pulled

her close. Chelsea smiled weakly. Everyone knew that her grandfather's sudden illness had taken the shine off the day. Still, she tipped her glass back towards Richard.

'Thank you,' she said. 'Thank you all for coming. This has been a lovely party.'

Chapter Five

Chelsea

Chelsea was supposed to be travelling back to London with Adam and Lily that night. They weren't planning to stay in the Midlands because Lily had to go to school the following morning and Adam had to go to work. However, after Granddad Bill was taken to hospital, Chelsea decided she ought to stay. Adam didn't argue with her decision. They both knew the unspoken reasoning behind it. Granddad Bill was eighty-seven. He suffered from dementia. He'd had a pacemaker for twenty-odd years. Every birthday Bill celebrated felt as though it might be the last. Though Jacqui had said otherwise on the phone, maybe this was serious. Maybe Granddad Bill would not come home from hospital after all.

So, Adam and Lily bade everyone goodbye and Chelsea stayed behind at Ronnie's. Once all the guests were gone, the party-related rubbish was quickly cleared away. One great thing about Ronnie's decision to buy paper plates was that tidying up meant simply tipping everything into bin bags instead of endless washing up. Sophie and Jack were brilliant. They both did all they could to help before Jack's bedtime. Sophie also offered to read Jack's story that night and, for once, Jack didn't protest. He was very good at understanding when something serious was going on. He knew this was not the time to push his luck with his usual request for 'another ten minutes' playing Minecraft or watching TV.

Ronnie and Chelsea ended up in the kitchen, which was where the family always seemed to convene at moments of crisis. Perhaps it was the proximity to the kettle that made it the perfect place to discuss weighty matters. The kettle had certainly seen plenty of use that day. Tea is the English answer to everything.

That evening, Ronnie and Chelsea sipped tea in silence. When Mark came back from returning Cathy Next Door's deckchairs and awning, he went straight to the fridge and found a stray bottle of Spitfire.

'Cathy Next Door says she wants you to text as soon as you get any more news about Bill,' Mark told his wife.

'We won't hear anything more tonight,' said Ronnie. 'Not now he's on the ward for the night. Not unless it's bad news.'

Ronnie's face crumpled. Mark stood behind her and wrapped his arms around her shoulders.

'He'll be all right,' he said. 'Granddad Bill lived through the Blitz. He fought on the beaches. He lived through raising you lot. He's not going to fade away overnight in a hospital ward.'

'But he will die, won't he?' said Ronnie. 'One day. And I can't help thinking it's not that far off now. He's not half so lively as he used to be. He's really gone downhill since the start of the summer.'

'No he hasn't,' said Mark.

'He has, Mark. There's no point denying it. He just sits there. He doesn't even watch TV like he used to. He hasn't belched "Stand By Me" in months.'

'That's a good thing, isn't it?' Mark tried.

'You know it isn't. It's a sign he's given up.'

Chelsea took a shuddering breath, which sounded like it might precede a sob. 'Don't say that,' she begged her sister.

'But it's true, Chels. We can't deny it any longer. He's on a downhill run.'

'Ronnie,' said Mark. 'Let's not talk about it tonight. There's nothing we can do from here. He's in hospital, which is the best place for him. And today is supposed to be a happy day. We're celebrating Chelsea's engagement.'

'Thanks, Mark,' said Chelsea. 'It was a lovely party. Even with the way things went at the end. Adam and Lily had a great time. We're all really grateful you made so much effort.'

'Do you have to wait so long to get married?' Ronnie suddenly asked. 'I mean, a whole year? Will it really take you that long to get organised? Couldn't you do it more quickly than that?'

Chelsea knew at once what Ronnie was getting at. She was trying to say that Granddad Bill might not make it through another twelve months.

'I don't know,' said Chelsea cautiously. 'It's not just my decision. I'd have to ask Adam.'

'He won't mind. I mean, he wants to marry you, doesn't he? He's not going to care whether it's in a year's time or next Wednesday morning. But it just wouldn't be the same if Granddad Bill wasn't there to see it happen.'

'We can't get married next Wednesday!' said Chelsea, eyes wide with panic.

'No. But if you really put your mind to it,' said Ronnie, 'you could be married by Christmas.'

Chapter Six

Bill and Chelsea

Granddad Bill spent just one night in hospital. After several tests, the medical staff decided that what he had suffered was nothing more than a faint. Probably brought on by the excitement of the party, the late summer heat and that bottle of Spitfire. From now on, said the doctor in charge of the ward, Granddad Bill must not be allowed booze. He had to take things easy. Jacqui and Dave promised Bill would not be allowed to deviate from the doctor's instructions at all. They were keen to get him home and into his own bed. As far as Jacqui was concerned, there is no worse place to be when you're ill than in a hospital.

'It's impossible to get any sleep on those wards,' she told Chelsea and Ronnie when she dropped by the house to pick up the serve-ware she'd brought over for the party. 'All those monitors beeping. All the old people groaning and moaning all night long.'

'And Granddad Bill belching his way through his songs,' said Ronnie.

'I wish he were,' said Jacqui. 'He's not himself at all.'

'See?' Ronnie mouthed at Chelsea over their mother's head. 'He's gone downhill.'

* * *

Chelsea went over to Jacqui and Dave's to see her grandfather before heading back to London. Jacqui was right that he wasn't himself. He spent much of Chelsea's visit staring into space. He didn't even look at the carefully drawn 'Get Well Soon' card Jack had insisted Chelsea take with her. Naturally, it featured a Dalek. This one was carrying a thermometer and wearing a hat with a red cross on the front.

It was awful to see Bill laid so low. It was much better when he was belching. It was even slightly better when he was talking about the Second World War. Or imagining he was fighting it all over again. It was difficult to cope with Bill's dementia, but this strange emptiness was new. It was almost as though his spirit had already gone. Only his body was left.

Chelsea could only hope her mum was right when she insisted that Bill would start to be more himself again now that he was home. He was just tired after his restless night in hospital, was what Jacqui said. Soon he would be up and belching with the best of them.

'OK, Granddad. I'll be up to see you again in a couple of weeks.' Chelsea kissed him on the cheek. He half-turned towards her but didn't look at her. He didn't seem to be seeing anything at all. Could he even hear her? 'I love you,' she added, just in case. As Adam always said, you can never tell someone you love them too often.

Then she went into the kitchen to say 'goodbye' to her mum. Dave was going to drive Chelsea to the station where she would catch a train back to London.

'Ronnie said she'd had a word with you,' said Jacqui.

'About what?' Chelsea was distracted by the sad state in which she'd found her grandfather.

'About the wedding. About maybe bringing it forward.'

'Oh, yes,' said Chelsea. 'She did.'

'I know it's not what you and Adam had planned . . .'

'We haven't really planned anything yet, Mum. We just picked an arbitrary date next year because that's the first thing people want to know after they've seen the ring.'

'Well . . .'

'I'm going to ask him,' Chelsea said. 'As soon as I get back to London. If Adam is happy to bring the wedding forward, then I certainly am. I don't see why we couldn't.'

Jacqui gave her youngest daughter a hug.

'Oh, you are good, Chelsea. I know it's not for us to influence you and Adam over such a big decision. I just want your Granddad to be there. He always worried about you, you know. He wanted to see you settled. Even if he doesn't really know what's going on any more, I like to think he'd feel better for having seen you get married. He's always loved you so much. You and Ronnie. And Annabel too.'

Chelsea felt tears springing to her eyes.

'He will see me get married, Mum. He will. Granddad Bill's not going anywhere.'

'Someone has to burp "Here Comes the Bride",' said Dave. 'Come on, Chelsea. There're roadworks near the station. You don't want to miss your train.'

A Christmas wedding.

The more Chelsea thought about it on the train back to London, the more she liked the idea. The choice of a September date twelve months hence had, as she'd assured Jacqui, really been quite arbitrary. A year just felt like the usual amount of time people took between getting engaged and getting married. Everyone seemed to understand and approve when Adam and Chelsea told them their engagement would last a year. But Ronnie was right. There was no real reason why they had to take twelve months. Chelsea and Adam were not teenagers who might need that long to really get to know each other and change their minds. Neither was Chelsea going to be a bridezilla who would need months and months to bring her complicated Pinterest boards to fruition. A December wedding was totally doable. Christmas was still twelve weeks away.

And there was no doubt it was a very romantic time of year. When she was back at the house she shared with Adam and Lily in South London, before Lily finished school and Adam came home from work, Chelsea spent a bit of time Googling 'Christmas wedding'. It opened up a whole new aesthetic. New flowers. New themes. New colours. As it was, Chelsea had always secretly felt she looked her best in the winter. She didn't have the sort of skin that went golden brown in the sunshine. She was always at the 'milk bottle' end of the spectrum, even with fake tan. A winter wedding dress would certainly suit her. She looked at a photograph of a bride in a white dress accessorised with a red velvet cape. Her bridesmaids were all dressed in red velvet too. Lily would definitely like that. Lily loved a bit of velvet and red was her favourite colour after pink.

By the time she went to pick Lily up from school, Chelsea was convinced that a winter wedding could work. All that remained was to persuade Adam to speed up their nuptial timetable. She decided she would talk to him that very evening, once Lily was in bed.

Chapter Seven

Chelsea and Adam

Lily took a long time to go to bed that night. She was full of news from school that she needed to discuss at great length. That morning, Lily's form teacher had announced that over the next few days she would be casting the class's nativity play.

'I want to be Mary,' said Lily.

Of course she did. Adam and Chelsea shared a look. Doubtless every other girl in Lily's class wanted to play Mary too and, like Lily, they all thought they deserved the starring role.

'There are other really good parts though,' said Chelsea, aiming to shore Lily up against disappointment. 'There are angels and kings and shepherds. Even the sheep are important. When I was at school, our class did a nativity play where I was the little Irish girl.'

Adam frowned in confusion.

'There was a little Irish girl at the nativity?' he asked.

'And a French girl and a Japanese girl and a girl from Germany. Apparently.' Chelsea smiled.

Adam raised an eyebrow.

Lily merely asked, 'What was your costume?'

'I had a green skirt and a white blouse and I carried a shamrock.'

'What's that?'

'It's the national emblem of Ireland. It's like clover.

A green plant with three leaves that are shaped like hearts.'

'Can you draw me one?' Lily asked. She fetched a piece of paper and a green felt-tip pen that had long since dried out.

Chelsea scratched out a shamrock. 'It's easy. Three hearts joined at the stem, see?'

'Yes,' said Lily. 'One for you, one for Daddy and one for me.' Lily took the pen from Chelsea and wrote 'C', 'D' and 'L' inside the heart shapes.

Three hearts. When Chelsea cleared the table that night, she carefully folded the piece of paper with the shamrock drawn upon it into her pocket. She would keep it for ever.

'Why did you play an Irish girl?' Adam asked, as they were washing up. 'That's a bit random. You're not Irish.'

'Actually, my great-great-grandfather was,' Chelsea informed him. 'And we couldn't all play girls from the West Midlands.'

'You should have been an angel,' said Adam.

Chelsea leaned across and gave him a kiss on the cheek.

'Urgh. Kissing!' said Lily, who had picked up her new horror of public displays of affection from her soon-to-be cousin Jack, who thought kissing was on a par with weeing in the street. She hid her eyes from the sight.

Lily was eventually persuaded that it was time for bed. She did her usual trick of calling out to Chelsea as she went back downstairs, asking increasingly random questions, just to get her to linger a little longer. However once Chelsea forced herself to say 'goodnight, Lily' to yet another question about shamrocks, the little girl settled down. She was out for the count when Chelsea popped her head around the door for a final check three minutes later.

Alone at last, Adam and Chelsea snuggled up together on the sofa and Chelsea chose that moment to bring up the question of moving the wedding forward. She had expected at least a little resistance but, in the end, there was none. When he heard about the conversations Chelsea had had with her mother and her middle sister since Granddad Bill's 'turn' at the engagement party, he sympathised entirely.

'Of course,' he said. 'I understand you want Bill to be there. He's your grandfather and you love him. We all love him. It really wouldn't be the same without him. And a Christmas wedding would be great. Very romantic.'

'Do you really think so?'

'I do. Absolutely.'

'And you don't think it will leave us too little time to get the whole thing organised?' Chelsea pressed.

'What's to organise? We're taking twenty people to Nando's, right? I'll bet they don't even need a reservation.'

Chelsea gave Adam a dig in the ribs.

'I'm joking,' he said. 'I don't see why it should be much more difficult than taking a year though. Let's do it.'

'I bet if we do bring the wedding forward for Granddad Bill, he'll live another ten years,' said Chelsea.

'Let's hope so,' said Adam. He gave her a squeeze. She needed it. Even though Bill had 'had a good innings' as the saying went, Chelsea was absolutely not ready to say goodbye. When is there ever a right moment to say farewell to someone you love? Her eyes welled at the thought of it but Adam soon kissed away her tears. He knew how to console her. That was one of the reasons why she loved him.

When she was sure that she wouldn't cry again, Chelsea called Jacqui and Ronnie to tell them the news. They were both delighted.

'Chelsea,' said Ronnie, 'you are a star. Mum's been worrying all day that we did the wrong thing by asking you to bring the wedding forward. She thought Adam would freak out. I knew he wouldn't. And it's going to be brilliant. A Christmas wedding. You might even get snow!'

'I'll go to the registry office tomorrow,' said Chelsea to Adam as they climbed into bed. 'Fingers crossed they'll have a spot for us.'

'Wow,' said Adam. 'We're going to be married by the end of the year.'

Chelsea very much liked the sound of that.

Chapter Eight

Chelsea

Married by the end of the year. Every time Chelsea thought about it, she felt a little flutter of delight and was compelled to look at her engagement ring – still so shiny and bright and perfect – the proof of Adam's promise.

Despite having decided to bring the wedding forward for fairly unhappy reasons, Chelsea did not mind the idea of a winter wedding at all. It wasn't hard to imagine how romantic it could be. And one advantage of a Christmas wedding was that the whole country would be decorated and ready to celebrate with them.

Adam and Chelsea decided to aim for the last Saturday before Christmas at the Marylebone Registry Office. They'd follow that with a party at Valentino's, a swanky Italian restaurant in London's Soho, which was where they had celebrated both their birthdays and the anniversary of their first meeting. Valentino's had become their special place. They'd make it a sit-down lunch. They probably wouldn't have an evening do. That close to Christmas, people would almost certainly have other plans. They could arrange dinner somewhere else for the immediate family though.

Chelsea was determined not to be a bridezilla, but once she started thinking about it, she discovered she had some very firm ideas about how her wedding should be and there were so many people she wanted to invite!

For the first time in a long time, Chelsea was glad to log on to Facebook. Usually spending time on social media left Chelsea feeling as sick as if she'd eaten a dozen Krispy Kremes. Everyone seemed to be having a better time than she was. But at last Chelsea had some excellent news of her own. After she posted a photograph of the newspaper containing the engagement announcement, her 'friends' went wild with their 'likes' and their messages of congratulation. People she hadn't seen or spoken to in years commented on her very happy status.

Even Colin Webster, the last man she'd dated before meeting Adam, sent her a private message asking 'who's the lucky man?' When she saw Colin's name in her inbox, Chelsea was gratified that for the first time since the fateful day she met him, her heart did *not* skip a beat. She responded to Colin's message with a short, chatty reply that ended 'I hope all's well with you.' And she meant it. In her blissed-out state, Chelsea genuinely wanted everyone to be happy. Even the rat-bag who had two-timed her and left her for a twenty-one-year-old heiress. She was feeling *that* magnanimous. Funny what love can do.

Right after she wrote to Colin, Chelsea began to pull together a guest list. Her ex wasn't on it, of course, but it was surprising how quickly it grew. Chelsea's family was quite large for a start. With both her sisters and their families, the number of immediate family members on Chelsea's side was eleven. That was before she even thought about cousins. Then there were her friends. She wanted to invite several of her former colleagues from

Society, the magazine where she had worked until it folded at the end of the summer. She was still in touch with some of the girls she'd been to school with. She had a handful of close girlfriends from university. By the time she'd written down all their names, that was another twenty. And they would need to bring other halves. As Chelsea had observed ruefully over recent years, she was the last of her mates to find love. And some of them had children. Should she and Adam have children at the wedding? Of course Lily and Jack would be there. And Baby Humfrey too (though he was still tiny and wouldn't really need to be catered for. Annabel would bring his lunch). Should they extend the invitation to the other guests' kids? Quickly scribbling down only those names she could remember, it wasn't long before she had another fifteen. There were bound to be at least five she'd forgotten.

Chelsea's guest-list soon skirted the hundred mark and she hadn't even started on Adam's side.

The funny thing was, as she wrote out her list, Chelsea realised that she actually wanted a big wedding. She wanted *loads* of people to witness the moment when she and Adam promised themselves to each other. It felt important to make their marriage a really big occasion. If she could broadcast her love for Adam to the whole world, then she would.

Adam's eyes almost popped out of his head when he saw the list his fiancée had compiled that afternoon. He quickly recovered himself however and smiled and nodded as Chelsea told him what else she'd been up to.

'I called the restaurant. They can close the whole

place for a private function so this many guests would be possible. If you don't think it's too much.'

'I want you to have whatever you want,' said Adam. 'This is your special day.'

'And yours too,' she reminded him. 'It's got to reflect the pair of us.'

'That's why we're having it at Valentino's. If only I'd taken you to Nando's for your birthday instead.'

Chelsea grinned and pushed Adam down into the cushions of the sofa so that she could kiss him all over.

'Kissing!' Lily shrieked with horror, when she came in to watch television and caught her dad and Chelsea canoodling. '*Again*! There is no escape.'

She fell to the floor in a dramatic fake faint. Another trick she'd learned from Jack Benson-Edwards.

Chapter Nine

Adam and Chelsea

On Sunday morning, Adam got a text while they were eating breakfast. Chelsea heard the ping of notification and, like Pavlov's dog, immediately turned to see what was going on. In a split second, Adam's face betrayed a couple of emotions. First: curiosity about who might be texting. He didn't get many texts except from Chelsea. Then something approaching worry. But he had rearranged his face into something more neutral by the time he told her:

'Claire's parents have said they would like us to have lunch with them.'

It had to happen. There was no way Chelsea could become Lily's official stepmother without meeting the parents of Adam's first wife, Claire, who had died of an aneurysm when Lily was just a few months old. Of course Claire's parents wanted to know who was going to be stepping into their dead daughter's shoes and taking over Lily's care. They had every right to know.

'Great,' Chelsea said when Adam told her about the invitation. 'Wonderful. Where shall we meet them?'

'At their house,' said Adam. 'I think that's the idea.'

'Right.'

'Claire's mum Frances is a wonderful cook.'

Chelsea nodded but her smile faltered. It wasn't what she had hoped for when she imagined her first meeting with Claire's family. Somehow, she thought that meeting on neutral ground might make it easier. But instead they would be going to the house in which Claire had grown up. The beautiful country house with the huge garden where Claire and Adam had held their own wedding reception for two hundred guests in an enormous marquee. A house that would be full of memories. Full of ghosts.

Adam immediately sensed Chelsea's unease.

'It will be fine,' he said. 'Really. Frances and Brian are nice people. And I know that they'll like you very much.'

Why would they? Chelsea wanted to ask.

'OK,' she said instead. 'Tell them I'm looking forward to it.'

Chelsea found it hard to fall asleep that night. For the past six weeks – since Adam proposed – she had been floating on a cloud of engagement bliss. Everything seemed easier and happier than before now that she and Adam were committed to a future together. But this invitation from Claire's parents reminded her that her marriage to Adam would not exist in isolation. It couldn't. It would always exist in the context of his first marriage to the woman who was Lily's mother.

How could Claire's parents possibly decide to like Chelsea given everything they'd lost?

Since Adam first told Chelsea about his dead love, Chelsea had tried not to think too much about her. Of course, there was no way that Claire could be air-brushed from the picture that was Adam's life but if Chelsea didn't have to think about her, she did her best not to.

It was hard however. Claire's photograph was still in pretty much every room of the house. Chelsea knew it wasn't appropriate to ask Adam to take the pictures down, but she would be lying if she said she didn't wish there weren't quite so many. There were wedding photographs on the bookshelves in the living room. There was a photograph of Claire holding newborn Lily on the mantelpiece in the dining room. There was another pic taken on the same day pinned to one of those padded notice boards in the kitchen. Sometimes it felt as if Claire was everywhere Chelsea looked. Beautiful Claire. Blonde and blue-eyed and slim and always smiling. Even when she'd just given birth, Claire managed to look photo-shoot ready. She made the Duchess of Cambridge look like a post-natal slacker.

That was Claire's trump card. Played long before Chelsea even laid eyes on Adam Baxter. Claire had captured Adam's heart *and* she had given him a daughter. A daughter whom everyone agreed was the very blonde blue-eyed image of her mother. Lily Rose.

Lily didn't talk about her mum very often. She was just a tiny baby when Claire died and her memories of the woman who had given birth to her seemed to be hazy. Though Chelsea knew that probably wasn't the whole truth. She believed that babies understood a great deal more than people gave them credit for. Take Annabel's younger child, Humfrey, for example. At just ten months old, he definitely recognised people he only saw from time to time. And it seemed he already had a fine sense of humour. There was definitely a hint of triumphant amusement in his face when he peed directly up in the air while Chelsea was changing his nappy.

What did Lily remember? Was she conscious of the magnitude of what she had lost? How had her experiences shaped her since? Chelsea wished she knew.

Lily was certainly a feisty little girl. Though she was fond of pink and fancied herself a princess (she was determined that one day she would marry Prince George, even if he would be a younger man), Lily could also hold her own with the boys. She ran circles around Jack. If they were up to something they shouldn't be, it was usually at Lily's instigation. She was confident and never afraid to state her opinion.

Chelsea remembered how Lily had been when they first met on the flight to Lanzarote. Adam and Lily were the last onto the plane that morning. When Lily found Chelsea sitting in the window seat, she had thrown a wobbly worthy of a fashion magazine editor discovering someone had usurped her in the front row. Finding out that Lily and Adam were staying in the same hotel had not exactly filled Chelsea with joy, but thanks to Jack whose insistence that Chelsea took him to the Kidz Klub kept putting her in Adam's orbit, a romance had blossomed. It was perhaps cemented when Adam rescued Sophie after the teenager, drunk on vodka, fell into the sea and almost drowned.

Back in London, as Adam and Chelsea's holiday romance became something more substantial, Lily had continued to be prickly and difficult for quite a while. When she thought about it properly, Chelsea put that down to self-defence. Lily was subconsciously trying to keep her dad's new girlfriend at a distance until she knew she could be trusted. She had grown a hard shell to protect herself.

Now, their relationship was very different. There was a moment – Chelsea thought she remembered it – when Lily finally started to believe that Chelsea was going to stick around. That was when she began to ask her to read to her at bedtime. It was when she started to give

Chelsea a kiss upon greeting her or saying goodbye. Now she was just as likely to run to Chelsea as Adam when she needed a comforting hug after falling over.

Lily could be stroppy. She could be selfish. Without siblings, she'd never had to share, after all. But she could also be deeply insightful. And funny. And kind. And so very, very lovable. She was a wonderful little girl and it was a privilege to be able to spend so much time with her. It was ridiculous of Chelsea to be jealous of Claire when Chelsea was the one who was getting to see Lily grow up. Claire's death had given Chelsea two wonderful gifts. Her husband and her daughter. A ready-made family. Claire's parents were part of that family too.

The day after Adam received the invitation to lunch, Chelsea ran a duster along the bookshelves in the living room. She picked up the wedding portrait of Adam and Claire and carefully buffed a smudge from the silver frame. She looked into Claire's eyes.

'What are you thinking?' she asked. 'Would you and I have been friends? Are you going to let me love Adam and Lily for the rest of my life? Because I will,' she said. 'I promise I will love them for ever.'

Chapter Ten

Adam and Chelsea

The following Friday, Chelsea spent a lovely day thinking about her upcoming nuptials. After dropping Lily off at school, she went into central London to visit a couple of wedding dress shops. It was a real thrill to feel she had the right to be in those places. When she walked in, she could proudly tell the assistants her wedding date at last. She felt as though she had finally been admitted to a very exclusive private club.

Chelsea didn't try anything on though. She had promised she would save that for a day later in the month when her mother and Ronnie could be there too. She merely browsed the rails, letting her fingers flutter over silks and chiffons and velvets. She felt like a small girl again. But this time she was allowed to have whatever she wanted.

She found one dress that she particularly fancied. The price tag announced that it cost three thousand pounds. Used as she was to the cost of high fashion, even Chelsea thought that was possibly a little bit out of her league. But maybe two thousand pounds wasn't. After all, she was only going to do the whole getting-married thing once and she would be the centre of attention. There would be photographs that would be around for years.

Over lunch, Chelsea got out her laptop and went

through her finances. She'd received a pretty generous pay-off when the magazine folded. Thanks to the contacts she'd built up over the years, she'd been able to get some good freelance work since. Just that week, she'd been commissioned to write two articles that would cover the minimum she needed for day-to-day expenses that month.

Unlike lots of brides, Chelsea would not be asking her parents for a contribution. She knew they didn't have it to spare. But with Adam's job as an architect and assuming she continued to get freelance work at the rate she had been, they could afford something a little bit special for their wedding day. The dress had to be the most special thing of all. However, Chelsea was counting her blessings *and* her chickens. Everything was about to change.

When Adam got in from work that night, he had a hug for Lily and for Chelsea as usual. He listened to Lily's long-winded explanation about something that had happened at school and smiled and laughed in all the right places. But Chelsea could tell that something wasn't quite right. His smile never seemed to reach his eyes. He was distracted.

As soon as Lily was bathed and in bed, Adam came back into the kitchen and got a bottle of beer out of the fridge. This was unexpected. Adam periodically went on a health kick which involved staying off the booze. Just a week earlier he'd told Chelsea he was going to have a month off alcohol in preparation for the parties ahead. Both the usual seasonal events and, of course, their wedding.

'Bad day?' Chelsea asked.

'You could say that.'

'What happened?'

'I think I need to drink this first,' he said.

Adam took a swig from his bottle.

'Will I need one too?' Chelsea asked.

'You might do.'

Chelsea opened a bottle of beer for herself and followed Adam into the living room. They sat down at opposite ends of the sofa. Chelsea wasn't sure whether Adam wanted her to be physically close to him right then or not.

'What happened?'

'Fred has decided to call it a day.'

Chelsea wasn't surprised to hear that. Fred, the owner of the architectural practice where Adam worked, was almost seventy-five. Most people in his position would have taken retirement by now.

'What does that mean?'

'It means I need to start looking for another job.'

'The company isn't going to carry on without him?'

'He's been looking for a buyer but, basically, no.'

'Oh, this is terrible.'

'It's not the best news we've had this year, that's for sure. But it might not be all bad. I've been thinking I should set up my own business for a while. Or join another practice as a partner.'

Chelsea nodded. She knew that Adam's career hadn't taken quite the path it might have done. Claire's death and the subsequent pressure of suddenly finding himself having to cope as a single parent had made it hard for him to progress through the ranks to partnership level. He'd always taken the less risky path. A guaranteed wage. Paid holiday and sick leave.

'How long do you have where you are?' Chelsea asked.

'End of the year. Unluckily for me, the jobs I've been working on are all in their final stages. It's not long but we can survive for a while on my redundancy cash. It does mean we need to rethink the wedding though. I'm sorry.'

Chelsea felt her heart climb into her mouth. It took less than a second for her to decide that this was the real reason for Adam's distraction. He was going to use his redundancy as the perfect excuse.

'You mean you don't want to get married any more?'

Her voice came out as a squeak.

'No!' Adam looked aghast. 'No, of course that's not what I mean, you silly moo. I just mean we've got to rethink the way we're going to do it. The plans you were making. That restaurant. All those guests. Some of them will have to go.'

'But I've sent out "save the date" emails to a hundred people. I can't just disinvite them.'

Chelsea regretted having said that the moment it left her mouth. The last thing Adam needed then was to feel under pressure about the wedding.

'But we can't afford to take them all to that restaurant for a sit-down meal. There's no way. This changes everything. I don't know when I'm going to find a new practice. You don't know what your income is going to be from one month to the next. If we can just take it easy on the wedding, the money we save will give us longer to think about where we're going from here. We've got to be sensible for a little while. That's all.'

'Of course. Of course we have.'

What else could she say? She had to be sensible. She

knew that. But that didn't mean she was happy about it. She clenched her fists, feeling her nails dig into her palms. She had to rein in the urge to cry.

'We can still have a great wedding,' Adam said. 'It just won't be quite so glamorous.'

'I don't care about glamorous,' said Chelsea, forcing herself to smile. 'The important part of the day is the bit where we say "I do". That's all that really matters.'

'I knew you would say that,' said Adam. 'And that is precisely why I love you.'

He kissed the tip of his finger and pressed it to the end of Chelsea's nose. It was a gesture he often made to Lily when she was being especially sweet. Chelsea knew she had to try to be sweet herself. She let Adam hug her again and she hugged him twice as hard back but, inside her, the tiny spoilt girl part of her was balling her fists and shouting 'it's not fair!' Her dream wedding was already out of the question.

Chapter Eleven

Annabel

Adam and Chelsea weren't the only ones experiencing their own personal credit crunch. Though from the outside, life in Little Bissingden chez the Buchanans looked as luxurious as ever, Richard and Annabel were also examining their budget very carefully.

'I keep reading that all the smartest people are shopping at Lidl,' said Richard, tapping the figure in the column marked 'groceries' on the spreadsheet he'd prepared for a 'family conference'. 'So why are you still spending the GDP of a small nation at Waitrose every week?'

'Darling.' Annabel was not convinced by Lidl. 'You wouldn't want to eat a Lidl chicken. Heaven knows what sort of conditions those animals have to live in.'

'Looking at the cost of the chicken on this receipt, I'd expect it to have been living in a suite at the bloody Savoy! Sweetheart, business has not been good and our portfolio is in the toilet. Either we need to cut back or we need to bring some more money in.'

Neither prospect was particularly appealing, but cutting back seemed especially bad. Annabel had to find a way to bring in more money.

Annabel hadn't worked for a very long while. She'd given up her last full-time job when Izzy was born. At the time, Richard had just been made partner at a law firm. Life was very good. It continued to get better – in material terms, at least – when Richard left the law firm and went into finance.

Annabel had thought about doing something when Izzy was sixteen. Not because they needed the money but because, if she was honest, she was starting to feel a little redundant as Izzy became an adult. Bored even. That had all changed quite dramatically when Izzy went to her first festival to celebrate the end of her GCSEs. She took some dodgy pills, was taken very ill and ended up needing a kidney transplant as a result. It was beyond awful. Annabel wouldn't have believed that a body could fail so quickly and so dramatically. Just a couple of tablets had almost robbed Izzy of her future. It was the first time she had ever taken drugs. In the game of Russian Roulette you play every time you take an unknown substance, poor Izzy had found the live bullet.

The months that followed seemed like a bad dream to Annabel now. All that time Izzy spent in hospital. The helplessness Annabel felt when she couldn't donate one of her own kidneys to her darling girl because she was unexpectedly pregnant with Humfrey. Meanwhile, Richard, with his sky-high blood pressure, was deemed to be too unhealthy. That was why, at the age of forty-three, Annabel had finally looked for her birth family – the Bensons – in the hope that they might offer a solution. It was a can of worms she hadn't wanted to open but a year later, Izzy was well (in the end, she received a kidney from an anonymous donor) and the Bensons had brought a great deal into their lives. Izzy and Sophie's close friendship and Annabel's own blossoming relationships with Chelsea and Ronnie were well worth her initial misgivings.

Yes, given the events of the past year, all thoughts of an organic candle company (Annabel's preferred entrepreneurial idea) had gone out of the window. In any case, when she'd actually looked into it, it seemed too much like hard work. All that melting and pouring. And she probably wouldn't be able to work out of her kitchen, as she'd thought when she was idly considering the plan, because of Health and Safety.

But if Annabel was going to try to bring some money in now, she still needed to find an occupation which could fit around Humfrey, who was still only ten months old, and Izzy's visits to the hospital to check on the condition of her transplanted kidney. It was less than a year since Izzy's operation. There wasn't an ordinary job Annabel could think of that would give her the time and freedom she needed to attend to the needs of her family and getting a nanny in full time would wipe out any of the money she made anyway.

Perhaps cutting back was going to be the easier option after all. The Buchanans had already done away with a few of the things they'd previously considered necessities for their lovely life. Since Izzy was taken ill, they'd cut back on holidays for a start. Annabel was too nervous to take Izzy far from the hospital where she'd received her new kidney. And while Humfrey was so small, it would really be no fun to take him on a plane. Skiing trips were definitely out now too. That saved a surprising amount of money. And Annabel was secretly relieved because, while Richard loved to ski, she had always preferred to take sunny holidays. As far as she was concerned, there was nothing very relaxing about any activity that required you to wear so many bulky layers and horrible boots that felt as though they were breaking your shins when you did them up. Izzy too had been equally unenthusiastic, even before her transplant. Maybe Richard could start going again when Humfrey was old enough to join him.

Then there were the cars. Ordinarily, Richard and Annabel upgraded their cars every three years. This year, they were going to hang on to the vehicles they already had. They were perfectly good after all. Likewise, Annabel didn't spend as much on clothes as she used to. Since Humfrey was born, they hadn't had so many nights out anyway.

But it would be nice to go down to London and have a shopping spree in Fenwick. Like in the old days. However, even going down to London was different since Richard decided that they had to rent out the flat they had kept there for his work. Now her husband caught the train back to Warwickshire, no matter how late he'd been at the office. The rent was being socked away for Humfrey's future school fees.

Annabel was fully aware that, despite all this, she had a wonderful life and very few people out there would feel sorry for her, but it was still a little worrying to see the bank balance dwindling and find herself having to think about the things she threw into the shopping trolley for the first time since she was a student.

She put a capsule in the Nespresso machine – Nespresso was yet another luxury she really couldn't bear thinking of being without – and set up everything she needed to brainstorm moneymaking ideas while Humfrey was having a nap. Sitting down with a pen and paper, she made a start.

What could they do with the assets they already had? The flat in London, which was the home Richard and Annabel first shared after they married, was already washing its face, with a nice corporate tenant. But what about the Great House – the Jacobean mansion the Buchanan family had renovated so lovingly? Was there any way they could make money from that?

Chelsea had once suggested to Annabel that the Great House would be a wonderful place for magazine shoots. It had appeared in an interiors magazine already. It was such a beautiful place. From the immaculate gardens to the pristine kitchen to the great room with its original oak panelling, the house could serve as a backdrop for all sorts of products from food to fashion. Or it could make a wonderful set for a television programme. The renovation had been done with diligent attention to historical detail. People often wrote to ask if they could come and see the graffiti left in the attic bedroom by the future Charles II and his brother James when they hid there as children during the English Civil War. From time to time, Annabel would allow a small group of interested history buffs to visit.

But as historically important as it was, the Great House was the Buchanans' home. Though Annabel had initially been intrigued when Chelsea told her about the sort of money that could be made by registering your home with a location agency, she'd been put off pretty quickly when she investigated the possibilities online and read about homes wrecked by careless camera crews. The Great House was full of expensive antiques that were simply irreplaceable, no matter how good your insurance. And she certainly wasn't prepared to have the decoration scheme she'd chosen so carefully altered on a whim to fit an advertising agency brief. Apparently they often wanted to repaint. The money just wasn't *that* good.

So, renting out the Great House itself was out of the question. But it wasn't the only building the Buchanans had in Little Bissingden.

While the Great House was being renovated, Richard and Annabel had also tidied up one of the attached farm buildings. It was an enormous tithe barn. Under the house's previous owner it had been allowed to get into a terrible state – disgraceful, really – but they had spent a small fortune on fixing the roof and the walls. It was no longer damp and dangerous but dry and, on a warm day, almost welcoming. For the moment, it was empty, apart from the bicycles she and Richard had bought in a moment of fitness fanaticism but never used. Planning restrictions had prevented them from turning the barn into a sort of granny flat but, so long as it had to stand empty, it would be the perfect venue for a party.

Chapter Twelve

Annabel

How do you turn a barn into a party venue? And would it be worth doing anyway?

A quick spot of Googling led Annabel to a house with a similar barn not ten miles away that was often let out as a venue for weddings. On the pretence of wanting to book something herself, she called them up. She was able to put on quite a convincing act, saying that her sister, who lived in London, had tasked her with seeking out venues close to Coventry. It wasn't entirely untrue. She really did have a sister who was getting married, after all. Annabel even used Chelsea's name and her prospective date – 19th December. She felt just a little guilty when the party planner – Mrs Heather – confirmed that, while it was very short notice, she could probably organise something and would cancel a hairdressing appointment so that Annabel could see the barn ASAP.

Annabel made the trip to inspect the house in the next village on Friday afternoon, taking Izzy, who was on an Inset day, with her for back-up and to act as another pair of eyes to spot the potential pitfalls. Humfrey stayed at the Great House with his grandmother Sarah, Annabel's adoptive mother, who would be staying for the weekend.

* * *

Annabel and Izzy rather enjoyed themselves, as Mrs Heather took them on the guided tour of the house and the attached barn and plied them with tea and homemade biscuits in her big country kitchen while they went through their imaginary checklist of items to find out what sort of services were being offered.

Talking to this experienced party planner soon showed Annabel aspects to the job that she hadn't even begun to think about. Having a suitable empty barn was just the start of it. Tables and chairs had to be hired, according to the size and format of the party: would it be sit-down or buffet? Likewise, a portable kitchen would need to be brought in. Mrs Heather explained that most catering companies could bring their own facilities for heating food. A bar would need to be set up. And, of course, you had to think about toilets. Again, the number you needed would depend on the number of guests and whether you wanted to make them single sex.

'That's the best option, if you want my opinion. The last thing we ladies want is a view of a urinal while we're touching up our make-up.'

Annabel agreed. Izzy laughed.

'And then there are portaloos and there are portaloos. You can have the kind that they have at a music festival, which are basically just big plastic tubs with those funny unbreakable mirrors you can't see anything in. Or you can go for the luxury option, with proper porcelain, brass-plated taps, real mirrors, curtains and a bunch of fresh flowers.'

'What's the difference in price?' Annabel asked.

The difference was quite staggering.

'Gosh. Why are they so expensive?'

'It's the waste disposal and the cleaning,' Mrs Heather explained. 'The festival-style ones are basically hosed down but the luxury loos – of course they require more attention.'

'Of course.'

Little things.

'I'll send you an email with the exact pricing breakdown,' said Mrs Heather, 'but I imagine that what you're looking at will be somewhere in the region of five thousand pounds for the hire of the venue and furniture. Another two for the toilets. Assuming you would go for the high end.'

'Absolutely,' said Annabel, feeling slightly horrified that she might look like the sort of woman who wouldn't go for the *high end* when it came to picking such essential facilities.

'Of course, things like table dressing will be extra.'

'Table dressing?'

'Yes. Most tables you hire these days are just plain MDF, not wood, so you really can't go without tablecloths. Likewise, the chair company I use does not automatically supply cushions.'

Mrs Heather revealed the cost of providing padded comfort for your guests' bottoms through over-long speeches.

'And you don't even get to keep the cushions afterwards?' Annabel joked.

'I'm afraid not. Plus there's a cleaning charge for any major mishaps.'

'So much has changed since I got married,' said Annabel. 'I don't remember there being so many choices. Or charges.'

'It's a proper industry these days,' Mrs Heather admitted. 'And I imagine this all sounds very expensive but I can assure you that these prices are in line with the average. Depending on the package you go for, however, I could probably offer a discount in the region of ten per cent.'

'Thank you,' said Annabel. Even at ten per cent off, the prices would still be horrific. 'This has all been very enlightening.'

'Of course you and your sister will want to digest everything I've told you and have a proper think about it, but I would urge you not to take too long. A couple of months isn't as long as you would imagine when there's so much to organise.'

Annabel assured Mrs Heather she would talk to Chelsea that very afternoon and they'd have an answer as to whether they wanted to go ahead in the next couple of days.

'I'll look forward to hearing from you,' Mrs Heather said.

'Wow,' said Izzy as she and Annabel got back into the car for the drive home. 'Five thousand pounds. To hire a barn. An empty barn! For half a day. Mum, that's crazy money. Our barn is at least as good as that one.'

It was true. And there was space behind it for the chemical toilets. And space in the small shed next to it to accommodate loads of chairs. Annabel was convinced that it would work out cheaper to buy chairs than to rent them. All they had to do was find a suitably neutral design that could work with every colour scheme. Likewise the tables Mrs Heather had shown them were no better than the sort of thing you could pick up in Ikea. If you had to cover them with tablecloths anyway, you might as well use pasting tables.

'And all that stuff about luxury toilets!' Izzy laughed. 'The conveniences. For two grand you should be able to get those Japanese ones that blow warm air on your bum.'

'Isabel,' Annabel admonished her daughter. But she agreed. 'Talk about spending a penny.'

The visit to Mrs Heather's barn had set Annabel's brain buzzing. This wedding business was a licence to print money and she was determined to get her own share of the action.

Later that evening, Annabel and Izzy talked to Richard about their adventure.

'Forget tightening our belts. We are sitting on a gold mine,' Annabel concluded. 'If we had a wedding or a party every weekend from May until the end of September, we'd easily make a quarter of a million a year.'

Richard nodded. 'But that's before you've thought about the cost of staff, of renting the tablecloths, of chemical toilets, of insurance . . .'

Annabel rolled her eyes as though her husband was just being a spoilsport.

'We have thought of all that actually and I still think it's worth investigating,' she said.

'Me too,' said Izzy.

Izzy was very excited by the idea. Having spent her summer holiday interning at a very boring solicitor's office, she had decided beyond doubt that a career in law was definitely not for her. A career in events management was altogether more exciting. She liked the idea of helping people create their ideal party.

'Well,' said Richard. 'It sounds as though you're both keen to explore this further. I'm sure I can help you with some seed money. Why don't you put together a proper business plan and we'll take it from there.'

'Yes!' Annabel gave Izzy a high-five.

'What are we going to call ourselves?' Izzy asked. 'The Party People? The People's Party?'

'Business plan first,' said Richard.

'Yes, boss,' said Annabel.

Chapter Thirteen

Annabel and Chelsea

Annabel was inspired. If Richard wanted a business plan, Annabel was going to give him a knockout one. She scribbled down a list of the variables involved and the very next day, she called Chelsea to ask her for the names of the most fashionable mobile catering firms in the country. This was the kind of useful information Chelsea had at her fingertips, having worked on *Society* magazine, which documented the best of everything. Chelsea trotted off a list of the glitterati's favourite canapé providers. Annabel scribbled them all down.

'Are you having a party?' Chelsea asked.

'No. I'm thinking of setting up a business,' said Annabel.

'In catering?'

Cooking was not Annabel's strong suit.

'Not exactly. How's the wedding planning going down there in London?' Annabel briefly changed the subject.

'Oh, you know . . .' Chelsea sighed.

'You don't sound very excited. I spoke to Jacqui. She said you've found your venue. That's half the battle. Getting the registry office and the venue you want on the same day without having too much time between the ceremony and the lunch.'

'We did get the registry office and we did find a venue, but we've had a bit of a set-back since then.'

'Oh.'

Chelsea told Annabel about the closure of the company where Adam worked.

'I'm sure it won't take him too long to find another job,' Chelsea said. 'But in the meantime, we've got to keep an eye on the budget and a sit-down meal at Valentino's for more than a hundred wedding guests is definitely not on the cards.'

'Oh,' said Annabel. 'Oh dear. Will you have to cut the numbers or change the format?'

'Both,' said Chelsea. 'The only problem is, because it's all been happening so quickly, I've already sent out my save the date cards. What's the etiquette for telling people not to bother saving the date after all?'

'I really don't know,' said Annabel. 'I'm sorry.'

'I'm just going to have to bite the bullet and tell some of them they're disinvited. Ugh. I don't know where to start. Who can I risk disappointing? If I were told to save the date for an invitation that never came – especially for a date so close to Christmas when people might have otherwise gone away – I don't think I'd talk to the person concerned ever again. I'm going to look like a right idiot.'

'Or . . .'

Annabel was having a light-bulb moment.

'Look, Chelsea, the reason I called you and asked you about those caterers is that you're not the only one who's having to do a spot of belt-tightening. Richard's bank has had a bad year and all the new government regulations mean his bonus is going to be a fraction of what we hoped it might be. He's got to take most of it in shares and the shares are worth less by the day. It's got so bad that *I* need to get a job.' There was a smile in Annabel's voice as she said that. 'But I'm practically unemployable, as you know. So the only option for me is to create my own little business.'

'Organic scented candles?' asked Chelsea, remembering conversations she'd had with Annabel in the past. Or hand-knitted baby shawls. Her entrepreneurial ideas were very middle class and chi chi. They were glorified hobbies, really.

'No,' said Annabel. 'Wedding planning. Well, party hosting. Here. In Little Bissingden.'

'In your house?'

Chelsea knew how much Annabel loved her beautiful home. It was hard enough for her to let her own children have free rein among the soft furnishings. Chelsea couldn't imagine her letting complete strangers anywhere near her precious antiques.

'In the tithe barn.'

'Ah.'

'It's the perfect venue. Big enough to have a sit-down meal for hundreds with space left over for dancing. And since we've had it renovated, it's very warm and dry and looks wonderfully rustic without any of the danger there was before. It's the perfect blank canvas for a wedding at any time of year. You could fill it with flowers in the summer, pumpkins in the autumn, Christmas trees in December . . .' Annabel paused. 'Can you imagine how lovely it would look all decked out with holly and ivy? Big candles. Red baubles. Fairy lights.'

Chelsea could indeed imagine it. Annabel had shown her round the tithe barn that summer. Now she pictured great boughs of greenery hanging from every beam.

'It would look fabulous,' she said.

'So, how would you like to be our test wedding?' Annabel asked.

'Test wedding?'

'We've got to start somewhere. Why shouldn't we start with you?'

'Seriously? Me and Adam?'

'Yes. We could easily accommodate a hundred people for a sit-down meal in the barn. It would be our pleasure. Between the two of us, Chelsea, I'm sure we could make the barn look really special. This way you get to have your big wedding with no need to disinvite anybody and Izzy and I get to see whether we really could be any good at the wedding planning lark.'

Chelsea laughed. 'I'm sure you'd be wonderful but . . . It's a big thing you're offering to do.'

'You'd be doing us a favour. Assuming you don't mind us using photographs of your wedding in our advertising.'

'Of course not.'

'Then will you think about it?'

'I will. And thank you. Thank you, Annabel! Thank you.' Chelsea couldn't quite believe it. 'This could be great.'

Chelsea put the idea to Adam that night. Just as when she'd told him that she wanted to bring the wedding forward by nine months, Adam was surprisingly unfazed by this latest development.

'And you don't mind that we won't be getting married in London?' she asked him again.

'I don't mind at all. I just want you to be my wife. I don't have any particular preference as to who does the ceremony. Or the party afterwards. But Annabel doesn't have any experience at this sort of thing, does she? Do you think she's ready for everything that might be involved?'

'Annabel will be a natural,' said Chelsea. 'I can't think of anyone better suited to all the bossing around that will need to be done.'

Adam agreed with that.

'And it will be easier for Mum and Dad with Granddad Bill.'

'Who is the reason we're having a Christmas wedding in the first place. Let's go for it.'

Chelsea called Annabel back first thing in the morning to tell her that she and Adam were delighted to accept her help.

'I think I'm almost as excited as when I planned my own wedding day!' Annabel laughed.

Chapter Fourteen

Everybody

Once Chelsea and Adam had accepted Annabel's offer, they were invited to the Great House for lunch that very weekend, so that they could have a proper look at the tithe barn and start to think about what form they might like the wedding to take. If they were not going to change their actual wedding date, then there was no time to waste.

Annabel got cracking with the preliminaries right away. First she called the council, to find out what sort of licence she would need to have music in the barn. Even though she was throwing a party for a family member, Annabel would not be cutting corners. She would be sticking to the rules. It would be a total disaster if she fell foul of her neighbours and the local authority before the business was even up and running. On Richard's insistence, she also investigated insurance.

'We can't have a hundred drunken people rampaging around without it,' he said. 'If someone trips over in the dark on their way from the barn to the portaloos, we could end up with a lawsuit that wipes us out.'

'Lighting between barn and portaloos' went on Annabel's list.

* * *

By the time Chelsea and Adam arrived for Sunday lunch, Annabel had made significant progress. She had even been to see the vicar at St Timothy's, the local church.

Annabel was already very close with the vicar, Father Malcolm. She was raised in a church-going family and though her belief had wavered over the years, especially when Izzy was ill and they were waiting for an organ donor, she was still a regular at church. She served on various committees. She was part of the rota of women who looked after the flowers and handed out hymn books. Annabel felt she could call in a favour or two.

When thinking about how her wedding day would proceed now that she wasn't having her reception in London, Chelsea had come to the conclusion that she and Adam would still get married at the registry office in Marylebone in the morning, then dash up the motorway for the party. Annabel had other ideas. She was envisaging a fairy-tale wedding for her sister and that had to start with a fairy-tale ceremony. Forget a registry office, no matter how illustrious the newly-weds who had previously married there. The beautiful Norman church of Saint Timothy in Little Bissingden was the perfect fairy-tale setting.

'Bring your sister and her fiancé to see me after the service on Sunday morning,' said Father Malcolm. 'And I will see what I can do.'

Unlike Annabel, Chelsea had not grown up in a church-going family. Jacqui and Dave identified themselves as Christian – Church of England – but they weren't actively religious, seeing the inside of their local church only when one of the children, or grandchildren, gave them a good reason to be there. As it stood, they hadn't been since Sophie did her last Brownie church parade. Jack was unconvinced of the joys of the scouting movement. He preferred Minecraft and *Doctor Who*.

Chelsea had picked up her parents' pattern of church-going – stepping inside only for weddings, christenings and funerals or when she was sightseeing on her holidays – which was why she had plumped for a registry office. It didn't seem right to her to marry in a church when she wouldn't otherwise be there. It felt hypocritical.

For that reason, Chelsea was a little wary when Annabel announced that Father Malcolm was expecting them.

'You think he'd marry us? Even though we're not part of his congregation?'

'I have some sway,' said Annabel.

'With him upstairs?' Adam asked in a joking tone. 'Could you put in a word for me about a new job while you're at it?'

Despite Chelsea's concern that he would view them as hypocrites, Father Malcolm was as warm and welcoming as Annabel had promised he would be. He explained that he wasn't in the habit of marrying people who weren't members of his congregation, but he would consider them if they were willing to spend some time at the church in the run-up to the ceremony. They were family of one of his most active congregation members after all.

Father Malcolm soon put Chelsea and Adam at their ease as he showed them the church and explained that he was actually the vicar of three churches in the vicinity and spent his Sundays dashing between them on his motorbike like a super-hero. He was every bit the modern cleric.

Once the church tour was over, Annabel remained to chat to Father Malcolm while Chelsea and Adam took a turn around the outside of the church.

'What do you think?' asked Chelsea.

'I think it would be wonderful to get married here,' said Adam. 'There's something about this church . . .'

'It does feel very welcoming,' she agreed. 'Not at all stuffy.'

'No. Not stuffy at all.'

'But is it wrong for us to do it here? It isn't what we planned.'

'Doesn't God laugh when people make plans?' Adam joked.

'So, you'll do it?' said Annabel, suddenly joining them and linking one arm through Chelsea's and another through Adam's. 'You'll come up here and go to the services where the banns are read?'

'We'll think about it,' said Adam.

'Don't think too long,' said Annabel. 'Oh, it will be great. Father Malcolm gives a lovely sermon. And can you imagine how lovely it would be to have your wedding photos here? I can just see this doorway decorated with an arch of Christmas greenery, accented with big red ribbons.'

Chelsea nodded. So could she.

Chapter Fifteen

The Benson-Edwards Family

It was impossible for Annabel to have Chelsea, Adam and Lily over without inviting their parents and Ronnie and her family too. They arrived in the afternoon and would be staying for tea. Jack and Lily greeted each other like the great friends they were becoming and immediately disappeared into the garden with Leander the Labrador, who played reluctant Piggy in the Middle as Lily and Jack threw his favourite ball between them. The game didn't last long before Leander slunk back into the house for a snooze instead.

Annabel had already given Chelsea and Adam the tour of the barn and a quick overview of how she thought it might work as a wedding venue. Now she went through the whole thing again for the benefit of Ronnie and Jacqui. Mark and Dave stayed in the kitchen with Granddad Bill and Richard. They were about as interested in wedding planning as the women in their lives were interested in the Premiership. A cliché, perhaps, but true. Adam, as the groom, was not excused.

Chelsea had been gushing with enthusiasm while Annabel showed her how the tithe barn might be adapted to her needs. After years of working on magazines, Chelsea was used to seeing empty spaces transformed into fairy-tale scenes. When she looked at the beams, she could already imagine the swags of winter greenery that might hang from them. Looking down the length of the barn, she could imagine tables covered in snow white cloths and decorated with more greenery and red and white candles. She imagined shiny red and gold baubles woven into the greenery or piled like snowballs as centrepieces. She could picture a great bower of fir and holly and ivy, beneath which she and Adam might cut their wedding cake. Jacqui said she could picture it too.

However, when Ronnie looked around the barn, she merely saw bare wood, and cobwebs, and dust.

'It's never going to be warm enough,' she said. 'Not in December.'

'We can hire space heaters,' said Annabel. 'They're pretty effective. Also, you have to imagine the barn full of people, generating their own heat. It will soon get pretty toasty in here once everyone is chatting and drinking and dancing.'

'And we could have blankets,' said Chelsea. 'For anyone who really started to feel the cold. I went to an outdoor concert at Hampton Court where they put a blanket on each seat.'

'That's an excellent idea,' said Annabel. She made herself a note on her iPhone. 'I'll have a look to see where we can source those.'

'But isn't all this going to mean it works out just as expensive as having a London wedding?' Ronnie asked. 'And more complicated? At least if you have your party in a restaurant, you don't have to find your own chairs. Or hire tablecloths. Or blankets. You're talking about a hundred blankets, Chels.'

'I would bear the cost of those, since they would be an investment for future weddings. And there's going to be a big saving on catering costs,' said Annabel. 'And loads on the wine.'

'That's true,' said Chelsea. 'Restaurants put a huge mark-up on alcohol. The cost you see on the menu is always at least double the cost of buying direct. Sometimes more. We'd avoid all that. On the amount the Benson side drink alone, we'll save a couple of grand.'

Ronnie snorted at that.

'You have to imagine it all decked out, Ronnie,' said Annabel. 'With holly and ivy and boughs of fir. Think of the smell of the pine! That's the scent of Christmas to me. And we can have seasonal music playing while everyone sits down for their meal. Perhaps we can even get someone to dress as Father Christmas to entertain the children.'

'That's an excellent idea,' said Chelsea. 'Jack and Lily would love that.'

'And you could travel to the church on Santa's sleigh,' said Ronnie.

'Ooooh!' said Chelsea.

Annabel nodded. 'Not bad.'

'I was joking,' said Ronnie. 'Reindeer stink.' Ronnie had found herself in close proximity to a reindeer a couple of years before, when she and Mark had taken Jack and Sophie to a 'winter wonderland' theme park for a day. She was astonished at how whiffy the reindeer was.

'OK. So perhaps we won't have a reindeer but the Christmas theme does give us all sorts of options,' said Annabel. 'We've definitely got to have crackers.'

'Oh yes,' said Jacqui. 'That'd be lovely. I'd like that.'

'We could offer Christmas pudding as dessert,' said Chelsea. 'And mince pies.'

Chelsea and Annabel were on a roll.

'I'm getting chilly,' Ronnie announced. 'I'll see you all back in the house.'

Chelsea watched her sister depart. She was momentarily worried that she'd somehow offended Ronnie but Annabel soon distracted her with the suggestion that they should have an actual Christmas tree as the centrepiece of the whole decorative scheme.

'We could get a twelve footer in here.'

Chelsea imagined the twinkling lights and forgot all about her other sister.

Chapter Sixteen

Jack and Lily

Ronnie was right about it being cold. The weather was distinctly autumnal that October afternoon. It wasn't long after Leander decided he'd had enough of playing Piggy in the Middle outdoors that his tormentors Jack and Lily followed him inside. Auntie Annabel found them some snacks but the other adults were too busy talking about the wedding to pay them much attention.

When the children started to play-fight by the Aga, Ronnie decided it was time to trust them to an electronic baby-sitter. She gave Jack the old first-generation iPad she'd taken off him earlier that day, because he was spending too much time playing Crossy Road – a horrible game in which the player had to get an avatar across several lanes of traffic, a river and a railroad without mishap. Jack's increasingly manic laughter every time an oncoming train squashed his character was more than a little worrying.

'Play one of your *nice* games with Lily,' Ronnie instructed him. 'How about Doodle Jump? Or the one where you have to join up the coloured squares.'

'Boring,' said Jack.

'Why don't you both go and watch some television?' Annabel suggested instead. 'In the media room. You know how to turn the TV on, don't you, Jack?'

Lily followed Jack into the Buchanan's den – the

'media room' – which was where the TV lived so that it didn't spoil the aesthetic of Annabel's carefully planned sitting room. ('The stateroom,' as Ronnie sometimes jokily referred to it.) They took with them a plate of biscuits and a couple of glasses of milk, to tide them over until teatime proper.

But there was nothing much on television that afternoon. To begin with, the children squabbled over the remote control. Lily gained possession by pinching Jack on the arm and quickly flicked through the channels. There was no *Doctor Who*, no *Simpsons* and definitely no *Frozen*. When they happened upon *Dora The Explorer*, the children both pulled faces.

'But you *love Dora The Explorer*,' Lily told Jack.

'No, *you* do,' said Jack. 'You want a *Dora The Explorer* book for Christmas. And a *Dora* hat. And a *Dora* outfit.'

'I do not!'

'Well, that's what you're getting,' said Jack.

'I am not!' said Lily, launching herself at him and pinning him onto the pillows.

'Say you like *Dora The Explorer* the best,' she said before she would release him.

Jack used all his strength to flip Lily over and demanded, with his fingers in her ribs threatening to tickle her, 'No, *you* say you like *Peppa Pig*!'

Lily capitulated. 'I like *Peppa Pig*!' she squealed. Giggling until they could hardly breathe, the children sat back up again.

Jack flicked through the television channels as though with him in control, the TV might offer something new.

'There's still nothing on,' Lily sighed.

Jack confirmed her view.

'What have you got on the iPad?' Lily asked. 'Show me Crossy Road.'

'Mummy said we shouldn't play it.'

'Nobody will know.'

Jack went along with Lily but, to his disgust, he discovered that his mother had deleted the offending app.

'What!' he exclaimed. 'I don't believe it!'

'Awwww,' Lily complained. She wasn't allowed violent games either.

'I can show you something else though,' said Jack. 'Look at this.' He prodded at the screen. 'I've been making videos.'

Jack showed Lily his work so far. When he'd been given the old iPad, which used to belong to Cathy Next Door (she was in the habit of upgrading her technology more often than NASA), he had quickly worked out how to use the movie function. He'd even figured out how to set the self-timer so that he could prop the little gadget up on his shelf and film without assistance. Lily watched with interest as Jack showed her a variety of clips of him in his bedroom, attempting daring stunts. Mostly, he would run full-pelt across the floor and do a headspring on his mattress, before landing more or less elegantly on a beanbag he had placed by the bed as a safety precaution.

At one point in one of the little films, Ronnie could be heard to shout, 'What are you doing in there, Jack Benson-Edwards? You sound like a herd of bloody elephants.'

'Nothing, Mummy!' said Jack, hurriedly switching off the camera.

Lily was quietly impressed by Jack's movie-making attempts. 'They're very good,' she said admiringly.

'If you hold the camera, I'll be able to get an even better shot. That would be awesome. You stand there. I can bounce off this settee.'

Lily's eyes widened. 'But we're at Auntie Annabel's house. You can't bounce on her furniture. What if she tells us off?'

'The adults won't know what we're doing,' said Jack confidently. 'They're all too busy talking about the boring wedding.'

'It is really boring,' Lily agreed. Her interest was confined to the bridesmaids' dresses. Talk of seating plans and catering went right over her head.

'Do you know how to use the movie app?' Jack asked.

In a matter of minutes, he'd taught Lily everything he knew and they were ready to make a proper film.

'OK,' said Jack, stripping off the brown zip-up cardigan his mother had made him wear that day because it had been a gift from Annabel for his birthday. Jack hated that cardigan. The collar came up too high and it was itchy. 'Are you ready?'

'I'm ready. I'm going to count to three,' said Lily. 'Then you run. One, two, three—'

'Wait! I'm just getting into position,' said Jack. 'And I have to do an introduction before I do the stunt.'

'All right,' said Lily. 'I'm going to press Record . . . Now!'

Jack raised his arms and addressed the camera in a deep and dramatic voice. 'Ladies and gentlemen, boys and girls, welcome to the Jack Benson-Edwards Show.'

Jack raised a cheer from his imaginary crowd.

'For my first trick, I am going to attempt a forward somersault. Please do not try this at home,' he added, paraphrasing something he'd seen on TV. 'This is very dangerous and you have not been trained.'

'A-one, a-two, a-three . . .' Lily counted.

Jack set off at high speed and did a handstand on Annabel's expensive and beautiful Osborne and Little-covered Knowle sofa. He came to a stop with his feet halfway up the wall, just short of a valuable print of Annabel's Oxford college.

'Watch out!' Lily cried.

Jack tumbled back to the floor.

'Ta-daaa!' he said and took a bow. Lily shouted 'cut!', exactly as Jack had told her she should.

Together they examined the film.

'Hmmm. We need to do it again,' said Jack. 'You didn't get all of me in. This time, follow me with the camera.'

'OK,' said Lily.

'I'm getting into place,' said Jack.

He shook out his shoulders and drew himself up to his full height. He went through his introductory spiel again. This time he tried an American accent. It was all over the place. East coast? West coast? Who knew?

'Ladies and gentlemen. Boys and girls . . . for my next daring trick . . .' etc. etc.

Lily counted him down and he started his run.

'Stopppp!' Lily shouted, just as Jack was about to take a leap. 'I didn't get that. I pressed the wrong button.'

'Oh, for goodness' sake,' said Jack, echoing his mother.

'Start again,' said Lily.

This time she managed to get a take but Jack wasn't very happy with it.

'You didn't get my feet in and it doesn't look very interesting.'

'What you did wasn't very interesting,' Lily countered. 'Perhaps you should do a back flip. Like those acrobats we saw on the cruise. That would be good.'

Jack and Lily's families had holidayed together that summer. Granddad Bill had won some money on the lottery and paid for the whole family to go on a Mediterranean cruise. The amazing acrobats on the ship had captured both children's imaginations.

Lily set up to film Jack again. Jack took his mark.

'Ladies and gentlemen,' he said in as deep a voice as he could manage. This time his accent was passably Canadian. 'Please put your hands together for the amazing, the exciting, the incredible . . . Jack Benson-Edwards!'

Jack approximated the noise of a crowd going wild again.

'A-one, a-two, a-three . . .' counted Lily.

Jack took another run at the sofa. For a change he turned at the last minute, in an attempt to land backwards. The result was that he missed the sofa altogether and landed straight on the floor.

'Ow. Delete that,' he said as he recovered himself.

'One more time,' Lily insisted. 'You nearly did it.'

This time Jack put everything he had into the perfect backwards flip. And it was pretty amazing. He turned like a professional long jumper. For a moment, he actually seemed to be suspended in mid-air. But, milliseconds later, he landed badly, brushing a foot along the mantelpiece and bringing down a great many of Annabel's expensive antique ornaments with him as he fell.

Chapter Seventeen

Jack and Lily

In many ways, it was a wonder that more was not broken. As it was, only the tiny china dog lay in two pieces on the edge of the fire surround. Everything else had landed on the altogether more forgiving sheepskin rug.

'Oh no,' said Jack.

'You broke it!' said Lily, as she stared at the shattered china collie. 'You broke it! That was expensive. I can tell.'

Jack picked the two pieces up and frantically tried to fit them back together.

'What are you going to do?' Lily asked.

Jack tried to prop the dog up on the mantelpiece again.

'You're going to be in massive trouble!'

'Don't tell on me,' said Jack, suddenly panicking.

'You broke it.'

'But you made me do the back-flip. I wouldn't have done it if you hadn't said. And you were filming me.'

'You told me to.'

'You should have said no.'

Lily could see how it was going to pan out. While Jack may have been the one who technically broke the dog by brushing it off the mantelpiece with his feet, they would undoubtedly both share the blame when the news of the damage got to the adults.

'We've got to hide it,' said Lily.

'But what if Auntie Annabel thinks it's been stolen?'

'There are lots of ornaments in here,' said Lily. 'She might not notice.'

'She *will* notice,' said Jack. 'And we'll be in even bigger trouble then. We're going to have to say what happened.'

'No,' said Lily. 'Auntie Annabel will shout.'

Jack agreed; though neither of them had heard Auntie Annabel shout before, the very idea of it was terrifying.

'My mum will *definitely* shout,' said Jack.

Lily nodded. Everyone had heard Ronnie shout at some point. Ronnie in a mood was not to be messed with.

'What are we going to do?' Jack wailed.

'Ssssh! They'll hear you. We can pretend Leander did it,' said Lily.

Leander had sneaked into the room while the children were filming. The dopey Labrador heard his name and responded with a cheery wag of his tail. He had no idea that the children were plotting to frame him.

'They won't believe us,' said Jack. 'Leander can't get up that high.'

That was true. Leander was much too fat to have reached the mantelpiece.

'I don't know what to do!' wailed Jack again.

'Let's put everything back where it was,' said Lily, ever the pragmatist. 'And hide the dog behind the other things.'

She carefully leaned the two pieces of the dog against the mirror. If you didn't look closely, you might think that the dog was still whole.

'Then, the next time we come here, we can bring some glue and mend it.'

Jack readily agreed. It might just work. It would have to.

Ten minutes later, when Izzy opened the door to the TV room, both younger children jumped out of their skins. Izzy recognised the signs of guilt at once.

'What are you two up to?' she asked.

'Nothing!' Jack and Lily chimed in unison. Their innocence was unconvincing.

'OK. If you say so. Tea is on the table.'

Jack and Lily followed Izzy back into the kitchen. They sat opposite each other and shared worried looks across the sandwiches. Neither ate as much or as enthusiastically as usual. They didn't chat as much as they usually did either. Ordinarily, it was hard to shut them up.

'What's up with those two?' Sophie asked her cousin Izzy, when Jack and Lily had been excused and disappeared into the media room again.

'I think I caught them playing doctors and nurses,' Izzy laughed.

At the end of the day, Jack pulled Lily close on the pretence of giving her a goodbye hug.

'The broken dog is our secret,' he said. 'We mustn't tell anybody!'

'I won't,' said Lily. 'Pinky promise.'

'Whoever breaks the promise gets impetigo,' said Jack.

Lily nodded. It was the worst punishment either of them could imagine.

Jack remained solemn in the car. It did not go unnoticed.

'Is Lily your girlfriend?' Mark asked as they drove back home.

'Noooo.' Jack covered his eyes to emphasise just how wrong his father was.

'Then what were you two whispering about as we were saying goodbye?'

'Nothing,' said Jack. 'We weren't whispering. Nothing happened.'

Ronnie turned round to look at her son. Jack was not very good at pretending innocence. He'd have made a hopeless spy.

'What have you done?' she asked.

'Nothing!' said Jack, his voice rising in panic. 'Nothing.'

'You don't look like you were doing nothing. Why are you being so moody?'

'Oh, leave him alone,' said Mark. 'He was just getting his first kiss, weren't you, Jack?'

Jack went completely puce at the thought but he realised that it was probably best to let his dad think he was right. That way, his mum might not continue to push for an answer. She wouldn't have to push much harder to get the truth. Jack stared out of the window all the way home, trying hard not to cry at the thought of the little broken dog. Having Auntie Annabel find out about the broken dog or having everyone think Lily was his girlfriend? He really did not know which was worse.

Chapter Eighteen

Ronnie

It had been a lovely afternoon at Annabel's but everyone in the Benson-Edwards' household could tell that Ronnie was not happy when they got back to their house in Coventry that night. She crashed around the kitchen while making Jack's bedtime snack of warm milk and a biscuit. She almost bit Mark's head off when he asked if she could put the kettle on and make a cup of tea while she was in there. Sophie decided it probably wasn't a good time to broach the subject of needing money for the school Christmas ball.

'Do you want me to make you a sandwich while I'm at it?' Ronnie asked when Mark dared to ask for that cuppa.

Missing that his wife was being sarcastic, Mark replied, 'No, that's all right, love. Annabel always puts on a good spread.'

Ronnie nearly dropped the biscuit tin at that.

'Of course she does,' Ronnie muttered. '*Annabel* gets everything right. She's the perfect hostess.'

She put three broken pieces of biscuit on Jack's plate. When she handed them to him, he started to complain that they were three small pieces that didn't actually add up to a whole, but even at his tender age, he recognised the inherent danger in that course of action right then.

'Thank you, Mummy,' he said instead.

'You finished sulking, have you?' Ronnie asked him.

'I wasn't—' Jack began to say. Then he stuffed a piece of biscuit into his mouth before any more words could leak out. He scampered out of his mother's way.

Ronnie made Mark his cup of tea and almost spilled it in his lap when she presented it to him where he sat on his leather chair in the sitting room.

'There,' she said. 'Just like Annabel makes it.'

Actually, it wasn't just like Annabel makes it. Annabel would have presented the milk separately, in a little china jug. Needless to say, Ronnie did not have a milk jug. In her house, the plastic bottle usually went straight on the table. That's if she hadn't slopped milk into a mug at the same time as a tea bag and poured hot water over the lot.

There were lots of things that Annabel and Ronnie did differently.

There was good reason for that. The two sisters were ten years apart in age and they had grown up in entirely different households. Ronnie hadn't even known that she had a big sister until she was thirty-two. Jacqui and Dave had revealed the painful secret of Annabel's birth and her subsequent adoption – when Jacqui was a teenager – on a family holiday to Lanzarote to celebrate Jacqui's sixtieth. The utterly unexpected news had hit Ronnie hard.

It was partly because Ronnie herself had been a teenage mum. On the one hand, she couldn't understand how Jacqui would have allowed herself to be parted from her baby, even if she was only seventeen and had no means of support. Despite things being very different back in the nineteen seventies. On the other hand, much as she loved her daughter Sophie, Ronnie could not help occasionally wondering how differently her life might have turned out had she not fallen pregnant at seventeen. Might she have gone on to university, as both Chelsea and Annabel had done? Might she have got herself a good job and married an architect or a lawyer instead of a kitchen-fitter? Might she be living in a house worth millions with a shiny Porsche Cayenne on the drive, instead of a semi with a rusting Ford Focus parked on the road outside?

When they first met, Annabel's wealth had definitely bothered Ronnie. Over the year that they'd known each other, she'd come to be less concerned by what she'd originally perceived to be Annabel's superiority as she realised that there were things she had that her elder sister didn't. Ronnie's daughter had her health, for a start. She knew how awful it had been for the Buchanans when Izzy was on dialysis and the wait for a transplant seemed endless. Annabel would have given away everything she owned so that Izzy could be well. Ronnie knew that. But now, for some reason, Ronnie was feeling uncomfortable again about all the material advantages Annabel had.

She thought back to that afternoon, when Annabel showed them around the barn. She wasn't showing off exactly. Ronnie couldn't have described it as that. But it was as though Annabel and Chelsea were suddenly speaking a different language that Ronnie didn't know. They talked about catering and lighting rigs and portable toilets. They discussed wedding favours, orders of service and table plans. Ronnie hadn't thought about any of that when she got married. She'd just booked the registry office and a room in the pub for afterwards. They'd had a buffet of sausage rolls and Scotch eggs bought at the cash and carry. Jacqui had made a load of cupcakes in lieu of the traditional three-tiered fruit-cake. The cupcakes were cheaper and easier. Chelsea's wedding was going to be very different indeed and it was all thanks to Annabel.

It wasn't just the wedding talk. Ronnie's comparative lack of education made her slightly insecure. When Annabel and Chelsea were talking about things she hadn't even considered, she felt embarrassed. When she felt embarrassed, she got belligerent. She knew it and yet she couldn't seem to help it. She didn't want to take out her frustration on her family and yet she always did. She hated herself for that. And that made her feel even less warm towards her long-lost sister.

Ronnie didn't even have to put Jack to bed that night. As soon as the clock showed eight, he appeared at the sitting room door and announced that he was going upstairs and he didn't need a story.

It crossed Ronnie's mind to ask 'why not' but she didn't. She didn't feel like reading a story. She wanted to sulk.

Chapter Nineteen

Ronnie

Unknown to Ronnie, while Jack went to bed early to avoid his mother's bad mood, he was still wide awake close to midnight. He could not sleep. Not while he was worrying about the broken china dog. He had been close to confessing but Lily had persuaded him not to. She was sure that anything in Annabel's house must be worth hundreds of pounds. Where would Jack get hundreds of pounds?

Jack's conscience kept him tossing and turning all night long. Several times he got up and went as far as the door of his parents' bedroom, ready to make his confession and throw himself on Ronnie's mercy (because Ronnie's wrath would surely be even worse than Annabel's). Lily was wrong. They would never get away with pretending the accident hadn't happened or, even worse, blaming it on poor Leander! At the last minute, however, he would chicken out and slink back to his room for another session of worry and panic.

He did sleep a little at last but fitfully and in the morning Ronnie was quite concerned. He looked peaky. She laid her hand tenderly on his forehead.

'Are you OK, Jack?' she asked. 'You feel a little bit hot. Perhaps you shouldn't go to school today.'

Jack sat up. Ordinarily, there was nothing he would have liked better than the chance to skip school but there was no way he could stay home with his guilty conscience.

'I'm all right,' he told his mother.

'Are you sure? You've got dark circles under your eyes.'

'No I haven't,' said Jack, jumping from bed.

Since Jack insisted he didn't want to stay home from school, Ronnie went to work as usual. She was part-time office manager at a funeral home, doing three days a week. People might think that working in a funeral home was a depressing sort of job, but, oddly, Ronnie found her occupation rather life-affirming. Meeting the funeral home's clients, who came to her at the very worst time in their lives, reminded Ronnie to count her blessings. It reminded her to love the people who meant so much to her as hard as she could while they were around to know about it. Never leave anything unsaid.

While Ronnie's boss was out, overseeing an especially important funeral, Ronnie caught up with her phone calls. First she called Jacqui, to find out how Granddad Bill was getting on.

'He's doing fine, love,' Jacqui said. 'He had a boiled egg this morning.'

The two women agreed that was a very good sign.

'And no funny turns?' Ronnie asked.

'No funnier than usual,' Jacqui assured her.

Next Ronnie called her little sister. Now that Chelsea was working from home, the sisters spoke over the phone much more often than they used to when Chelsea was in an office and worried that being caught making personal calls might cost her her job.

Ronnie launched straight to the point of the conversation.

'So you're really having your wedding at Annabel's?' she asked.

'Yes. I think it's going to be great.'

'I didn't think you wanted a church wedding.'

'I didn't either but the vicar was so nice and the church at Little Bissingden is so pretty and, if you think about it, the village does have a connection to Adam and me. It is the place where he asked Dad for my hand in marriage, after all.'

'By the war memorial,' Ronnie reminded her. 'Not in the church.'

'Well, we can't get married at a war memorial, can we?'

'But what about your London wedding? The Marylebone Registry Office. You wanted something that reflects your life, you said. That's what you were going for. That's what you always dreamed of.'

'I know but we underestimated the cost and now Adam's being made redundant. We couldn't afford a big London wedding. This way, we still get to invite everybody we want. And that's what matters in the end. We just want to be surrounded by all the people we love. It doesn't matter if that's not in the city. And Mum is pleased, isn't she?'

'Probably,' said Ronnie. 'Anything Annabel does is all right by her.'

Chelsea ignored that. 'It's so much simpler when you think about it,' she said. 'You and Mum are just down the road. Adam's little brother can get there really easily from Birmingham.'

'It isn't that easy to get to Annabel's house from ours,' Ronnie complained. 'There are roadworks on the bypass all the time.'

'But it's easier than getting to London, isn't it? And

it will be cheaper. You won't need a hotel. I'm really happy with the idea. And so is Adam.'

'Well, that's what matters,' said Ronnie.

'Yes,' said Chelsea. 'It is.'

Chelsea was determined to end the discussion there. 'Are you going to come to the wedding fayre next weekend?' she asked.

'If you want me to,' said Ronnie.

'Of course I do.'

'If I won't be in Annabel's way.'

'Ronnie,' Chelsea sighed. 'I want you there. I'll see you at Mum's place next Saturday.'

Why was Ronnie being so strange about it? Having Chelsea get married in Annabel's village would be far more convenient for everyone in the Benson family. None of them would have to travel far. There would be no need to find hotel rooms for the night. It made much more sense as far as Granddad Bill was concerned. Chelsea raised Ronnie's weird behaviour with Adam.

'She's jealous,' said Adam.

'Of me getting married? She's already married to Mark.'

'Of you getting married at Annabel's. She knows it's bound to trump the engagement party. It was all right when you were going to have your reception in a restaurant but now you've pitted sister against sister.'

'Don't say that,' said Chelsea. 'That's ridiculous.'

'Your sisters are ridiculously competitive with one another,' said Adam. 'Every time we see them together, they're both fighting for your attention.'

'Mine?'

'Yes. Yours.'

Chelsea found that hard to believe. She'd always felt

in Ronnie's shadow and Annabel didn't seem like the kind of woman who ever fought anyone for attention.

'I'll just have to make sure Ronnie feels properly included. I'll make a point of taking her views into account next Saturday. Are you sure you don't want to come to the wedding fayre too?'

'If it's all right with you,' said Adam. 'Much as I want to be really involved in the whole wedding organisation, I'll let you make that particular outing into a girls-only treat.' The emphasis Adam put on 'treat' let Chelsea know he regarded it as anything but.

Chelsea playfully tossed a scatter cushion at his head.

Chapter Twenty

Chelsea and her sisters

The wedding fayre Chelsea had chosen to attend was at a hotel on the outskirts of Coventry. She didn't expect it to be particularly inspiring, but it was close to both her parents and her two sisters. To make the most of the trip, Chelsea caught a train to the Midlands on Friday afternoon and spent the evening with her parents and Granddad Bill.

Thankfully, Bill seemed a little more like himself on this visit. When Chelsea poked her head round his bedroom door to say 'hello', he was sitting up in bed watching Sky Sports. Bill loved Sky Sports. They'd got it so that he could follow the Premiership but he didn't only watch football. He would watch anything. When Chelsea arrived on Friday afternoon, Bill was watching competitive lawn bowls. Even though in real life he had once declared bowls as a sport for 'old ladies', he didn't seem to mind watching it on TV.

'All right, Granddad Bill?' Chelsea asked. 'I've brought you a cup of tea.'

'I've won the bloody lottery,' Bill responded. 'That's a lovely cuppa.'

Chelsea sat with him for a while and was grateful to hear him talk about the action on screen. Chelsea had no interest in the competitive lawn bowling whatsoever, but it was far better to have Granddad Bill going on about the ridiculousness of a ref's decision in a sport of which he had only a sketchy understanding than have him staring into space or lost in the past, talking about the Second World War as though it were still happening. When Granddad Bill was having one of those turns, Chelsea occasionally found it frightening.

At nine o'clock in the evening, Jacqui and Dave put Granddad Bill to bed in the well-orchestrated routine they had honed since they converted the dining room into Bill's bedroom some three years before. Chelsea found the whole thing a little melancholy – Granddad Bill had always been such a big, strong man – but she was glad to see that Bill was so well loved and cared for. She hoped she would be able to be so patient and kind if the time came when her parents, or even her parents-in-law, needed her help. She prayed that moment was still a long way off.

Once Bill was in bed, Chelsea joined her mum and dad in the sitting room. Dave flicked through the channels, complaining there was nothing to watch, as usual, despite the astronomic cost of the Sky subscription. Jacqui and Chelsea had more important things to do than watch the television. Chelsea was very pleased to have her mum almost to herself for a little while. Normally, when she saw her parents, one or both of her sisters was there too. Though Ronnie lived just a couple of streets away and saw their mother pretty much every day, she always seemed to need Jacqui's attention more, even if Chelsea was only on a short visit. And if Jack was there, well, then nobody really got a chance to get a word in edgewise. It was the Jack Benson-Edwards Show from the minute that boy woke up. Not that they didn't love him for his exuberance and endless enthusiasms.

Sitting next to her mother on the sofa, with neither of her sisters to compete with, Chelsea felt as though she was twelve years old again. Back then, before she was allowed out on a Saturday evening, she and Jacqui would sit together and fill in the crossword in the back of the copy of *Best* to which Jacqui treated herself at the end of the supermarket shop. To fuel their endeavours, they would share an enormous bar of Dairy Milk. Tasting a square of Dairy Milk could always transport Chelsea back to those Saturday nights.

'Got any chocolate, Mum?' Chelsea asked now.

'If your dad hasn't eaten it all.'

He had.

Dave, having spent what seemed like half an hour going through every channel, announced that he was going down the road for a pint.

'Just the one,' he assured his wife.

'Heard that before,' said Jacqui. 'Just don't end up in a ditch on your way back.'

Dave assured Jacqui and Chelsea that he would be back within an hour, and then he headed for the pub.

Chelsea and Jacqui remained on the sofa. Now that Dave had relinquished the remote control, they quickly did find something worth watching – their definition of 'worth watching' being quite different from his. It was a rerun of a recent episode of *Long Lost Family*, the programme that reunited people with family members they hadn't seen in years. Typically, because a baby had been removed from a family at birth.

Jacqui loved to watch *Long Lost Family*. When the series started, long before she herself was reunited with the baby she'd given up for adoption – Annabel – the reunions she saw on the show had given her hope. They'd also made her feel slightly less bad about the decision she had made forty years before. Hearing the stories of other women who had relinquished their babies, she recognised their guilt and shame and, in seeing them find forgiveness from the children they had lost through no real fault of their own, started to forgive herself.

Chelsea and Jacqui watched the show in reverent silence. Jacqui could never stop herself from crying at the moment when a birth mother was reunited with a long-lost child. It reminded her so sharply of the moment she first set eyes on Annabel as an adult. How tense she'd felt before it happened. How oddly prosaic it was in the end. Just two grown women meeting in a bland hotel restaurant over tea and scones. That first meeting had not actually gone terribly well for her and Annabel. Jacqui was too anxious to act normally. Annabel was trying hard to remain aloof. They were practically strangers, after all, and they didn't have an awful lot in common. It had taken a good few subsequent meetings for the ice to melt and the subtle ways in which they were alike to assert themselves.

While Jacqui sniffed her way through another happy ending, Chelsea cuddled up to her, just as she had done when she was small, long before she and Ronnie even heard about Annabel and understood why their mother was so moved by films and television programmes in which people were brought back together with their loved ones. Even *The Littlest Hobo*, the American show in which a stray dog goes from town to town, changing the lives of the people it meets, could have Jacqui in floods of tears. Until Annabel tracked the Bensons down, Jacqui had relived her loss every day. Now Chelsea understood. Jacqui stroked her youngest daughter's hair.

'I am so lucky to have had you three girls,' Jacqui

said in a moment of sentimentality. 'Being your mother is the best thing that ever happened to me.'

'Aw, Mum. Surely going on a cruise is really the best thing that ever happened to you,' she joked.

'Being on a cruise *with* my daughters,' said Jacqui. 'And my grandson and the little girl who is going to be my step-granddaughter soon. We're so happy to be welcoming Adam and Lily into the family.'

The mention of Lily brought a flicker of worry into Chelsea's eyes. She sat up.

'Are you OK?' Jacqui asked.

'Mum, I'm really nervous about becoming Lily's step-mother,' Chelsea admitted. 'I don't know what to do.'

'You've been doing very well so far,' Jacqui pointed out. 'That little girl loves you, I can tell.'

'I hope so. But once Adam and I are married and it's official, I wonder if things will change. Are we having a honeymoon period? When she knows that I'm around for good, will she start to resent me?'

'Why would she resent you?'

'I don't know. Because I'm not . . .' Chelsea started to say 'because I'm not Claire' but she stopped herself. Instead she asked, 'What's the secret to being a good mum? I wonder if I've missed out on something I can never catch up with because I didn't actually carry Lily in my body. I'm worried that I'll never be able to love her enough to make up for what she's lost. Her real mum.'

There was a moment of silence as Chelsea's last sentence hung in the air.

'You could speak to Sarah,' said Jacqui at last.

Chelsea knew at once to whom she was referring. Sarah was Annabel's mum, the woman who had stepped in to become Annabel's mother when Jacqui gave her up for adoption.

'I think she'll tell you that it doesn't make a difference at all. You don't have to give birth to a child to love him or her with all of your heart. Motherhood isn't something that can only begin when you conceive a baby. Sarah is no less Annabel's mother than I am just because she didn't give birth to her.'

It was the first time Chelsea had heard Jacqui talk so candidly about Annabel's relationship with the woman who had raised her. The woman Annabel called Mum. Jacqui was always Jacqui to her eldest daughter. Sarah was the only 'Mum' Annabel would ever have in her life.

'Sarah loves Annabel. She was there for her all the way through. She was the one who Annabel went to when she needed comfort. She still is. My biological connection to Annabel will never trump all those years they had together. The care that Sarah gave to her. The happy times they had. The arguments they had when she was a teenager.'

'Did Sarah tell you about those?' Chelsea was curious.

'Oh yes. It sounds as though Annabel was just like Ronnie. A complete pain in the whatsit from the age of fourteen on.'

'I've got all that to look forward to,' Chelsea mused. 'Lily as a teenager. Can you imagine?'

'She's certainly going to be a challenge but you'll get through it together.'

'How do you parent a teenager?'

'Same way as you train a tiger. Carefully.'

Chelsea laughed.

'But you've got ages until you have to worry about that and you'll know what to do when the time comes,' Jacqui continued.

'I don't know. I just wish I were more like you, Mum.

I wish I knew what I was doing. You always seemed to.'

'Nobody knows what they're doing. Every parent / child relationship is different. We're all making it up as we go along but you'll succeed with Lily because you care.'

'I do care,' Chelsea confirmed. 'I love her so much more than I ever imagined possible.'

'I know.'

'It stings my heart when she gets upset. About anything! If someone says something horrible to her at school or she's sad about something she's seen on television.'

Jacqui nodded. 'That's being a mum.'

'But it's such a responsibility.'

'All the most worthwhile things in life are.'

'I'm so frightened of letting her down, Mum.'

'That's precisely why you won't.'

Jacqui gave her daughter a hug.

'You can talk to me about it any time, you know. Lily is going to be my granddaughter too. We're a team in this. We're a family.'

Just then, Dave returned from the pub. They hadn't expected him back before closing time.

'Was no one you knew there?' Jacqui asked.

'No. I saw Cathy Next Door,' he said. 'She challenged a bloke none of us had seen before to an arm wrestle.'

'Did she win?'

'Put it this way, his mate is driving him to A and E to get his shoulder put back where it should be.'

Chelsea and Jacqui were appalled.

'She doesn't know her own strength, that woman,' Jacqui observed. 'Like you.' She touched Chelsea lightly on the end of her nose. 'Like you.'

* * *

Chelsea slept in her childhood bedroom that night. When she turned out the bedside lamp, she noticed that the glow-in-the-dark stars she and Ronnie had stuck to the ceiling when they were around eight and ten years old respectively were still there, still sending out a feeble green shine after all that time. The sight of them made Chelsea smile as she remembered how happy her childhood had been. She thought about how much her parents had done to make her feel loved and cared for. It wasn't about getting her into the right school or buying her the right clothes or taking her to the right theatre productions. It was the simple stuff that mattered. The cuddles. The way they listened to her hare-brained schemes over the kitchen table. The respect they gave her views. The way they always let her know they were on her side. Chelsea didn't have to think of something new and exciting to do with Lily every day. She just had to be there. Be consistent. Be engaged.

She was trying to do that. She made an effort, when she and Lily were together alone, to keep her phone tucked away so that she could always give Lily her full attention. She tried to answer all the little girl's questions. She did her best to transmit an aura of unconditional love even when Lily was doing *her* best to drive Chelsea bonkers.

Being a de facto parent to Lily was very different from the life Chelsea had lived before. With no children to keep her from living exactly as she'd liked, she'd worked long hours and, when she wasn't working, spent almost as much time in bars, gossiping with her girlfriends about the various useless men they were dating. It was hard to think about everything in the context of another person. Two other people. Everything Chelsea did was now run through the filter of how it would affect the two people who would be her next of kin from the end of December.

She had expected to find it stifling. Instead, she found it made her happier than she had ever been. A little anxious from time to time, but definitely happier overall.

She texted Adam. 'Please give Lily a bedtime kiss from me.'

'She sends one back,' Adam replied.

The thought made Chelsea smile.

Chapter Twenty-One

The ladies

The following morning, Ronnie, Jack and Sophie arrived just after breakfast. Mark was working that weekend, raking in the overtime while he could ahead of an expensive Christmas, so the plan was that Jack would stay with his grandfather and great-grandfather while the Benson family women went to the bridal fayre. Jack, however, had other ideas. He could see Granddad Bill and Dave any day of the week. In fact, he did see them most days as Jacqui often picked Jack up from school so Ronnie could work longer hours at the funeral director's. Auntie Chelsea's company was much more rare and therefore more precious. Especially since Chelsea didn't spend so much time with Jack that she didn't pay what her nephew considered to be due attention when he talked about *Doctor Who* or Minecraft. Chelsea had actually managed to give Jack the impression that she was as keen on Sonic Screwdrivers as he was.

'I'm coming with you to the fayre!' said Jack, grabbing hold of Chelsea's waist and attempting to spin her around.

'You won't enjoy it,' said Sophie to her little brother. 'It's going to be all about dresses and flowers and girls' things.'

'I don't care. I like girls' things actually,' said Jack to Chelsea, ignoring his sister. 'I talk about girls' things with Lily all the time.'

Chelsea nodded. 'That's good to hear.'

'Girls' things are just as interesting as boys' things,' Jack continued. 'Everybody is the same.'

They started the equality message early at Jack's school.

'Fine,' said Sophie. 'See if you're still saying that when we make you try on a bridesmaid's dress.'

'A bridesmaid's dress?' Jack echoed.

'Well,' said Chelsea. 'That's not a bad idea. You're nearly the same size as Lily so we could try the dresses she might wear on you. It would certainly help me to get a better idea of what to buy.'

'Nooooooo!' Jack abruptly let go of his aunt, thundered out of the kitchen and went screaming up the stairs to hide on the landing.

'Actually, Jack,' Ronnie called up to him. 'You better had come with us. I don't know why I didn't think of it,' she said to Chelsea. 'He needs an outfit too. They'll probably have something for boys there.'

'I was thinking velvet knickerbockers,' said Chelsea.

Jack peered down into the kitchen from between the bannisters, horrified.

'But they would have to be the same colour as the bridesmaids' dresses. I wonder if they make them in pink.'

Jack let out another wail. 'I don't want to come with you after all. I don't like girls' things. I'm staying here with Granddad Dave and Granddad Bill.'

Down in the kitchen, Ronnie and Sophie gave each other a high-five.

So the women of the Benson family piled into Ronnie's car without Jack and drove to the Midland Court Hotel.

They met Annabel and Izzy at the venue. Annabel was taking her new role as wedding planner very seriously. She was carrying a clipboard, pink and glittery. Freshly bought from Paperchase for the occasion. Ronnie raised her eyebrows at that.

'Izzy and I have already done an initial tour of the whole fayre,' said Annabel when they caught up with her. 'I've marked on the brochure the stalls I think will be of most interest. We don't want to waste any time. There are some real amateurs in there.'

'Says the wedding professional,' Ronnie muttered. Jacqui gave Ronnie a nudge with her elbow to warn her to shut up.

'Thank you,' said Chelsea. 'That was a good idea.'

'Well, let me tell you, I already have wedding cupcake fatigue,' Annabel confided.

The women paid the entrance fee of two pounds per person – 'though why we have to pay to allow people to sell to us, I do not know,' Annabel complained – and went inside. The Midland Court Hotel was a fairly typical conference-style place. Three stars and no thrills. It was hard to imagine being especially excited about having a wedding there, but the first stall they came to was that advertising the hotel itself. They were offering a special wedding package for a thousand pounds, which entitled the wedding party to bring fifty guests and included a sit-down meal, a champagne toast *and* a wedding cake.

'Now *that* is a serious bargain,' said Ronnie. 'Me and Mark should have done that.'

'I dread to think what you get for twenty pounds a head including champagne and wedding cake,' Annabel scoffed. 'The three courses are probably a Scotch egg, a sausage roll and a Kit Kat.'

'That's what some people like,' said Ronnie.

'But not Chelsea.' Annabel beamed in her youngest sister's direction. 'I know we can do better than that for her. OK. There's no need for you ladies to see this first room at all. It's basically all about wedding entertainment. Bands, singers, impressionists. None of them are particularly impressive. I don't think Chelsea wants a Simon Cowell impersonator to be master of ceremonies for a start.'

'A Simon Cowell impersonator?' said Ronnie. 'Is he any good? This I have to see.' Off she went.

Annabel smiled tightly.

'Perhaps it's best if we split up and go our separate ways for half an hour,' said Chelsea, knowing that Ronnie was never going to let Annabel tell her what she did or did not need to see. 'How about we do that, and then meet up again here? We can all report on what we think might be of interest.'

'I feel as though Izzy and I have already narrowed the options down quite effectively,' said Annabel. 'I thought we might save you some time. But if Ronnie wants to duplicate our efforts, then . . .'

Ronnie reappeared. 'Mum, Chelsea, Sophie. You've got to come and see the Simon Cowell guy. He's really good. And he's got a dog that can impersonate Pudsey. He can do incredible tricks. You could have a Pudsey ring-bearer, Chels. How about that?'

Reluctantly, Annabel agreed to Chelsea's suggestion that the party split and reconvene half an hour later.

Chapter Twenty-Two

Chelsea

Chelsea soon began to think Annabel was right. None of the entertainers in the first room were the kind of acts Chelsea would have wanted for her wedding. The Simon Cowell impersonator was one of the better performers on offer. Though who wanted Simon Cowell at their wedding? Would he rig up a big illuminated cross over the top table and use it to cut short the father of the bride's speech? No thanks. Chelsea had never seen the appeal of Simon Cowell in real life. She hated his sneering, eye-rolling brand of criticism. She couldn't understand why so many people thought it was fun to see genuinely talented (or even the utterly deluded) wannabes humiliated on live television.

Neither did she want someone impersonating David Dickinson to be her master of ceremonies, though she thought he might amuse Adam. She'd caught him watching *Bargain Hunt* on a number of occasions. But what a career path to take – impersonating a D-list star. Chelsea wondered how the man had come to think it might be a good idea. What had he really hoped to be when he was growing up?

As well as the impersonators, there were many hopeful singers, taking it in turns at a microphone by the fire doors. While Chelsea circulated with Jacqui, they heard a passable Cher, a pretty good Michael Bublé and an appalling Lady Gaga.

'Michael Bublé did a Christmas album,' Jacqui pointed out. 'So he'll know all the classics.'

'Mum, you do know he's not the actual Michael Bublé, don't you? I think I'd rather have a singer who isn't pretending to be someone else.'

Suddenly, Ronnie rent the air with a whistle.

'Over here,' she shouted across the room to Chelsea and Jacqui. 'Quick!'

Ronnie was talking to a man who appeared to be dressed as Captain Jack Sparrow from *Pirates of the Caribbean*.

'You've got to see this. Do your impression,' Ronnie instructed the man when Chelsea and Jacqui came over.

'If the miners don't strike copper soon,' said the man, 'by Christmas we'll all have starved.'

Jacqui and Chelsea were confused. He wasn't anything like Jack Sparrow. And yet Ronnie seemed to be delighted. The man handed Chelsea his card.

'Oh, you're a Poldark impersonator,' Chelsea read. 'Now I get it.'

'He's good, isn't he?' said Ronnie.

'My girlfriend usually does Demelza,' Poldark told them. 'But we had an argument last night so she refused to come along today. I think it'll blow over though.'

'Right,' said Chelsea.

'We sing Cornish folk songs and stuff.'

'That would have been good to hear,' said Ronnie. 'Mum loves *Poldark*. So do I.'

'Perhaps you can be my Demelza instead,' the man winked.

'Ooooh, saucy,' said Ronnie.

Everyone could tell she was pleased. Ronnie took one of the impersonator's cards for herself.

As they drifted away from the poor woman's Poldark, Chelsea said to Ronnie, 'Who has Poldark and Demelza at their wedding? I bet they were doing Jack Sparrow and Keira Knightley this time last year.'

'Got to admire his enterprise,' said Ronnie. 'I bet he's very popular.'

She looked back in admiration. Poldark winked at her again. It made her giggle.

'Ronnie!' Jacqui exclaimed. 'You've got a perfectly good husband at home.'

After half an hour, as arranged, all the women reconvened in the lobby. Izzy and Sophie had not been taking the fayre terribly seriously. They'd mostly targeted the wedding favour stalls and had come away with an impressive haul of luxury chocolates.

Annabel, meanwhile, fanned out a handful of business cards.

'These are from the stalls I thought might be of interest to you. I've narrowed them down quite a bit since my first look round. What did you find?' she asked Ronnie.

'I found love,' Ronnie joked.

'She found a Poldark impersonator,' said Chelsea.

'Oh, Mum,' Sophie rolled her eyes. 'You're obsessed. It's embarrassing.'

'And I had a look in the cake room. There's one stall giving away whole cupcakes,' Ronnie told her sisters. 'Instead of measly samples.'

'I'm going to pass on that,' said Annabel, patting her stomach. Which was looking much flatter than it had done even a fortnight before, Ronnie thought. Her sister must be on a very effective diet. Or starving herself. Ronnie immediately wished she hadn't tried out three cupcake flavours.

'Well, come and look at them anyway,' she said. 'I think they look really nice.'

'Personally,' said Annabel, 'I think the tower of cupcakes had its day about three years ago.'

Which was two years before Ronnie had a tower of cupcakes at her own wedding.

'They're a bit of a lazy option,' Annabel continued, perhaps forgetting her sister's reception. Perhaps meaning to make a dig. It was hard to tell. 'It doesn't take much skill to make cupcakes. That's why they became so ubiquitous. Whereas a proper traditional wedding cake with sugar flowers—'

'Like the flowers you made for my engagement cake, Mum,' said Chelsea, quickly jumping in. She had noticed that Annabel's anti-cupcake speech was making Ronnie narrow her eyes.

'Yes. Now those were really lovely. That sort of thing takes a lot of talent.'

Jacqui beamed. 'I'd like to make the cake for your wedding, Chelsea,' she said.

'I can do the base,' said Ronnie. 'I did the base for the engagement cake, remember.'

'And it was delicious. Then that's settled,' said Chelsea. 'We don't need to look at cakes at all. Good.'

'But it's a big responsibility,' said Annabel. 'Making a wedding cake. An engagement cake is one thing but—'

'Mum and Ronnie can do it,' Chelsea insisted.

'Their engagement cake was the best I've ever tasted.'

Ronnie smiled. Round one: Ronnie Benson-Edwards.

Later that day, back at Ronnie's house, Chelsea tipped all the leaflets she had collected at the fayre out onto the kitchen table. Jack was very pleased with the wedding chocolate samples his sister had brought back for him.

'Don't stuff it all in your mouth at once!' Ronnie wailed as Jack did exactly that. 'That single chocolate costs two pounds.'

'Wow!' said Jack, talking with his mouth full. 'Two pounds! I could have two whole Kit Kats for that.'

'Is the chocolate much better than Kit Kat chocolate though, Jack?' his grandmother asked.

Jack looked contemplative as he finished chewing.

'Not really,' he said. 'And it's got bits in.'

'We won't be having those then,' said Chelsea, letting Jack have the one she had been saving too. 'I was thinking of having them for after the wedding dinner.'

'You could have Kit Kats instead,' said Jack, pleased with his solution. 'You can get them at the cash and carry.'

'You know what, Chels, I think you should go down the cash and carry for the lot of it,' said Ronnie. 'I couldn't believe the prices people were charging at that fayre. Seems like the minute you stick "wedding" in front of something, it's suddenly twice as expensive. I mean, why are wedding flowers so much more expensive than a normal bunch of flowers? And why are they any better? My flowers looked perfectly fine.'

'They did,' Jacqui agreed. 'They looked lovely, in fact.'

'Anyway, I've got good contacts in the floral world, Chelsea. Don't forget that.'

'If you don't mind having table decorations that spell out the words "Rest In Peace",' said Sophie.

'The florists we use at work can turn their hands to anything,' said Ronnie. 'You saw what they did for me. They don't just do funeral stuff.'

'Auntie Chelsea knows that, Mum. I was making a joke.'

'Well, it wasn't very funny,' said Ronnie.

'Thank you, Ronnie. I'll keep it in mind, though Annabel has suggested we do the flowers ourselves and I think that might be a good idea. It would certainly be cheaper. We can pick up everything we need at the flower market for the wholesale price. Since it's going to be Christmas, we're going to go for something along that theme with pine and holly anyway.'

'People could hurt themselves on holly,' said Ronnie.

'Only if they're total morons,' said Sophie. 'Or drunk.'

'It takes some skill,' Ronnie persisted. 'To make floral arrangements look good.'

'Annabel did a course in flower-arranging,' Jacqui interjected. 'She does all her own flowers at home. They always look lovely, don't they? I think she's got the eye.'

'I just don't see how having the wedding at Annabel's is going to save you money,' said Ronnie. 'If cash is really tight, why don't you go for the package the hotel itself was offering? Nothing wrong with that. A thousand quid. Fifty guests. Three-course meal and champagne. And cake. Though I still think Mum should make the cake.'

'Ronnie,' said Chelsea. 'I know what you're getting at but I really don't want to marry in a place that looks like it should be tacked on to a motorway service station. And I want more than fifty guests. I've already asked twice that many people to save the date. We can get at least a hundred in the barn.'

Jacqui nodded. 'Probably more.'

'Don't let Annabel railroad you,' said Ronnie. 'She's not the one who'll be paying it off for years. I know which kind of wedding I would go for.'

'The opposite of whatever Auntie Annabel suggests,' Sophie observed.

Chapter Twenty-Three

Chelsea and Jack

Because she was staying at Ronnie's house that night, sleeping on the sofa bed in the sitting room, Chelsea had the honour of putting her nephew Jack to bed. Before he would go to sleep, however, he needed a story.

'I'm feeling Christmassy,' he mused. 'Read me something about that.'

'It's only October,' said Chelsea.

'It's forty-three sleeps until I can start opening my Advent calendar,' Jack observed.

'That's more than six months in dog years.'

Still Chelsea looked through the books on Jack's shelves, which contained a surprisingly large number of seasonal books, and pulled out her own Christmas favourite, *The Snowman*. How that book had enchanted her when she herself was a child. She loved to see The Snowman's smiling face. And the little boy, wasn't he just like Jack?

When Sophie was Jack's age, not long after baby Jack was born, Chelsea had taken her niece to see a theatre production of *The Snowman*. The audience, both young and old, were rapt. And when it came to the scene where The Snowman melts, Sophie had cried out 'No!' with such anguish it broke everybody's hearts. Now, when they recounted the story, Chelsea and Ronnie laughed about it, of course. But it was a magical moment. Chelsea wondered if she and Adam could get tickets to take Lily and Jack to see the play that year. There was a small window in a child's life when they were old enough to go to the theatre but still young enough to be entranced by a Christmas tale.

Anyway, Jack enjoyed the way Chelsea read *The Snowman*, though he noticed when she tried to skip a page and he grumbled that she wasn't doing 'a voice' for Father Christmas. Apparently, when Mark or Ronnie read the story, they adopted a deeper voice for Santa's lines.

'How do you know Santa's got a deep voice?' Chelsea asked. 'He might be really squeaky.'

'Don't be silly,' said Jack, with the certainty of childhood.

'OK, that's it,' Chelsea said when she finished the book. 'You need to get some sleep.'

'Auntie Chelsea?' said Jack. 'I've got something important to ask you.'

'What's that, sweetheart?'

'Did you decide what I'm going to be wearing for the wedding? Did you really decide I'm going to wear knickerbockers?'

'Hmmm.' Chelsea suppressed a smile. 'Well,' she said. 'We did look at some knickerbockers and they would look awfully good on you. And they do go with my wedding colour scheme . . .'

'Nooooo!' Jack sat up, slapped his own forehead and slumped forwards from the waist as though he'd just been told some really bad news.

'So, I did ask the lady who was selling them how much it would cost for her to make a pair of knickerbockers especially for you. In velvet. In a dark-red that is really almost a pink.'

Jack wailed again.

Chelsea enjoyed his dramatic reaction for just a moment before she added, 'But unfortunately, they would cost a hundred million pounds.' Everything expensive in Jack's world cost a hundred million pounds. 'So I told her that you'll have to wear something else instead. Something like a James Bond suit.'

'Yes.' Jack gave a fist pump. 'Thank you, Auntie Chelsea.'

'Though maybe we can find cheaper knickerbockers somewhere else,' she mused.

'If you make me wear knickerbockers, I will fart all the way into the church,' Jack threatened.

'As long as you can do it to the tune of "Here Comes The Bride",' said Chelsea, 'that's fine. Now, go to sleep.'

She made to leave the room.

'Auntie Chelsea?'

'Yes?'

'Can I ask you one more question?'

Chelsea recognised the delaying tactic that Lily deployed on almost a nightly basis. 'Just one,' she said.

'OK. How much does a china dog cost?'

'That's a funny question. Are you thinking of buying Mummy a dog for Christmas?'

He nodded.

'Well, it depends on the dog. And the size.'

'Just a small one,' said Jack.

'Hmmm. I should think you could get one for a couple of pounds.'

'Is that the most expensive kind?'

'I shouldn't think so. The most expensive kind might be thousands of pounds. If it was an antique, like some of the ornaments at Auntie Annabel's.'

Jack's smile faded.

'Thousands of pounds. That's more than hundreds?'

'Yes,' said Chelsea.

Jack's forehead wrinkled.

'But Mummy wouldn't want one that expensive,' Chelsea tried to reassure him. 'I'll help you look for something a bit cheaper next time I visit.'

Jack was on the point of confessing about the shattered china ornament but then Ronnie came up the stairs.

'Is he giving you trouble?' she asked.

'No. Not at all,' said Chelsea. 'He was just saying that he's ready to go to sleep.'

Jack lay down and pulled the covers up to his nose.

Thousands of pounds. When Auntie Annabel finally discovered that the dog was broken, Jack was going to be in trouble for a year. He'd be paying off the damage until he was a grown up. There'd be no Christmas presents. No birthday presents. Not even any Easter Eggs. Jack had to make a plan to pay the money back and quickly.

Money was on Jacqui's mind too. When Chelsea and Ronnie came back downstairs, Chelsea joined her in the sitting room while Ronnie unloaded the washing machine.

'I'm sorry you can't have the wedding you really wanted, love. You know, a wedding in London at that restaurant you like to go to. Your dad and I, well, we wish we were able to help you out more. We should have saved some money from Granddad Bill's lottery win and put it aside for your marriage.'

'Mum,' said Chelsea. 'Don't think like that. I'm thirty years old. You don't have to find me a dowry. Besides, a wedding in the barn at the Great House is something a lot of brides would kill for. Once Annabel and Izzy start charging for her services, I won't be able to afford them. Believe me, there's going to be no cutting corners. We just won't be paying the ridiculous premiums all those people at the wedding fayre charge.'

'I know. Fifteen pounds to put a bit of ribbon round a chair!' said Jacqui. The concept of 'chair-dressing' was still boggling Jacqui's mind. 'Your dad and I never had to think about that sort of thing. Talk about money for nothing.'

'Exactly. But thanks to Annabel, I can save on all of that. I'll do my own chair-dressing for nothing more than the cost of the ribbon. And you're making the cake.'

'I've been thinking about that,' said Jacqui. 'I don't know if I'm up to it.'

'What do you mean?'

'I'm not sure my cake-making skills are what they should be. Not for a wedding.'

'You made the cakes for Ronnie's wedding.'

'I know, but they were cupcakes and, like Annabel says, cupcakes aren't really the thing any more, are they? She's right, I think. Everyone's fed up of them.'

'The cakes you made for Ronnie were wonderful. Everybody loved them. And our engagement cake! Those flowers were beautiful, Mum. Everybody said so.'

'I know you're having your wedding at your sister's house but you still want it to look professional. All of it. Adam's family will be expecting that.'

'Adam's family aren't snobs, Mum.'

'But he went to private school and everything. His friends won't want a cake made by me.'

'But I do,' said Chelsea, placing her hand on her mother's arm. 'I can't think of anything more special.'

'If you're sure . . .'

'I am sure.'

'Only Annabel didn't seem too keen.'

Chelsea was just beginning to get an inkling of the politics involved in planning a wedding.

Chapter Twenty-Four

Chelsea

Back in London, Chelsea described the wedding fayre to Adam. He laughed at the descriptions of the terrible cakes and the appalling impersonators and was suitably outraged by the cost of chair-dressing.

'Chair-dressing? Is that even a thing?'

'There are people out there making a six-figure living from it,' said Chelsea.

'I always knew I was in the wrong profession.'

Adam looked crestfallen for a moment. Chelsea knew that while she'd been at the wedding fayre, he had been working on his CV. It was a bad time to be made redundant in any profession, but in a profession such as his, which was extremely sensitive to the economy, it was awful.

'Have you got any leads?' Chelsea asked. She knew that Adam had sent an email to all his old uni friends, asking them if they'd heard about any vacancies. Adam shook his head.

'Maybe it's the wrong time of year to be looking,' she suggested. 'Nobody thinks about much else but planning for Christmas from this point forward, do they? Maybe it's best to start again in January?'

'Perhaps you're right but I feel better knowing my CV is already with a few headhunters. And if that doesn't work—'

'We'll set up Benson and Baxter's Bridal Accoutrements,' suggested Chelsea. 'Chair-dressers to the stars.'

'Are you going to stay a Benson after we get married?' Adam asked.

'Benson Baxter has a ring to it,' said Chelsea.

'That would make you CBB,' said Adam.

'CBeebies!' trilled Lily, entering the room. 'Can we have it on, please?'

Chelsea handed over the remote control.

Chelsea didn't tell Adam about the conversation she'd had with Jacqui about the cake. If only Annabel hadn't been so dismissive of the towers of cupcakes. She must have forgotten that was exactly what Ronnie chose for her wedding. Not because it was easier but because it was less expensive.

It also occurred to her that maybe Ronnie had a point about the cost of letting Annabel take charge. Was having the wedding at Annabel's really going to work out that much cheaper than if Adam and Chelsea had gone with their original plan? It was obvious that Annabel wanted to make this wedding a showstopper so she would have something amazing to show future clients. But would Adam and Chelsea be footing the bill? And in more than the obvious ways? Chelsea didn't want to fall out with anybody over this wedding. There was no doubt that tensions were already developing.

The weekend after the wedding fayre, Chelsea had to turn her attention to one of the most important pieces of wedding planning. What was she going to wear? Also, what was she going to make her bridesmaids wear? And Jack? Chelsea had ruled out knickerbockers – though she thought they would look extremely cute – but she had to think of something special.

Annabel had immediately offered her support for the bridal outfit shopping trip. As did Ronnie.

'You'll have to take both of them,' said Adam. 'If you take one and not the other, you'll never hear the end of it.'

He was right, of course. She had to take them both.

Meanwhile, Chelsea was reminded that there was something else to worry about, other than upsetting her sisters.

'Frances called while you were in Coventry,' said Adam. 'To confirm our lunch in November.'

So it was definitely happening.

'She wanted to know if you have any dietary requirements.'

'That was thoughtful of her,' said Chelsea. 'But isn't it a bit soon to be worrying about what to cook?'

'I don't suppose there's much else in the diary,' said Adam.

Adam's comment reminded Chelsea that Claire had been Frances and Brian's only child.

'She also wanted to know if I could take Lily up to their place next weekend. For a sleepover. She said they'd like to see more of Lily if they can.'

Chelsea wouldn't argue with that.

'And Frances did ask if we wanted to stay overnight when we go up for lunch, but then she remembered that they only have two guest rooms.'

'Isn't that enough?'

'Not while you and I aren't married, apparently.'

Chelsea felt herself blush. It hadn't occurred to her that was still an issue for anybody in the twenty-first century. And then she felt a little angry that Frances had raised the possibility at all. It seemed as though she never intended to have them stay. What she really wanted to do was remind Chelsea that she wasn't Adam's wife yet. Chelsea was about to say as much to Adam. She didn't.

You're overthinking this, she told herself.

'That's fine,' she said out loud. 'We can drive there and back in a day.'

Chapter Twenty-Five

The sisters

So, once again, Chelsea spent a Saturday with both of her sisters. Though there were dozens of wedding shops in London, Chelsea made the drive to the Midlands, where Annabel knew of a little boutique that could make Chelsea a bespoke dress in double-quick time and, hopefully, at half the price of any place in the capital.

It was worth a look. Chelsea was discovering that three months was not long to plan a wedding after all. At least, it was not long if you weren't able to buy your wedding dress off the shelf. The budget was set at eight hundred pounds. Chelsea knew that wasn't much when it came to wedding dresses – definitely not in London – but Annabel assured her that her friend would be able to do something wonderful within that range.

Had she a little longer, she might have made her own dress but, while she loved to sew, she wasn't sure that she could create quite what she wanted with her skills. She certainly wasn't confident she could get the boning on a bodice right. She also didn't have a lot of experience with lighter silks and satins. She foresaw hours of frustration as she tried to learn how to sew those sorts of fabrics without ripping them.

She also wasn't entirely sure what sort of dress she wanted.

Chelsea had a fairly clear idea of what she did *not*

want her wedding dress to be. She did not want a strapless dress. She did not want the skirt to be too puffy. She quite liked the idea of a Grace Kelly-style gown with a lace body. However, she was willing to throw all of her preconceived ideas out of the window if someone could persuade her to do so.

The boutique Annabel took them to certainly looked promising. The dresses in the window were a cut above the strapless monstrosities Chelsea had expected. And they were displayed very tastefully. The window was dressed for autumn, with fake autumn leaves scattered around the mannequins' feet. There was a nod to Halloween too, with a small arrangement of pumpkins.

Elaine, the woman who ran the boutique, welcomed Annabel warmly. It turned out that, like Annabel, she was a governor at Little Bissingden's tiny primary school. Since they were friends, Elaine quickly brought out a bottle of prosecco for Chelsea's party.

'Before we start,' she said, 'I think we should toast the bride.'

Chelsea basked in the warm wishes of Elaine, of her sisters and her mum. It was nice, being engaged. People were very warm towards a bride-to-be.

'Now,' said Elaine. 'What sort of dress have you been thinking about? What would be your dream frock for your big day? What colour? White? Ivory? Red?'

Chelsea opened her mouth to speak but in the time it took her to mould some of her thoughts into a sentence, both Annabel and Ronnie jumped in.

'I think she should go for white,' said Annabel.

'Cream is best with her colouring,' Ronnie said.

Chelsea laughed nervously.

'I think you could wear either,' said Elaine diplomatically. 'Depending on how you do your make-up. Do you have a preference, Chelsea?'

'I don't,' she said. Though it was closer to the truth to say that she didn't dare have a preference right then. She had hoped Annabel and Ronnie would get on with each other that afternoon. Minutes in, they were already disagreeing.

'Perhaps it's best if you have a wander around and pick out a few dresses that speak to you. Feel the fabric. That sort of thing. There are plenty of catalogues too. If we haven't got exactly what you're looking for here, we can order something in. Or we can make something from scratch. Though I know we don't have long. When is the wedding date again?'

'Nineteenth December,' Annabel jumped in while Chelsea was still trying to pluck the answer out of her head.

'Nineteenth. Yes. December. That's it.'

Chelsea placed her prosecco glass back on the tray and stood up to survey the rails. 'I don't know where to start,' she said. 'It's like being inside a pillow, with all the frills and flounces.'

Annabel suddenly had an idea. 'Why don't we all choose a dress each? That would be a good way of making sure Chelsea tries on lots of different styles.'

'But won't she know what suits her best?' asked Jacqui.

'Perhaps. But I also know that Chelsea is a very modest kind of person and so she might hold back from something truly spectacular. We, on the other hand, will be able to give an objective view. What do you think, Chelsea?'

'There's no harm in trying something a bit different,

I suppose. But Ronnie, you're not to use this opportunity to take out your revenge on me for borrowing your clothes without asking when we were teenagers.'

'As if I would,' said Ronnie. 'I'm going to choose you something just right. I know you, little sister.'

'Mum,' said Chelsea, 'you'll have a look for something too, won't you?'

'If you think I won't get it wrong.'

'Jacqui,' Annabel tutted. 'This isn't about getting it *wrong or right*. We're just experimenting. We're using all our skills to help Chelsea make the most of her wedding day. Choose freely. After all, if Chelsea hates the dresses we pick, she doesn't have to wear them. This is just about coming up with some suggestions to stop her from feeling overwhelmed.'

Annabel's idea was a sound one but it didn't really stop Chelsea from feeling overwhelmed. It was hard to see what any of the dresses were really like, because they were hung so close together. Chelsea would spot what she thought was a good bet, then discover that she was in fact looking at two dresses crammed too tightly together and she'd fallen for the bodice of one and the skirt of another.

She thought back to how she had helped Ronnie to choose her wedding dress. They'd done everything online, ordering a handful of frocks from Monsoon's wedding collection. Ronnie had tried them on at home and sent back those that didn't work. It suddenly seemed a much easier way to do it than this. Having both her sisters and her mothers in attendance was making Chelsea feel too self-conscious to take the time and the care she might otherwise have done. She didn't want anyone to get bored. She especially didn't want Ronnie and Annabel to have time to get on each other's nerves. The potential for disaster was paralysing.

Fortunately, Chelsea's companions were being less reticent. Annabel had soon pulled out *two* dresses that she thought would be contenders. Jacqui shyly added a heavily embroidered number to the pile. And Ronnie chose something that looked like Katie Price might have designed it.

Chelsea started to laugh, but a look from Ronnie told her that her sister had not chosen her cream satin number ironically. She really did think it might be Chelsea's style.

'OK,' said Chelsea, following Elaine into the changing room. 'Nobody is to laugh at me when I come out.'

Nobody laughed when Chelsea emerged in the first of the four white dresses – Jacqui's choice. Jacqui, however, let out a little cry.

'Mum?' Chelsea was worried.

'Oh, it's OK, love. It's just that I think I'm going to burst into tears. Oh, Chelsea! I can't tell you how lovely it is to see you in a wedding dress at last.'

'It's pretty weird for me,' said Chelsea, looking at her reflection in the mirrored wall of the salon.

Elaine helped Chelsea onto a low stool, so that the skirt of the dress could be seen to its best advantage. Then she pinched the fabric of the bodice to show Chelsea how different it might look when it had been fitted to her figure.

'And we'd have to take a little length off the skirt, depending on the height of your shoes,' Elaine explained.

Up on the stool Chelsea posed for her team, who quickly went into *Britain's Got Talent* judges' mode.

'I like it,' said Jacqui. 'It would look lovely if you wore your hair up so everyone can see the detail on the back.'

'It's not bad but I think it would be better in cream,' said Ronnie.

'It does come in cream,' said Elaine. 'Would you like to try the cream one on?'

Annabel was Simon Cowell. 'No, no, no,' she said. 'It totally swamps her. That neckline is much too busy. I think it would be much better for Chelsea to have a plain neckline so she can wear a delicate necklace. She's got lovely collar bones and a very fine neck.'

'What?' Ronnie scoffed.

'She does have nice collar bones,' said Jacqui, quickly capitulating. 'I should have thought of that. She would look better in something more delicate. You're right.'

'I don't think you should write that dress off so easily,' said Ronnie, suddenly changing her tune so that it was just that little bit more different from Annabel's.

'Try the next one on,' Annabel instructed.

'Try my cream one,' said Ronnie.

Jacqui's choice of dress was quickly on its way back to a hanger and out of contention.

'But, Mum, I do think it was a good start,' Chelsea said to put her mother at ease.

It was true that the dress Jacqui had chosen was slightly too big and, Elaine admitted as she helped Chelsea out of it, the particular alterations it had needed might have ruined the whole aesthetic.

The dress that Ronnie had chosen was definitely not too big. Chelsea breathed in while Elaine heaved the two sides of the bodice together at the back and hooked them into place.

'I can't breathe,' Chelsea said.

'It will start to loosen,' said Elaine. 'I think.'

And it was strapless, which was definitely not on Chelsea's wish list. However, when Elaine said, 'it gives you an excellent décolletage,' she was prepared to suspend her judgement for a moment or two.

Elaine helped Chelsea back into the main salon.

'Now that's more like it,' said Ronnie.

'She looks like she's going to faint,' said Annabel.

'I feel like I'm going to faint,' said Chelsea.

Jacqui leaped up. 'Then sit down.'

'I'm joking, Mum. Though it is a little snug.'

'It looks amazing,' said Ronnie. 'Exactly what I thought it would look like on you. It shows off your figure a treat. You'll knock Adam dead when he sees you walk into the church wearing that.'

'I should think half the congregation would drop dead if they saw Chelsea in that dress,' commented Annabel. 'Isn't it just a little . . . obvious?'

Chelsea crossed her arms over her all-too-bare chest while her sisters discussed the merits of dress number two.

'If you've got the figure for it, I say show it off,' said Ronnie.

'Isn't it better to hint rather than shout?' said Annabel. 'It's a wedding. She's promising herself to one man for the rest of her life, not auditioning for a new one.'

'What do you think, Chelsea?' Jacqui tried to put the spotlight back onto her youngest daughter.

'It's nice—' Chelsea began.

'But you don't feel comfortable in it,' Annabel interrupted. 'I can tell. The way you're crossing your arms across your chest says it all. You feel too exposed.'

'It's quite cold in here,' said Chelsea. 'That's all.'

'The temperature hasn't changed since you were in the last dress,' said Annabel.

'That one had a bit more fabric,' said Jacqui.

'You're only young once,' said Ronnie. 'You've got a

magnificent figure, Chels. Get out there and show it. You'll look back on your wedding photos in years to come and be glad you did. I wish I'd got married while I still had a waist.'

'What's the time, Mum?' Chelsea changed the subject. 'I know you want to be back home for tea-time.'

'That's all right, sweetheart. Your dad said he'd get Granddad Bill's supper tonight. We've got all the time in the world.'

Drat, thought Chelsea.

'Give us a twirl,' said Ronnie.

Chelsea dutifully turned so that the other women could see the back of the dress.

'It's giving her a roll of back fat,' said Annabel. 'It's too small.'

'We can get a size up in by the end of the week,' said Elaine.

'I wouldn't bother,' said Annabel.

Ronnie shot her a poisonous look.

'Your sisters have got very strong opinions,' Elaine observed as she released Chelsea from Ronnie's choice.

'Yes,' said Chelsea. 'Sometimes it's a bit like being stuck between two lionesses.'

'Just remember that it's your choice that matters. Neither of them is the bride. They're not the ones getting married. Don't let them bully you into a dress you don't want.'

'I won't,' Chelsea promised.

'And you do not have back fat,' Elaine added.

'I'm so glad you said that.'

'This one next?'

Elaine held up the first of Annabel's choices. It was quite old-fashioned. It had a full skirt and a nice narrow bodice but it also had leg of mutton sleeves of the kind that hadn't been seen since the early nineties. Since Annabel herself got married, in fact, Chelsea realised as she put the dress on. Annabel had basically chosen one of her two picks because it reminded her of her own wedding outfit.

'It's quite . . .'

'Sleeves are coming back,' said Elaine.

Chelsea stepped out of the changing room.

'That's great,' said Annabel, straightaway. 'You look very elegant in that one.'

'Oh my god,' said Ronnie. 'You can't wear that thing. The eighties called, they want their wedding dress back.'

'It's a vintage style,' said Annabel.

'It does remind me a bit of Princess Diana,' said Jacqui.

'See?' said Ronnie. 'Even Mum thinks it's old-fashioned.'

'I didn't say old-fashioned. Things come back into style, don't they, Annabel?' Jacqui offered her support to her oldest daughter.

'Exactly,' said Annabel. 'And I'm sure Chelsea will be able to give it a fresh new take, with all her fashion savvy.'

Chelsea pulled a face which suggested that all the fashion savvy in the world was not going to make Annabel's first choice of dress work.

'I think it would have to be worn ironically,' she said. 'And I'm not sure that I want to wear my wedding dress ironically.'

'Exactly,' said Ronnie.

'Fine. I see what you mean. Take it off,' said Annabel.

Ronnie was triumphant.

There was one more dress to go. Annabel's second choice was very different from her first. It was much lighter than all the others. It didn't have a floor-length skirt. Chelsea could envisage herself being able to put this dress on without the assistance of all her bridesmaids. Still Elaine helped her into it. It was covered in delicate beading.

'Done by hand,' Elaine said.

'Oh, lovely!' said Annabel, clapping her hands together.

'Nope,' said Ronnie. 'That is completely wrong.'

'What are you talking about? It fits her perfectly.'

'It's the wrong colour and it looks like something an Amish woman would wear. To a funeral.'

Chelsea studied the dress in the mirror as her sisters continued to argue its merits.

'It's a great shape,' Annabel insisted. 'Very nineteen twenties. It merely suggests that Chelsea has a knockout figure. It doesn't take out a billboard advertisement saying "great tits". Much more suitable, if you ask me.'

'It makes her look as though she doesn't have any tits at all.'

'Excuse me,' said Chelsea. 'I can hear you both, you know. Be kind.'

'I think it's nice,' said Jacqui, doing her best to remain neutral.

'That's the one,' said Annabel.

'I really preferred the other one,' said Ronnie. 'My choice. Though even Annabel's first choice, with the puffball sleeves, was better than this thing. This one, it's got no shape to it.'

'Of course it's got shape to it. The one you liked is actually too tight. And strapless really isn't right for someone of Chelsea's age. Or any age, for that matter, if you're getting married in church. In the winter. It will be very cold. And it's tacky to show so much skin in the house of God.'

'She can wear a cloak.'

'She won't want to wear a cloak for the actual ceremony.'

'Chelsea, sweetheart, which one do you like?' Jacqui asked in desperation. 'Because that's all that matters, isn't it? What Chelsea likes. She *is* the bride.'

'I'm not sure,' said Chelsea, not wanting to come down on either side. In actual fact, neither of the dresses that her sisters were so excited about felt like the right one to her. Ronnie's choice was too revealing but Annabel's choice was way too staid. Chelsea didn't want to look like Katie Price on her fifth short-lived marriage but neither did she want to look like a novice nun about to become a bride of Christ.

'She wants to be able to look back at her photos and be proud of how good she looked,' said Ronnie.

'On the contrary, she wants to look *timeless*,' Annabel insisted. 'Strapless just screams early noughties. It's going to look as dated in ten years' time as you think my puffball sleeves look now.'

'You're trying to make her look like you.'

'Well, I'm sure I don't know what you're trying to make her look like,' Annabel countered.

'Ladies,' Chelsea interrupted. 'I'm going to take this one off. Then I suggest we all go for a nice cup of tea. I'm going to need a chance to think about this.'

'You haven't got long,' said Elaine, when she and Chelsea were alone in the changing room. 'We've got to order the dress you choose in and do alterations. But you do have at least a week.'

'Thank you. I'm beginning to think that the only way I'm going to get away with this is to choose something entirely different from what either one of them wants to see me in. Maybe I should go for a Bianca Jagger trouser suit.'

'That would work,' Elaine assured her. 'Look. I see this all the time. This is what weddings are like. They always end up being about just about anything other than the two lucky people who are actually tying the knot. Instead, they become a flashpoint for long-standing family grievances. Or people try to have their dream wedding by proxy. We get a lot of mothers of the bride, who try to persuade their daughters to get the dresses they would have liked to wear themselves. And there's *always* rivalry where there's sisters. I once had a pair of twins have a punch-up right there in my salon.'

'Seriously?'

'They were having a joint wedding but they wanted to wear different dresses. Of course, they fell for the same one. It was like having two toddlers in the shop. In the end, they managed to rip the dress and, as far as I know, they both went to their joint hen night with black eyes.'

'I hope it won't come to that with Annabel and Ronnie. But all this makes we wonder if we should just elope.'

'And that can cause families to be estranged for years!' Elaine exclaimed. 'Be very wary about depriving the people who love you the opportunity to see you get wed. Anyway, aren't you having your party at Annabel's house?'

Chelsea nodded. 'She's being very generous.'

'All the same, make sure it's your day. Not hers.'

Chapter Twenty-Six

Chelsea

Chelsea was glad to get on the train back to London that night. Who knew that getting married was so stressful?

Adam didn't know it, that was for sure. He'd already booked his morning suit. It took him less than half an hour to find what he wanted and put down a deposit at a gentleman's outfitters near Clapham Junction. Chelsea decided that perhaps she would go online for the bridesmaids' dresses. If that day was anything to go by, it was going to be insanely stressful to have to make another visit to the bridal salon with her sisters, her mother, her nieces *and* Lily in tow. Just the thought of it was enough to make her head start to ache.

'Let's have a day off from the wedding,' Chelsea suggested on the Sunday.

Putting the wedding planning firmly to one side, she, Adam and Lily went for a long walk in Richmond Park, followed by a pub lunch. It felt like a proper holiday. It was especially nice to spend the day with Adam and Lily alone. It reminded Chelsea that all the fuss and bother about the wedding was going to have a wonderful outcome. She'd have her own little family.

While they were walking in the park and Lily dashed ahead to jump into a pile of autumn leaves, Adam told Chelsea how the visit to Frances and Brian's house had been. He had taken Lily up there on Friday night and they'd both stayed for a sleepover.

'They're the same as they ever were,' he said.

'Do they talk much about what happened?' Chelsea asked. 'About Claire?'

'I think we all try not to. It's been six years. We focus on Lily now instead. On the future. Brian and Frances aren't the kind of people who believe in talking endlessly about the things that make them unhappy. They're from a different generation. Stiff upper lip and all that.'

'What was it like the first time you met them?'

'I was petrified. It meant a great deal to me that they liked me. Claire had told me all about them, of course. She was so proud of them both. They were successful. Cultured. Rich. I was desperate that they should think me good enough for their little girl.'

'And how did it go?'

'It was an absolute disaster. I made a complete tit of myself. I couldn't think of a thing to say that wasn't a stupid joke. I was convinced that they hated me by the time Claire and I went back to London. I certainly knew their dog hated me. He bit me on the hand when I tried to pat him on the head.'

'My family must seem very different.'

'Yeah. I was lucky I didn't have to go through the whole meet-the-parents thing with them because I knew them already.'

Adam had met almost all of Chelsea's family during the week in Lanzarote to celebrate Jacqui's sixtieth. They'd had no idea how much he and his daughter would come to mean to them at that time.

'You don't have to worry about using the wrong cutlery where my lot are concerned.'

'Don't put them down like that. Your family are different from Claire's but it still matters to me enormously that they like me,' said Adam. 'Just as much as it mattered when I met Frances and Brian. They're your family. They're going to be mine.'

'I'm glad you said that,' said Chelsea.

'You're not nervous about meeting Claire's parents are you?' Adam asked.

'Of course I'm not,' Chelsea lied.

The following day, Lily ran out of school brandishing a piece of paper full of instructions.

'Chelsea,' said Lily. 'I've got some very good news.'

'What's that?'

'Today at school we started practising for the nativity play. I can't be Mary this year because I got an order mark for scribbling on Catlin's Maths book at the beginning of term, but Miss Hahndorf said I can be an angel instead.'

'That follows,' said Chelsea. 'Which angel? Angel Gabriel?'

'No. Angel Gabriel is boring. He just has to stand there and say stuff. I'm going to be one of the Harold angels.'

'The *Harold* angels?'

'Yes. The ones in the song. Hark the Harold angels.'

'Ah, you mean the *Herald* angels.'

'Harold angels, yes. There were three. And we've all got to have wonderful costumes. I told Miss Hahndorf that you are very good at sewing.'

'Oh?'

'And she said it would be very nice if all three Harold angels matched.'

'Right . . . Do you mean to say you volunteered me to make three costumes, Lily?'

'Yes,' said Lily brightly.

'Thanks.'

'My pleasure,' said Lily, copying a phrase she'd heard Adam's mother say. She skipped towards the car.

Thank goodness Lily was not upset that she'd been passed over for the part of Mary. Mostly, it was due to the costumes. Lily had quickly established that there was much more opportunity for a really special outfit when you were an angel. Mary, well, she had a certain look. Humble. Plain. Modest. Saintly, in a word. Pale blue or white dress. Blue headdress. You really couldn't deviate. You certainly couldn't add sequins to a Mary costume. An angel could totally have sequins, however. And glitter. And feathers.

'And silver shoes!' said Lily. 'And a little silver purse on a string to go over my shoulder.'

'What would an angel need a purse for?' Adam asked when Lily made her wish list over the kitchen table. 'I don't think they ever have to buy anything.'

'But they might need to *give* someone some money,' said Lily. 'If they're in trouble.'

'Good point,' said Chelsea.

'Can we draw the outfit after dinner?' Lily asked.

'You bet,' said Chelsea.

It was great fun. Chelsea loved to draw almost as much as Lily did. Lily had Chelsea draw the outline of a 'Lily' figure. Lily then added the frock. She couldn't do arms and hands, but Lily could certainly do bows and flounces. It wasn't long before she had designed herself an ensemble that was worthy of the last dress in a Vivienne Westwood catwalk show.

'I want this in silk,' she explained to Chelsea.

'Silk is expensive,' said Chelsea.

'And?' was Lily's reply.

When they had finished drawing, Lily practised her carolling in the bath. 'Hark the Harold Angels' was fast becoming a new classic. Adam and Chelsea couldn't help smiling when Lily sang, 'Risen with helium' rather than 'healing in his wings.'

'It does make sense,' Adam had to concede.

'I can't believe I've got to make three angel costumes,' said Chelsea, once Lily was in bed. 'Three! Those other mothers better both buy me a bottle of gin. Two bottles, if I've really got to try to replicate all that flouncing.'

By the following afternoon, Chelsea would be clothing a fourth celestial being.

Chapter Twenty-Seven

Jack

Over in Coventry, Jack had won the part of the Archangel Gabriel in his own school's nativity play. Jack was very happy with that. He hadn't wanted to be Joseph.

'I'm too young to have a baby,' he told his dad.

'I know how that feels,' said Mark.

Just as at Lily's school, parents were expected to provide the children's costumes, though there were a few stock items for some of the parts. The pale-blue Mary frock had clothed three generations of young Coventry girls. There was one 'real' crown for the king with the biggest speaking part. And the donkey outfit had been handed down through the years as well. It smelled like it.

Unfortunately for Ronnie, angel costumes seemed to have a particularly fast turnover. White wasn't a great colour in which to dress seven-year-olds with a penchant for blackcurrant juice. The previous year's Angel Gabriel had left the costume for that part looking as though it had been worn to go paintballing. No amount of Vanish would bring it back to a suitably angelic state. When she heard what she would have to do – that is, make a new one – Ronnie was straight on the phone to Chelsea.

'I can't bloody sew,' said Ronnie.

'What about the time you cut up that velvet dress when Jack was one of the three kings? He told me that was fantastic.'

'I didn't *sew* anything. I just cut out a square and made a hole in it for his head. It was only a tabard. And nobody noticed once he had his crown on. This time he's got a speaking part. *The* speaking part. Everyone is going to be looking at him.'

It was true. No matter what people thought, the Angel Gabriel was the part that proved you were best in class. Forget Mary and Joseph, the principal shepherds or the three kings. As Gabriel, you got the highest point on the stage. You got the spotlight. You got the flippin' wings.

'You've got to help me, Chelsea. You made that *Arabian Nights* costume for Jack in Lanzarote. An angel is no sweat for you and you're already going to be doing one for Lily.'

'And two of her mates.'

'What? How did that happen?'

'Lily volunteered me.'

'Well, if you're making outfits for two children you don't even know . . .'

'I'll make Jack's costume.'

Ronnie was effusive with her thanks. And what was one more? When Chelsea had a wedding to plan and a dress of her own still to find. Talking of which. . .

'Have you decided on your wedding dress yet?' Ronnie asked. 'You know you looked best in the one I chose, right?'

'Thanks,' said Chelsea. 'But I'm going for something completely different from all the dresses you, Mum and Annabel picked out.'

'What's it like?' Ronnie asked.

'You'll have to wait until the day.'

In the end, Chelsea had found her perfect dress in a vintage shop in London. She'd dropped in to look on her way to pick Lily up from school. She'd spotted the dress right away, though the shop was packed to bursting. It was as though it called to her. The girl who was manning the till that day didn't know much about it. Fortunately, Chelsea did. She recognised the hallmarks of a Givenchy dress at once. Though the label had long since been removed, there was no mistaking the quality. It was just right for a winter wedding. The silk was heavy and the beading was exquisite. The moment she put it on, she knew it was for her. And because the woman who owned the shop didn't know how special the dress really was, Chelsea got it for a bargain price. At three hundred pounds, it was well inside her budget, leaving her more to spend on the bridesmaids. And Jack.

As she continued on her way to Lily's school, swinging the dress in an old Dorothy Perkins bag (the vintage shop didn't have its own bags yet) Chelsea decided that the dress was her reward for having her sisters squabble in the bridal salon. Having found it gave her an enormous boost. She was one step closer to making her dream day come true.

Chapter Twenty-Eight

Everybody

Halloween quickly came and went. Lily attended an early evening fancy dress party held by one of her school friends, dressed as Elsa from *Frozen*, which was still really her favourite film despite her worry that perhaps it was a little bit babyish. There were older girls in Lily's class who had pronounced it 'over' but, fortunately, they were not invited to the bash. There was another little wobble when Adam pointed out that Lily didn't look very scary, but Chelsea helped out by opening her make-up bag. Moments later, Lily had a powder-white face and two dribbles of lipstick 'blood' falling from the corners of her mouth.

'Zombie Elsa,' Chelsea announced.

Lily was very pleased with that.

Meanwhile, in Coventry, Jack went trick-or-treating in the close where the Benson-Edwards' family lived. Dressed as a ghost with an old sheet over his head, he joined a trio of small boys, all neighbours, who were watched from a very close distance by their parents and forbidden from knocking on the doors of any houses which did not announce their willingness to play the game with a lighted jack-o'-lantern in the window. And there was to be absolutely no tricking, much as Jack pleaded to be allowed to throw an egg at Cathy Next Door's house after she scared the life out of the young revellers by answering the door dressed as the angel of death complete with real scythe.

'For fuck's sake, Cathy,' Ronnie complained as the children scattered.

'It was my grandfather's,' Cathy said.

'Whatever,' said Ronnie. 'I don't suppose it's even bloody legal.'

Cathy somewhat made up for it by loading down the petrified children with extra-long bars of Cadbury's Dairy Milk (after the scythe had been put away and Jack had been persuaded that his favourite neighbour had not really turned psycho killer). Thankfully, the rest of the evening progressed without incident, unless you count Mark getting belly ache from helping himself to a little too much of his son's sugar-laden haul.

'It's appendicitis,' Mark insisted, when Ronnie refused to show him any sympathy.

'It's wind.'

After Halloween came Bonfire Night. Chelsea, Adam and Lily went to watch the fireworks in Battersea Park. As they filed back to the nearest train station with the crowds afterwards, they came close to Battersea Dogs Home and Adam confirmed to Lily that they would indeed be getting a dog the following year. Lily was delighted. Chelsea wanted to squeal too. Having a dog had been one of her own long-held wishes.

'I want one like Pudsey!' Lily announced. They'd recently watched Pudsey the movie on DVD. Bang went Chelsea's hope of having a lurcher. She didn't mind too much though. Any pup would do. She would love it just the same.

Up in the Midlands, Ronnie and the Benson-Edwards were invited to Annabel's big house in Little Bissingden to celebrate 5th November. Sophie and Izzy watched over Jack as he played with sparklers. They cooked jacket potatoes and toasted marshmallows over the embers of the bonfire. Then Richard and Mark put on a serious firework display in the house's enormous garden. They were both closet pyromaniacs who liked nothing more than playing with matches. Leander stayed inside for that, having been given half a sedative tablet that made him totter around the kitchen as though he was stoned.

Everyone was so impressed by Richard and Mark's fireworks that it was decided that the men would put on another display for Chelsea's wedding.

'It can be our wedding present to her,' Mark said to Ronnie.

'We've already got her an ice cream machine,' said Ronnie.

'We can keep that,' Mark suggested.

'Yes! Ice cream every night!' Jack agreed. 'Auntie Chelsea would much prefer fireworks.'

Richard and Mark bumped fists. The upcoming wedding was suddenly one hundred and fifty per cent more interesting for them both.

Only Granddad Bill didn't enjoy Bonfire Night. He never really had. It came at the wrong time of year for him. In combination with the change of seasons and the scent of winter on the air, it took him to a place he didn't want to remember. It took him back to the Blitz.

Granddad Bill was particularly difficult that November. Jacqui and Dave declined Annabel's offer to join her fireworks party because they were worried how Bill might react to the sound of an explosion. Instead, they stayed home and turned the TV on extra loud to cover the noise of their neighbours' celebrations. Bill was spending more and more time in the past these days, going over and over the last time he saw his brother Eddie. He wanted to talk about how they had been playing cricket in the garden and Eddie promised to teach him how to be a better batsman. There was no way he would let himself get killed by Hitler when there was still so much important work to be done on Bill's batting technique.

When Granddad Bill first began to suffer from dementia, Jacqui and Dave had tried to gently bring him back to the present by putting him straight on the things he seemed to have forgotten. It was heart-breaking to keep having to tell him that his wife and his beloved brother were both long dead, but Jacqui and Dave assumed that was what they should do.

They'd recently decided that they wouldn't do that any more. When Bill was transported back to the nineteen forties and imagined himself a small boy again, what was the point of telling him that he was really an eighty-seven-year-old whose brother would not be coming to play cricket that night because he had died in the Blitz seventy-five years earlier? Jacqui and Dave were tired of seeing Bill newly bereaved with each telling of the story. Wasn't it just cruel to keep putting him through it?

So, the night of Annabel's bonfire party, Jacqui told Bill he didn't need to worry about the explosions he could still hear above the telly because his bedroom was actually a specially converted Anderson shelter. Dave and Jacqui joined him there at his insistence, until the bangs and whizzes stopped. They assured him that the old lady and the dog who usually joined him in the shelter were safely installed in one a little further down the street. And Eddie, Eddie his brother, his hero, would be perfectly safe. He was with their father. Of course they had both taken their helmets and their gas masks. They knew how to stay out of trouble. Hadn't they always come home before? Hitler wasn't having them.

'I don't know how long I can keep doing this,' said Jacqui to Dave, when Bill finally agreed that he could hear the 'all clear' and lay down on the pillows to sleep.

The local media coverage of the seventy-fifth anniversary of the Blitz only confused Bill more. The historical reports in the papers felt like new news. Back in the summer, budding journalist Sophie had interned at a local free magazine called *County Class*. She'd written an article on the Blitz for the November issue. It was illustrated with photographs of her great-grandfather as a lad, as he was when the bombing happened, and earlier that year, with Jack standing beside his wheelchair. Bill decided that the new picture of himself with Jack was in fact a photograph of him with his own great-grandfather. He was incredulous when Jacqui tried to tell him that he had three granddaughters and four grandchildren. He simply would not believe he was in his eighties.

But then there were moments when Bill knew exactly when and where he was. And that was what his family had to cling to.

'It won't be so bad if Bill's in 1940 when Chelsea gets married,' Dave suggested. 'We can tell him there's no beer because of rationing.'

It was an attempt at a joke. Nobody felt like laughing.

Fourteenth November – the anniversary of the night Coventry's cathedral was destroyed by the Luftwaffe

– passed quietly in the Benson household. Jacqui made an executive decision to skip over the date on her magnetic kitchen calendar. They had forty-eight hours of the thirteenth instead, before moving straight to the fifteenth.

They praised Sophie for her intelligent article when they saw her but they didn't show it to Bill twice.

'You've done him proud though,' said Dave. 'If he didn't have the dementia, he would have told you so himself.'

Seventy-five years. How could such an old memory stay so fresh for so long? And while more recent memories were slipping from Bill's mind like the leaves dropping from the trees in the park.

It would have been a very melancholy winter indeed, were there not Chelsea's wedding to look forward to.

Chapter Twenty-Nine

Chelsea

If Jacqui and Dave had dreaded the arrival of 14th November, Chelsea was dreading 15th November even more.

It was time for Sunday lunch with Claire's parents. Though Adam had reassured her time and again that Claire's parents were lovely people who wanted only the best for Lily and himself, Chelsea couldn't help expecting the worst.

She had seen pictures of Claire's parents. There were plenty in the wedding album, which lived on the shelf in the living room. Brian, Claire's father, did look like a friendly sort of person. He had a big smile. Frances looked a little trickier. Even on her daughter's big day, she looked distinctly aloof. She was very upright and elegant. Her hair was perfectly coiffed. She put Chelsea in mind of an old-fashioned Tory politician's wife, who could wither plants with a disapproving gaze and take down a potential terrorist with her handbag.

'Really,' Adam insisted. 'She is so much friendlier than she looks.'

Good, thought Chelsea. Because she doesn't look friendly at all.

Chelsea may have been feeling sick with nerves about the upcoming lunch, but Lily was very excited about going to see her maternal grandparents. Because they lived in the countryside in Rutland two hours' drive from London, she didn't seem them anywhere near as often as she saw Adam's parents, who were just down the road in Richmond. Over breakfast Lily was full of the delights of going to Grandma Frances' house.

'They've got a dog,' she said.

'That's the one that bit me,' said Adam. 'On its last legs now.'

'And there's a summer house in the garden.'

'Sort of a shed,' Adam explained to Chelsea. 'Full of spiders.'

'And a lake.'

'More of a pond.'

'And there's a rocking-horse.'

Claire's rocking-horse, presumably. As she buttered her toast, Chelsea had a sudden mental image of a wooden horse in an attic, rocking wildly though there was no rider in sight. No living rider, anyway. She shuddered.

'And Grandma Frances always lets me eat the cake mix,' Lily continued.

'She's an excellent baker,' said Adam.

She would be, thought Chelsea.

It took Chelsea a long time to dress that morning. Dressing to meet your loved one's parents for the first time was tricky enough. But dressing to meet the parents of your beloved's dead wife? There were no handy online guides to that one.

First, she pulled out a navy-blue pencil skirt and a white blouse that she hadn't worn in years. It was a very conservative ensemble. It had nothing whatsoever to do with fashion, unlike most of Chelsea's wardrobe.

'Do I look OK?' she asked Adam when she came downstairs.

'Well, yeah. Perfect for a job interview,' said Adam.

'Right. Thanks.' That was as good as a 'no'.

Chelsea went upstairs and changed into a blue cashmere jumper and a pair of plain grey woollen trousers. She accessorised with ballet flats and a very sober necklace of black beads. Still very conservative. An accountant on an away day, was what Chelsea thought when she looked at herself in the mirror. It was a very boring outfit. But Adam knew better than to pass comment this time. He just said, 'Are you ready to go?'

They had to be on the road.

Chelsea felt her nerves rising like a bubble in her oesophagus all the way down the M4. Meanwhile, Lily chattered happily about visits to Grandma Frances past. Did Adam remember the year there were ducklings on the village pond? What about the time the dog stole all the sandwiches off the table when they were having lunch in the garden? Would Grandma Frances let her play with Claire's dolls house again?

'I expect so,' said Adam.

'But I have to be very careful with it,' Lily told Chelsea. 'Because it belonged to my mummy and she was very careful with it when she was my age. It's an antique.'

'I don't think it is an antique,' said Adam. 'It's just a Barbie house,' he added to Chelsea.

Chelsea stretched the corners of her mouth in a smile as a sort of response. Owning a Barbie house had been one of Chelsea's childhood dreams. She had never had a proper dolls' house. When she was growing up, there wasn't enough money for real Barbie dolls, let alone their expensive accessories. Ronnie and Chelsea had

Barbie-a-likes bought from the market stall for a fraction of the price and instead of a store-bought dolls' house, they had piled three cardboard boxes on top of each other. Their dad had helped them to cut out windows and doors. They'd decorated the insides. Chelsea remembered the pictures she had drawn straight onto the cardboard walls. Had she ever had the chance to play with a real Barbie house, she would have been careful with it too.

Crazy. Chelsea felt a stab of envy at the thought of Claire's old toys.

The journey to Frances and Brian's house was at the same time too long and much too brief. It was long enough to give Chelsea time to worry herself into a real funk. It was too short to snap herself out of it. When Adam turned into the village, Chelsea almost asked him to drive around the block a couple of times but he couldn't do that. Lily had recognised her grandparents' village. She was brimming with excitement. She pointed out all the familiar landmarks.

'There's the duck pond, Chelsea. Can you see it? That's the farm where my mummy kept her horse.'

'She had a Shetland pony,' said Adam. 'For about six months before they sold it on. She wasn't a natural horsewoman.'

'It must have been very nice to grow up here,' Chelsea responded to Lily's excited chatter about her mother's early life.

The village was straight from a picture postcard, unspoiled by the march of time. It was the kind of place where people looked after their properties. Woodwork was painted every couple of years. Hedges were kept in check. Cars were washed every weekend.

Chelsea contrasted the village with the street she'd grown up on in Coventry. The people who lived there were kind and generous people but they had to work too hard to have time to keep their homes looking so lovely. There was little point in polishing cars that lived on the street and were falling apart. Chelsea knew that as children, she and Claire would not have had much in common. Claire might not even have been allowed to play with a girl from the wrong side of town.

And now they were at the house.

The home Claire had grown up in was beautiful. It was an Edwardian mansion, almost as grand as Annabel's house in Warwickshire. A Virginia creeper climbed the walls and curled around the big sash windows. The front garden was perfectly manicured and there was a classic Jaguar in the driveway. It looked as though it had been cleaned just that morning.

'Brian loves that car,' said Adam.

'Granddaddy's car is more than a hundred years old,' said Lily proudly.

'Not quite, sweetheart.'

'It's certainly very lovely,' said Chelsea. 'The house and the car.'

'Come on then,' said Adam, putting the handbrake on and patting Chelsea's knee. 'Let's get it over with.'

Chapter Thirty

Frances and Brian

Lily had already unfastened her seat belt and was eager to get out. Adam jumped out and opened the passenger door for her. There was a child lock.

Chelsea unclicked her own seat belt much more slowly. She remained in her seat, taking a few deep breaths. She checked her reflection in the mirror in the back of the passenger sunshade. She dabbed away a fleck of mascara that had flaked off onto her cheek. She wasn't wearing much make-up. She'd decided that 'modest' was the best look to go for. Inconspicuous. Determined not to cause offence. But she was an offence in herself, wasn't she? She was the woman who had taken Claire's place.

Adam tapped on the passenger window to hurry her along.

'You look great,' he reassured her.

Lily was skipping ahead to the door. Her grandfather Brian had opened the front door and swept Lily up into his arms. She squealed with delight.

'Granddaddy!'

Chelsea followed Adam up the path. He put out his hand to her but she didn't take it. It didn't feel quite right. Not here. Not in front of Claire's family. Chelsea's stomach was churning. She felt far more anxious now than she did the first time she met Adam's own parents.

There seemed to be so much more resting on this moment.

'You must be Chelsea,' said Brian.

He smiled broadly and warmly. Chelsea shook his hand. So far so good.

'Frances is just taking her pinny off.'

The smell of something delicious floated out from the kitchen. Lily was already heading in that direction calling, 'Grandma Frances, we're here!'

'Come in. Come in.'

Brian ushered Chelsea and Adam into the hall.

'How was the traffic?' he asked them. 'Not too bad I hope. The road works on the ring road are finished now, thank goodness. They were adding at least half an hour. Ridiculous.'

Chelsea recognised the traditional male opening gambit. If in doubt, talk about the traffic.

'We had a very easy run,' said Adam.

'Car still running well?' Brian asked.

'It is.'

'Been thinking about changing Frances' car sometime soon,' said Brian. 'She says she'd like an Audi.'

'Good cars,' Adam agreed.

Chelsea's focus was still on the door to the kitchen. Lily had run straight in there. Chelsea could hear her giggling at something her grandmother had said.

'We're very glad you could come here today,' Brian said to Chelsea. 'We've both been looking forward to meeting you.'

'And I've been looking forward to meeting you,' Chelsea lied.

At last, the moment arrived.

In person, Frances was every bit as intimidating as Chelsea had imagined. Despite the fact that she'd been in the kitchen all morning, when she finally came into the living room to meet Chelsea, she looked as though she had just stepped out of an editorial meeting at *Vogue*. It was hard to believe that she had ever been sporting a 'pinny' over the immaculate cream silk blouse she was wearing. Her blonde hair was coiffed, just as in the wedding photographs. Her make-up was perfect. Her manicure was immaculate. Chelsea, who was well used to sizing up other women and to being sized up herself, got all that in a couple of seconds. In the world of fashion magazines, you had to know your enemy.

Frances smiled when she and Chelsea were introduced, but Chelsea was sure that the smile didn't get as far as Frances' eyes and her handshake was light, as though she didn't want to touch Chelsea at all.

'We're so happy to meet you,' she said. 'Adam has told us a lot about you.'

'All good, I hope,' Chelsea said. She wished she hadn't. Too glib, Chelsea. Too glib.

The visit kicked off with drinks in the sitting room. It was exactly as Chelsea had imagined. It was tasteful in an old-fashioned way. The curtains and cushions were a subtle gold chintz. Chelsea perched on the edge of the seat she was offered. It was hard to keep her balance. The seat itself was deep and inviting, but Chelsea was still hell-bent on making a good impression and sinking back into the cushions would not help her do that. She kept her back straight and her knees pressed neatly together.

Brian offered Chelsea a gin and tonic. She gratefully accepted.

The artworks on the walls were as well chosen as the soft furnishings. Mostly landscapes. Watercolours. There were a couple of porcelain ornaments on the mantelpiece. A pair. A shepherdess and a young farmer. Pink-cheeked and eternally flirting.

While Brian and Adam continued to talk about the route they'd taken that morning, Chelsea attempted to curry favour with Frances by complimenting her beautiful home.

'That's a particularly lovely watercolour,' she said, pointing out a beach scene.

'Thank you. Claire painted that for us. I think it was on her first holiday with Adam after they became engaged.'

Chelsea nodded. What could she say?

'Do you paint, Chelsea?'

'A little. I like to draw. Figures. Fashion.'

'Fashion?' said Frances, as though Chelsea had said 'bums'.

The conversation stuttered. Chelsea tried not to gulp at her gin while Frances' questions brought to mind a scene out of Jane Austen. Do you paint? Do you play an instrument? Do you cook? What does your father do?

That was a tough one. For the moment, Dave wasn't doing all that much, having lost his job when the furniture store he was working at closed. That week he'd been accepted as a self-employed delivery driver for the Christmas season though, so Chelsea fudged her answer.

'He's in transportation,' she said.

Frances, thankfully, didn't press for details. Her attention was distracted by the sound of a timer going off in the kitchen.

'I must just check the lunch,' she said.

Chelsea relaxed the moment Frances left the room

with Lily following behind her. Lily was in awe of her glamorous grandmother. Chelsea was in fear.

'Lunch is served,' said Frances, returning from the kitchen all too soon.

Chelsea followed her through into the dining room. Yet another room which was lined with photographs of Claire. Claire as a baby. Claire as a schoolgirl. Claire on a horse. Claire taking her degree. Claire as a bride. Claire as a bride. Claire as a bride.

Chelsea chose a seat on the window side of the table.

'Actually,' said Frances, 'I would rather you sit there.'

Her tone made Chelsea wonder if she had inadvertently sat in Claire's place. That would be just perfect.

Lily helped her grandmother bring things to the table. At the Bensons', everything was plated up in the kitchen, straight from the pan. Here the food was presented in beautiful porcelain serving dishes with proper serving spoons. Heirlooms. The food did look delicious and Chelsea felt the urge to dive in. She knew what the urge was. It was the same one that used to drive her to the fridge after she'd rowed with her old boyfriend Colin or had a terrible day at work. When she was nervous or scared or otherwise upset, her stomach would always begin to growl. To silence that growl, she would have to stuff her face. Then she would have a brief moment of relief, before a different kind of anxiety kicked in and she hated herself for being so greedy. That was when she would throw up.

Beneath the table, Chelsea dug her fingertips into her thigh, bringing her consciousness to that sensation in the hope that she could distract herself for long enough that the anxiety would subside. It was no good. She had to eat. It was a compulsion. As soon as Adam had passed Chelsea the gravy, she picked up her knife and fork and tucked in.

'I thought we would say grace,' said Frances, fixing her with a look.

Chelsea felt herself shrivel in shame. Why hadn't Adam warned her that Claire's parents said 'grace'? She bowed her head towards the table, grateful at least that she could do that to disguise the raging blush that covered her cheeks. But she would not have long. Frances gave a very quick vote of thanks to the Almighty.

'For what we are about to receive, may the Lord make us truly thankful. Amen.'

'Amen,' everyone else echoed.

'Right,' said Frances, and she seemed to be aiming it right at Chelsea. '*Now* we can start.'

Chapter Thirty-One

Chelsea

Though the meal smelled and looked wonderful, Chelsea had suddenly lost her appetite. This was a new one for her. She pushed the food around her plate, avoiding the peas in particular. She was sure that if she tried to eat them in the 'proper' way, on the back of the fork, they would end up rolling all over the table.

'You don't seem to have eaten very much,' Frances commented, as Adam and Brian were already looking for seconds.

'I'm sorry,' said Chelsea. 'It was delicious but—'

'So many young women have eating disorders today,' said Frances, suddenly and unexpectedly heading into deep water as far as Chelsea was concerned. 'You must come across it all the time, working in magazines. Personally, I think it's attention seeking.'

'I don't think it's that at all,' said Chelsea.

'In my day, people didn't have anorexia or bulimia. And self-harming. How did that start? Ridiculous. How can one possibly feel better after cutting oneself? It makes no sense whatsoever. It's just a fad.'

Chelsea winced. 'I don't think it's that simple.'

'Then where has it come from? Why didn't the people of my generation and my parents' generation cut themselves if it really does work?'

'I don't think this is a conversation we need to have at Sunday lunch,' said Brian.

Lily had been talking to her father and grandfather, but now she was looking at Frances to find out what was taboo. Frances, thankfully, took the hint and turned her attention to dishing out seconds.

Chelsea was enormously relieved not to have to put Frances straight. She looked to Adam for a supportive shared glance. He didn't give her one. He just asked Brian something about the improvement works on the by-pass to get the conversation at that end of the table moving again.

Chelsea got through the rest of the lunch by not saying very much at all. Frances seemed to have forgotten her, focussing instead on Adam and her granddaughter.

Unlike his wife, Brian was the consummate host. He kept a careful eye on Adam and Chelsea's glasses. They were never allowed to run dry. Adam, however, was allowed to say he'd had enough because he was driving. Chelsea was not.

'You haven't got to go to work tomorrow,' Brian pointed out as he refilled her glass again.

'Yes. Adam tells me you're not working right now,' said Frances. The hint of condescension was clear.

'Actually, I am working,' said Chelsea. 'Freelance. It seemed the right time to try being self-employed. I may not have to leave the house in the morning any more but I still have to get things done.'

'But no one will know if you don't change out of your pyjamas first, eh?' said Brian. He meant it as a joke.

'I'm sure Chelsea changes out of her pyjamas,' said Frances. 'Don't you?'

'Sometimes she doesn't,' Lily piped up.

'Lily,' said Chelsea. 'That isn't true.'

Lily just gave a smirk and a shrug.

'It isn't true,' Chelsea echoed hopelessly.

And then Chelsea had a coughing fit. It wasn't just a polite little coughing fit, either. It definitely wouldn't be hidden behind a napkin. It happened when she took a sip of wine and it went down the wrong way.

'I've got to go,' said Chelsea, pushing back from the table so that she could run for the bathroom.

'Don't dash off,' said Brian. 'That's how people die. Locking themselves in the bathroom.'

That would be just fine, Chelsea thought. Anything would be preferable to continuing to sit there while Frances made snide asides.

'Chelsea!' Adam called after her. 'Brian's right. Don't lock the door.'

Chelsea didn't lock the bathroom door but she didn't come out. Not even when everyone else was gathered in the hall.

'As long as she's still coughing, she's still alive,' said Frances, loud enough for Chelsea to hear. 'Come back to the table, Lily. There's no point all of us being out here letting lunch get spoiled.'

Only Adam remained. He knocked on the door.

'Can I come in?'

Chelsea looked at her reflection. The coughing fit had robbed her of what little composure she'd been able to hang onto throughout that awful lunch. Her eyes had run and her make-up was all over the place. She opened the door so that Adam could join her.

'Are you all right?'

She wasn't sure whether he was shocked or disgusted by the way she looked.

'I'll live,' said Chelsea. She tried to fix her mascara with a piece of wetted toilet paper. She had proper make-up remover pads in her handbag but that, alas, was still on the floor beneath the dining table. 'I'm sorry. I've done nothing but show you up the whole time we've been here.'

'What are you talking about? Anyone could have a coughing fit. Especially with the wine Brian's serving. It's like paint-stripper.'

'But what about grace? I can't believe I just dived in and started eating. I wish you'd warned me. You should have said.'

'I have never heard Frances say grace before in my entire life. I was just as surprised as you were.'

'Lily didn't seem to be.'

'Perhaps it's something they do for her. To try to keep her from turning into a little savage.'

'As she would do under my care,' said Chelsea.

'What do you mean by that?' Adam asked.

'She thinks I'm incompetent. She thinks I sit in my pyjamas all day.'

'Who does?'

'Frances.'

'She doesn't. That's not what anybody thinks,' said Adam. 'Come on. We need to get back to the table. Frances is waiting to bring out the pudding.'

'Can we go straight afterwards?' Chelsea asked. 'We don't have to hang around for tea, do we? Will you tell them you've got an appointment in the morning or something like that?'

'I will,' Adam promised.

Chelsea followed him back to the dining room and took her seat again. Pudding, thank goodness, was a chocolate mousse. Nothing especially choking about that. But it tasted dry in Chelsea's mouth. She abandoned the dish after two mouthfuls.

'Dieting?' Frances asked as she took Chelsea's dish away.

The small worried voice inside, the one Chelsea tried so hard to suppress, immediately whispered 'Do I need to?'

As he had promised, Adam made their excuses as soon as Lily had finished her third helping of pudding. He claimed he had an eight o'clock meeting the following morning. Chelsea was pretty sure he hadn't told Frances that his job was coming to an end. Lily complained at having to leave but Frances soon put a stop to that.

'Daddy has an important meeting. And I'm sure Chelsea has things to do as well,' she added as an afterthought.

Lily hugged her grandparents goodbye. Brian had a hug for Chelsea too. Frances most definitely did not.

'Good luck in all that you do,' said Frances, as she shook Chelsea's hand.

It was a strange thing to say. On the surface it was nice enough, but Chelsea heard it as a dismissal. It was as though Frances wasn't planning to have to see her again.

Chapter Thirty-Two

Chelsea and Adam

'Well, I thought that went OK,' said Adam, as they drove out of the village at last.

Chelsea didn't respond. She just smiled tightly and nodded. Could Adam really think that the day had gone well? Frances hadn't thawed at all over the course of the four hours they'd spent there. Brian tried so hard to compensate for Frances' *froideur* that in the end he got rather drunk. Lily obviously, picking up on the atmosphere, had been more difficult than she had been in months.

Did it matter?

Chelsea had an awful feeling it did. Was Adam suddenly looking at her and seeing second best? She reran the afternoon through the cinema of her mind. Why had Frances made that crack about eating disorders? And dieting? Had Adam actually told Frances about Chelsea's struggle with bulimia? Chelsea wanted to ask him but, at the same time, she couldn't bear the possibility that he might have betrayed her confidence in that way and handed Frances the perfect reason to decide that Chelsea was not good enough.

Chelsea rested her head against the cool glass of the car window and watched the headlights of the cars flashing by on the other side of the motorway.

Back at home, Adam soon put Lily to bed. The little girl was surprisingly compliant. She was tired after all the excitement. Chelsea was tired too.

With Lily asleep, Chelsea and Adam settled down in the sitting room. Chelsea was still replaying the whole day over and over like a horror film on a loop. She saw Frances' face when she made that crack about eating disorders. It just wasn't possible that she didn't know. Frances must have known exactly how hurtful that comment would be. She wouldn't have bothered to make it otherwise.

Chelsea had to ask Adam what he'd told them.

'Oh, Chelsea,' Adam responded. 'You don't really think I would do that to you? I would never, ever betray your confidence like that. If Frances meant to try to hurt you at all, which I'm sure she didn't, it was just a stab in the dark. Maybe it was about your career in magazines. I promise you, she has no idea about your private life at all. I would never have said anything about that.'

Chelsea searched Adam's face for confirmation that he was telling the truth. She believed him. She had to.

'She hates me.'

'She doesn't.'

'I wanted so much for her to like me, Adam. I'm frightened that she's going to try to turn you against me. She doesn't want you to marry me.'

'Look, Chelsea, Frances and Brian are always going to be part of my life. They're Lily's grandparents and it's important that she retains her connection with Claire's family. But they do not have veto over any part of my life. They certainly don't get to tell me who I'm going to marry.'

'But we're so different. My family is nothing like

them. How can you want to be with someone like me from a family like mine after . . .'

Chelsea couldn't bring herself to say 'Claire'.

'I'm from a different class,' she trailed off.

'Chelsea,' said Adam. 'I don't know another woman on this earth who has as much class as you do.'

'You know what I mean.'

'I do and it distresses me to hear you say it. I hope I've never given you the impression that sort of thing matters to me. Knowing which knife to use at a fancy dinner table doesn't make someone better than somebody who doesn't. Going to the 'right' school doesn't make you more intelligent or worthy or more deserving of respect than someone who went to the local comp. Having notable ancestors or pots of old money doesn't make people kinder or more loving or more lovable. The way someone speaks or dresses or eats their peas. None of those things are important. What's important is what goes on in here.'

Adam tapped his heart. Then sat up straighter and held Chelsea's face in his hands so that she couldn't look anywhere other than at him as he spoke.

'I love you and I'm going to marry you, Chelsea Benson. It's really as simple as that.'

Chelsea curled up in Adam's arms. But she couldn't help looking towards the shelf, from whence Claire looked down upon them both. Her steady gaze seemed triumphant.

'Hold me tighter,' Chelsea asked her fiancé.

Chapter Thirty-Three

Everybody

The next couple of weeks went by in a flash. Plans for the wedding were coming on nicely. Chelsea was receiving lots of RSVPs in the positive. Together with Annabel, she had chosen a caterer and planned a suitably Christmassy menu. Turkey and all the trimmings. Christmas pudding for afters. Up in Coventry, Jacqui and Ronnie had already made the fruitcake base for the three-tier wedding cake they had planned. Jacqui spent most evenings making white sugar flowers.

Chairs and tables had been ordered. Tablecloths had been bought. The portaloos had been reserved. Annabel had negotiated hard with the portaloo providers, reasoning that she would be using their services many times over the years to come. As a result, she had secured Chelsea the deluxe version for festival slop-bucket prices. Annabel was proving to be very good at the business of haggling. When he saw the figures, Richard admitted that he had underestimated her business savvy.

Next, Richard and Mark got together to plan their surprise for Chelsea and Adam. They were both very excited about the firework display. With a budget more than five times that they'd spent for Bonfire Night, they bought a huge array for Chelsea and Adam's big day. They were given very strict instructions about how they should be kept when they arrived at the barn. Richard and Mark enjoyed the lecture, which underlined how dangerous their undertaking could be. That made it all the more exciting, of course.

Soon it was December. Lily and Jack opened the first doors on their respective Advent Calendars. Chelsea had bought them matching chocolate-filled calendars by Lindt. Lily wrote her Christmas list. It was long and extensive and annotated with websites where everything could be found.

'Father Christmas doesn't need website addresses,' said Chelsea.

Lily gave her a look, which may or may not have been meant to let Chelsea know that she had rumbled the truth about Saint Nick. Chelsea chose to ignore it. That would have been a real pity. Chelsea was sure she'd believed in Father Christmas until she was eight at the least. There were some very sophisticated little madams in Lily's class, however, and they weren't afraid of telling the less-mature children how things really were. Chelsea was dressing two of the little madams for the nativity play.

On 2nd December, the other angels came for tea, with their mothers, so that Chelsea could have them try on their costumes. Their behaviour, once they were high on chocolate, was far from angelic. Fortunately, Chelsea very much enjoyed the company of their mothers, whom she hoped would be useful allies for the future. It was always a good idea to have someone you could call upon to pick your child up from school if you found yourself unable to do so. And with the angel costumes, Chelsea was certainly racking up a lot of school credit.

The bridesmaids' dresses also arrived. As an acknowledgment of Annabel's well-meaning attempt to help find the wedding dress, Chelsea ordered all the bridesmaids' dresses from Elaine's shop. Adam was told to stay out of the way while Lily tried hers on. Chelsea wanted both her dress and the bridesmaids' dresses to be a surprise. Lily's frock was exactly as Chelsea had imagined the first time she considered a Christmas wedding. White silk with a smocked bodice and a red velvet cape to match. Lily loved it. She loved the little red leather ballet shoes Chelsea had bought to go with it even more.

'I want to wear them now!' she said.

Fortunately, she was persuaded that would not be a good idea.

And then it was 4th December, a very big day in the wedding calendar. Both Adam's stag do and Chelsea's hen party would be happening a little earlier than was traditional. The run up to Christmas was a busy time for everybody and thus they picked 4th December in the hope that everyone they wanted to attend would be able to come along.

Adam was going to be spending his stag night in London with his brother, his best mates from uni and his dad. Chelsea would be driving up to Coventry to spend her official last night on the town as a single woman with her mother, her sisters and her nieces.

Lily would be spending the night with Frances and Brian.

'Will you drive her there on your way to Coventry?' Adam asked.

Chelsea could hardly say that she would rather stick pins in her eyes than have to see Frances again. Frances was, after all, doing Chelsea a big favour, taking on the responsibility of childcare so that Adam and Chelsea could celebrate the end of their single lives.

'Of course I will,' she said.

Adam hugged Chelsea hard. 'Just remember not to drop your aitches,' he said.

Chelsea gave him a playful dig in the ribs. As the weeks had passed, that awful Sunday lunch had receded in Chelsea's memory. She and Adam had had several conversations since which had largely put Chelsea at ease about what Frances thought of her. The wedding was the most important thing on Chelsea's mind right then.

Chapter Thirty-Four

The ladies

Chelsea and Lily got to Rutland around lunchtime. It wasn't the first time they'd met, so Chelsea, having spent much of her adult life in a luvvy-media type world automatically went to kiss Lily's grandmother 'hello'. She realised too late that she had made a mistake. Frances froze. When Chelsea pulled back, she saw that the expression on Frances' face was something close to horror.

'I did think that Adam would bring Lily up,' she said.

'Well,' said Chelsea, 'it made much more sense for me to do it, since I'm on my way to Coventry for my hen party.'

'Ah yes. Coventry. That's where you grew up.'

'It's a great city,' said Chelsea. Never mind that she had left the town as soon as she possibly could. She was going to defend it from Frances.

'I can't say I've ever been there,' Frances replied. 'Just driven around it. Will you stay for a cup of tea?' she asked. But the invitation seemed so rote that Chelsea was sure it wasn't genuine.

'I should press on,' she said. 'My sisters are expecting me.'

'Well, have a good time,' said Frances.

'Did you get Adam's email about Lily's nativity play?' Chelsea asked. 'I know she very much wants you to be there.'

'Will you be there?' Frances asked.

'Of course.'

Chelsea was sure she saw a flicker of disappointment in Frances' eyes at that. She was glad she had an excuse to get away.

She felt her mood lighten with every mile she drove towards Coventry and away from Frances' house. It helped that the radio show she listened to for most of the journey was full of Christmas classics. She loved the cheesy old favourites. Even 'Mistletoe and Wine', the cheesiest Christmas song of all time, had the power to lift her heart. When 'Last Christmas' by Wham! was played, Chelsea sang along at the top of her voice, remembering how she'd sung the song as a teenager, drinking underage at the local pub. Though the tune was almost as old as she was, it was still a go-to song for every girl who ever found herself without someone to kiss under the mistletoe. It was even better to be able to sing along knowing that at last she'd found 'a real love' just as the lyrics said. George Michael knew how to write an anthem.

The Christmas music made the journey to Coventry seem to pass in record time. Chelsea hoped she hadn't set off any speed cameras in her haste to be away from Frances and back with the people she knew really loved her.

Ronnie's house was already decorated for the season. As children, the Benson girls had bemoaned the fact that they were never allowed to put up Christmas decorations before the start of the school Christmas holidays. It was the way it had always been, Jacqui told them. As a child, she'd had to wait until Christmas Eve.

Now that she was an adult and could make her own rules, Ronnie barely waited until December before she got the decorations out. Her husband Mark, fortunately, was in agreement that Christmas should be celebrated for as long and as loudly as possible.

'Decorations cost money,' was his rationale. 'If you only use them for two weeks a year, you're not getting your proper money's worth.'

So the Benson-Edwards family always decorated their house on the first of December. It didn't matter whether it fell on a weekend or a weekday. The first of December was when their Christmas lights went up. All over the house. Inside and out.

At three o'clock that December afternoon, it was already beginning to get dark and gloomy but there was no danger that Chelsea would not be able to find Ronnie's house in the twilight. Number 15, Three Spires Close glowed like a beacon. Like a radioactive beacon.

This year, Mark had truly outdone himself as far as the exterior decorating was concerned. There were some fantastic new additions to the illuminated characters on the lawn. The inflatable Father Christmas was there for the fifth year running. Now three reindeer joined him, each with glittering antlers and a flashing red nose, and an enormous snowman, which put Chelsea in mind of the marshmallow monster in *Ghostbusters*.

It was lucky for Mark and Ronnie that their neighbours were in on the joke. Although it was still so early in the Christmas season, there was hardly a house on their little cul-de-sac whose occupants hadn't entered in to the spirit of things and put up their decorations early. Cathy Next Door was neck and neck with Mark and Ronnie when it came to having the most heavily decorated semi. She had festooned the front of her property with enough lights to confuse the air traffic going into nearby Birmingham airport. A full-size model of Santa's bottom and legs waved from the chimney pot, as though the old chap was stuck head first.

It was naff but it was all very good fun and it was in a good cause. The following weekend, the street would be hosting a special street party in aid of the local children's hospice. The previous year, hundreds of visitors had come from all over Coventry and the West Midlands to see the lights and to buy mince pies and mulled wine provided by the residents. It was a lovely new tradition. Jack enjoyed it enormously and Chelsea would have taken Lily to help him man the Benson-Edwards' mince pie stall had it not clashed with Lily's own school Christmas fair.

Jack had heard Chelsea's car pull up to the kerb and was soon jumping up and down at the sitting room window, waving at his aunt. He jumped in time with the Father Christmas on a spring, which hung from the curtain rail. That model of Father Christmas was twice as old as Jack was.

'You're here!' said Jack when Chelsea reached the front porch. 'I've been waiting for you all day. I need some help with my Christmas list.'

'What? You mean you can't think of anything to put on it?' asked Chelsea. 'I'm amazed.'

'No. I need help spelling "fire extinguisher". Mummy says that if I don't spell it right, Father Christmas won't know what it is and he won't be able to bring me one.'

'Why do you want a fire extinguisher for Christmas, Jack?' she asked. Though looking up at all the bulbs glittering on the front of the house, as she stepped in, Chelsea thought that a fire extinguisher might not be such a bad idea for a Christmas gift after all.

'At last,' said Ronnie, joining them in the hall. 'Are you ready for tonight?'

'Ready as I'll ever be.'

'Is that what you're wearing?' Ronnie asked.

Chelsea looked down at her outfit with irritation. She knew that question meant her sister didn't approve of her jeans and jumper combo.

'I've got a dress in my bag,' she said.

'Good. And I've got some stuff for you to put on as well.'

Chelsea wasn't sure she liked the sound of that.

Chapter Thirty-Five

Chelsea and Ronnie

If Annabel was going to be planning Chelsea's wedding, then the duty of arranging the hen night had to go to Ronnie and Ronnie was determined to make it a night to remember.

'Just as long as we don't have to go to the Tollgate,' said Chelsea, remembering the pub where she'd done much of her underage drinking.

'No way!' said Ronnie. 'We're sending you off in style.'

But Ronnie's idea of style was a long way from Chelsea's. Ronnie sent Jack upstairs to find 'a plastic bag with a crown on it'. Jack brought the bag down and Chelsea winced as Ronnie pulled out the hen party accoutrements she had picked up at the cash and carry. A pair of learner plates. A veil. A plastic tiara. A pair of plastic handcuffs. A plastic wand tipped by a flashing penis . . . There wasn't a single hen night cliché Ronnie hadn't bought into.

'Don't look, Jack,' said Chelsea as she hurriedly stuffed the penis wand back into the bag.

'Is it a sonic screwdriver?' Jack asked his aunt, all innocence.

'No, I'm afraid it isn't,' said Chelsea.

'Awwww,' Jack complained. 'Can I have a go with the cufflinks?'

He meant the handcuffs, of course.

'I hope there's not going to be a stripper,' said Chelsea, while Jack went off to arrest his father.

'You'll have to wait and see,' said Ronnie, in a way that immediately suggested there would indeed be a stripper.

'Oh great,' said Chelsea.

It wasn't going to be a huge party. But Ronnie had gone to the effort of getting in touch with some of Chelsea's old friends from school, who still lived in Coventry. They were going to meet them at the club later on. First, a much smaller group would be going to a restaurant near Warwick for a nice civilised dinner. If it was possible to have a civilised dinner when one of your number – Ronnie, to be exact – was planning to wear a rubber hat shaped like a condom.

'Mum!' said Sophie. 'You cannot go out like that. You're totally showing us all up.'

'Don't be such a square. Your Auntie Chelsea is getting married. We've got to celebrate properly. We thought this day would never come.'

'I knew she'd get married one day,' said Sophie, jumping to her aunt's defence.

'Thank you, Sophie,' said Chelsea. 'I appreciate that.'

'I did too,' said Jack, appearing in the kitchen. He still had the handcuffs. 'I knew you would get married, Auntie Chelsea. Mummy . . .' He paused to take in his mother's head-gear. 'What is your hat supposed to be?'

'It's the finger off a rubber glove,' said Sophie, thinking quickly. 'Take it off, Mum. Seriously. Before Jack asks any more questions.'

'Why don't you want me to ask any more questions?' Jack asked his sister.

'Just don't, OK? There's nothing going on that you need to know about. Not yet.'

That was a mistake. Jack was immediately intrigued.

'Why does Auntie Chelsea have to wear a number plate? And why is she called a hen?'

'I don't know,' said Ronnie. 'She just is.'

She pulled a bottle of M & S prosecco from the fridge. 'Right. Let's get this party started!'

She poured out three glasses. One for her, one for her sister and one for her daughter. Jack insisted on having a glass of his own – albeit filled with Sprite – so that he could join in with the toasts.

'To my little sister,' said Ronnie. 'Settled at last but definitely not *settling*.'

'That's a good one,' said Chelsea.

'What does that mean?' Jack asked.

'Settling is what I did when I married your father,' Ronnie told him.

'That's not fair, Mum,' said Sophie.

'I'm joking. You know I love your dad. In fact, Chelsea, what I wish for you is as happy a relationship as me and Mark have had.'

'That sounds good to me.'

There were more toasts. Ronnie drank most of the prosecco. Chelsea went upstairs to get changed into her frock. There was a brief panic when Jack handcuffed Sophie to the handle on a kitchen cabinet and no one could find the key, but soon everyone was ready to go.

Chelsea joined Sophie and Ronnie in the taxi. They swung by Jacqui and Dave's house to pick their mother up. As Jacqui got into the car, Ronnie handed her a pair of 'comedy' deely-boppers, crowned with two willies on springs.

'Oh,' said Jacqui. 'Thank you. I think.'

'You don't have to wear them until we get to the club,' Chelsea assured her mother.

Secretly, they were all hoping that by the time they got to the club, Ronnie's bag of awful accessories might have been left behind somewhere. At the restaurant. In the back of a cab. Anywhere.

'Annabel chose the restaurant,' said Ronnie as they drove into town. 'I told her you wouldn't want anything fancy but she insisted. That's why we've got to get a few drinks in first,' she added as she passed Jacqui a bottle of WKD from the stash she'd brought with her. 'It costs a fortune, the place she picked.'

It was a restaurant that held bad memories for Ronnie. It was the place where she and Annabel had gone for dinner back when they first met, when Ronnie tested as a match for Izzy and everyone thought Ronnie would give her new-found niece one of her kidneys. That night, in the restaurant, Ronnie had tried and failed to tell Annabel that she really wasn't sure she could go ahead with the operation. She had her own children to think about. She couldn't take the risk. The restaurant, with its memories of that time, was not a place that Ronnie was especially keen to revisit.

But this was Chelsea's hen night and Annabel claimed it was a place that Chelsea very much wanted to go to. And so they were going.

Chapter Thirty-Six

The ladies

Annabel and Izzy met the others at the restaurant. They both looked chic and elegant in little black dresses. Annabel's was a classic. It had a boat-neck and fell to her knee. It was obviously expensive. Izzy's, which came from All Saints, was rougher and more edgy, as befitted her age. Sophie was wearing something almost identical in navy blue. The girls had bought the dresses together. Sophie spent the money her parents and grandparents had given her for passing all her GCSEs with spectacularly good grades.

A waitress took their coats. She was having a busy night. The restaurant was serving a special Christmas menu for the whole of December. The beautifully decorated main dining room was full of parties. Lots of local businesses had chosen to hold their Christmas bashes there. As a result, the place was buzzing. The atmosphere was lovely but not too rowdy. At least, not yet. As far as Chelsea was concerned, Annabel had made exactly the right choice.

But Chelsea's party was not going to be in the main dining room. For 'special reasons', Ronnie explained, they were going to be in a smaller room upstairs.

Once they were at their table, it transpired that Annabel had also been stocking up on hen night-related nick-nacks. There were no more plastic penises, though.

Annabel had gone with a very sweet red and white confetti theme. She'd also bought everyone a party favour in the shape of a Christmas present, each one containing a mini bath bomb decorated to look like a Christmas pudding. It was all very tasteful.

Chelsea waved her penis wand at her eldest sister.

Annabel blushed.

'Gosh, that's—'

'Exactly what you should be carrying on a hen night,' said Ronnie. 'I've got a pair of penis deeley-boppers for you.'

All six women chose to eat from the Christmas menu that night. A smoked salmon starter followed by traditional roast turkey and finishing up with a slight variation on the theme: Christmas pudding ice cream. They continued to drink bubbles. Sparkling water and champagne.

The conversation mostly revolved around ribbing Chelsea for things she had done in her childhood. It wasn't just the turkey that was getting a roasting. Chelsea went crimson as Ronnie recalled some of their childhood exploits. No one knows how to embarrass you like your sister.

Indeed, Ronnie was about to embarrass Chelsea in a big way.

It was while they were eating the Christmas pudding-flavoured ice cream that he arrived. The waitress came over to the table and whispered in Ronnie's ear. Ronnie grinned widely.

'Now we're going to have some real fun,' she said.

Up until this point, the music in the restaurant had been relatively quiet and muted. An inoffensive mix of Christmas carols. Suddenly, someone turned the music up. The Christmas tunes were drowned out by the *Poldark* theme tune.

Chelsea, Annabel and Jacqui looked at each other in confusion. Sophie covered her eyes.

'Oh, Mum. You didn't.'

Izzy tried to pull Sophie's hands away.

'You don't want to miss this!' she cried. 'This is going to be epic.'

Suddenly, a figure appeared in the doorway. He was dressed in leather breeches and a billowing white shirt. He wore knee-high boots. His hair was long, dark and curly. In his right hand, he carried an old-fashioned hobby horse: a stuffed head on a broomstick, which he stuck between his legs as he cantered into the room.

'I've left Demelza,' the man announced in a very ropey Cornish accent, 'and come to carry Chelsea Benson away on my 'orse.'

It was the wedding fayre Poldark.

'Is he supposed to be Poldark?' Annabel asked Jacqui. 'Looks more like the little one from Cannon and Ball with that hair.'

The *Poldark* theme segued into every male stripper's anthem – Right Said Fred's 'I'm too sexy'.

'Oh wow,' said Chelsea as 'Poldark' began to dance. 'Just wow.'

'I didn't know he did stripping,' said Jacqui.

'He's just added it to his repertoire,' said Ronnie. 'His Demelza never did come back after that argument so he had to diversify.'

Poldark strutted around the room, which wasn't easy because the table was large and the room really wasn't. There was barely half a metre of space. He paused by Chelsea, thrusting his pelvis suggestively in her face.

This time Chelsea covered her eyes. Sophie was still peeping through her fingers.

'Mum, Mum, how could you do this to us all?' she asked her mother.

'Shut up,' said Ronnie. 'Your Auntie Chelsea loves it.'

Honestly, Chelsea really didn't know where to look. Poldark straddled her lap as he began to unbutton the cuffs of his billowing white shirt. Then he started to undo the buttons down the front. Never mind that the real Poldark would have worn a shirt that went straight over his head. Pervy Poldark licked his lips and looked into Chelsea's eyes. With all buttons undone, he whipped the shirt off and whirled it around. When he let go of it, it sailed through the air to land on Annabel's half-eaten ice cream.

'Ugh,' she said. 'I won't be able to finish that now.'

Oblivious to the disgust behind him, Poldark continued to shimmy closer to the bride-to-be. He suggestively cupped his own pecs.

'I wouldn't do that if I were him,' Izzy whispered to Sophie. 'Talk about highlighting his man boobs.'

It was true that this Poldark wasn't exactly a 'hard body'. He'd been eating too many of Demelza's pies.

'My eyes,' said Sophie. 'I will never get over this.'

'I'm too sexy' cut straight into 'You're the one that I want' from *Grease*. It was a curious medley. Then Poldark started to undo his boots. They were zipped. Again, he lost points for lack of attention to detail. But what he lacked in historical accuracy, he made up for in enthusiasm. He whirled one of the boots around his head, like Dita Von Teese with a stocking. Everybody ducked.

And all the women in the room, apart from Ronnie, averted their eyes when Poldark dropped his trousers.

'Just tell him to put his pasty away,' squeaked Sophie.

Thank goodness Poldark was persuaded against an encore.

'You're entitled,' he said. 'That's what's been paid for.'

'Oh no,' said Chelsea. 'I think you've worked hard enough.'

Ronnie handed Poldark an envelope with his fee. He gathered his clothes and his hobby horse and headed for the gents'.

'I thought he'd be better at dancing,' Ronnie complained once he'd gone.

'Ronnie, he was great,' said Jacqui.

'Every woman wants a Poldark stripper,' said Chelsea.

'It was that or Father Christmas,' said Ronnie.

'Nooooo,' said Sophie. 'Father Christmas doesn't take his clothes off! Mum, that would have traumatised me.'

'And me,' Izzy agreed.

'Why? You don't still believe in Father Christmas, do you?'

'Auntie Ronnie,' Izzy deadpanned. 'What are you trying to tell me?'

'I'd like to propose a toast,' said Annabel, in an attempt to bring the conversation back to a higher level. 'To Chelsea. We're all so happy for you. Adam is a very lucky man.'

The women all raised their glasses.

'I wonder what Adam and his gang are doing?' Chelsea mused.

'Who cares?' said Ronnie. 'They can't be having anywhere near as much fun as we are. And there's more to come.'

Sophie and Izzy grimaced at one another. By downing a full glass of champagne when she toasted her little sister, Ronnie had officially crossed over from tipsy to flat-out drunk.

While the older women finished their coffee, Sophie and Izzy made a trip to the ladies' to retouch their make-up for the trip to the nightclub ahead. Izzy was only just eighteen. Sophie was officially still too young to go clubbing but everyone hoped that she would sneak in if she arrived with respectable adult company. They would make sure she stayed out of trouble.

While the girls were reapplying powder and highlighter and lip-gloss, Ronnie swayed in. She had that plastic bag with her again.

'Put this on,' she said to her daughter as she pulled a black T-shirt out of the bag. On the front of it was emblazoned 'Chelsea Benson's Hen Night'. On the back, 'Last chance for a quickie.'

'Mum,' said Sophie. 'There is no way I'm wearing that. No way.'

'Yes you are. Stick it on over your dress. I've got them for everybody.'

'Mum, I'm serious. This is really nasty. Last chance for a quickie? We'll get harassed.'

'Izzy,' said Ronnie. 'You'll wear one, won't you?'

Izzy winced. 'It's not really my style, Auntie Ronnie.'

'It's not about style. It's about looking part of a team. It's so we can all find one another in the nightclub.'

'We don't need T-shirts for that,' said Sophie. 'Especially not black ones. You won't be able to see anyone in the dark.'

'Just put them on. They cost me five pounds each.'

'That much?' said Sophie.

'Just stick it on,' whispered Izzy diplomatically. 'We'll take them off as soon as we get to the club. They'll keep us warm on the way there. It's freezing outside.'

Sophie followed Izzy's lead. 'This is so embarrassing. Please don't let us see anybody we actually know before we can take these off again.'

Ronnie emerged from the toilet cubicle in her own shirt. The bawdiness of the words was emphasised by the contours of her ample chest.

'Right. Come on, you two. We've got to get the others dressed up as well.'

Jacqui caved immediately. She recognised that Ronnie was just trying to make the party go with a swing and pulled her T-shirt on over her frock. Chelsea too accepted her T-shirt, which was extra-special, with glittered writing where the others had plain pink.

'Thank you,' she said, using the expression she'd honed through years of working at magazines. She was good at hiding her feelings when she thought something was a bad idea.

Only Annabel wouldn't be persuaded. She picked up the T-shirt that Ronnie had given her and held it at arms' length as though to better read the writing.

'That will never fit,' she said.

'I made sure they were stretchy. Just put it on.'

'Ronnie, this won't even go over my head,' Annabel insisted.

'I got you the same size as I got myself,' said Ronnie, perhaps knowing that Annabel would likely believe she was smaller than her sister. 'If it fits me then it must fit you.'

'I'm still not wearing it. It won't go over this dress. I don't want to crease it. If I was wearing a skirt and a top, perhaps.'

'Suit yourself,' said Ronnie, suddenly. So suddenly that everyone was a little surprised. They'd expected her to push much, much harder to make Annabel dress up. Perhaps she thought she'd met her match. 'I'll call a couple of taxis to take us to the club, shall I? Then we should ask for the bill.'

'Already sorted,' said Annabel.

'What? I didn't put any in for me and Sophie.'

'It's all taken care of. It's my hen night gift to Chelsea.'

'Thank you,' said Chelsea. 'It's really very kind of you, Annabel.'

Chelsea gave her eldest sister a squeeze and a kiss on the cheek.

Ronnie glared at the back of Annabel's head.

Chapter Thirty-Seven

Ronnie and Annabel

The taxis arrived pretty quickly. It was that golden moment when everyone who was going out for the night had gone out and it was still too early for the big rush home. But there was bad news when they reached the club. Ronnie had planned ahead. She'd gone online and added the names of everyone in the hen party to the VIP guest list and, indeed, their names were on the door. But the door was shut.

Cathy Next Door, who never knowingly missed a party, was waiting for Ronnie and the rest of the gang at the top of the street. The area around the club was bedecked not with Christmas decorations but with police tape.

'They've closed the club,' said Cathy.

'What happened?' Ronnie asked.

'I don't know. Stabbing, I reckon.'

'Stabbing?' Chelsea and Annabel said in unison.

'Or a glassing. Or maybe just drugs. An ambulance took someone away about ten minutes ago.'

Izzy and Sophie shared a look of concern. Izzy's experience with a bad E had shaped her whole life in a moment. Her subsequent kidney failure and transplant had influenced her cousin's decision that she would never touch a drug that wasn't prescribed.

'Ugh,' said Chelsea. 'Sounds like we're lucky to have been a bit late.'

'Are they going to open it again, do you think?' Jacqui asked.

'Depends if someone died,' said Cathy Next Door. 'If it was just a superficial stabbing, then I expect they'll clean up and let everyone in. Don't want to lose out on the Christmas crowd. But if someone died it becomes a murder investigation, doesn't it?'

Cathy Next Door looked as though she rather hoped it would.

'Oh dear,' said Chelsea. 'Let's hope whoever went off in the ambulance is OK.'

'I'll call Scott and get him to tune into the police radio and find out,' said Cathy.

'Isn't that illegal?' Annabel asked.

'They listen to us,' said Cathy Next Door. 'We need to keep tabs on them too.'

While Cathy fished for gossip, Ronnie was busy rallying the troops via text message. Chelsea's school friends Jade and Chloe had actually been inside the club, having arrived as soon as it opened, but everyone had been ejected when the trouble kicked off. They were at the other end of the street, cut off from Chelsea and the rest by the police tape. To join them, they would have to make a very long detour. They didn't know whether it was worth it. They were nearer to the bus station at their end of the road. They were sorry about the hen night, but had ultimately decided to go back to Chloe's rather than hang about in the cold.

'Ah well,' said Annabel. 'I suppose that's it for the night. Probably for the best. I don't know about you, Jacqui, but I'm completely bushed.'

'I am a bit tired, yes,' said Jacqui. And she was eager to take her hen night T-shirt off too. It may have been full of Lycra, but it was still cutting off the circulation under her arms.

'Where else can we go?' asked Ronnie.

'I think it might just be time to go home,' said Annabel.

'Have a nice cup of tea . . .' dreamed Jacqui.

'No way! We've got to go dancing!' said Ronnie.

'I agree with Annabel and Mum. Let's call it a day,' said Chelsea.

'What are you talking about?'

'We've had a great night. We had a great meal. We saw Poldark take his clothes off. We don't need to go on anywhere else.'

'Chelsea, you only get married once!' said Ronnie. 'This is your one and only hen night. Let's have another drink.'

'Really, I think I've had enough,' Chelsea said.

'You've hardly had anything.'

'I had at least three glasses of wine.'

'Exactly. You've hardly had anything. Come on. Let's go over there.'

Ronnie pointed to a very dodgy-looking pub that was already heaving with the revellers who'd been kicked out of the nightclub. 'I'm going to get you some shots.'

'Chelsea doesn't want any shots,' said Annabel.

'Oh yeah? Who asked you?'

'I'm just repeating what she said. She said she's had enough.'

'You're Chelsea's mouthpiece now, are you?' Ronnie asked.

'Ronnie, it's fine, really,' said Chelsea. 'But I don't want any shots. I think I'd rather go back to Mum's and have a nice cup of tea.'

'Me too,' said Sophie. 'I'm really cold.' She was almost glad she had that awful T-shirt on.

'Lovely,' said Jacqui. 'I may even be able to offer you some cake, if your dad and Granddad Bill haven't already got at it.'

'You cannot be serious!' said Ronnie. 'Tea and cake on a hen night?'

'Oooh, I could just do with some cake,' said Cathy Next Door.

'Then come back with us,' said Jacqui. 'You're very welcome.'

'What kind of cake is it?' Sophie asked.

'It's one of those red sponges. Red velvet cake is what it's called. It's chocolate flavour. First time I've made it. I think it turned out OK.'

Everyone but Ronnie agreed that chocolate-flavoured red sponge sounded like a very good idea.

'I've got some mince pies too,' Jacqui added. 'But they're shop-bought.'

'I don't care if the mince pies were made by bloody Mrs Christmas herself. We can't go home! It's only ten o'clock,' said Ronnie, full of indignation. 'The night is young.'

'But we're not,' said Annabel.

'Ha!' said Jacqui. 'That's funny, that is.'

Ronnie scowled.

'I think we should head towards the centre to get some taxis,' Annabel continued. 'There are too many people hanging around here. We'll never get one. We should also try to get a head start. Once everyone gets fed up of waiting for the club to reopen, there'll be a rush.'

'Good idea,' said Jacqui.

She and Annabel made to start off in the direction of the taxi rank.

'No,' said Ronnie. 'We can't go home now.'

'Ronnie,' said Annabel. 'We're all very grateful for your attempts to get us into this club, but I think we're all also secretly very pleased that it isn't open.'

'Oh really. You're the spokesperson for everyone now, are you, Annabel? You can't not be in charge, can you?'

'What are you talking about?' Annabel asked.

'Take Chelsea's wedding. You've just muscled in on everything. You're not really interested in Chelsea. I've been her sister since the day she was born. You hardly know her.'

'And you think you do? Didn't you see how mortified she was by that stupid penis wand?'

'Actually,' Chelsea began, 'the penis wand was OK.'

Ronnie and Annabel both turned and glared at her. This was not the moment to interfere.

'You're just using her to test your wedding business,' Ronnie went on. 'You're not really interested in what she wants. You've overridden her preferences at every turn.'

'That's not true!' Chelsea interrupted again. 'The wedding is going to be exactly what I want.'

'Look at you,' Ronnie continued to attack her older sister. 'In your posh frock and your old lady shoes.'

Izzy and Sophie raised their eyebrows at each other in shock.

'Too classy to wear one of my T-shirts. That sums you up, that does. You think you're better than the rest of us. You always have done and you always will. But you're not that much better, are you? You took the money you were offered from Granddad Bill's lottery win and now you've got to get an actual job. Welcome to the real world.'

Earlier that year, Granddad Bill had won forty thousand

pounds on the lottery. The bulk of it had been divided among the great grandchildren, including Izzy and Humfrey, despite the Buchanans' wealth. Ronnie hadn't seemed to mind at the time, insisting that all the children should be treated equally regardless of their parents' status. Now the truth of Ronnie's feelings was coming out.

'Ronnie, I don't know why you feel the need to be so nasty all of a sudden,' said Annabel.

'I've been feeling the need to be nasty all night. I saw how you rolled your eyes when the stripper arrived.'

'I think we *all* rolled our eyes at the stripper.'

'I hid mine,' Sophie piped up.

'I forked out a hundred quid for that,' said Ronnie.

'Then you were ripped off,' said Annabel. 'Look, Ronnie. I don't want to argue with you—'

'No. You'd rather whisper and snigger behind my back.'

'No one is whispering and sniggering.'

'Right,' Ronnie growled.

'That's it!' said Jacqui suddenly. 'I can't cope with this. I won't have you two fighting. I'm going home, Ronnie. Chelsea, please walk me to the taxi rank.'

'Of course, Mum.'

'I'm coming too,' said Annabel. 'Izzy?'

Izzy shrugged. As if she had a choice.

'Can I get a lift with you, Grandma?' Sophie asked Jacqui.

'Turning my own daughter against me now!' Ronnie railed.

'Mum,' said Sophie. 'For heaven's sake. You're steaming drunk. No one's turning against you. I just don't want to stand in the middle of the street for the rest of the night listening to you having a rant about nothing. It's freezing.'

'Cathy,' said Ronnie. 'You're staying with me, aren't you?'

Cathy Next Door hummed and hawed – the cake was a huge draw – but then she said, 'All right. I will. It's not every night I get to go clubbing. I've been looking forward to it.'

'See?' said Ronnie. 'See?'

'We'll see you back home, Mum,' said Sophie.

The rest of the party headed for the taxi rank, leaving Cathy and Ronnie to queue for the club which did actually reopen within ten minutes of the others giving up and going home.

'Can't have been a fatal stabbing then,' said Cathy, with just a hint of disappointment, as they joined the queue to go in.

Chapter Thirty-Eight

Chelsea and Ronnie

The following morning, Chelsea woke up with a headache but it wasn't because of the booze. She knew that. She'd actually lied to Ronnie about having had three glasses of wine, because every time Ronnie's back was turned, Chelsea would secretly ask the waitress to bring her an empty glass to replace the one her sister had topped up. No, Chelsea had a headache because of Ronnie.

The argument at the end of the night, when Ronnie squared up to Annabel, was still clanging around her brain. Ronnie was so much in the wrong. She had been absolutely vile to their big sister though Annabel, walking with Chelsea and Jacqui and the girls back to the taxi rank, had assured them all that she really wasn't upset.

'Ronnie just had a few too many. We all say stupid things when we're drunk.'

And truthful things, thought Chelsea. *In vino veritas.*

Jacqui quickly agreed with Annabel. 'When she wakes up in the morning, I bet she'll be really embarrassed. She'll probably call you, Annabel love, to tell you that she's sorry.'

'I hope so,' said Chelsea, but knowing Ronnie of old, she somehow doubted it.

'Let's not let it spoil what's been a wonderful evening,'

said Annabel. 'We all had a great time at the restaurant.'

'Oh, it was lovely,' said Jacqui. 'Thank you so much for getting the bill, Annabel.'

'It was unbelievably kind of you,' said Chelsea.

'It's just my gift to you, Chelsea. My little sister. You deserve to be treated.'

'I certainly feel as though I've been spoiled,' said Chelsea. 'Even with the visit from Poldark.'

'Now *that* is something I don't think any of us will ever forget,' said Annabel.

The morning after, Chelsea found herself wishing that Annabel had not picked up the bill. Or, at least, found some way to do it more discreetly. Or pretended she'd had a whip-round. It was undoubtedly Annabel's extravagant generosity that had started Ronnie off. She'd unwittingly initiated another competition in which Ronnie simply could not compete. Ronnie had wanted the whole evening to be *her* homage to Chelsea, right down to the cheesy stripper.

Chelsea checked her phone. There was a text from Adam confirming that he'd got home from the stag do safely and wanting to know how her hangover was. Chelsea sent him an emoticon of a smiley face with its tongue sticking out. She hadn't told him she wasn't planning on drinking, so of course he assumed she was waking up feeling like something the cat dragged in.

There was a text from Annabel, thanking her for a lovely evening. Chelsea responded with an emphatic. 'No. Thank YOU! You made it really special.'

And then there was a text from Ronnie.

'We need to talk,' was all it said.

Chelsea groaned. She wondered if Ronnie could even remember half of what she'd said the previous evening. That was probably what she wanted to talk about. She wanted Chelsea to reassure her that she hadn't been an idiot. Well, there was no way Chelsea was going to reassure her about that, because Ronnie had been a first-degree idiot of the highest order and, as far as Chelsea was concerned, she needed to know it.

It had always been the plan that Ronnie would come over to Jacqui's that morning, bringing Jack for a Christmas costume fitting. Chelsea was looking forward both to spending time with her nephew and seeing him wearing the angel's costume she had created. It was subtly different from the one she had made for Lily. The shape of the tunic was straighter and there were certainly no sequins. He would have had a pink fit at the slightest hint of glitter.

Jack came in first. He was brandishing a piece of paper.

'This is my speech for the show,' he said.

Ronnie followed him. She was wearing sunglasses. Jacqui and Chelsea shared a glance.

'What?' said Ronnie. 'It's bright out there.' She winced as she took the glasses off. Her eyes were still half closed.

'What time did you get in?' Jacqui asked.

'We stayed out until the club shut,' said Ronnie. 'Cathy Next Door knows how to have a good time. Unlike some people I could mention.'

'Don't mention them,' Chelsea warned her.

Jack had gone from the kitchen to the front room where Granddad Bill and Dave were watching football highlights. He stood in front of the screen to deliver his speech.

'And lo,' he said. 'I bring great tidings of great joy.'

On the television, someone scored a goal.

'Get out the way,' said Dave. 'We can't see who's winning.'

Jack brought his angelic tidings back into the kitchen.

'Where's my costume?' he asked.

Chelsea indicated the garment bag, which was hanging from the hook on the back door where Jacqui usually kept her apron and her gardening cardigan.

'Fantastic,' said Jack.

But his enthusiasm was short-lived.

'It's a dress!' he exclaimed. His voice was full of horror.

'It's not a dress. It's a tunic,' said Chelsea.

'It's a dress.'

Jack was not happy.

'I was expecting trousers,' he said.

'People didn't wear trousers in the olden days,' Jacqui tried. 'They all wore tunics. And the Romans just wore sheets. Remember the ones we saw at the Colosseum?'

Jack recalled the gladiators in their tunics. 'I suppose this is sort of like that,' he said, gingerly fingering the hem.

'Stop moaning and put it on,' said Ronnie. 'Your Auntie Chelsea has gone to a great deal of effort for you. I think it's just right.'

Jack slipped the tunic over his head. There was something about the plain white robe that did immediately make him look a bit angelic. Even though he was scowling.

'It's a little bit long,' said Chelsea. 'I'll have to pin it up.'

But the tunic was not the best of it. Chelsea had also made Jack's halo and wings. She'd modelled them on an angel that she saw in a painting in the Victoria and Albert museum. The halo was not just the band of silver foil or tinsel on a coat-hanger as had been the norm back in Chelsea and Ronnie's day. Chelsea had made a full moon of foil-covered cardboard.

'Oh, doesn't he look lovely,' said Jacqui.

'Now, let's hear that speech again,' said Chelsea.

'Earthlings!' Jack began.

'I don't think you're supposed to say earthlings,' said Ronnie.

'Ladies and gentlemen, boys and girls . . .'

Ronnie handed Jack the speech written on a piece of paper.

'I bring tidings of great joy.'

Jacqui clapped her hands together. 'My grandson, the Angel Gabriel.'

Chelsea pinned the hem of Jack's tunic and he changed back into his jeans and T-shirt. He hung around in the kitchen in hope of some biscuits, but he was soon bored by the women's conversation about the upcoming wedding and went back to bothering Dave and Bill in the other room.

'I'll give you great tidings,' the women heard Dave shout. 'Stand to the side of the telly! We just missed a Coventry goal!'

Chapter Thirty-Nine

Ronnie and Chelsea

With Jack out of the way, tormenting the menfolk, Ronnie and Chelsea could have a proper conversation at last.

'About last night,' Ronnie began.

Chelsea gave a weary smile.

'I'm sorry you had to see that,' her sister continued.

'It's OK,' said Chelsea. 'Emotions were running high.'

'It was your special night and I didn't want to spoil it.'

'You didn't. There's lots of good stuff I remember much more clearly. All that funny headgear. The visit from Poldark. That was really good.'

'I know. But I mean the rest of it. Anyway, I am sorry. You didn't need to be in the middle of that.'

Chelsea squeezed her sister's hand and gave her a kiss on the cheek.

'You're forgiven. Have you talked to Annabel?' she asked.

'Why would I want to talk to Annabel?'

'To say what you just said to me.'

'What?'

'That you're sorry. Sorry for having a go at her.'

'That wasn't what I was saying. I was saying sorry *you* had to watch us argue. But she kicked it off.'

'Oh, Ronnie,' said Chelsea. 'She really didn't.'

'What are you talking about? She was winding me up all night.'

'How?'

'From the minute we met her at the restaurant, she was at it. You saw the way she curled her lip when I said where we were going afterwards. Not good enough for her, was it?'

'She didn't curl her lip.'

'You must have missed it. The way she looked at my hen party gear, as well. Like it was covered in germs. And don't even get me started on the way she reacted to Poldark.'

'She laughed, like the rest of us.'

'She *sneered*.'

'Why are you being like this, Ronnie? You and Annabel have been getting on really well lately. You've spent loads of time at hers this year. Izzy and Sophie adore each other.'

'Izzy's different. She's more like her dad.'

'Look, whatever you think, Annabel was not trying to wind you up.'

'She tried to *show* me up. Paying for everyone without asking. She didn't give me a chance to pay my way.'

'By paying in the restaurant, she was trying to do something nice for *me*. Me! On *my* hen night. And Mum. She wanted to treat Mum. And shouldn't you be happy? She bought your dinner too.'

'To make a point.'

'What point would that have been?'

'Look at me, is what she was saying. I can afford to buy dinner eight times over in this shit hole.'

'Ronnie, do you really think that was Annabel's intention? Isn't it just possible that she wanted to treat me – me, the bride-to-be – on my hen night? It's not all about you.'

'Is that what you think? That I think this is all about me?'

Chelsea took a moment to follow the sentence.

'That's certainly how you're acting,' she concluded.

'She's using you, Chelsea, and you can't even see it. She's using you as a guinea pig for her wedding business and she's using you for your media contacts. She doesn't know anything about blogging. She doesn't know how to get featured in a magazine, but you do.'

'Well, maybe that is part of the equation but I really don't care. Thanks to Annabel, Adam and I are going to have the wedding we wanted. We're going to be able to invite all the people we want to see.'

'I had everybody I wanted at my wedding and I had mine in a pub.'

'That was your day, Ronnie. This is mine. And Annabel is helping me make it just how I always dreamed it might be.'

'Well I'm not coming to the wedding if you're getting married at her house. Simple as that.'

'Fine,' said Chelsea.

'Is that all you're saying?'

'What else am I supposed to say?'

Ronnie stood up. 'Jack!' she shouted. 'Jack! Come on! We're going.'

Just at that moment, Jacqui, who had popped out to the corner shop to get extra bread in case Jack and Ronnie stayed for lunch, came back in.

'Where are you going?' Jacqui asked Ronnie, as her middle daughter pushed past her without saying goodbye. She was dragging a bewildered-looking Jack by the hand.

'Ask Chelsea,' Ronnie spat over her shoulder as she headed out the door.

Chapter Forty

Jacqui and Bill

Jacqui was disappointed but unsurprised by the way Ronnie had reacted.

'She didn't mean it,' she said. 'Of course she didn't. It was just the heat of the moment. You know what your sister's like. She's always been dramatic.'

'I hope you're right, Mum. But what if she stops Jack and Sophie from coming?'

'She wouldn't dare. Sophie's almost a grown-up and there's no way she'd keep Jack at home. He can't not go to his favourite auntie's wedding. And I can't believe Ronnie will stay at home on the day itself. No way. There's still two weeks to go, love. She'll have forgotten all about her argument with Annabel by then. Ronnie won't miss her little sister's wedding.'

It was the last thing any of them needed. Especially Jacqui. Though her mum tried to put a brave face on it, Chelsea could tell that she was feeling under strain. Jacqui hated arguments. Ronnie had always been fiery but, having grown up with her, Chelsea had mostly learned how to prevent a small disagreement from becoming a full-blown estrangement. Annabel did not have the advantage of thirty years of experience of Ronnie Benson. Also, Annabel was not inclined to back down for the sake of keeping the peace. It was like a clash between two dinosaurs. Both of them bone-headed.

Jacqui had other things on her mind too.

Knowing that Chelsea had enough on her plate with the upcoming wedding, Jacqui had not talked much about how Bill was getting on. The truth was, he wasn't getting on very well at all. Earlier that week, he'd had another turn and he seemed to be spending more and more time in the past and Jacqui was seriously worried.

Everyone had been so proud of Sophie's piece about Granddad Bill's wartime experiences in *County Class* magazine but it was hard to live through them with him night after night, as had been happening lately. Jacqui was beginning to dread going to bed, knowing that before dawn she would be woken by the sound of Granddad Bill crying out for his brother Eddie.

Eddie Benson was his younger brother's idol. Eddie was six years Bill's senior and was getting ready to go off to fight when the Nazis began their Blitz on Coventry. Because he was still waiting to go off to the front line in Europe, Eddie was at home on the night of the raid the Luftwaffe nicknamed 'Moonlight Sonata'. When the sirens sounded, he joined his and Bill's father in the centre of Coventry. He was in the department store, Owen and Owen, when it took a hit.

Years ago, back before dementia struck, Bill had told Jacqui how he had reacted upon hearing that his brother had been killed.

'I didn't believe it. I couldn't believe it. He told me he was going to come back for me. The last time I saw him, we were playing cricket in the garden. It was November but he said I needed to get a head start on the next season, I was that bad. He was bowling. He was laughing at my batting style and when the air raid sirens went off, he promised me he was coming back because he was going to sort my swing out. I didn't worry as I waved him off because I'd seen him go off before and every time he came back like he promised. He wouldn't leave our mum and me.

'Mum was worried that he would get killed if he went to France. Turned out he got killed in a department store two miles from home. Bloody funny thing that was. He hated shopping, did our Eddie. You wouldn't have got him to go in there any other way. But he went in to help the people who were stuck there get out and go somewhere safer. He died trying to save other people.

'When it finally sunk in, what had happened, I went crazy. I went outside and I yelled at the sky. And even when the siren started going off again, I stayed there shouting. I wanted the Nazis to get me too. I had to be carried into the shelter. Mum was in pieces. She wanted to die as well. It was the worst night of my whole bloody life.'

That was the night Bill kept going back to now. Not the night of the Moonlight Sonata raid itself, but a few days later when he finally had to accept that Eddie wasn't coming back. He wasn't going to be pulled from the rubble alive.

As he drifted off to sleep, Bill's tired old brain heard the sound of the siren across the years and roused him in a panic. He would get out of bed and scream at the sky. 'Come on, you bastards. Come on. Why don't you take me too?'

Jacqui and Dave would be woken by the commotion and rush to Bill's room to try to calm him down before he hurt himself. Inevitably, once he started shouting, he also started flailing. After the third time it happened, Jacqui had taken down all the framed photographs on the mantelpiece to keep them safe. They Bill-proofed the room so that there was next to nothing in there but the bed and an armchair. Even that didn't keep Bill from harm. He cut his forehead when he fell and caught his temple on the door handle. It was terrible. At her very lowest ebb, Jacqui even asked the family doctor whether it might be time for Bill to go somewhere where he could get professional support around the clock. An old people's home.

The doctor gave Jacqui all the numbers to call to find Bill a place in a council run home but, in the end, she and Dave decided they would just have to soldier on. Jacqui had been worried sick by a series of newspaper articles about abuse of the elderly by care home staff. She could not bear the thought of Bill being at the mercy of people who wouldn't love and look after him like his family did. People who would only know him as an old man with dementia, rather than the vibrant, beloved patriarch who had always put his family first.

Jacqui loved Bill with a devotion unusual in a daughter-in-law because of one thing in particular. Having got back together with Dave after almost a decade apart, she told Bill what had happened in the interim. Specifically, when she told him about giving Daisy up for adoption, he had not judged her. He had been kind and understanding. He had kept her and Dave's confidence through the years. But he had also from time to time, let Jacqui know that he thought about Daisy just as she did and that he believed one day she would be part of their lives again. When Daisy – now Annabel – did return, Bill was over the moon.

Bill was a good man. One of the best. He deserved the best from those who loved him. Jacqui would keep him at home.

As the wedding drew ever closer, Jacqui was praying for two things. The first was that Bill would be there to see Chelsea get married to Adam. The second was that they would all have a good night's sleep the night before.

Chapter Forty-One

The Benson-Edwards Family

'Mum,' said Sophie, when Ronnie announced her intention to stay away from the wedding at the tea table. 'Don't be so daft. You can't miss Chelsea's wedding.'

'Just you watch me.'

'You'll regret it,' said Sophie. 'I'm definitely going. You can't stop me.'

'Are you going to leave home the same day?'

Sophie rolled her eyes. Mark smiled awkwardly. Jack was open-mouthed with distress.

'But I'm the pageboy. I've got to go. Do I have to leave home too?'

'Probably,' said Ronnie. 'But you're still small enough to get work as a chimney sweep. You'll be OK.'

'Ronnie,' said Mark. 'Don't scare the boy.'

'I see,' said Ronnie. 'So you're all with Annabel, are you? Fine. I know where your loyalties lie.'

She stormed off.

Sophie rolled her eyes and went to her bedroom to Skype Izzy and find out how the aftermath of the big hen night row was playing in her house. The cousins agreed that they would never behave like such idiots when they reached middle age.

Meanwhile, Mark spent the next half hour assuring Jack that everything would be all right. Of course his mum wouldn't really make him leave home if he was his Auntie Chelsea's pageboy. Didn't Jack remember how Ronnie had threatened to cancel Christmas the previous year? She hadn't, of course. She just liked to let off steam.

'You'll understand when you grow up,' Mark said. 'Women aren't always like us, Jack. And sometimes, the best thing you can do when they're having a bit of a rant is say nothing.'

'Say nothing. Like when you see someone who looks weird in John Lewis.'

'Exactly,' said Mark.

'Or at the bus stop.'

'Quite. If you think your mum is acting strange, you must never, ever say so. Least said, soonest mended. If we all just carry on as normal, pretty soon your mum will be happy as Larry again.'

'Who's Larry?'

'Someone who must have liked a laugh.'

Jack was relieved for having had a little talk with his father.

'All right now, Jack?' Mark asked.

Jack nodded.

'But Dad?' he piped up. 'There's one other thing I want to ask you about.'

'What's that, son?'

'If you did something wrong and didn't tell anybody about it and nobody found out, would Father Christmas still know?'

'What have you done?' Mark asked.

'Nothing,' Jack said quickly. 'I was just asking.'

Mark squinted at his son. His look was sceptical.

'I should think Father Christmas would know, yes.'

'Is it better to say what you've done before Christmas, then?'

'I reckon so.'

'What if you didn't mean to do it?' Jack asked. 'What if it was an accident?'

'If it was an accident, then you'd probably be forgiven.'

'And still get all your presents?'

'Depends . . . You'll have to be more specific.'

Jack teetered on the edge of confession again. But it had recently occurred to him that a very long time (in dog years certainly) had passed since he and Lily were filming stunts in Annabel's TV room. His conscience battled with his pragmatism. Surely the broken dog would have been found by now and surely, if Auntie Annabel thought Jack was to blame, he would have heard about it. Maybe he had got away with it. Maybe Leander had taken the rap after all. And, what's more, Jack wasn't entirely convinced by Mark's view that Father Christmas would know anyway. The previous year, Father Christmas hadn't picked up on the fact that Jack had called his teacher 'Mrs Fatty Bum'. Mrs Bryant heard Jack's insult and told him off in front of the whole class but she had decided against telling Mark and Ronnie. They hadn't found out and neither, it seemed from the pile of presents Jack found downstairs on Christmas morning, had Santa.

Or maybe Santa had known about the name-calling. And maybe he considered the telling off from Mrs Bryant was punishment enough. Just as all these months of feeling guilty (when he remembered) about breaking Annabel's ornament had been awful. Yes. Guilt was a burden in itself. For all those reasons, on the subject of the china dog, Jack decided that his best option was to continue to keep quiet.

'But why do you want to know all this?' Mark asked, his suspicions roused.

'One of the girls in my class called the teacher Mrs Fatty Bum,' Jack said.

'Ha!' Mark laughed. 'That's a good one. And pretty accurate, too. But it was a very naughty thing to do,' he added as a 'good parenting' afterthought.

Chapter Forty-Two

Annabel and Richard

In the Great House, Annabel was still unaware of Ronnie's bombshell announcement about the wedding (Izzy knew, thanks to Sophie, but decided that it was best not to say anything. Like Ronnie, Annabel had a tendency to 'shoot the messenger'). She had spent the morning feeling a little annoyed that Ronnie hadn't called to apologise but by teatime, she'd pretty much forgotten the row. She was of the opinion that Ronnie would call her when she felt like it. There was no point brooding until it happened.

After supper, Annabel and Richard took Humfrey into the TV room. They were going catch up on the latest episode of *Masterchef*. Humfrey was being a little fractious that evening. He had a tooth coming through and every time Annabel tried to put him down to sleep, he wailed with great indignation until she picked him back up again. While Richard cued up the programme, Annabel walked Humfrey around the room. She paused by the mantelpiece, noticing that the ornaments were oddly bunched up towards the mirror that hung behind them. As she held Humfrey close with one arm, she used her free hand to move the ornaments into a more pleasing composition. She didn't think anything of it. The cleaning lady was often moving stuff about.

Eventually, Annabel picked up the head of the china

dog that had been on Jack's conscience for so long. She held it towards Richard.

'We really ought to get this little dog glued back together, you know. How long has it been since Izzy knocked it off the mantelpiece?'

'About twelve years,' said Richard.

'Really? We've had a broken ornament on display for all that time,' Annabel sighed. 'What must people think? I'm going to sort it out tomorrow.'

'Mmm-hmm,' said Richard. 'Programme's ready.'

Annabel replaced the little dog's head next to its body and sat down next to her husband. She handed Humfrey over.

'Your turn.'

Chapter Forty-Three

Jack

While Annabel and Richard were watching a recording of *Masterchef*, Jack was also watching television. Sunday nights meant *You've Been Framed* in the Benson-Edwards house. After *Doctor Who*, *You've Been Framed* was probably Jack's favourite television programme. He never got tired of seeing people fall off ladders or walk into doors.

'What I don't understand,' said Sophie, as she said every time she saw the show, 'is why people are filming half these things in the first place. I mean, why would you be filming someone going up a ladder to fetch a tin of paint down from a shelf?'

'They're all set up,' Mark agreed.

'What do you mean?' Jack asked. 'What's set up?'

'It means that these people aren't falling off ladders and walking into things by accident. They're just pretending for the cameras.'

Jack frowned. That didn't sound quite right to him.

'Oh, would you look at that!' Sophie exclaimed as someone walked backwards towards the edge of a swimming pool as though to get into a better position for a holiday snap. 'And we're supposed to believe he didn't know he was going to fall into the water?'

'Yeah,' Mark agreed. 'That was an obvious one.'

Little Jack was silent but he was suddenly watching everything very closely indeed.

At the end of the show came the usual spiel, explaining that each clip used would earn the person who had sent it in £250. Though Jack had watched the show a great many times, this was the first time he had really noticed what was said about the submissions process.

'So, people make those videos up?' Jack asked his sister for clarification. 'They don't wait for something to happen?'

'No,' said Sophie. 'They want to make some money by sending in a clip so they set up a stupid scenario. It's the only explanation for half those clips. They're all fake.'

'How do you fake falling off a ladder?'

'The same way you fake climbing up a ladder. It's just acting.'

'And falling into a pool?'

'You just walk backwards, like that man did. He must have practised it. He knew he was perfectly safe.'

'How do they get dogs to knock people over?'

'Pocket full of sausages.'

'And a horse to stop so they fall over its head?'

'They know what to do with the reins.'

For every scenario, Sophie had an answer.

It was a little like discovering that Father Christmas didn't exist (except that Jack was still a way off discovering that). Jack's conversation with his sister about how there was a never-ending supply of prat-falls for *You've Been Framed* both disillusioned him and fired his imagination. The most important thing he learned was that the people at *You've Been Framed* did not seem to discriminate between the genuine and the staged.

Every one of those clips had earned someone two hundred and fifty pounds. If Jack had two hundred and fifty pounds, he could use it to pay Auntie Annabel for the broken china dog. His debt would be settled and he could play the Archangel Gabriel with a clear conscience.

When he went to bed that night, Jack waited until his mother had closed the door, then he got out his secret notebook from beneath the bed and a pen with which to write in it.

'Films for You've *Bin* Framed' was the title. Now all he had to do was think up the perfect stunt.

Chapter Forty-Four

Chelsea and Lily

While Chelsea and Adam were enjoying their respective hen and stag dos, Lily had a lovely weekend with her Grandma Frances and Granddaddy Brian. She was full of news when she got back to London. Thankfully, Adam had done the pick-up so Chelsea did not have to face Frances again. After dealing with Ronnie, another frosty encounter with Claire's mother was the last thing she wanted or needed.

But Chelsea couldn't just put the fact that Lily had stayed with her maternal grandparents out of her mind. Especially not when Lily presented her with a carrier bag – a Jaeger carrier bag – that was overflowing with white tulle and lace.

'What's this?' Chelsea asked.

'It's an angel costume. Granny Frances says I should wear it in the play.'

'Oh.'

Chelsea pulled the tulle out until it revealed itself to be the skirt of a dress. It had clearly been in the bag for some time. Perhaps in the attic. It was crumpled and smelled musty.

'It was Mummy's.'

Chelsea nodded.

'OK. Well,' she held the dress out at arms' length. 'It's very nice.'

It was also very small. Claire must have been younger than Lily was now when she wore it. Chelsea was mightily relieved by that. It immediately solved the problem of whether or not Lily would be wearing it in the end of term play. She wouldn't. There was no way it would fit. Lily wasn't especially big for her age but she was certainly too big for Claire's cast-off.

'Can I wear it?' Lily asked.

'Well,' said Chelsea, 'it's a bit small for you. Also, don't you want to look like the other angels? That's why I made three identical dresses.'

'Not necessarily,' said Lily. Chelsea couldn't help smiling. 'Grandma Frances told me you must always try to stand out.'

'She's right,' said Chelsea. She folded the dress carefully. 'But I'm not sure the nativity play is the moment to do it. I'll talk to Daddy about it.'

Chelsea hoped he would see the problem at once but, even after she explained, Adam couldn't seem to see what the issue was.

'If Frances comes to the nativity play and Lily isn't wearing Claire's dress, she's going to be disappointed,' she clarified.

'But you've told me that it's too small.'

'It is. But—'

'Don't worry about it. Frances will understand. She must know that Lily is taller than Claire was at that age.'

'I don't want her to think that I'm refusing to let Lily wear the dress because I don't want her wearing something that used to belong to her daughter.'

'Why would she think that anyway?'

Despite the awfulness of that Sunday lunch, Adam simply refused to believe that Frances was somehow trying to set Chelsea up for a fall. Chelsea wanted to think that he was right but she had spent her entire life negotiating relationships with tricky women. From the moment she was old enough to say 'Ronron', her childhood name for Ronnie, she knew that almost every gesture one woman made to another could be read in several ways. It was very hard to accept that Frances just thought she was being helpful.

While Adam went online to refine his CV, Chelsea took Claire's angel costume into the spare room she had been using as her office and sewing space. Three identical white tunics hung from a laundry rail in the corner. Chelsea had been so pleased with the way they'd turned out. Now she spread the old dress, with its carefully smocked bodice, out on the table for a moment. Then she balled it up and stuffed it back into the bag in which it came.

Chapter Forty-Five

Jacqui

Chelsea had another nativity appointment before Lily's. If she was still invited. Ronnie had not called Chelsea since she stormed out of Jacqui's house. Jacqui had heard from her but she hadn't seen her middle daughter. Ordinarily, Ronnie would drop by her parents' house at some point every day. Despite this, Jacqui was adamant that it should be business as usual.

'You've got to come to Jack's nativity, Chelsea. You made his costume. You'll want to see him in it.'

'You can send me photos, Mum. Ronnie's his mum. If she doesn't want me there then I can't just gate-crash.'

'She hasn't said she doesn't want you there.'

'But she hasn't confirmed that she does.'

Christmas in the Benson family always seemed to be a time of trouble. Jacqui wondered when she had last truly looked forward to Christmas without there being some kind of stress in the background. Or firmly in the foreground, as it was that year. As a child, of course she'd enjoyed the festive season. Even as a teen, she'd been enchanted. Everything changed once Daisy / Annabel was born. Jacqui had been a naïve seventeen-year-old at the time but as soon as she'd given birth, she felt as if she had lived a century. After that awful day when she said goodbye to her first baby, even the happiest Christmases with Chelsea and Ronnie were tinged with a melancholy as she wondered how her eldest daughter would be celebrating the day. Then, when Annabel came back into her life, there was more trouble when Ronnie and Jacqui fell out over what Ronnie perceived as Jacqui's favouritism towards the daughter she'd given away.

And now this.

Jacqui loved all her daughters equally and she did her best not to take sides when they argued but, right now, it was difficult not to want to knock some sense into Ronnie.

Tired of waiting to hear and sensing that Chelsea would probably not take the initiative, Jacqui sent Ronnie a text.

'Is Chelsea invited to Jack's nativity play?'

'If she wants,' was the response.

Jacqui called Chelsea right away with the good news.

'She doesn't want me there. I knew it,' was Chelsea's response.

'She didn't say don't come,' said Jacqui. 'So I say you should. Once she sees you there, she'll soften up, I'm sure. And you can ask her to come to the wedding in person. Maybe she'll relent when she sees you.'

'Oh, Mum. I do really want her to be at the wedding. She knows that, doesn't she?'

'Of course she does. It's just that Ronnie seems to need more telling she's wanted than the rest of us.'

Jacqui had decided that was the issue with Ronnie. She was insecure. That was why she was so quick to see a simple observation as an insult.

Jacqui was going to have to tell her what a silly way that was to be. One day.

Chapter Forty-six

Chelsea and Ronnie

So Chelsea drove up to Coventry and to Jack's school. Seeing Ronnie's car parked on the street outside, she took a deep breath. She was running slightly late and she got into the school hall just as the headmistress was giving a speech, welcoming everyone to the performance. Scanning the room, Chelsea was relieved to see that her mother was sitting in the back row and she had her handbag on an empty chair.

'I was saving this for you,' Jacqui confirmed. Chelsea slipped in beside her. 'Ronnie's down the front.'

'Have you spoken to her?'

'I got here late,' said Jacqui.

'I probably shouldn't have come.'

'Rubbish. She'll be pleased.'

'Ladies and gentlemen, I give you the year two Nativity . . .'

A child sitting three seats along, who could not have been more than four, ssshed Chelsea and Jacqui.

'That told us,' whispered Jacqui.

The play began.

The little girl playing Mary came onto the stage carrying a broom. She dutifully swept the floor of her parents' courtyard and was suitably surprised and then rapt when Jack appeared to tell her about God's plan for her.

Jack really was the perfect angel. His face, so round and sweet, shone from beneath his halo (from a distance, the cardboard covered in aluminium foil did the celestial job quite perfectly). You could see the excitement in his eyes. Jack loved being on the stage. He was a natural, milking every line of his speech to great effect.

The whole play went wonderfully well. Hardly any prompting was required. There was no horsing around. All the children took their roles very seriously as suited the solemnity of their tale. There was just one impromptu moment of comedy when the two children playing the donkey briefly came apart and the bottom half stumbled blindly into the scenery, making the stable wall rock.

Though Jacqui said she'd heard there had been a fight between the shepherds and the kings while everyone was getting ready in the school gym, you couldn't tell as they gathered in the classic nativity tableau for the finale. The children all looked towards Jack with expressions of awe as he delivered his final speech heralding 'great joy'. Then they sang 'Away In A Manger' with such sweetness that Chelsea had to dab her eyes.

There were three curtain calls and much enthusiastic bowing.

'Jack has been practising his bowing for weeks,' Jacqui explained. Chelsea could imagine that. Jack's favourite parts of any show were those moments when he interacted with the audience directly – either with his floral introductions or his extravagant farewells. He couldn't get enough applause.

The audience at the primary school that afternoon went one further and gave the nativity cast a standing ovation. Jacqui even put her fingers in her mouth and whistled.

'Mum,' said Chelsea. 'I never knew you could do that.'

'I'm a woman of hidden talents,' Jacqui joked.

After the end of the show, Chelsea went straight across to Ronnie.

'I'm sorry I didn't come and sit next to you,' she said. 'I got here a bit late.'

'That's all right,' said Ronnie. 'I wasn't saving you a seat.'

'OK,' said Chelsea, recognising the snub. 'That's fine. Jack was very good, wasn't he? He completely nailed his speech.'

'He's a very clever boy.'

'He is.'

Ronnie wasn't warming up.

'Have we fallen out as well? Are you still determined to stay away from the wedding?' Chelsea came straight to the point.

'I'll come to the ceremony,' said Ronnie. 'But I won't come to the reception. I don't want to see that woman.'

'Ronnie, "that woman" is our sister. Annabel really doesn't know what this is all about. I wish you two would be friends again.'

'If she wasn't related to us by birth,' said Ronnie, 'we never would have met, let alone become friends.'

It was clear that she was going for a mega-grudge this time.

'Look, Ronnie, there's nothing I want more than to have everyone I love at my wedding,' said Chelsea. 'That means you *and* Annabel. It would mean an awful lot to me if you could just get over yourself for one day and come along.'

'Get over myself?' Ronnie reared away. 'Get over myself? And what exactly do you mean by that?'

Chelsea rolled her eyes.

'This is my wedding we're talking about. Possibly the most important day of my life so far. Why are you so determined to spoil it?'

'I won't be spoiling anything. I'm staying away precisely so I don't spoil your special day. Or Annabel's special day, as it seems to be turning out.'

Chelsea opened her mouth to protest. An argument was narrowly averted when Jack came bouncing over, still dressed as Gabriel.

'You were wonderful,' his aunt told him.

'I was, wasn't I?' he said modestly. 'I'm going to be an actor when I grow up.'

'I thought you were going to be Doctor Who,' said Chelsea.

Jack looked at his aunt as though she was daft.

'Doctor Who *is* an actor, silly,' he said. 'Where's Grandma? I want to know what she thought of my performance.'

'Get Lawrence Olivier,' Ronnie said.

Jack spotted Jacqui and disappeared in her direction.

'Please, Ronnie. Just come to my wedding. You don't have to talk to Annabel. I just want you both there.'

'I can't do it.'

'OK. But I'm going to keep your place on the head table empty,' said Chelsea. 'So if you change your mind . . .'

'I won't change my mind.'

'And that's your final word?'

'It is,' Ronnie said.

'Then it's not only Annabel you've fallen out with,' said Chelsea. 'Ronnie, you really are a complete pain in the arse.'

Chelsea left her sister, mouth open with shock, and went to find their mother.

Chapter Forty-Seven

Chelsea and Sarah

While she was up in Coventry, of course Chelsea had to go to the Great House and discuss the progress of the wedding preparations. She also wanted to visit Father Malcolm at the church. Perhaps he could say a prayer to make Ronnie come to her senses. Ironically, Chelsea had worried that planning such an important event together might strain her relationship with Annabel but, if anything, the opposite was true. They worked very well together and Chelsea did not feel shy about telling Annabel exactly what she wanted. They were becoming very close, which made it doubly hard that Ronnie was being so stubborn about making up.

Sarah was at Annabel's house that evening. When Chelsea walked into the big warm kitchen, Sarah was sitting at the table with Humfrey on her lap. She was trying to persuade him to eat his supper. Humfrey was playing the usual baby tricks on her. He would appear to be ready to accept a mouthful of whatever she was offering him, then, at the last minute, he would turn his head away so that instead of going into his mouth the plastic spoon would dent his pillow-soft cheek and the food would end up all over the place.

Leander the Labrador, needless to say, was close at hand, waiting for the inevitable moment when the food would drop to the floor. For every pound in weight that

Humfrey gained as he grew, Leander was gaining two.

Chelsea liked Sarah, Annabel's adoptive mother, very much. Given the circumstances in which they had come to know each other, Sarah might have been frosty towards the Bensons – especially since she had only recently lost her husband to illness and might reasonably have been feeling insecure – but she was warm and welcoming and very generous. Since getting to know them, Sarah had put Sophie and Jack on her Christmas list, treating them as though they were her grandchildren alongside Izzy and Humfrey. Sarah had also been very kind to Jacqui. She had opened her heart to her. Jacqui was very grateful to be able to talk to Sarah about the years of Annabel's life she had missed.

Sarah had even made Jacqui a special photograph album containing copies of pictures from every year of Annabel's life. The last picture in the album was Jacqui's favourite (and became Chelsea's too when she saw it). It was a family photograph of the Bensons and the Buchanans united, taken the previous Christmas. Richard had set up his camera on a proper tripod and used a timer so that nobody was left out. In the middle of the group, Jacqui and Sarah flanked Annabel. Both of them gazed down on Humfrey in her arms. He was just nine days old when the picture was taken. Annabel had been just nine days old when the social worker came to take her from Jacqui in the mother and baby home.

The picture completed the circle.

Sarah was keen to know how Chelsea was getting on in the run up to the wedding. She also wanted to hear about Jack's nativity play and about the costumes Chelsea had created for all the little angels.

'And how is Lily?' Sarah asked. 'Is she doing well at school?'

Conversation about Lily led Chelsea to confess her difficulties with Frances. Sarah listened quietly and nodded in sympathy. But Chelsea soon realised that Sarah's sympathies lay as much with Frances as they did with her. When she heard about the dress Frances wanted Lily to wear in the nativity play, Sarah's eyes welled up.

'I think I might have done the same in her position,' she admitted. 'I can't begin to imagine how much it must hurt to have lost a daughter.'

'I understand that,' said Chelsea. 'But I still can't help feeling she's making a point.'

'Oh, Chelsea. I know it's hard but you just have to believe that whatever Frances is doing that upsets you, it isn't because she dislikes you or thinks you're not worthy of marrying Adam and being Lily's step-mum.'

'Well, maybe she's right. Maybe I'm not. I'll never be Lily's biological mother, after all.'

'That doesn't matter.'

Chelsea winced as she realised what she'd just said.

'I know what you're trying to say,' Sarah said, 'but I don't agree that needs to be an issue. I remember when we brought Annabel home. We just put her on the floor between us, in her basket, and gazed at her. We couldn't quite believe she was ours. We loved her from the moment we laid eyes on her. In fact, I think my heart opened even before then, when we got the letter telling us that she'd been born.

'Motherhood isn't just about the act of giving birth. I believe that all of us have what it takes to be a good mother, even if our biology defeats us. What it takes is pure love. I know you have that in you. I can tell. Frances will come round to knowing that too.

'But it's not going to be easy for her. Just like it hasn't been easy for me, seeing how Annabel has become so well integrated into your family. There's jealousy, of course. But there was also a desire on my part not to see my daughter hurt again. Frances will be thinking that sort of thing too. She wants to protect Lily. And Adam too, I'm sure. And she wants to protect Claire's memory. Maybe you need to do something to show her that you're not going to whitewash her daughter from Lily's family history once you're the new Mrs Baxter.'

'How can I do that?' Chelsea asked. 'Seriously, what on earth can I do or say?'

'I've got an idea,' said Sarah. 'You say that Claire's old angel costume doesn't fit Lily. But perhaps there's some part of it you could use. How about you took some of the lace and stitched it around the hem of the new dress? Or used it to make a fancy collar? That way, Frances would see that you understood and appreciated her gesture. Which was not intended to upset you,' she repeated carefully.

'You know, that's a really good idea,' said Chelsea. 'I can do that. The lace on Claire's dress is certainly lovely. It would be brilliant if I could find a way to use it on Lily's new costume.'

'See?' said Sarah. 'Frances will really appreciate that. I know I would.'

'Thank you, Sarah. It's been so useful to have this talk.' Chelsea gave the older woman a hug.

'Family life is a minefield,' said Sarah. 'But you'll get through it in one piece. Want to have a quick cuddle with Humfrey?'

'I thought you'd never ask,' said Chelsea.

'Good. I think my grandson may have just filled his nappy,' Sarah smiled as she handed him over.

Chapter Forty-Eight

Chelsea, Adam and Lily

Chelsea stayed at the Great House that night. When she got back to London on Saturday afternoon, Adam and Lily were in the sitting room surrounded by cardboard boxes.

'At last!' said Lily when Chelsea let herself in. 'I thought you were *never* going to come home.'

Adam and Lily had been to collect the Christmas tree that morning. They hadn't done an especially good job of choosing. The tree they had brought home was tall but it was distinctly lop-sided. One side of the tree was pretty full and well shaped. The other side looked as though it had come off worse in an argument with a hedge trimmer.

Chelsea gave Adam a look over the top of Lily's head. It was a look that said, 'WTF?'

'I chose this tree,' said Lily. 'Because Daddy said it looked terrible and how could the people at the Christmas tree shop possibly hope to sell it? And then I thought the tree would be left all alone on its own on Christmas Day and so I decided that we should take it instead.'

'And that is how we ended up with the crappiest Christmas tree in Christendom,' said Adam.

Lily's eyes were wide. 'Daddy, don't swear!'

'Well, I think it's lovely,' said Chelsea gamely. 'And

if we stand it in the corner, with the bald side facing towards the wall, no one will know it's only got half the branches it should have.'

'And Father Christmas will think I'm extra good for choosing the tree that nobody else wanted,' said Lily.

Lily insisted, since she and Adam had been waiting for *hours* for Chelsea to come home, that the decorating should start right away. Chelsea wasn't even to have time to hang up her coat or make a cup of tea. Lily started barking instructions. Chelsea and Adam were to get the boring bits of the decorating done so that she could add a flourish with the baubles. That meant that the adults had to position the tree in the corner (being careful to hide the bald spot) and hang the fairy lights.

'Let's test them before we put them on the branches,' said Chelsea, remembering far too many Christmases at the Benson house when they would discover only after festooning every branch with baubles and tinsel that the fairy lights which had gone on first refused to spark into life. It had almost become part of the Benson family Christmas ritual. The great switch on. A moment of huge excitement followed by crashing disappointment when the tree remained in the dark. Then Dave and Granddad Bill would have to go to work, systematically tweaking every fairy light bulb to find the loose connection that was keeping the whole string from working. These days, with the children having long since left home, Jacqui and Dave had a fake tree with the fairy lights built into the branches. So far it had done three Christmases without a glitch.

The fairy lights for Lily's tree were in perfect working order. Thank goodness. Lily was impatient to get on with decorating the branches.

While Adam and Chelsea made sure that the lights were draped evenly from the highest branches to the bottom, Lily put a CD of Christmas songs on the stereo. She sang along to 'Rudolph the Red-nosed Reindeer'.

Chelsea soon forgot how tired she had felt on the train back from the Midlands. Lily's energy was infectious. Soon she and Adam were singing along as well, laughing their way through Hark The Harold Angels again.

'*Risen with helium in his wings . . .*'

'Where's the fairy?' Lily asked. 'We haven't finished the tree until the fairy is on the top!'

Adam put his hand to his forehead.

'Lily,' he said. 'Don't you remember? Last year when we were putting the tree away, the fairy fell on the floor and she broke.'

Lily's face lengthened. She did remember.

'Oh no!' she said.

'And we said that we would have to buy another fairy to replace her.'

'But we haven't got one,' said Lily. 'What are we going to do?'

'Perhaps we could use one of your dolls?' suggested Chelsea. 'There must be one who looks like an angel.'

'But I want to play with them all,' said Lily. 'I need them.'

'Then we'll have to think of something else,' said Adam. He pulled a cardboard star out of the bottom of a box.

'How about this?'

'That's rubbish,' said Lily, with her characteristic tact.

'I made that,' said Adam. 'When I was your age.'

'In the Victorian times,' Lily commented. As far as she (and Jack) were concerned, anything that had happened prior to their lifetimes was classified as Victorian. Or even Roman, as in the case of a tin soldier that had belonged to Granddad Bill as a boy.

'I've got an idea,' said Chelsea. 'You know how Auntie Annabel has her old teddy bear on top of the tree? Perhaps we could use my teddy this year. Just until we can get a new fairy.'

Lily agreed it was an excellent idea. Auntie Annabel's Ted was a legend to Lily. The old bear, a gift from Jacqui to Annabel when they were parted just after Annabel's birth, had been Annabel's constant companion. Then Izzy's. Now the bear belonged to Humfrey but Annabel had allowed Jack and Lily to take Ted with them on their holidays that summer. That was nearly the end of Ted's story. On a day trip from the cruise they were taking, she'd been stolen by a monkey in Gibraltar, making it home only because Jack had insisted on giving her a Paddington-style label. A kind stranger had found her and posted her back to the UK, minus some stuffing but still recognisably her beloved self.

Lily loved Annabel's tradition of using Ted instead of a fairy. So, Chelsea's childhood ted got to sit in the highest branches of Lily's tree with a piece of tinsel wrapped around his head. A lop-sided tree crowned with a filthy ancient teddy bear. It wasn't exactly *Homes and Gardens* but it was perfect.

Later, with Lily in bed, Chelsea and Adam admired the tree alone.

'I feel as though Christmas has started now,' said Chelsea.

'Christmas only really starts with Baileys,' said Adam.

'Good point.'

'Do you fancy one?'

'I'd love one,' said Chelsea. 'But I don't think I'll have one just now.'

Adam tipped his head to one side.

'Bit of a headache,' Chelsea said. 'It was really hot and busy on the train.'

While Adam watched television, Chelsea got out Lily's nativity costume and Claire's old dress and set to work on making the alterations that Sarah had suggested. Claire's dress was beautiful and there was a huge double margin of lace around the hem of the tulle skirt that would be easy to reuse. Carefully, Chelsea unpicked the stitches that held the lace to the tulle. She also snipped off the little pearl buttons. She would use those too. Just a little while later, the lace was adorning Lily's new dress. Chelsea had put one row around the hem and used the rest to make a frilly Edwardian-style collar. She used the buttons down the back in place of the plain white buttons she had dug out of her sewing box. The end result was rather lovely. The old lace gave the new dress a subtle vintage feel. She had no doubt that Lily would be the best dressed of the Harold Angels now (though she had always intended to put new lace around the collar and hems of all three dresses).

Added to that, Chelsea felt good about what she had done. It was very satisfying indeed to have been able to refashion the old dress into something new. But Chelsea felt most pleased about having been able to take Frances' gesture and come to an accommodation with it. Chelsea had included Frances and Claire in the making of Lily's nativity costume without feeling edged out. It helped Chelsea to think of Frances a little more kindly and reassured her that, in the future, they could work together for Lily's happiness.

Chapter Forty-Nine

Chelsea and Lily

The following Wednesday was the day of Lily's nativity play and the last day of her school term.

Lily was up very late on the Tuesday night. She was full of excitement. It was hard to persuade her that she should go to bed. In the end, Chelsea fell back on the threat she had promised herself she would never use.

'Lily Rose Baxter, if you don't go to bed *right now* then I will have to tell Father Christmas to put you on his naughty list.'

'Noooo!' Lily exclaimed. The idea of not being on Father Christmas's nice list this close to the big day was too much to bear. 'Promise you won't tell him,' Lily made Chelsea swear.

'I won't tell him,' Chelsea confirmed. 'If you get into your pyjamas right now. And clean your teeth. And get into bed. And go to sleep.'

'I'll do all of that,' said Lily.

Chelsea wasn't looking forward to the day when Father Christmas no longer held such power. She suspected that Jack was already beginning to question the big man's existence. When she'd told him that she had a direct line to Father Christmas on her phone, Jack had insisted on sending him a text there and then. Chelsea had hurriedly inputted the speaking clock into her contacts and filed it under 'Father Xmas'. When

Jack actually called the number and got the message, Chelsea managed to persuade him that the speaking clock was in fact Father Christmas's answering service, which was naturally overloaded at this time of year. Jack seemed convinced, though for how long?

Adam came home late from the office. While the company was winding up, it was all hands on deck, making sure that projects were properly finished or handed on. Adam looked exhausted when he walked into the kitchen, where Chelsea was carefully pressing Lily's angel dress one last time.

'Is it too early for Baileys?' he asked.

'That kind of day, eh?' Chelsea sympathised.

He nodded. 'But there was some good news. I got a call back from Jarvis and Jones.'

Chelsea looked up. Jarvis and Jones were one of the firms that Adam had on his dream list of places he'd like to work.

'Fantastic. When do they want to see you?'

'That's the thing. They want to see me tomorrow.'

'But . . .'

'I won't be able to go to Lily's nativity play,' said Adam.

'Could you not put the interview off until another day?'

'I can't start asking them to arrange their plans around me. As I understand it, the big boss is jetting straight off on his holidays after interviewing me so if I don't go in tomorrow, he won't be able to see me until January. It would be great if we didn't have to wait until then to find out whether I've got a chance at Jarvis and Jones.

If I could go to Lily's play tomorrow and do the interview later, I would, but I don't think I've got any choice but to show my enthusiasm for J and J by turning up tomorrow, no matter how short notice.'

Chelsea agreed and understood. It was an awful choice to have to make. Lily would not have many nativity plays. But if Adam didn't find a new job, nativity plays would be the least of their worries. Chelsea's freelance income would just about cover the mortgage payments on their house. Added to that, the firm was one that Adam had long admired. They were doing interesting work that could take Adam's career to another level. It was the chance of a lifetime.

'Lily will understand,' said Chelsea. 'And I'll be there.'

'And so will Frances and Brian. Frances texted me today to confirm that she and Brian will take Lily straight back to theirs after the play.'

Lily was going to have a sleepover with her grandparents.

'I'll take her overnight bag with me,' Chelsea confirmed.

'Is that her angel dress?' Adam asked, seeing the carefully folded garment on the ironing board. Chelsea confirmed that it was. She explained how she'd followed Sarah's suggestion to customise it.

'It looks lovely,' said Adam. 'It was a great idea to use the lace from Claire's dress for the collar. Frances is going to be pleased with that, I'm sure.'

'I hope so.'

'She'll love it,' Adam insisted.

On the morning of the play, Lily insisted on trying her costume on one more time before breakfast. She wanted to wear it *for* breakfast too. Chelsea didn't argue with her. There was too much to do. All she asked was that Lily tried to make sure she didn't spill anything on the pure white tunic with its frilly lace edges. Lily duly tucked a tea towel into the neck of the dress so that she could eat her toast and honey without worrying about crumbs or stickiness.

Chelsea did not eat any breakfast. She really didn't feel like it. She had woken up that day feeling somewhat nauseous. That was probably to be expected. The wedding was less than a week away. What bride wouldn't be nervous? And then there was the upcoming encounter with Frances. That was enough to make Chelsea's stomach churn.

'Look!' said Lily, carrying her plate to the dishwasher. 'I managed not to get my dress dirty at all.'

Just after she said that, she dropped her cup of juice on her pristine white silk ballet shoes.

Because of the nativity play, school was starting slightly later than usual so Chelsea and Lily were able to make a detour to buy a new pair of ballet shoes on the way in. While they were in the shop, Lily somehow managed to persuade Chelsea that she needed another red pair too. Chelsea agreed. She'd already bought one pair for Lily to wear at the wedding. It was probably a good idea to have a standby in case there was a repeat of that morning's juice disaster on the wedding day.

The atmosphere in the school was electric as dozens of small children looked forward to their big moment on stage. The noise in the classroom that had been designated as a changing room was tremendous. Despite the school's strict sugar ban – no sugary drinks or sweets were allowed during the school day – most of the youngsters were bouncing off the walls with excitement. It wasn't just that they were going to be in the school play. They had come to the end of term.

Chelsea felt gratified to be greeted so warmly by the mothers and fathers of Lily's classmates. Everyone cooed over the angel outfits that Chelsea had created for Lily and her friends. The mothers of the two other angels were gushingly grateful and had clubbed together to buy Chelsea a very expensive bottle of champagne for her trouble.

'This is beautiful,' said Susie, the mother of Lily's closest school friend, as she watched Lily do a twirl. 'Where did you get the lace, Chelsea? It's just exquisite. I didn't see anything like that in Peter Jones.'

Chelsea duly explained the origins of the lace trimming.

'Oh, that's lovely,' Susie cooed. 'That makes it really special. I bet Lily's grandma will be really chuffed you thought of that.'

'Oh yes,' said Madeleine, who also had a child in Lily's class. 'It's such a nice idea. I would never have thought of that. You are clever. I'd have just chucked the old dress in the bin.'

'I couldn't do that,' said Chelsea. 'It was a sort of heirloom.'

'You've done the right thing,' said Susie. 'It brings the past and the present together. Oh! It's making me quite tearful just thinking about it.'

'You've been crying all morning,' Madeleine commented. 'Are you up the duff?'

'Nooo. It's just . . . it's just seriously emotional, isn't it? Seeing your child in a nativity play? I know I'm going to sob all the way through it.'

'I'm not going to sit next to you then,' Madeleine said.

'I'll sit next to you,' said Chelsea. 'Because I am definitely going to cry at some point.'

'Ladies and gentlemen!' The headmistress clapped her hands together. 'The play is about to start. Would you all please take your seats in the auditorium? The children are looking forward to showing you everything they've learned.'

'OK?' Chelsea asked Lily. She straightened her new lacy collar.

Lily nodded. 'I'm so excited, I might wet my pants.'

'You're not going to wet your pants, are you? Do you need to use the loo?'

'Chelsea!' Lily laughed. 'I was joking!'

'Very funny. I'll see you afterwards. Be the very best angel you can be.'

Chapter Fifty

Chelsea and Frances

Frances and Brian were not in the auditorium when Chelsea sat down between Susie and Madeleine. Susie handed them each a Kleenex.

'Just in case,' she said.

Adam's former in-laws arrived just as the bell rang to announce that the performance was about to begin. Chelsea caught sight of them right before the lights dimmed. She waved to let Frances know where she was sitting but Frances either didn't see her or didn't care to acknowledge her presence. Chelsea hoped it was the former. Frances did wear glasses.

Chelsea felt Frances' presence in the room all the way through the first half of the play. She did her best not to turn round to see whether she was in fact staring daggers at the back of Chelsea's head. That's what it felt like. She sat up straight, with her hands folded in her lap. Unimpeachable.

'Are you OK?' Susie whispered to her while Mary and Joseph were making their long journey to Bethlehem courtesy of a stuffed model donkey on wheels. 'Is your back hurting?'

Chelsea tried to sit a little more casually. She remembered what Sarah had said about Frances not meaning to hurt or insult Chelsea by the things she'd said at lunch and by sending Lily home with Claire's nativity costume. It wasn't actually about Chelsea. She had to keep that at the forefront of her mind. They were both in the school hall that afternoon for Lily. They both loved the little girl and that should be something that brought them together.

Still, Chelsea was nervous about the inevitable meeting at the end of the play. She chewed on a hangnail.

'Please let Frances like the dress,' she quietly prayed.

It seemed like an age before Lily and her fellow 'Harold' angels made their appearance, announcing the good news to the shepherds, one of whom picked his nose throughout the speech. Lily spoke up loud and clear. She remembered all her lines. When she wasn't speaking, Lily scanned the room for faces she recognised. Chelsea gave her a thumbs-up that made her beam with delight.

Eventually, the story came to its climax, with everyone gathered in the stable. 'Away In A Manger' was sung, just as at Jack's school, but when that came to an end, the children quickly segued into 'Hark the Herald Angels'. Lily sang her loudest. Her little face was shining with pride and happiness. She sought Chelsea out and gave her a sneaky wave.

No one clapped harder than Chelsea as the children took their bow. And, just as she'd predicted, she had a little cry as well.

'Right. Time for a glass of wine,' said Susie, as she put away her Kleenex and went in search of her daughter.

'Lily was great,' said Madeleine. 'And she had the best costume in the whole play. Next year, I'm paying you to do mine. Though I doubt Zach will ever get a leading role.'

Zach was the nose-picking shepherd.

Chelsea gathered her things together and went to

look for Frances and Brian. Now that everyone was standing up, she couldn't immediately see them. As she headed in the vague direction of where she had last seen them, she was waylaid by one of Lily's teachers, Mrs Waterman. Mrs Waterman was full of praise for Lily's performance. And her outfit.

'Fabulous costume, Chelsea. So unusual. You've really got a talent.'

'Thank you.'

Chelsea was about to explain the origin of the beautiful lace that adorned Lily's dress when she was interrupted by Frances and Brian.

'Oh, Mrs Waterman, these are Lily's grandparents, Frances and Brian Smithson.'

'Your parents?' Mrs Waterman asked. She had met Lily's paternal grandparents, but this was the first time that Frances had been to a production at this school.

'Heavens, no,' said Frances, wincing at the suggestion that she might be related to Chelsea. 'I am the mother of Lily's mother, Claire.'

Chelsea held a tight close-mouthed smile through the explanation. Mrs Waterman shot her a consoling glance.

'Well, didn't Lily do well today?' the teacher said.

'Her mother had a talent for acting,' said Frances.

'And Lily's costume is beautiful. I was just telling Chelsea that she has a real talent for sewing.'

'Or vandalism,' said Frances.

Mrs Waterman looked confused as she absorbed what Frances had said. Chelsea stiffened in horror. Brian laid his hand on his wife's arm.

'Come on, Frances,' he said. 'Let's not—'

'Let's not what? Let's not tell Chelsea what we think?'

Frances turned so that she was facing Chelsea directly now.

'I gave Lily her mother's dress so that she could wear it exactly as her mother did. In one piece. I did *not* send it to you so that you could take your scissors to it and rip it to bits to adorn that rather basic little shift you were expecting my granddaughter to wear. You've ruined something that was very precious to me and to Lily. You might at least have had the decency to tell me what you were intending to do before you went ahead. Can you imagine how awful it was to see my daughter's dress torn up like that? How could you be so selfish? The sheer arrogance of your actions is breathtaking.'

'Frances,' Brian tried to intervene. 'Please.'

'No, Brian. Chelsea needs to know what she's done.'

'It was just an old dress,' said Brian. 'We've got lots of Claire's old dresses.'

'It was the dress *our daughter* wore to play the Angel Gabriel when she was Lily's age.'

'It's been in the loft for years.'

'Shut up, Brian,' said Frances. She turned the guns back on Chelsea, who was by now blushing furiously and trying not to shake. 'What did you do with the rest of it?'

'I was very careful,' said Chelsea. 'When I took the lace off. I didn't touch the dress itself. I can stitch it all back together.'

'I don't want you touching anything of Claire's ever again.'

'I'm sorry, Frances. But the dress was too small for Lily to wear as it was. I thought that taking the lace from Claire's costume and adding it to the bigger dress would be a good way of incorporating your memories and—'

'I think that's a lovely idea,' said Mrs Waterman, going to Chelsea's aid. 'Bringing a little bit of the past into the present and at the same time making Lily's costume uniquely hers.'

'You don't know what you're talking about,' said Frances coldly. 'Chelsea cut that dress up out of spite.'

'I assure you I didn't. I wanted to . . . I was trying to do what you wanted. She couldn't wear the dress as it was.'

'I want my memories to stay intact!' Frances blustered.

By now, a small crowd had gathered. Frances was not keeping her voice down. She continued to berate Chelsea for having ripped up Claire's dress. Chelsea struggled not to cry. Mrs Waterman and Brian both begged Frances to be reasonable and see that Chelsea had only tried to bring a little of Claire's spirit to Lily's costume.

'It was thoughtless and utterly selfish. You deliberately set out to upset me,' Frances insisted.

'Nothing could have been further from my intention,' Chelsea said, almost in tears.

And then Lily came rushing into the hall. She'd been in the changing room, putting her day clothes back on. She was waving a Christmas cracker.

'Chelsea! Chelsea! You've got to help me pull this,' she said.

'Why don't you ask Granddad?' said Chelsea. 'Grandma and Granddad are going to take you straight to their house,' she continued. 'I've brought your suitcase with me in the car. If we all go outside now, I'll hand it over.'

'When will you pick me up?' Lily asked.

'I think your dad will be picking you up,' said Chelsea.

She never wanted to see Frances ever again.

Susie and Madeleine caught up with Chelsea in the car park after Frances, Brian and Lily had gone.

'Sheesh!' said Susie. 'Was that your mother-in-law?'

'Worse.' Chelsea explained her relationship to Frances.

Susie winced.

Madeleine gave her a hug. 'You need some wine,' she said. 'Come with us back to Susie's house. Sauvignon Blanc will make everything better.'

'I can't even have a drink!' Chelsea complained.

'OMG,' said Susie.

Of course Susie and Madeleine understood at once.

Chapter Fifty-One

Chelsea

Susie and Madeleine tried to persuade Chelsea to come back to Susie's house anyway – she didn't have to drink alcohol – but Chelsea told them she had to get home. She watched them go but didn't actually leave herself for another hour. She sat in the car in the school car park, waiting for the shaky feeling that had come over her when Frances launched her attack to pass. While she was there, she answered emails and text messages from Annabel and Ronnie on her phone. Though Ronnie was still determined that Annabel had wronged her and they would not be making up, it seemed she was at least going to be true to her word about letting Jack and Sophie take part in the ceremony. Thank goodness. Chelsea hoped that was a sign that Ronnie was softening. She was still optimistic that by the time the day of the wedding rolled round, Ronnie would be unable to resist joining in.

But for the first time since Adam proposed, Chelsea was not looking forward to her wedding day. She had hoped that in using the lace from Claire's dress to complement Lily's, she was building a bridge. Instead, she seemed to have unwittingly torched one. Frances had not apologised for her outburst in the school hall. She had gone to sit in the car, while Brian and Lily walked with Chelsea to hers, so that she could hand over Lily's bag.

Brian had been apologetic.

'It's hard for her,' he said. 'This time of year. So many memories. It's hard for me too.'

Yet Brian still tried to behave like a human being, thought Chelsea angrily. She had completely lost faith that she would ever be able to make Frances like her. And yet she would always be in her life. So long as Chelsea was married to Adam. So long as she was Lily's stepmother. Could she face that animosity? Would it get worse?

Chelsea gripped the steering wheel and laid her forehead against the cold black plastic. Of course it could get worse.

The house was quiet and empty when Chelsea finally got home. Adam had gone straight from his interview to the old office. There was still much to do there before the Christmas break. Poor Adam was under so much stress as he tried to find himself a new job that Chelsea had already decided she could not tell him about that afternoon's debacle. Not yet. Thank goodness Lily had missed most of it.

Walking into the sitting room, Chelsea picked up the picture of Adam and Claire at their wedding and addressed her spirit-world rival.

'I want you to know that I'm not going to be put off,' she said. 'I love Adam. I love him every bit as much as you did. And I love Lily too. And if you'll only let me, I will love her as though she were my own for the rest of my life. I will take care of her and be there for her and never let her down. I just want the chance to prove I'm the right woman for them both. I will be a good wife and mother. I know I can be. I know I can.'

But Chelsea wasn't really talking to Claire. She was talking to the photograph of someone long gone but the person she really wanted to convince was Frances. Would that ever happen?

Chapter Fifty-Two

Bill

Chelsea phoned Jacqui.

'How did Lily's nativity play go?'

Chelsea filled her mum in on Lily's fantastic performance as one of the three Harold Angels (everyone in the family had taken to calling them the Harold Angels now). Like Charlie's Angels, only hairier, was what Dave said to Lily when she told him. Thank goodness Lily thought that was funny. Chelsea did not tell Jacqui about the incident with the dress and that Frances seemed to have gone out of her way to humiliate her. But Jacqui was no fool. She knew that Frances was planning to be at the show and she sensed that something must have happened to upset Chelsea. She quickly got the true story out of her youngest daughter.

'It doesn't matter. It doesn't matter if she decides she's never going to like you. You just have to keep loving Adam and Lily. They're the ones who matter. Families are difficult.'

'Talking of difficult families . . .'

'Ronnie and Annabel,' Jacqui sighed.

'Still no sign of them making up?'

'It's the only thing I've got on my Christmas list,' said Jacqui. 'Apart from Granddad Bill not having a turn on your wedding day.'

'Is he OK, Mum?'

'He's doing fine,' Jacqui lied.

Just that afternoon, while Frances was giving Chelsea a dressing down, Bill had had another turn.

After a quiet couple of days, Jacqui was daring to hope that Bill would make it to the wedding. That afternoon, she was reminded of the unpredictability of his illness. Bill was having a nap in his chair in front of the television. Then, all of a sudden, he was half awake and back in the war.

Jacqui could not console him. His grief over the death of his elder brother was as brand new and as fresh as the day he first heard of it. When she tried to hold him, to stop him from hurting himself in his confusion, he shook her off. In doing so, he stumbled and caught the side of his head on the mantelpiece – the bare mantelpiece – as he fell.

The knock to his head seemed to calm Bill down just a little. Jacqui managed to get him back into his comfy chair and he stayed there while she called for an ambulance. They arrived swiftly. Dave always used to joke that the ambulances waited on the corner of their street because of the serviced old people's flats at the other end of it. If that was the case, Jacqui was very glad of it.

The paramedics loaded Bill into the back of the ambulance and he was taken to A and E. There he was patched up and Jacqui sat next to him in the waiting room until Dave finished work and was able to fetch them and bring them home. Once home, Bill went straight to bed.

Jacqui had to broach the subject with Dave.

'I don't think Bill's going to be well enough to go to the wedding,' she said.

'He'll be there,' said Dave.

'But perhaps he shouldn't be. What if he goes off on one in the middle of the service? It'll be a disaster.'

'He won't,' said Dave. 'Not if he stays awake during the service. You know it's when he's just waking up that he's at his worst. We can give him some coffee or something. We can make sure he doesn't drop off.'

Jacqui wasn't sure. 'Oh, Dave. What have we done? We made Chelsea bring her wedding forward for Bill's sake. If he's not there or he is there and he ruins everything, it will all be our fault.'

'You can't think like that. You've got to think positive. It's all going to be OK.'

Having spoken to Chelsea about her run-in with Frances, Jacqui was in a reflective mood.

She laid out her 'mother of the bride' outfit on the bed, wanting to make sure that it was as clean and well pressed as when she last took it out. She hadn't bought anything new for Chelsea's wedding. She couldn't afford to. She was going to be wearing the outfit she wore when Ronnie got married. It wasn't actually even new then. Jacqui had bought the Jacques Vert ensemble for her first face-to-face meeting with Annabel. It was an outfit with memories, all right.

Funny how a scrap of fabric could come to represent so much. Jacqui's heart swelled towards Chelsea, her darling youngest daughter. Too sweet and kind for her own good. But her heart also went out towards Frances, Lily's grandmother. She knew how the perceived destruction of that angel dress must have hurt. Chelsea was going to have her work cut out for her with Frances, for sure.

Jacqui tried on her outfit. Thankfully, it still fitted. If anything, it was perhaps a little looser than it had been when she last wore it to see Ronnie marry Mark. Jacqui hadn't been trying to lose weight deliberately, but she had definitely been under stress since Chelsea's engagement party, which now seemed so long ago.

She sat down at her dressing table and picked up her own wedding photograph. She and Dave had a very small wedding. Registry office, followed by a meal at the Beefeater, which was just about the smartest place you could go to back then. Jacqui didn't even have a proper wedding dress. She wore a green velvet number she had picked up in Bon Marché. Dave wore a borrowed suit because he couldn't imagine needing to wear one again. He certainly didn't need one for work. They didn't have many wedding guests. Jacqui was estranged from her parents because she felt they had forced her into giving Daisy up for adoption. Dave's mother had died when he was a teenager. But Bill was there, smiling wide for the camera, showing his unwavering support for them as they embarked on their new life together. Bill was the very heart of the Benson family.

He had to be at Chelsea's wedding too.

Chapter Fifty-Three

Adam and Chelsea

Lily had gone to stay with Frances and Brian because she would not be seeing them over Christmas. It was helpful because, in theory, Adam and Chelsea could finish getting ready for the wedding, which was now only three days away. But it wasn't going to be all work. Unbeknownst to Chelsea, Adam had other plans.

They weren't going to be going far, but he had booked them into a central London hotel for the night. Just a little break from reality. A bubble bath. A glass of champagne. A bed that someone else had to make. It was perfect. When Chelsea worried out loud that it was an extravagance they couldn't afford, Adam explained that his parents had contributed towards the treat as an early Christmas gift. Chelsea was very grateful to her future in-laws. They seemed to like her, at least. She was very happy that Sally and Graham were going to be part of her life.

Thanks to the Baxters' generosity, Adam and Chelsea had dinner at the restaurant where they had their first date – Bocca Di Lupo – in Soho. For old times' sake, both Chelsea and Adam ordered exactly the same as they had on that day almost fifteen months before. Only this time, Chelsea didn't panic when her pasta arrived. On her first date, she had immediately regretted ordering spaghetti because in the time between seeing the dish on the menu and seeing it in front of her, she had forgotten how difficult it was to eat spaghetti elegantly. That didn't matter so much any more. Adam had seen her with pasta down her top more than once.

And Adam confided that he wasn't worried this time that the dish he'd ordered turned out to be full of garlic.

'I was devastated on our first date because I thought it would put paid to any chance of a kiss.'

'Except that my pasta was super-garlicky too, so neither of us could tell how much the other stank,' Chelsea reminisced.

They even ordered the same wine, though Chelsea asked the waiter to stop after he'd poured her half a glass.

'Do you remember what I was wearing that night?' she tested Adam playfully.

'I wasn't looking at what you were wearing. I was transfixed by your beautiful eyes.'

'Oh.' Chelsea gave a fake frown. 'To think I spent three days planning that outfit.'

'Really? And that's what you came up with?'

'So you do remember!'

'Er . . . Something black?' Adam suggested.

'It was blue. Navy blue. A knee-length lace dress by Diane Von Furstenberg that I really couldn't afford. I might have taken it back to the shop the next day if I hadn't spilled red wine all over it,' Chelsea joked.

'I remember that,' said Adam. 'You were waving your arms around. Getting quite animated. The wine went everywhere.'

Chelsea blushed.

'It was charming. I loved seeing you get enthusiastic like that.'

'I wish I could remember what I was waffling on about.'

'You never waffle on,' said Adam. 'Though I remember thinking that I was talking too much that night.'

'I could have listened to you for hours. I didn't want that night to end.'

'Me neither.'

'Who would have thought we'd be here just over a year later, days before our wedding?'

'I would have thought it,' said Adam. 'I think I knew on some level the very moment I laid eyes on you.'

'On the plane?' Chelsea recalled their real first meeting.

'Yes. On the plane.'

On that Sunday morning at Gatwick airport, Chelsea was furious about having slept through her alarm the previous day, thereby missing her original flight and having to buy a new ticket; it had cost her so much cash she could ill afford to lose. Now, it seemed like the best investment she had ever made.

Chelsea and Adam reminisced about the moment they first locked eyes.

'I thought I had the whole row to myself. But I wasn't too disappointed when I saw you coming down the aisle. Little did I know you weren't flying alone.'

Lily was too small to be seen as she preceded Adam down the aisle. But she made her presence felt as soon as she saw Chelsea.

'I want the window seat!' Adam did his best Lily impression.

Lily, who had been dressed in a fairy outfit at the time, crossed her arms and glared at Chelsea until Chelsea moved to sit in the aisle. Things got much worse in the air, when Lily squirted the contents of her drinks carton all over Chelsea's borrowed dress.

'What was it you were reading that day?' Adam asked.

'Before I sat down next to you and you hid it in your handbag?'

Adam loved to tease Chelsea about her in-flight reading. That day she had been reading a self-help book called *From Booty Call To Bride*.

'Well,' said Chelsea. 'It sort of worked.' She winked.

After dessert – they shared a chocolate pudding, just as they had done the first time they ate there together – Adam ordered them each a glass of champagne. This was a deviation from the script but he felt very strongly that they needed to toast their future properly.

'To us,' he said.

They chinked glasses.

'To our bright and brilliant future. Which is looking very much brighter and more brilliant as of this afternoon.'

Adam was pleased with the way his interview had gone at Jarvis and Jones. He'd had great feedback from his friend on the inside. He thought he might even hear official good news before Christmas.

'To us,' Chelsea echoed his toast. She took a sip and put her glass to one side.

'Aren't you going to finish that?' Adam asked five minutes later.

'No,' said Chelsea. 'I think I've had enough today.'

Adam hadn't noticed that Chelsea had barely touched the red wine he ordered to go with their main course too. He shrugged and finished her champagne for her.

'I've just had a funny thought,' said Adam.

'What's that?'

'Tonight. This dinner. This is our last date.'

'What? Don't say that!'

'I don't mean we're never going to have a date night

again,' said Adam. 'But the next time we go out like this, it will be as man and wife.'

Chelsea nodded.

'Sounds good to me.'

'You've changed my life, Chelsea Benson.'

It was the sort of evening that Chelsea had always dreamed of. As they stepped outside the restaurant, they heard the sound of a carol drifting towards them on the cold night air. The volunteers of the Salvation Army were out in force that night, providing both entertainment and emergency first aid to the city's revellers. Piccadilly Circus was heaving with people determined to celebrate the season.

Chelsea leaned into Adam's side and rested her head on his shoulder as they paused to listen to the Salvation Army band play 'Silent Night'.

'This year, we'll be spending our first Christmas as a proper family,' she said.

Chapter Fifty-Four

Chelsea and Frances

The night in a hotel was wonderful. Magical. When Adam and Chelsea woke up, they ordered breakfast in bed.

But with every minute that passed, Chelsea was getting closer to having to be somewhere she definitely didn't want to be. She was getting closer to having to pick Lily up from Frances and Brian's house.

It had always been the plan. Chelsea had to travel to Little Bissingden to oversee the last few wedding arrangements with Annabel. She needed to take lots of stuff along with her, not least her wedding dress, the bridesmaids' dresses and Jack's dreaded pageboy outfit (he was still under the impression it would be in a terribly girly colour). Frances and Brian's house was a relatively small detour from Chelsea's route to the Midlands. It made sense for her to pick Lily up and take her with her to stay at Annabel's. School had finished. Plus Lily would enjoy the wedding preparations and the opportunity to spend some time with Jack.

Meanwhile, Adam would work his last few days at his old job before driving up the night before the wedding itself.

Chelsea could think of nothing she wanted less than to see Frances again. Not after their encounter at the nativity play when Frances made it perfectly clear that she had no interest in forming any kind of relationship with her grandchild's future stepmother. Chelsea still felt the sting of Frances' angry, dismissive words, delivered in front of Lily's teacher (and several parents) to add insult to injury.

But there was no way Chelsea could shirk this duty. Even though she had told Lily that Adam would be picking her up, Chelsea had always known that, in the end, she would be the one to go to Rutland. She needed to take the car to Coventry. Adam needed to be in London. Lily needed picking up. To make Adam do a round trip just because she didn't want to see Frances would have been unreasonable, wouldn't it?

Chelsea could only hope that Frances had a similar dread of their ever meeting again and would tactfully remain out of sight while Brian brought Lily and her things out to the car.

Chelsea and Adam checked out of the hotel after their lazy breakfast and one last, long cuddle as an unmarried couple. They took a taxi back to the house. Adam helped Chelsea load everything she needed into the back of the car. He kissed her goodbye.

Adam still didn't know about the argument in the school hall. Perhaps he would have insisted on picking Lily up himself if he had known. Chelsea considered telling him as they said their farewells. She decided against it. He had enough on his mind. Instead she assured him that she would give Frances and Brian his best wishes and even pick up a little Christmas gift for them on the way there.

She gave herself a pep talk for the whole drive. It didn't matter what Frances thought of her. It really didn't. Adam loved her. Lily loved her. Adam's family loved her. Chelsea even had the feeling that Frances' husband Brian thought she was OK. Were they all wrong? All those lovely people?

Rationally, Chelsea knew that Frances' view did not override the warmth and kindness she felt from everybody else but she still had to fight hard to squash the little voice inside her that said that Frances' opinion was the only important one. Chelsea had always been like this. It didn't matter how much good news she heard, she only ever wanted to believe the bad news. Her counsellor had pointed that out to her many, many times. Chelsea knew it was the truth and yet somehow she couldn't persuade her heart to act accordingly.

Chelsea was a perfectionist. Of course she believed that she should be able to make things right. It was hard for her to accept that Frances didn't like her. In all probability, Frances might never come to like her. In fact, Frances flat-out hated her. That was the only thing Chelsea could see as she drove the hundred miles from London to Rutland. Frances' opinion of Chelsea was a one-star review amongst all the five-star raves. She knew every word of criticism by heart. She could almost feel Frances' angry words hitting her face.

'Selfish. Sheer arrogance. Spite.'

Chelsea flinched at the all-too-clear memory.

To make things worse, she was starting to feel sick again. Properly vomitous. Though it was tempting, she really didn't want to throw up on Frances' feet the minute she opened the door. Now she prayed that Frances wouldn't come to the door anyway. Please let her send Brian out.

At last, Chelsea pulled into the driveway of the big house, where Claire had grown up in such privilege. She turned off the car engine but continued to sit in the driver's seat for a few moments, breathing deeply and trying to gather herself so that Frances wouldn't know she was in the least bit bothered. Selfish, arrogant and spiteful were not words that applied to Chelsea, she reminded herself one last time. It didn't work. Chelsea would have sat in the car for the rest of the day had not Lily looked out of the window. Spotting Chelsea sitting there on the drive, Lily waved and banged on the glass to get her attention. Soon Frances was looking out with her. Plastering on her biggest smile for her beloved Lily and her nemesis, Chelsea got out of the car.

Chapter Fifty-Five

Chelsea and Frances

Chelsea carried the poinsettia she had bought at the service station en route ahead of her like a shield. With everything that was going on at work and the wedding planning, Adam had forgotten to buy Brian and Frances a Christmas present so Chelsea had to make do with the offerings at the local service station's branch of Waitrose. Along with the poinsettia, she bought a box of biscuits in a smart faux-Victorian tin. Jacqui would have liked it. She hoped Frances would feel the same way.

'You shouldn't have,' said Frances as Chelsea handed them over. She got the feeling that Frances meant that quite literally. And she was probably right. If it's the thought that counts when it comes to gifts, should you even think about giving a present to someone you know doesn't like you? The biscuits were a lazy choice and Chelsea certainly hadn't been feeling full of the joys of the season when she picked out the poinsettia. The plant looked as though it embodied her real feelings. The red leaves were droopy and slightly ragged.

'I'm sorry I'm a little late,' said Chelsea. 'There was quite a bit of traffic. People heading out of London to go home for the holidays, I suppose.'

'That's fine. We treasure every extra minute we get with Lily,' said Frances. 'I'm sure there isn't a grandmother in the world who thinks she gets enough time with her grandchildren.'

Chelsea interpreted Frances' words as a dig, of course.

'Adam says he's sorry he couldn't come today,' said Chelsea. 'He's got an awful lot to do in London before the end of the year.'

And the wedding, Chelsea thought but didn't say.

'He does work very hard,' said Frances. 'But I'm quite glad you came instead.'

Really? Chelsea definitely couldn't believe that.

'You must come in and have a cup of tea.'

Said the spider to the fly.

'I'm sure you're busy getting ready for Christmas,' said Chelsea, taken by surprise. 'I don't want to keep you.'

'But Lily and I have made a cake. You must come in and try some.'

'Yes,' said Lily. 'We made it especially for you, Chelsea. You've got to have it.'

'And you're letting the heat out by making us stand here on the doorstep,' Frances added.

Chelsea could not refuse after that.

She followed Frances and Lily into the kitchen. There was indeed a cake on the side. A chocolate sponge. It was still on the cooling rack, fresh from the oven. It did smell delicious and Chelsea was suddenly feeling strangely ravenous. For once, she didn't think it was purely down to nerves and the vestigial remains of her issues around emotion and food.

'Grandma measured the ingredients but I mixed them,' Lily explained. 'And she let me lick the bowl.'

'I see,' said Chelsea.

'You're giving away our secrets, Lily-Belle,' said Frances indulgently.

'Oh, I've told Chelsea that you've let me eat the cake mix before. It's not true that it goes hard in your stomach if you eat it before it's cooked.'

'Who said that?' Chelsea asked.

'Jack did,' said Lily.

'I think that's what Auntie Ronnie says to Jack so she doesn't have to share the mixture with him,' said Chelsea. Jack also believed that Twix bars contained alcohol, which is why you can't have them until you're eighteen. According to his mum.

'Lily,' Frances interrupted. 'Will you please go down to the shed and tell Granddad that Chelsea is here, dear? I know he'd like to say hello as well.'

'All right,' said Lily. 'But don't cut the cake without me.'

'We'll wait for you,' Frances assured her.

When Lily was gone, Frances turned to Chelsea with a serious look on her face. Now it was going to happen. Now they could stop pretending that they hadn't gone head-to-head in a primary school hall in front of hundreds of other people.

'Chelsea,' said Frances. 'I'm very glad we've got this chance to be alone together. When I saw that it was you and not Adam in the car, I asked Brian to keep Lily occupied for a little while when you came in. He's going to try to keep her busy for at least ten minutes.'

'Oh.' Chelsea tried not to look frightened. Ten minutes was more than long enough for a row.

'Sit down. You're making the place look untidy,' Frances said.

Chelsea took one of the chairs at the kitchen table. She perched on the edge of it, feeling as though she was back in the headmistress's office at school, waiting to be reprimanded for something she hadn't done.

Frances sat down opposite her. She pinched the bridge of her nose. It was not a gesture that made Chelsea any more confident about what was to come. It was the gesture of someone who knew they had to do something awful and needed to gather the energy. What was she about to say? Was it possible that Frances could stop the wedding? Was she about to announce that she and Brian were going for custody of their grandchild to keep her out of Chelsea's incompetent clutches?

Thankfully, it was neither of those things. It was something Chelsea hadn't expected to hear from Frances' lips at all.

'I wanted to apologise.'

'Apologise?'

If Chelsea sounded surprised, it was because she was flabbergasted.

'Yes.'

It was the very last thing Chelsea was expecting.

'For the other afternoon. In the school hall.'

Chelsea started to say that Frances did not need to say 'sorry' – her English politeness breaking through even though she wanted that apology with every fibre of her being – but Frances cut her short.

'Oh, you're very sweet, Chelsea, but I know when I've acted like a fool. I've been unfair to you all along. From the moment Adam told me that there was someone new in his life, I was ready to hate you without knowing anything about you at all. I'm afraid that when you three came for lunch all those weeks ago, I was frosty and unkind.'

'You weren't,' Chelsea began to protest weakly.

'There's no need for you to say that, Chelsea. Brian told me I was. I *know* I was. And as for what happened at Lily's nativity play . . .'

Frances took a deep breath.

'I was unforgivably rude and in front of Lily's teacher to boot. I don't know what I was thinking.'

Chelsea looked down at the pattern on the oilcloth that covered the kitchen table.

'I saw Lily wearing that dress you'd made, trimmed with the lace from Claire's dress, and I suddenly saw red.'

'I should have asked before I did what I did,' said Chelsea.

'Perhaps you should have,' said Frances. 'But to accuse you of all those awful things as a result – that wasn't fair of me at all.'

'I should have realised how much it meant to you that the dress remained as it was.'

'But it's just a thing, Chelsea. A few bits of cloth sewn together. Of course it doesn't matter.'

'But it was Claire's dress.'

'Her dress, yes. It isn't Claire herself. I reacted much too strongly.'

Chelsea didn't know what to say.

'When we got back home that night, after Lily went to bed, Brian and I had a long and very difficult conversation. He told me I was being ridiculous. And not just about the dress. There are too many things like that frock in this house. Since Claire died, this place has become like a museum. I thought that by keeping all Claire's old clothes and toys, I was respecting her memory. There's a whole room of toys up there that I know Lily would love to play with but I have never let her loose because I worried something might get damaged. As if keeping all of Claire's old things intact could ever bring her back. What you did was right. You tried to make Claire's past a part of Lily's present by using the lace.'

'That's what I hoped to do.'

'And just this morning, I let Lily go into Claire's old bedroom and I left her in there to play exactly as she liked. I didn't hover over her. I didn't tell her that anything was out of bounds. I mean, if Claire were still alive, I wouldn't be bothered about the leg dropping off some old Sindy. Claire said goodbye to those old toys long before she died. I'm sure Brian and I would have got rid of most of them by now and redecorated Claire's room as a guest room. That's what we were planning to do, the year she passed away.'

Frances pulled out a lace-edged handkerchief and dabbed at her eyes.

'Keeping Claire's things exactly as she left them is keeping all of us frozen in time.'

'But I understand why,' said Chelsea.

'Do you? I overreacted to seeing Lily in that dress for so many reasons. It was difficult to see Lily in her nativity play without having Claire by my side. She should have been there. I know she would have been proud. I was so sad by the thought that she wasn't there and then suddenly I was angry. Perhaps you can imagine how difficult it was for me to look around the school hall and see you, taking my beloved Claire's place. It just didn't seem right or fair. I felt the same way when you and I first met. When you came here for lunch. I was furious with you for not being my daughter. By daring to assume her role in her family. You even sat in her place at the dining table.'

Chelsea winced as she remembered that moment.

'I wanted to march you out of the house and tell you never to come back again.'

'That's understandable.'

'But it's irrational. How would doing that make me

feel any better? How would it change things? It wouldn't bring Claire back. You weren't to know that was Claire's place. Just as you were not responsible for what happened to my daughter. Nobody was. Her death was just one of those accidents of fate. And it's been more than six years since she died. I can't pretend she hasn't been properly mourned. I certainly can't say Adam rushed into filling the space she left behind. He was devastated by Claire's death.'

'He loved her very much,' said Chelsea. 'He still talks about her all the time.'

'I am glad to hear that,' said Frances.

'He'll never forget her,' Chelsea continued. 'And I'm not replacing her. In a funny way, I think Claire and I will be parallel wives.'

Frances gave a small smile.

'Life goes on,' she said. 'Brian told me he's determined to make the most of it. We have our memories and we have our beautiful granddaughter. Brian said I should be happy to see Adam settled with someone like you. He said that what's good for Adam is good for Lily. Of course he is right about that.'

Good old Brian, thought Chelsea. She hadn't been wrong when she decided that Brian quite liked her.

'And over these past few weeks, seeing how you are with Lily, I can see that Brian is right. You love her, don't you?'

'I do. With all my heart.'

'And she loves you back. Every second word that comes out of her mouth is "Chelsea". She talks about you all the time. She's so excited about the wedding and not just because she's getting a new dress. She thinks you're the best thing since sliced bread, my dear.'

Chelsea blinked back tears at the thought of Lily,

who had once been so prickly towards her, actually singing her praises.

'Having you around has changed our granddaughter for the better. I can see that very easily. She's calmer when you're nearby. She's happier too, I know. You make her feel secure and cared for. That's reflected in the way she is.'

'I do the best I can.'

'You're doing wonderfully. As difficult as it's been for me to see another woman taking the place of my daughter in Lily's life, it can't be easy for you to have to deal with our side of the family. One set of in-laws is bad enough, but it's as though you've inherited an extra set.'

'I feel very lucky,' said Chelsea.

'I hope that one day you'll mean that,' said Frances. 'I will try not to get in your way too much, Chelsea. I think that Claire would have approved of the way you and Adam are doing things. Adam really was the love of her life, you know. She said she knew from the moment she met him. But because she loved him so much, I can also tell you that she would only want him to be happy. You make him happy. She would like you.'

'I'm very glad you said that.'

'So, I hope you'll accept my apology and that we can start again. As friends.'

'Of course.'

The two women shook hands.

'And I've decided I want you to have this.'

Frances unhooked the thin gold bracelet which encircled her narrow wrist. She tipped it into Chelsea's open palm. 'This belonged to my mother-in-law. She wore it at her wedding to Brian's father. I wore it at mine. Claire borrowed it for her wedding too. It might not be your style, exactly, but every bride needs something "old".'

'It's beautiful,' said Chelsea. It was. The chain was especially finely wrought.

'Let me help you put it on,' Frances said.

Chelsea held out her wrist so that the bracelet could be looped around it.

'All I ask is that when the time comes, you pass this bracelet on to Lily.'

'Of course I will.'

Lily solemnly processed back into the kitchen, singing another misheard carol. '*The first Noel, the angels did say, was to frighten poor shepherds in fields as they played.*'

Frances and Chelsea shared an indulgent smile.

'I'm looking forward to Christmas,' Lily announced. 'But, most of all, I'm looking forward to being a bridesmaid.'

'And I shall look forward to seeing the pictures,' said Frances.

'You can still come,' said Chelsea. 'If you want to. There's plenty of room in the church.'

Frances shook her head.

'You can send me the photographs.'

Chelsea didn't push it.

As promised, Frances and Chelsea had waited for Lily to return before cutting the cake. Brian joined them. The kettle went on and the four shared a cup of tea and a slice of chocolate sponge like any happy family. Lily made sure the conversation didn't flag for a second, as she explained her theory as to how Father Christmas could make it around the world in a single night.

'It's because his sleigh is made by Jaguar,' she said. 'They are the fastest cars in the world.'

'That's right,' said Brian.

It was easy to guess where Lily had picked up that idea.

'Also, the reindeer are special racing reindeer, crossed with horses.'

And finally . . .

'Houses without chimneys have their Christmas presents delivered by Amazon.'

'Come on, my Harold angel,' said Chelsea to Lily after this revelation. 'We've got to go to Auntie Annabel's to help her with the decorating for the wedding.'

'Hooray!' said Lily.

'Have a wonderful day,' said Frances. And this time the hug she gave Chelsea felt very heartfelt indeed.

Chapter Fifty-Six

Chelsea and Lily

Chelsea's moment with Frances had left her feeling warm but also just a little melancholy. She was pleased and felt vindicated that Frances had apologised for the incident at the school but she also knew what an effort it must have been for Frances to set aside her grief and to embrace the woman who would become Lily's stepmother. She wished she might have persuaded Frances and Brian to come to the wedding, but she also knew that was too much to ask.

Chelsea had been feeling oddly raw lately. The strangest things could have her crying. She dared not look at Facebook in case someone had posted a video of a puppy doing something cute. Even worse would be a video related to someone's endeavours for charity. How was it that human kindness could suddenly feel physically painful? The sight of an elderly gentleman collecting money for charity at the service station where she picked up that tatty poinsettia had made Chelsea's eyes sting. She was grateful that she would have Lily in the back of the car for the rest of the drive to Coventry. Had she been on her own, Chelsea would have been wetter than the weather with tears.

Lily would keep up the chatter all the way. She insisted that Chelsea find the compilation of carols she had uploaded to her iPhone (they were going to use them as background music at the wedding reception) and play them through the car stereo. They sang along together to all the old favourites. 'Jingle Bells'. 'Away In a Manger'. 'Silent Night'. Hark the *Harold* Angels. From now on, Jesus would always be 'risen with helium in his wings' to the members of Chelsea's household. Chelsea wasn't certain she could even remember the proper line any more.

'Do they have Christmas in heaven too?' Lily suddenly asked, when they were about half an hour away from Frances and Brian's house.

'Of course they do,' said Chelsea.

'Then can we send my mummy a present?'

Chelsea turned the music off for a moment so she could hear Lily properly.

'What sort of present?' she asked.

'Granny Frances said she always liked Dairy Milk. We could get her some of that.'

'We've got some in the car,' said Chelsea.

'But *where* should we send it?'

'I've got an idea,' said Chelsea. She remembered that on their first drive to see Claire's parents, Adam had pointed out Claire's old school. It was a famous school locally. Growing up on the other side of the Midlands, Chelsea had been aware of it. And now they were within five minutes of the place. Chelsea fiddled with the sat nav and soon had a fast route to the place.

'Let's go to Mummy's old school,' she said.

Term had ended and the school was empty, of course. Chelsea parked outside and together with Lily, she peered through the wrought-iron gates at the grand building beyond.

'If we leave the chocolate here, Mummy will know where to find it,' Chelsea suggested.

She helped Lily to write a Christmas card. She had a box of them in the boot, ready to write at the last minute if she realised she'd forgotten anyone from the Coventry gang. Lily chose a card decorated with a robin. They were her favourite birds, she said.

Together, they sealed the card and placed it, with the bar of chocolate, on top of the stone pillar to the left of the gate. Chelsea wondered if she was doing the right thing, by indulging Lily's idea that her mother still existed somewhere. The chocolate would no doubt end up being eaten by a groundsman, or a passing stranger, or an animal. The card would probably be blown away, trampled underfoot, forgotten. But Chelsea felt this was a powerful ritual for Lily. It helped her to connect her present with her past. Plus, Chelsea wasn't so sure that death really was the end. Having listened to Father Malcolm's sermons, she definitely hoped it wasn't.

And just as they were about to get back into the car, a curious robin alighted on the stone post to see what they had left behind. If signs existed, that seemed to be a very good one. Chelsea scooped Lily into her arms and gave her an enormous hug.

Chapter Fifty-Seven

Everybody

When Chelsea and Lily arrived at the Great House, it was already a hive of activity. Jacqui had been there since breakfast time. Dave had stayed at home with Bill, who needed to rest up if he was going to make it to the party in good health. Mark had brought Sophie and Jack over.

'We wanted to help,' said Jack.

'Ronnie was fine with it,' said Mark.

'But she's not coming?'

'She's covering for somebody at work.'

Chelsea had the feeling that wasn't true but she didn't question her brother-in-law on it.

'Mum is giving out jobs,' said Izzy of Annabel. 'You've got to go to her for instructions. We're on wedding favour duty. Me, Sophie and Jack. Lily, you can help us if you want.'

Izzy indicated the three big tins of Quality Street in the middle of the kitchen table. Having tried a ridiculous number of 'high-end', 'hand-made', 'artisanal' wedding chocolates at insanely steep prices, Chelsea and Annabel had come to the conclusion that it would actually be better to go for a true Christmas classic. A tin of Quality Street was certainly an important part of Christmas in both the Benson and the Buchanan homes.

'OK,' Izzy said to Jack and Lily. 'You've got to take

three chocolates, wrap them in a circle of cellophane – ' Sophie was cutting out the circles ' – and tie it so it makes a little bag. For that, we're using this ribbon. And you are not to eat more chocolates than you wrap up, Jack Benson Edwards.'

Jack's eyes were wide and innocent.

'He can have the strawberry creams,' said Sophie.

Izzy could go along with that. She passed Jack an opened tub of chocolates and he dived in to look for the pink ones. Jack was the only person in the family who liked strawberry creams. That was partly because he was the youngest and everyone else had staked his or her claims to the other flavours long before Jack came along.

'Nobody likes strawberry creams,' said Lily.

'I do!' said Jack, coming up with two at once. Seeing Jack so transported with delight, Lily said she would deign to try one.

'Now I like strawberry creams too!' she announced with her mouth still full.

'Oh dear,' Sophie mouthed to Izzy. Jack would not appreciate the competition. Thankfully, Lily quickly decided that she liked the orange creams too.

'Then you can have the orange ones, Lily, and you can have the strawberry ones, Jack,' Izzy quickly adjudicated.

Lily and Jack were pleased with that arrangement. They set to work and were soon treating Sophie and Izzy to a medley of their favourite Christmas songs. And not one of them with all the right lyrics. The older girls found it hard not to laugh as Lily sang out, 'Oh come, *holly* faithful! Joyful and *try am vent*,' while Jack followed up with, 'Oh come let us *ignore* him, Christ the *Law*.'

While the children worked on the party favours, Chelsea followed Jacqui outside. The portaloos were being delivered and wheeled into position under Richard's watchful eye.

'Gosh, these are fancy loos,' said Jacqui, as they took a quick tour of the first cabin to be set up. 'This is nicer than the caravan your Granddad had in Littlehampton.'

It was certainly much nicer than Chelsea had expected.

'These loos are brand new,' Richard explained. 'Annabel insisted. You should have heard her on the phone. I tell you, they should send her in to negotiate the UK's new EU agreement.'

Chelsea and Jacqui could imagine it.

'We're not going to have those vile silk flowers,' said Annabel, as she joined them. She tugged at a vase containing three silk roses, which was velcroed to the shelf on which it stood. 'The floral arrangements in here need to match the ones in the barn.'

'Of course,' said Jacqui.

'How are you, lovely?' Annabel asked Chelsea. 'Are you feeling excited yet? Nervous? Sick to the end of your toes?'

'I'm feeling pretty good, as it happens,' said Chelsea. Nobody needed to know about how the last couple of days had been. She was feeling good now.

'I must say,' Annabel continued, 'you look absolutely radiant. You'll have to tell me what moisturiser you're using.'

Next, they headed into the barn itself. The place was teeming with more workers, putting up tables and setting up a stage for the band that would be playing throughout the evening.

'Chelsea!' Sarah waved from the far end of the barn. Chelsea was very glad that Sarah had accepted their wedding invitation and was throwing herself into helping with the preparations. She knew that Jacqui was thrilled by Sarah's inclusion too. 'Thank goodness you're here. Now we can start with the decorations. We need your expert eye.'

In one corner of the barn were enormous piles of pine branches and holly.

'You wouldn't believe how hard it was to find holly with berries on it. The birds have been stuffing themselves. I hope that doesn't mean we're in for a hard winter.'

'But wouldn't it be nice if there were snow for the wedding,' said Annabel.

'Only if the guests have got here first,' said Sarah.

'And if it clears so that we can get rid of them all afterwards,' Chelsea added with a smile. 'You don't want to end up having everyone snowed in at your house, Annabel.'

'Well, there's plenty of food. And booze. Richard and Mark spent the best part of a day at Victoria Wines. I think they tested everything.'

Just then, Mark appeared. He was carrying a big metal box.

'What's that?' Chelsea asked.

'Er . . . nothing,' said Mark, immediately alerting her to the fact that it was something interesting. 'I mean, just something for the band.'

Chelsea nodded.

'Shall we make a start on the arrangements?' Sarah asked.

She handed each of the women a fat spool of red ribbon. It would be no small task to transform the greenery and ribbon into wreaths.

'I've brought all my gardening gloves,' Sarah explained, as she divvied out four pairs. 'You don't want to handle holly without gloves on.'

'You're not wrong, Mum,' said Annabel as she backed into a pile of greenery to let one of the band members through and was prickled through her jeans for her trouble.

While Chelsea and Jacqui tried to figure out where to start with the holly, Malcolm the vicar arrived. He came bearing an enormous ball of mistletoe.

'From the churchyard,' he said. 'Can't have a Christmas wedding without kissing.'

'Thank you,' said Chelsea. 'That will have pride of place over the entrance.'

'And how are you getting on?' Father Malcolm asked. 'It's an anxious time for the bride-to-be.'

'I'm very excited,' said Chelsea. 'And I know Adam is too. We're very grateful to you for agreeing to marry us.'

'The church is open,' said Father Malcolm. 'You're welcome to visit whenever you like.'

'I'll be right over,' said Chelsea.

'Oh yes,' said Annabel. 'We need to measure up for the bower over the church door.'

'Your decorations will certainly help make the church look beautiful for Christmas,' said Father Malcolm.

'Do you want a drink while you're here, Malc?' Annabel asked. 'Mark and Richard have been testing Christmas cocktails for the party.'

Father Malcolm smiled. 'I don't mind if I do.'

Chapter Fifty-Eight

Chelsea

A little later, Chelsea did go across to the church. She went alone. Annabel and Jacqui would be bringing the floral arrangements for the church over later. Father Malcolm was still in the tithe barn, helping Mark and Richard narrow down the cocktail contenders. In the weeks running up to the wedding, Chelsea had visited the church whenever she was in the Midlands – not just when the banns were being read – and had come to appreciate it as a place of peace and calm, where she could forget about the stress and tension that accompanied planning her big day. She relished her private moments at St Timothy's. The very walls seemed to exude comfort and love and she couldn't wait to be married there. She knew that Adam felt the same way.

The heavy church door was closed but unlocked. Chelsea pushed it open slowly, knowing that if you rushed it, the door hinges would squeal in protest. She didn't want to announce her arrival like that because, inside, the village choir was practising for the Christmas services ahead. Little Bissingden was very proud of its choir and justly so.

As Chelsea crept in, they were singing 'O Come All Ye Faithful'. Their voices were full of gusto and joy. Chelsea was very happy to hear the carol. She and Adam had actually chosen it as one of the hymns to be sung during their wedding ceremony. The singing and the sound of the organ were so loud and energetic, they seemed to vibrate in Chelsea's chest.

When that carol was finished, however, the mood changed.

Chelsea recognised the 'Coventry Carol' within three notes. It was Chelsea's favourite. Not often heard but never forgotten. The minor key of the sixteenth-century traditional sent shivers through Chelsea that afternoon. She waited at the top of the apse, staying out of sight as the choir sang Mary's lament over Herod's slaughter of the Innocents and the sorrow to come. While she listened to the plaintive melody, Chelsea instinctively crossed her hands over her stomach.

'*Lullay, lullay, thou little tiny child . . .*'

As the choir sang, Chelsea thought about the mothers in her own life and the sacrifices they'd made for their children. She thought about Jacqui at seventeen years old. Alone and frightened, giving up her first baby for adoption. Was there ever a lonelier, more awful experience? She thought about Sarah and her unhappy struggle with infertility before she adopted Annabel. She thought about the open-heartedness with which Sarah had faced letting Annabel look for her family of birth all those years later. She thought about Annabel, fighting like a lioness to get Izzy a kidney transplant. Then she thought about brittle and broken Frances, losing her only daughter in such a sudden and brutal way. She thought about Claire, torn from the child she and Adam had longed for.

Chelsea felt so many emotions welling inside her as the choir sang sweetly of Mary's love for her baby. She was thankful and fearful. Joyful and apprehensive. She was standing on the edge of a completely new life. The love she felt for Adam and for Lily made her feel terribly vulnerable and raw. But she was excited too about the years to come in the heart of her very own proper family.

The choir finished singing. Chelsea looked down at her belly. Then she closed her eyes and prayed that Christmas would bring news of a very special gift indeed.

Chapter Fifty-Nine

Mark and Richard

Mark and Richard were properly excited about Chelsea and Adam's wedding reception. While the women of the family busied themselves with making the barn look wonderful, the two men had tested six different cocktails for the big night. A vile concoction of Baileys and cream was quickly ruled out as was a horrible twist on a piña colada (the twist being Baileys instead of coconut milk). They plumped instead for a variation on a champagne cocktail, which they called 'A Festive Fizz' and a souped-up Sangria, which became a 'Santa's Sledgehammer'. Cocktails chosen, they turned their attention to their spectacular firework display.

The men had retreated to the small shed at the back of the barn to inspect their bounty, which had been delivered just that morning. They took the safety precautions very seriously. They both wore safety goggles. Mark had lots of protective clothing from his work. You didn't want to go sawing through MDF without safety goggles, that was certain.

Even with the atmosphere of danger, Richard and Mark were having a great time. Perhaps it was because of the atmosphere of danger. They had chosen the music – 'O Come All Ye Faithful' – and now they were working out which firework should be let off when. 'O Come All Ye Faithful' turned out to be great firework music with plenty of crescendos they could use to great effect.

They'd also chosen where the display would be set up. The Great House had a vast garden so it was easy to find a suitably open spot far enough from the house for safety but close enough for an excellent view.

The fireworks could not be set up too far ahead of time, though. The weather had been iffy the past few days and they didn't want anything to get damp. There was also the matter of wind direction. If, on the day of the wedding, the prevailing wind was blowing in a different direction to the way it had been for the past few days, they would have to rethink the site. So, for the moment, all the planning had to be done on paper.

'You know what?' said Mark. 'If you do lose your job at the bank, Rich, you and me could set up a firework display business.'

'That's not a bad idea,' said Richard. 'I don't know how I ended up in banking in the first place. Or law. Why did I study Law? I always wanted to be a stuntman.'

'Me too,' said Mark. 'When I was a kid, I used to practise my wheelies for hours on end. I was going to get a motorbike as soon as I could afford one. I had it all planned out. I was saving up for lessons. Then Sophie came along.' He was silent for a moment. 'I wouldn't change that for the world though.'

The men continued to plot the sequence in which they would light the various rockets and Catherine Wheels. If they occasionally disagreed, they soon came to a compromise. They got along very well. They understood each other and felt no need to compete. They allowed each other to indulge in the fantasy of who they might have been, had life turned out differently. Were they not married to Ronnie and Annabel. On the subject of the sisters' on-going feud, they were sanguine.

'Ronnie will come round,' said Mark. 'She won't be able to stand being at home on her own while everybody's here having a party.'

'I've said to Annabel, she should just phone Ronnie up and apologise. She can't miss Chelsea's wedding. Doesn't matter who said what. They're both as bad as each other.'

'I bet that went down well.'

'I had to make my own tea that night,' Richard admitted.

'Women,' Mark agreed.

'What did they fall out about anyway?'

'Annabel dissed Poldark or something,' said Mark.

'I have no idea what that means,' said Richard.

'Exactly.'

'Catherine Wheel next?' Richard suggested.

'Good choice, mate. That's just what I was going to say.'

Each firework was taken out and inventoried, then put back into the safe metal box.

'Where are we going to leave these tonight?' Mark asked.

'I don't know,' said Richard. 'I'm not sure we should leave them in here though. We should probably put them in the garage. Totally out of the way. And we can lock it.'

Mark agreed.

'What have we got left to finish the routine?' he asked.

'There's this one,' Richard pulled out an enormous rocket. 'I thought we should try to make this go off during the very last line of the song.'

'Chri-eye-st the Lord?' sang Mark.

'That's the one.'

'Richard,' said Mark. 'This display is going to be epic.'

The two grown men bumped fists.

Chapter Sixty

The ladies

By seven o'clock in the evening, the barn was looking absolutely beautiful. Sarah, Jacqui, Annabel and Chelsea had done a magnificent job of turning the greenery and ribbons into a Christmas display worthy of any top London hotel. Chelsea was delighted. Annabel too. She took hundreds of photographs for the website advertising the tithe barn she aimed to set up in the New Year.

Jacqui hugged her youngest daughter as they surveyed their handiwork.

'It's really happening,' she said. 'I can just imagine you walking in here in your dress, with all your bridesmaids and your page-boy around you.'

'I can see it too,' said Chelsea.

'Where is the dress?' Annabel asked.

'In the back of the car,' said Chelsea.

'You need to get it out and hang it up.'

'I'll do that when I get back to Mum's.'

But Annabel insisted. 'I've got a proper steamer. I was using it on the drapes.'

Annabel had bought some old red velvet drapes to close across the barn doors once everyone was inside, in an attempt to stop some of the draughts. She'd also cobbled together a number of screens, behind which caterers could deal with dirty plates and the rest. 'If you get the dress out now, we can give it a quick steam, then you can lay it on the back seat of the car for the trip from here to Jacqui's.'

'Actually, that is a good idea,' said Chelsea. 'A steamer is the one thing I forgot to bring.'

Jacqui helped Chelsea bring her dress, still wrapped in its garment bag, out of the car and into the barn. They brought the bridesmaids' dresses too and the little suit with the velvet jacket that Jack would be wearing in his role as pageboy. Carefully, they hung the clothes from a rail. Annabel had bought four rails to put in one corner of the barn as a makeshift cloakroom. Having worked on a magazine and attended many photo shoots, Chelsea knew exactly what to do with a steamer.

'But you're all to go away while I've got my dress out,' she said to Jacqui, Annabel and Sarah. 'I want it to be a surprise.'

The other women agreed not to watch while Chelsea unpacked her wedding gown.

Pulling the dress out of the bag and seeing it hanging on the rail, Chelsea felt the same thrill she'd felt when she discovered the dress in the vintage shop. It was truly beautiful and she couldn't wait to put it on again. She had found a lovely antique shawl too and, of course, the perfect shoes. They were new. And ruinously expensive. Jimmy Choos.

Carefully, Chelsea ran the steamer down the skirt. It wasn't actually all that creased considering it had spent most of the day in her car, and Chelsea erred on the side of caution. Better a few creases than accidentally damaging the fabric by getting a spot of boiling water on it. Annabel's steamer wasn't the very best kind and it hissed and spat like a kettle while it was warming up.

But soon the dress was ready. She did the same to the velvet gowns she had chosen for Izzy and Sophie and the little velvet frock Lily would wear. Jack's outfit was less delicate and could be ironed.

Job done, Chelsea unplugged the steamer and pushed the garment rail behind a screen so that the wedding dress could hang in perfect peace until it was time to lay it on the back seat of the car again. She joined her mother, sister and Sarah in the main hall. They were busy laying out the place cards on the table. It was all going very smoothly. Had Ronnie been there, she would definitely have tried to switch people around. Ronnie couldn't help meddling.

Chelsea sighed. It was sad that Ronnie wasn't there but Chelsea had long since decided that she'd done everything she could to persuade her sister that it was important she attend the whole wedding. They would save her a place. If she decided not to take it, that was her problem. Ronnie was forever cutting off her nose to spite her face. Chelsea would not let it ruin her day. She joined the others.

'Let's just light a few of these candles to see the effect,' said Annabel. 'I've got plenty of spares.'

Jacqui, Sarah and Chelsea watched eagerly as Annabel lit the candles on a magnificent standing candelabra. She'd found it in a junk shop in France many years before. Its shabby chic style – it was made of wood – didn't fit with the refurbished big house and she'd thought about throwing it out but, with a coat of gold paint, it was perfect for a wedding in the barn. Annabel was very glad she'd decided to keep it.

With the candles lit and the main lights turned off, the barn was transformed into a magical fairy banqueting hall. Chelsea hugged her sister, her mother and Sarah in turn. They'd all worked so hard to make her dream her reality. She simply could not wait to get married.

Chapter Sixty-One

Ronnie

While her sisters prepared for the wedding, Ronnie really had been at work, just as Mark had said. She was covering for Marie, the woman who did the days Ronnie couldn't do. That week Marie was recovering from a hysterectomy.

Ronnie went into the office for nine o'clock as usual. Her first duty was to check the floral displays in the reception, making sure to remove any and all dead leaves and petals. There was something especially awful about dead flowers in a funeral director's reception and Ronnie's boss was obsessive about keeping those flowers fresh. Normally, they were lilies but for December, they were poinsettias. Ronnie was not particularly fond of the plants with their strange red leaves but she made sure they looked presentable all the same. They were as Christmassy as the place was going to get.

The day was pretty quiet. Ronnie busied herself with dusting the marble samples that people used when choosing headstones. She straightened up the leaflets about funeral planning and sent out a couple of invoices.

At half past four, just as Ronnie was thinking about getting ready to go home, a last-minute visitor rang the doorbell. Ronnie pressed the button that unlocked the door and the woman came in.

* * *

The visitor was distraught. That wasn't so unusual. Ronnie's job meant that she often met people in a state of distress or confusion. Guiding the woman straight to a chair, she put on her best bedside manner and asked how she could help.

It took a long time to get the story out. At first Ronnie thought the poor woman must be coming to report a death. Eventually, Ronnie realised that she was there to visit a deceased relative who was already at rest in the funeral home's little chapel of rest.

Offering her arm, Ronnie led the woman inside. She had grown used to this part of her duties, but it still moved her to see her clients coming face to face with their dead loved ones for a last goodbye. Ronnie remained close by unless she was asked to leave. Sometimes people fainted.

The woman, who said her name was Jill, didn't want to linger by the coffin long but when she and Ronnie were back in Reception, she seemed to want to stay and talk.

'She was my sister,' Jill explained. 'But I haven't seen her since 1995. I didn't talk to her for twenty years. Can you believe it?'

'What happened?' Ronnie couldn't resist asking. Even in the midst of her own estrangement from Annabel, Ronnie was slightly outraged by the idea of not seeing your own flesh and blood for two decades.

'I can't even remember,' said Jill. 'We were always having little arguments. That's the way it was even when we were children. Always falling out. Always bickering. But we'd usually make up fairly quickly. Then one day we didn't. The way that argument started has completely gone from my memory. But it must have felt serious back then because I decided I wasn't going to back down for once. And neither would she. And before you knew it, a year had gone by. And then another. And then she moved and changed her phone number so I couldn't even get hold of her to apologise if I wanted to. I found out she was dead on the Internet. I was trying to find her address for a Christmas card. I found her death notice in the local paper instead.'

Ronnie grimaced.

'Why did we let it go on for so long?' Jill asked rhetorically.

'It must have been a serious argument,' Ronnie tried to console her.

'Nothing's so serious that you should lose a sister over it,' said Jill. 'There were so many things over the years that I wanted to share with her. So many moments when I should have tried harder to get back into contact. And now there'll never be another chance to tell her how much I've missed her. Don't ever let pride get in the way of happiness. At the end of the day, family is all any of us has got.'

Ronnie nodded. She felt a blush creep over her cheeks.

'Thank you,' said Jill. 'For listening to me. You'll look after my sister won't you, while she's here?'

Ronnie confirmed that she would.

'And if you've got a sister of your own, make sure you tell her you love her tonight.'

Jill's visit had certainly given Ronnie food for thought. As she drove home, she couldn't help thinking about her whole family, over at Annabel's, setting up the barn for the wedding. She should have been there. She should be at Chelsea's wedding reception too. Letting herself into the empty house – Mark and the kids were still in Little Bissingden – she took out her phone and decided it was time to send Annabel a text. As far as Ronnie was concerned, Annabel was still in the wrong, of course, but Jill was right. You shouldn't let pride get in the way of happiness. Ronnie was prepared to back down for Chelsea's sake. However, she didn't have time to finish composing her text before Annabel called her.

Chapter Sixty-Two

Lily and Jack

This is how it happened. Lily and Jack were bored. They'd finished filling the bags of wedding favours hours ago. Since then, they'd just been told to 'keep out of trouble'. To begin with, they kept out of trouble by downloading Crossy Road, the game they weren't supposed to play, onto Sophie's iPad. Mark had forgotten to put Jack's own iPad in the huge kit bag Ronnie gave him to take to Annabel's. Sophie was persuaded that it was better to risk Jack breaking her iPad than listen to him moaning all day. The game got boring. They were banished to the TV room.

The first thing they both did was check that the dog was still there. In two pieces, but propped up to look whole, on the mantelpiece.

'They haven't noticed,' Jack said with relief.

'But they will,' said Lily.

Jack knew she was right. At some point, the mantelpiece would be dusted. He was surprised it hadn't happened already. The mantelpiece in his house was dusted every single week without fail. He often had to do it himself. He would have expected his Auntie Annabel to be at least as house-proud as his mother.

'Do you think I should tell Auntie Annabel today?' Jack asked. 'It's getting near Christmas. If I get told off today, Father Christmas might have forgiven me by Christmas Eve.'

'Noooo,' said Lily. 'She might shout.'

'But if we don't say what happened, we might not get any presents. Father Christmas knows everything.'

Lily agreed. It was a grave situation indeed.

'Do you watch *You've Been Framed*?' Jack asked his soon-to-be cousin.

'Sometimes,' said Lily. 'At Grandma's house. Daddy says he doesn't really like it.'

'Did you see that they will give you two hundred and fifty pounds if you send them something funny?'

Lily nodded.

'If I had two hundred and fifty pounds, then I could pay Auntie Annabel back for the dog and she wouldn't be able to get angry.'

'It's more than two hundred and fifty pounds,' said Lily. 'I bet it's a million pounds. It was so old.'

Jack remembered the conversation he'd had with his Auntie Chelsea about Auntie Annabel's antiques.

'Then I'll have to make a lot of videos.'

'Hundreds,' said Lily.

'That will take years!'

'I'll help you,' said Lily suddenly. 'The dog was a little bit my fault too.'

Jack was touched by Lily's admission.

'And when we've finished paying back for the dog, we can spend the rest of the money!' Lily continued. Her grasp of maths was just as shaky as Jack's. 'I'm having a new dolls' house.'

'I'm having the latest version of Minecraft,' said Jack.

'And a pink car.'

'And a new set of *Doctor Who* miniatures.'

It was a brilliant plan.

Jack and Lily were convinced they had stumbled upon the perfect way to set things right. A subtle variation on the scheme that had got them into trouble in the first place. Jack would do his usual somersault onto the sofa, but this time he would get it wrong deliberately in a hilariously funny way. Quite what that 'hilariously funny way' would entail wasn't exactly clear. Jack hoped that it would come to him as soon as he started jumping. Once again, Lily was to be the camera operator, recording all the pratfalls.

'OK,' she said. 'On your marks, a-one, a-two, a-three . . .'

'Ladies and gentlemen, boys and girls,' Jack reprised his introduction.

He tumbled onto the sofa again and again in pursuit of the perfect shot. Each time, he and Lily would review the footage and she would say, 'But it's not really funny, is it? How can we make it funnier?'

That was the million-dollar question.

'Pull a face. Make a farting sound. Pretend you've done a poo in your pants,' were some of Lily's better suggestions.

Jack prepared himself for take twenty. Lily counted him down. Jack ran across the television room, faster than ever before. This time, instead of doing the usual simple flip, he first leaped into the air for extra height. And this time, when he came back down, the landing really wasn't funny.

'Owwww!' Jack clutched at his elbow and howled.

'Brilliant!' said Lily, the mini-Hitchcock, as she kept the camera rolling. 'Keep shouting,' she said. 'This is really funny.'

'It's not funny,' said Jack. 'I've hurt my arm.'

'No you haven't. You're just pretending.'

'I have hurt it. I've hurt it really.'

Jack tried to get up from the floor. When he put

pressure on the arm he'd been clutching, in order to lever himself to his feet, he promptly collapsed. Lily laughed some more. This was brilliant footage as far as she was concerned. Jack's super-realistic collapse would make *You've Been Framed* gold. Two hundred and fifty pounds was in the bag. But then Jack fainted. Lily dropped the old iPad and set up a wail of her own.

'Chel-sea!'

Chapter Sixty-Three

The grown-ups

The adults were all in the barn but Sophie and Izzy, who were in the kitchen redoing the wedding favour bags that Lily and Jack hadn't quite got right, recognised the sound of a real emergency at once. They raced to the TV room where they found Jack on the floor and Lily screaming her head off.

Sophie got down on her knees next to Jack.

'Jack! Jack! Can you hear me? Jack?' She gently patted his face.

Jack's eyes fluttered open.

'Jack?'

'What happened?' Izzy asked.

Lily started to cry as she told the story. 'Jack was bouncing off the sofa. He went too high. He fell over. He said he hurt his arm.'

'It looks broken,' said Sophie, doing her best to examine the damage without causing Jack any pain.

'Noooo!' Jack wailed, as Sophie gently touched his elbow.

'Keep still,' Izzy told him. 'Don't try to move.'

'Get my dad,' said Sophie. 'And Grandma. And Chelsea. And anyone else who might actually know what to do.'

Izzy set off at speed to the barn. Leander followed behind her, eager to be in on the action, like a Labrador Lassie.

As Izzy charged into the barn, she took the adults by surprise. She panted out the problem. Chelsea, Annabel, Sarah and Jacqui were soon on their way to the house. Annabel yelled for Richard and Mark. They were just about to carry the huge box of fireworks over to the garage. Instead, they set them down on one of the tables in the main barn and followed the women at once.

Everyone was so focussed on going to Jack's aid that no one remembered to blow out the lit candelabra. And nobody heard it topple over as Richard, the last one out, let the barn door close with a bang.

In the TV room, Annabel issued instructions while Jacqui and Chelsea crouched down beside Jack and tried to comfort him in his agony.

'Sophie, we need to get hold of your mum,' said Annabel.

'My phone's out of battery,' Sophie wailed.

'Then I'll call her. Izzy, you call an ambulance. We have to get him to A and E.'

'It might be quicker for one of us to drive him to hospital,' said Richard.

'Good idea,' said Chelsea. 'Mark? Are you sober?'

He wasn't quite.

'Richard?'

Richard shook his head.

'Then I'll drive,' Chelsea decided. 'You men will have to carry Jack to my car.'

'I didn't mean to break the dog, Auntie Annabel,' Jack mumbled. 'I was going to pay you back.'

'What's he on about?' Annabel asked.

'Must be delirious from the pain,' said Chelsea. 'Now, Jack, Daddy and Uncle Richard are going to lift you up. Put your good arm around Daddy's neck.'

'You're going to be all right, sweetheart,' Jacqui told her grandson. 'Mummy's on her way.'

'Are you sure you're OK to drive?' Annabel asked Chelsea. 'Do you know where you're going?'

'Sat nav,' said Chelsea.

'I'm coming with you,' said Sophie.

'Me too,' said Izzy.

'You can't leave me behind!' said Lily.

'We'll have to take two cars,' said Annabel. Ronnie had not picked up Annabel's call but having heard the message she had left, she was now calling back.

Everyone in the TV room could hear Ronnie's loud anguish even though Annabel had the phone pressed to her ear.

'Just meet us at the hospital,' said Annabel. 'Everything is going to be fine.'

Seconds later, they heard the explosions from the barn.

Chapter Sixty-Four

Everybody

The surprisingly flimsy candelabra had fallen over as the barn door slammed shut in the wind. It knocked over a table as it fell. On that table was the box of fireworks. The box was not locked – as per the strict safety instructions – so that as it hit the floor, it popped open, spilling those expensively large fireworks everywhere. Then the one candle that had not gone out when the candelabra fell over set light to the edge of the tablecloth. As the tablecloth smouldered, it in turn set light to a Catherine wheel. Once the Catherine wheel was alight and spraying sparks as it whizzed untethered across the floor, the barn was all but history.

Everyone gathered by the back door of the main house and looked in the direction of the noise. Richard and Mark soon guessed what was happening.

'It's the fucking fireworks!' said Mark.

'What fucking fireworks?' asked Chelsea.

'They were supposed to be your wedding surprise!'

'Oh no.' Chelsea covered her eyes.

'We can't worry about that now. Put Jack in the back of Chelsea's car,' said Annabel, trying her best to remain calm and keep control of the situation. 'Chelsea, go to the hospital. Jacqui, go with her. Take Lily and Sophie. We'll stay here and sort everything else out. Izzy, get the fire extinguisher from the kitchen.'

But by the time Mark and Richard had carried Jack to safety, the impromptu firework display was in full force. No kitchen fire extinguisher was going to do the job. There were further fire extinguishers inside the barn, of course – they were a health and safety requirement – but right then they were useless. None of the assembled adults dare go anywhere near the barn or attempt to open the door in case a loose rocket came flying out. While Izzy called the fire brigade, Annabel berated her husband.

'How many bloody fireworks are there?'

'We wanted to give Chelsea a good send-off,' Richard said helplessly.

It was certainly a display that none of them would ever forget.

It took the fire brigade almost half an hour to arrive, by which time the whizzing and banging had all but stopped and a proper blaze had taken hold. Annabel could only watch in despair as the firemen turned their hoses on full force. The jig was up. The water would ruin anything that had escaped being burned. She could only be thankful that nobody had been in there when the place went up.

Unable to go anywhere near the barn as it smouldered, Annabel, Richard, Izzy and Mark retired to the kitchen of the Great House away from the heat and the smoke. Humfrey, miraculously, had slept through the whole thing, closely guarded by Leander. The four adults sat around the kitchen table saying nothing. Annabel was too shocked even to start blaming Richard for not having put the fireworks in a more secure place. Later, when the shock wore off, she would accept that he had been intending to put the fireworks somewhere safe. Fate, in the form of Jack's accident had taken over.

When Ronnie texted to say that Jack had been seen and everything would be OK, Richard said, 'Thank goodness for that. Now we need a drink.' The wedding wine may have been in the barn, but Richard found a very nice bottle of Krug in his cellar.

Chapter Sixty-Five

Jack

Jack had broken his arm. When Jacqui and Chelsea carried him into the hospital, with Lily and Sophie close behind, and Jack saw his mother, he burst into fresh anguished tears.

'She's going to tell me off,' said Jack.

But Ronnie had only kisses for her son.

'You donut,' she said, when he told her what had happened, with Lily filling in the details about the china dog. 'Why didn't you just say the day you broke it? You definitely get your brains from your dad.'

While the staff at the A and E department attended to Jack's injury, getting him X-rayed and having the break set in a cast, Chelsea and Jacqui remained in the waiting room with Lily and Sophie, getting reports from the Great House by text.

They knew it was going to be bad news for the wedding. They were all smiles, however, when Ronnie brought Jack back into the waiting room with the bright-blue cast on his arm. A playful nurse had tied a piece of tinsel around it.

'The doctor said that Father Christmas might feel sorry for me and bring me extra presents,' was the first thing Jack told his grandma.

'Did she now?' said Jacqui.

Ronnie rolled her eyes, though both Jacqui and

Chelsea knew that Ronnie would almost certainly pull out the stops to make up for Jack having to wear a cast on Christmas Day.

'And will Auntie Annabel forgive me for the dog because of my broken arm?' Jack asked Chelsea.

'I'm sure she will,' said Chelsea. 'I'm also sure it's the last thing on her mind right now.'

Chelsea's mind was certainly elsewhere.

'Fire brigade gone but not allowed in barn,' was the latest text.

Chelsea had asked if Annabel could send a picture, so that she could start to get her head around what was going on back in Little Bissingden. Annabel had wisely ignored that request.

'Phew,' said Jack.

'Will she forgive me too?' asked Lily.

Jacqui gave Lily a hug. 'Oh, you children are too precious. Look at you both. You're my little angels. Auntie Annabel will just be glad you're both safe. She won't worry about her china.'

'I suppose we ought to go. I can look after Jack from now on,' said Ronnie. To Chelsea she added, 'You should get back to Annabel's to finish tarting up the barn for the wedding.'

'Actually,' said Chelsea. 'There's a bit of a problem with that.'

Chapter Sixty-Six

Everybody

Chelsea and Lily spent the night at Jacqui's house. It wasn't until the following morning that Chelsea was able to go back to the barn and find out just how comprehensive the damage had been. She was surprised to find that she could smell smoke on the air as she turned the car off the dual carriageway towards Little Bissingden. She prayed that she was actually only smelling someone's seasonal bonfire. The fire couldn't have got that serious, could it? That she would be able to scent the smoke from so far away? They had called the fire brigade so quickly.

When Chelsea arrived, Annabel, Richard, Izzy and Sarah were all in the kitchen. Izzy bounced Humfrey on her knee. She had a smile for her little brother but otherwise the mood was sombre.

'How bad is it?' was Chelsea's first question.

'Well, they got here in time to save the barn but I'm afraid that everything that was inside was absolutely ruined.'

Including Chelsea's wedding dress.

Annabel and Chelsea went out to the barn together. They didn't go inside it. They were still waiting for a visit from the building inspector to let them know that it was safe. However, the fire crew had brought an awful lot of stuff outside in an attempt to minimise the loss. It was arrayed around the front of the barn like the remains of a garage sale. Chelsea spotted her dress – or rather what remained of it – right away. And there were the bridesmaids' dresses. All four of them looking like rags. And Jack's little suit. Smudged with ash and tattered, it might have worked as a costume for a school production of *Oliver!* It definitely would not work as a pageboy outfit for what should have been the wedding of the year.

Around the clothes were other filthy rags that had once been tablecloths. Charred chairs and tables. Smoked greenery.

'It actually smells quite nice,' said Chelsea in an attempt to leaven the atmosphere. 'All that burned pine. Very Christmassy.'

'I am so sorry,' said Annabel. 'I don't know what to say.'

'It was an accident,' said Chelsea. 'A ridiculous accident.'

'It's like that song about the old woman swallowing the fly. The unintended consequences of my not having glued that silly little dog together when it broke the best part of twelve years ago.'

Chelsea had brought her sister up to speed with the incident that led Jack to be bouncing off the sofa in the first place.

'You never could have foreseen this. No-one could.'

Chelsea fingered the skirt of her dream wedding dress. It was grey with ash from the fire crew's water, but some of the sequins and little beads still shone. Bravely, Chelsea thought.

'I can tell it was a very special dress,' said Annabel.

'Yes,' said Chelsea. 'It was. But it's just a thing, isn't

it?' She remembered Frances and the little lace angel dress. 'Just stuff. The only thing that matters is that everyone is safe.'

While Chelsea and Annabel stood outside the barn, looking at the detritus that was once a wedding party, Father Malcolm joined them. He embraced Chelsea warmly. 'This must be hard to see,' he said. Chelsea agreed. 'But the wedding must go on. The church is still ready to welcome you and Adam on Saturday morning.'

Chelsea nodded. 'We'll be there.'

Chapter Sixty-Seven

Chelsea and Jacqui

Though she had assured Father Malcolm that she would be at the church on Saturday morning, by the time Chelsea got back to her parents' house, her gung-ho spirit had gone missing. The first thing she said was, 'It's a disaster. We're going to have to cancel the wedding.'

'Not the wedding,' Jacqui pointed out. 'The reception, perhaps, but not the wedding itself.'

Chelsea's face crumpled. 'But we can't ask people to come all the way up here if we've got nowhere to have the reception, Mum. At first Annabel thought we could move it into the Great House but everything smells of smoke and there are health and safety issues with all the debris from the barn everywhere. How can we invite people to a wedding without a party?'

'It doesn't matter. They'll still come for the ceremony. People will understand.'

'And I've got no dress.'

'You can buy a dress. There's still a whole day. Would it take that long?'

Chelsea gave Jacqui a look to suggest that she knew nothing about buying wedding dresses. Finding a decent dress to wear to lunch with a bunch of old friends could take Chelsea hours. Finding the dress in which she was supposed to say her wedding vows? What a nightmare. She thought back to the awful afternoon in the wedding dress salon and how lucky she had felt to find the perfect solution in a vintage shop instead. She started to tell Jacqui all the reasons why it wouldn't work. She and Adam absolutely had to put the wedding off and start again.

'Well, I suppose you could cancel the whole thing if you think that's for the best,' said Jacqui. 'But what happened to all that stuff about it being about the marriage and not the wedding? Of course you can still have the service. The church didn't burn down as well.'

'I just feel . . . I feel like perhaps it's an omen. I was so looking forward to having the reception in the barn. It was all coming together so well. I should have guessed that it couldn't work out for me. Of course it wouldn't. I was never meant to get married.'

'Chelsea Benson. I don't think I've heard anything so stupid in my life,' Jacqui snapped. 'Can you imagine what Adam would think if he heard you talking like this? Believe me, once you've been married for as long as I have, you'll see that not being able to have a party is nothing compared to some of the things you'll go through. You're bloody getting married. Of course you're meant to. Even if you have to get married in a dressing gown, you're getting married tomorrow. Don't you even think about doing anything else.'

But of course she wouldn't be getting married in a dressing gown. While her mother looked after Lily (Adam would not be coming up to the Midlands until that evening), Chelsea went into Solihull to see what she could cobble together there. Jacqui had offered to go with her but Chelsea said that she wanted to shop alone. She could work much more quickly that way and, heaven knows, she didn't have much time.

She started in the dress department of John Lewis. It

was depressing. There was certainly plenty to choose from but nothing that floated Chelsea's boat. Through her work, Chelsea was familiar with the very best of designer fashion. She knew about fabrics. To see so much synthetic tulle in one place made her depressed. And why was everything strapless? It was baffling to Chelsea that it had become the norm. Doubtless the wedding dress manufacturers were happy with the situation because they were saving money on fabric and the cost of having those missing sleeves sewn up. What had become of the sleeve specialists, Chelsea wondered for the moment. They'd probably all moved on to boleros.

Chelsea left John Lewis in a state of despond. She felt the same as she exited Monsoon half an hour later. There were plenty of long dresses there and she tried quite a few of them on, but there seemed to be something wrong with every single one of them. Most of them didn't have sleeves, again. The seams weren't sewn straight. The waistband hit at a strange height. There's nothing like a badly sewn bias-cut dress for clinging in all the wrong places.

Chelsea ended up buying a plain cream shift dress in Marks & Spencer and a red pashmina to throw over the top for a festive touch. With a rose stuck behind her ear, she would look OK.

Just OK.

She went back to John Lewis and stopped by the Chanel counter to buy herself a cheering lipstick. She wasn't in the least bit surprised to discover that they didn't have any of her usual colours. It was that sort of day.

Chelsea texted Jacqui to say that she was not going to be back for lunch. 'Still got a few dress shops to look at!' she lied. In reality, she just wanted a bit of time to herself.

She went into Pizza Express. The restaurant was packed with people treating themselves to lunch at the end or beginning of their Christmas shopping trips. Everyone seemed to be in high spirits. It was hard to get through the restaurant thanks to all the shopping bags which were piled high around each table, full of gifts that would be forgotten within days or, worse, returned to the store they'd been bought at for credit.

Chelsea was grateful at least that she didn't have to re-do her Christmas shopping. The presents she'd bought for her family were all safely tucked up in Jacqui's spare bedroom. The gifts she'd chosen for Adam and Lily were back at their house in South London.

As she picked at a pizza, Chelsea considered the situation. 'I shouldn't be so spoilt,' she told herself. 'I'm still getting married. I may have to do it in a dress I wouldn't have chosen in a million years but that doesn't make a difference to the fact that I'm marrying the love of my life.'

There in Pizza Express, Chelsea suddenly realised that the big wedding she'd imagined was about more than wanting to have all her friends around her. Specifically, it was about wanting her wedding to Adam to be at least as big and spectacular as his first wedding had been. If Claire had two hundred guests, then Chelsea wanted that many guests too. It was all about making sure people realised that this was just as important a marriage as Adam's first had been.

But she couldn't say that to Adam. She couldn't say it to Jacqui, or Ronnie, or Annabel, or anybody. Chelsea felt ashamed as she realised the motivation behind her grandiose plans. The fact that they would not now come to fruition felt like punishment for being so silly. It was all that she deserved.

Chapter Sixty-Eight

The Benson-Edwards

Back at Ronnie's house, there were more wedding outfit issues. Jacqui was trying to solve the issue of Jack's cast. When they learned that Jack's official outfit had gone up in smoke, Jacqui had suggested he wear the suit he wore to his parents' wedding the year before. They'd bought the jacket with growing room. It would probably be OK. But the cast on his elbow would not fit through the jacket sleeve and it wasn't simply a matter of cutting the sleeve off. For some reason, the jacket had particularly small armholes. It looked very elegant, but it was no good for Jack's broken arm. Jacqui turned the jacket inside out and had Jack try to get his wrist and the start of the cast through the sleeve hole. She could tell at once that there was no point ruining the jacket.

'Even if we cut the sleeve off,' Jacqui told Ronnie, 'we'd have to cut the sleeve off the shirt as well and he can't go into the church with half a shirt on. He'll freeze. And he'll look like a trucker.'

'I'd quite like to look like a trucker,' said Jack.

'I bet you would,' said his mother. 'But it's not what Auntie Chelsea would want.'

'What's he going to wear instead?' asked Jacqui. 'He hasn't got any T-shirts that aren't covered in *Doctor Who* stuff. We can't cut the arm off his school jumper. He needs it for next term.'

'I *could* wear one of my *Doctor Who* T-shirts,' said Jack. As far as he was concerned, this was getting better by the minute.

'No you can't,' said Ronnie.

'Auntie Chelsea likes *Doctor Who*.'

'Not at her wedding. We'll have to make an emergency dash to Marks,' said Ronnie.

'No!' Jack could think of nothing worse than an emergency dash to Marks & Spencer. 'I can't go to Marks & Spencer's with a broken arm.'

'Then it's lucky I've got a better idea,' said Jacqui.

Jack would not wear the dreaded pageboy outfit after all. The one outfit that would fit, without any alterations, was the costume he had worn for the nativity play. His Angel Gabriel get-up. It had loose wide sleeves, perfect for flapping about while addressing the Virgin Mary. Even if you were wearing a cast.

Jack was delighted.

Ronnie wasn't sure.

'It's perfect,' said Jacqui. Sophie agreed.

'It's not fair,' said Lily, when she heard.

'Why not?'

'I want to wear my angel outfit too.'

'Why not?' said Jacqui. 'At least then you'll both match.'

A quick phone call to Adam and it was done. He threw Lily's angel outfit into his case.

Adam got out of work early that day and was in Coventry sooner than expected. When Ronnie met him at the station, Adam revealed he had been busy with his mobile on the train.

'I've been in touch with all the guests I know and told them that there isn't going to be a reception. I've told them that we'll understand if they can't be bothered to come all the way up here for just the church service.'

'Adam,' said Ronnie. 'There is no way you're not having a party.'

'But Chelsea's right. It's too late. I called all the hotels in the area this morning to see if there was anywhere that could take a group the size of ours at such short notice and they're all completely booked up. It's Christmas. Everyone is hosting a party.'

'Not at my house, they're not. You had your engagement party there. Why shouldn't you have a reception there as well?'

'Ronnie, that's very kind of you but we'd invited more than a hundred people.'

'I know. That's why we're having a meeting.'

Ronnie and Adam drove to the Benson-Edwards' house where quite a gathering had formed around Ronnie's kitchen table. Annabel and Izzy were there (Richard was at home with Baby Humfrey). Mark was there, with Jack, Sophie and Lily. Jacqui was taking orders for tea. Dave was minding Granddad Bill. Cathy Next Door was there. She was armed with a clipboard. Cathy's husband Scott was leaning against the fridge, looking shy. Dev and Sangita Pandey, who lived on the other side of the Benson-Edwards and were fond of Ronnie's little sister, were there too. There was lots of excited chatter.

When she saw that Ronnie and Adam had arrived, Annabel called the meeting to order. Adam was surprised to see that Ronnie was allowing Annabel to take charge.

'Right, everybody,' said Annabel. 'We haven't got long. Ronnie, Jacqui and I have put our heads together and this is what we need to do. Let's start with the food . . .'

Food was relatively easy. The caterers who had been booked for the tithe barn could set up a van in Mark and Ronnie's cul-de-sac and prepare the wedding breakfast using portable ovens. They should probably have got some sort of permit from the council, but Ronnie was of the opinion that if enough of the neighbours were invited to the party, nobody would complain.

'You'll have to make sure Mr Evans gets an invitation in that case,' said Cathy, name-checking the only householder in the cul-de-sac who did not join in the annual Christmas light fest.

On the beverage front, the fire had largely wrecked the wine that Adam and Chelsea had chosen for the wedding but Richard had ordered wine, water and other drinks from his trusted supplier. Naturally, it being Christmas, the wine merchant was incredibly busy but Richard was a loyal customer and a friend so his order would be expedited. It would be arriving at any moment to be hidden in Mark's garage until it was needed. Party supplies – tablecloths, Christmas crackers and such – were Annabel's area. She and Izzy would drive to the cash-and-carry as soon as the meeting was over. Together with Cathy and Scott Next Door, Dev and Sangita would meanwhile drive to a farm on the outskirts of Warwickshire to pick up a brace of Christmas trees and assorted greenery for the decorations.

Because there was a chance that Chelsea would want to call in at her sister's house that evening, most of the real action would have to wait until the following day.

While Ronnie, Jack and Sophie were at Jacqui's house, getting dressed with the bridal party, Mark and Cathy Next Door would swing into action. Since Mark would have to be at the church fairly early (he was one of the ushers), Cathy had been tasked with coordinating the troops and overseeing the transformation. Cathy was delighted to be involved. And there was nothing she liked more than having a secret to keep. Though, having been entrusted with the secret that Mark was planning to propose on the family holiday two years earlier, Cathy had nearly caused a marriage break-up by incessantly texting Mark to find out whether he'd done the deed.

While Chelsea was in Solihull, she had no idea what was unfolding in Three Spires Close.

By the time Chelsea got back from her shopping trip, calling into Ronnie's as expected, the Pandeys, Cathy and Scott were long gone. As were Annabel and Izzy. Adam, Mark, Jack and Lily were playing Minion Monopoly in the living room. Sophie, Jacqui and Ronnie sat at the kitchen table looking innocent.

'Did you get a dress?' Ronnie asked.

Chelsea brandished her Marks & Spencer bag.

'Aw,' said Ronnie. 'I'm sure you'll still look great.'

What Chelsea didn't know is that in a break in that day's flurry of activity to prepare the secret wedding reception, Ronnie had been through the list of invitees and tracked down Serena, one of Chelsea's former colleagues at *Society* magazine. When *Society* folded, Serena, who had been the fashion editor, had moved on to A La Vent, an Internet fashion blog. If anyone could get hold of the perfect wedding dress at short notice, it would be her.

Ronnie had felt oddly nervous as she called the fashion

journalist up. Though when they were fighting, Ronnie often told Chelsea that her job was silly and contributed nothing much to the general good of the world, she was secretly in awe of people who worked in the mysterious 'media'.

Ronnie was amazed to find that Serena was so warm and that when she heard about Chelsea's predicament, she said she would be delighted to help. In fact, it would be a pleasure.

'I'll ring round a few people and see what I can find,' she said. 'I'm sure lots of people will want to help. Chelsea is very well loved.'

Two hours later, Serena texted Ronnie to say that she would be bringing five dresses up to Coventry the following morning.

For now, that was a secret. It was hard for Ronnie and the others to see Chelsea looking so downbeat that night, but they were sure that the element of surprise would make Chelsea's wedding day even more special.

Adam and Lily were staying with Mark and Ronnie at Three Spires Close that night. Both Adam and Chelsea liked the old tradition wherein the bride and groom did not see each other the night before. Even if they weren't exactly blushing young virgins, they felt the need for a symbolic new start.

'Tomorrow is going to be perfect,' Adam promised his bride as she left to spend her last night as a single woman at her mum and dad's.

Chapter Sixty-Nine

Chelsea

At last the day of the wedding had arrived. Chelsea woke and looked at the Marks & Spencer shift dress that was hanging on the back of the door. What had she been thinking? It was the least interesting item of clothing she had ever bought. She began to regret not having gone for one of the embellished slip dresses in Monsoon after all. There was nothing festive about the plain cream crêpe that would have looked more appropriate in a boardroom than in the aisle of a church. It was *Apprentice*-chic.

Too late now.

There was a knock at the door. Jacqui was doing her early morning tea round. She had already taken a cup in to Granddad Bill. Now she was delivering one to her daughter. White. Two sugars. Chelsea hadn't taken sugar in her tea since she left home ten years earlier, but that morning she accepted it gratefully.

'Thanks, Mum.'

'It's the big day,' said Jacqui. 'How are you feeling? A bit nervous, I bet. I've told your dad and Bill to stay out of the bathroom until you've been through so you don't get held up.'

'Thanks, Mum,' said Chelsea. 'Though it's not as though I've got a lot of tarting up to do.'

She looked at the dress again. It seemed more disappointing than ever.

Chelsea drank her tea and got up. Downstairs, Jacqui had put on the Christmas tree lights to lighten the early winter gloom. When she walked into the living room, Chelsea had a flashback to her childhood. Jacqui was not one to change her Christmas decorations according to that year's most fashionable colour scheme. There were baubles on that tree that had been in the Benson family for decades, including the hand-decorated baubles bearing the names 'Ronnie, Chelsea, Mum and Dad' that Jacqui had made in a flurry of creativity after watching someone make personalised ornaments on breakfast television. They looked a little sad now. The glitter that had covered them had largely fallen off. All the same, Chelsea was glad to see her own named bauble twisting in the draught she had made by her entrance.

How many Christmas mornings had Chelsea woken up in this house, full of excitement? On Christmas Eve, Chelsea and Ronnie would usually temporarily suspend hostilities. No matter what they had been fighting about during the day, on Christmas Eve, the sisters would treat each other with ultimate care and respect. They would talk kindly to each other in the hope that this very last-minute display of sisterly love might convince Father Christmas that they had been good all year after all.

They would even say their prayers – something that Jacqui and Dave had never suggested or insisted upon. Ronnie would lead. They would kneel down between their two beds and Ronnie would try to remember the

Lord's Prayer. Failing that, she would say something like, 'Dear God, thank you for Mummy and Daddy and Granddad Bill and we have been good all year so please tell Father Christmas to come to our house.'

'Amen,' Chelsea would chime enthusiastically.

Then they would lay awake, giggling, for as long as they could.

One year, they tried to gather evidence that Father Christmas actually existed. Chelsea left out a piece of paper and a pen with the message, 'Dear Father Christmas, if you exist, please write your name here.' The girls were astonished to discover, next morning, that Father Christmas had written his name. Neither of them noticed the similarity between Santa's signature and that of their father. Years later, Ronnie revealed that she had noticed the resemblance. In fact, she said, she'd already known by that point that Santa was a myth. She'd just chosen not to disillusion Chelsea.

Good old Ronnie. She'd been really kind since she heard about the fire. She was even being civil to Annabel again. And now that there was going to be no wedding reception, Chelsea no longer had to worry about the possibility there would be an empty chair where her middle sister should have been.

Chelsea remembered how beautiful the barn had looked in the brief moment between completion and conflagration and sighed.

Ronnie was one of the first people to arrive at Jacqui's house that morning. She brought Jack and Lily with her, both carrying their angel outfits. That was part of the new wedding plan Chelsea had known about. At least the children would look sweet, thought Chelsea, as she put the shift dress on in her bedroom.

'You're not wearing that!' said Ronnie when she saw her on the landing.

'Ronnie,' said Chelsea. 'Don't give me grief. This is the best of a very bad bunch. I am wearing it. I don't have any choice.'

'No, seriously. You're not wearing that. Serena!' Ronnie shouted to someone downstairs.

'Coming!'

'Serena's here? Why didn't she go straight to the church?'

'Because I asked her to come here first.'

'But . . . why?'

'Why?' Serena echoed. 'You'll see.'

Chelsea's old colleague puffed her way up the stairs. It wasn't that she was unfit. It was that she was laden with garment bags.

'I did a mad dash around everyone we know and pulled together every white, cream and silver dress I could find. Everyone was so sad to hear about the fire, Chelsea, darling. They all wanted to help. Now, I've got my personal favourites of course, but I'm sure that one of them will jump out at you.'

Serena paused to look at the plain cream shift dress.

'Yikes. Were you really planning to wear that? Your sister was right. Thank goodness she called.'

Chapter Seventy

Ronnie, Serena and Chelsea

That was the moment at which everything changed and Chelsea began to believe she might just get her dream day after all.

Together, Ronnie, Serena and Chelsea unbagged all the dresses Serena had called in from their fashion designer friends. Chelsea's spirits began to lift as each of the dresses spilled forth. Suddenly, her and Ronnie's childhood bedroom was transformed into an Aladdin's cave. Silk and satin and sequins draped over every available surface. Jack poked his head around the door to see what was going on. In his good hand – the one that wasn't in a cast – he held a piece of toast slathered in peanut butter. Lily was close behind him. She had Nutella on a piece of croissant.

'Out!' said the three women at once, before Jack and Lily had the chance to touch anything with their sticky fingers.

'I don't know where to start,' said Chelsea. She was beginning to feel tearful at the sight of so much kindness made into dresses. She had never thought to ask her old fashion world friends for help. She wouldn't have believed that they would be so generous now she couldn't really do them any favours in return.

'Well,' said Serena, looking at the frocks she had

hustled together. 'To be honest with you, I think this Cavalli is fabulous but it is going to be way too short for church. Perhaps you can change into it for the reception.'

'We're not having a reception,' said Chelsea. 'I thought everyone had been told. We're just going to have some tea and mince pies in the church hall. The village pub is closed for refurbishment and the church hall doesn't have a licence for alcohol.'

'Oh. Oh well,' said Serena, strangely unbothered by the news. 'Never mind. Probably better for everybody anyway. I haven't had a day off booze since the beginning of the month. The party season, eh?'

'I know . . .' Ronnie agreed.

'Why don't you try this dress first?'

Serena handed Chelsea a dress by an up-and-coming designer she was especially keen to champion. 'It doesn't have much hanger appeal but the tailoring is perfect.'

'Nah,' said Ronnie. 'Too plain.'

Chelsea watched Serena to see if she took offence. She didn't. 'You know what, Ronnie, I think you're right.'

Instead, Ronnie drew Chelsea's attention to a dress by Mebus, the designer whose dress Chelsea had pinched from the fashion cupboard at work and subsequently ruined on the trip to Lanzarote where she first met Adam. 'This is beautiful,' Ronnie said.

It was a work of art. The shape of the dress was simple but the embellishment was anything but. Chelsea could only imagine how many hours must have gone into sewing on the tiny beads, one by one.

'I remember this dress,' said Chelsea. 'It's from a collection three years back. Didn't Edie Campbell wear it at the end of the show?'

'That's the one,' said Serena.

'Gosh, she looked amazing.'

'And you will look even better,' said Ronnie.

'And it's by the same designer as the dress I was wearing on the day Adam and I first met.'

'Fate!' Serena declared.

Chelsea gleefully stripped off the plain cream shift dress. Her fairy-tale transformation was about to begin.

The dress by Mebus fitted perfectly, skimming over Chelsea's curves in a sexy yet suitably subtle way. It would have been a little long with the plain cream courts Chelsea had bought in a panic at M & S but with the embellished satin Charlotte Olympia shoes that Serena had brought along in her emergency bridal-wear kit, it was just right.

With the dress on and a scarf draped around her neck to protect it from stray hair products and make-up, Chelsea sat down at the dressing table. She laughed at the sight of her reflection in the mirror that she and Ronnie had decorated with Barbie stickers twenty years before. It couldn't have been further from a posh London salon. But Ronnie and Serena were determined that Chelsea would look every bit as good as a supermodel when she walked up the aisle.

Ronnie fixed Chelsea's hair in a romantic up-do while Serena did her make-up. Chelsea had always been in awe of Serena's skill with a liquid liner and she was delighted to submit herself to her friend's handiwork. Ronnie was equally keen to let Serena do her face too.

While Ronnie and Serena had been making Chelsea's bridal dreams come true, Izzy and Sophie had been helping Jacqui to dress Jack and Lily. The angel outfits had been checked for stains and carefully pressed. The wings had been fluffed up. The halos had been polished. Well, given another layer of kitchen foil for extra glitz.

When the children were ready, they treated their dressers to a round of 'Hark the Harold Angels', complete with helium in his wings.

Then Jacqui shooed them out of her bedroom so that she could put on her mother-of-the-bride kit, making it subtly different from when she wore it to Ronnie's wedding with the addition of a scarf that had been a birthday present from Annabel.

Soon everyone was ready except the bride. They all gathered in the kitchen to await her arrival. Jacqui was busily taking photographs of everyone. It was rare to have Dave looking so smart. Granddad Bill had been persuaded out of his carpet slippers and into a proper pair of shoes for the first time in years. He was on good form. He seemed to know who everyone was for once, without needing to be reminded. He even tried to teach Jack and Lily how to play the spoons. Everyone was hopeful that he would make it through the whole day without a funny turn.

'You all right, Granddad Bill?' Ronnie asked him.

'My youngest granddaughter's getting married today,' he said. 'I've won the bloody lottery. Now where is she?'

Jacqui glanced at her watch, which prompted Bill to begin a uniquely gaseous rendition of 'Get Me To The Church On Time'. It wasn't long before everyone joined in. Jack and Lily gave Granddad Bill a run for his money on the belching front.

'Wow,' said Serena, when the music stopped. 'I have never heard it sung like that before.'

At last, Chelsea descended the stairs. Until that moment, nobody but Ronnie and Serena knew which dress she would be wearing. When she saw her daughter, Jacqui immediately burst into tears. Dave and Bill both smiled goofily. Sophie and Izzy actually gasped in awe. Not only did Chelsea look beautiful, she was very much on trend.

'You look like a *real angel*,' said Lily, in much admiration.

Even Jack agreed.

'I like it,' he said. 'You look a bit like one of those statues in *Doctor Who*.'

'Ja-ack,' the women chorused.

'I can't believe that's my little girl!' Jacqui sobbed.

'Thank you,' Chelsea said to Ronnie and Serena. 'I can't tell you how grateful I am. To think I was going to get married in an office outfit. I never would have imagined this. You've made me look so much better than I dared to hope. I feel just like a princess.'

Jack made gagging sounds. Lily elbowed him in the ribs. More gently than usual, because of his broken arm, but enough to make him shut up just the same.

'Look at the time,' said Jacqui. 'Is everybody ready? The car for the bridesmaids will be here in ten minutes. Ronnie, you're going with them. Serena, we can fit you in with me and Bill.'

'Thank you,' said Serena.

A tooting from outside announced that the first car in the bridal cortège had indeed arrived. Mark's boss had loaned them his Mercedes, just as he did for Mark and Ronnie's wedding. Dave and Chelsea would be following later in Richard's Aston Martin. Thankfully, the car had remained unaffected by the fire as it had been safely tucked away in the garage (where the fireworks should have been). Meanwhile, Jacqui, Bill and Serena piled into Dave and Jacqui's Renault which was specially fitted out for Granddad Bill's wheelchair. Jack and Lily had decorated the wheelchair with red and gold tinsel. Granddad Bill complained that they weren't the Coventry City colours but seemed to understand that they were meant to match Chelsea's wedding scheme, not his favourite team.

While the bridesmaids piled into the Mercedes, Jack ran back in to give Chelsea one last kiss.

'After today,' he began, 'You will still be my auntie, won't you? Even though you'll be Lily's stepmum?'

'I'll always be your auntie,' said Chelsea.

'And you'll still love me as much as you used to.'

'I love you more and more every day. Without you, none of this would be happening,' she added, remembering how Jack's insistence on visiting the Kidz Klub in Lanzarote had brought her back into Adam and Lily's vicinity.

'What did I do?' Jack asked suspiciously.

Chelsea kissed him on the top of the head.

'Quick. Everyone's waiting for you,' she said.

Jack ran for the car – carefully, because of his arm – halo bobbing.

Chapter Seventy-One

Chelsea and Dave

At last only Chelsea and Dave remained alone in the house. They had fifteen minutes to themselves before Richard arrived to take them to the church. They sat at the kitchen table – the same table that had been in the house since Chelsea was small – with two glasses of champagne. Chelsea took just a tiny sip of hers, not wanting to spoil her lipstick (at least, that was her excuse). Dave knocked his back. 'Dutch courage,' he said. 'I've never walked down the aisle of a church before.'

That was true. He'd married Jacqui in a registry office and he'd given Ronnie away in a registry office too. There had been a small aisle at Ronnie's wedding but it was nothing like the one at the church in Little Bissingden. And, of course, he hadn't been at Annabel's wedding at all. She'd been given away by Humfrey, her adoptive father.

'Just don't step on my dress,' said Chelsea.

'It's a lovely dress,' said Dave. 'I don't know much about clothes but you look like a princess to me.'

'Thanks, Dad.'

'You're all princesses to me, you know. My three girls. Ronnie, Annabel and you. Sometimes I look at you, Chelsea, and wonder how you came to be so wonderful. How you came to make such a success of your life. You didn't get much help from me.'

'Are you joking, Dad?'

'I wish I was. I couldn't help you get into university or give you contacts in the media or anything like that. You did it all by yourself.'

'But you gave me the foundation. You and Mum together. You gave me the love and stability I needed in my childhood to help me take the risks later on. I didn't need you to find me work experience at the *Sunday Times*. I just needed your love and support and you've always given me that. I've always felt loved, Dad. That means more than anything.'

'You are loved, Chelsea. And I know that Adam loves you too. I'm glad you're marrying him. I wouldn't let it happen if I didn't think he was a good bloke. Heaven knows you've picked a few losers in the past.'

'Dad.' Chelsea did not want to be reminded of her dating fiascos right then.

'All that matters is that you've got it right this time. Adam is a very lucky man.'

'Thank you. I feel very lucky too.'

A blast from the horn announced the arrival of Richard in his Aston.

'Oh my goodness,' said Chelsea. 'This is it! I'm going to get married at last.'

She threw her arms around Dave's neck and he picked her up and whirled her around, just as he'd done when she was a little girl.

Chapter Seventy-Two

Chelsea and Adam

Chelsea entered the church of St Timothy in Little Bissingden to the tune of 'Sheep May Safely Graze'. At the hundreds of weddings she'd attended as a singleton, it had always been her favourite processional. She liked the quiet joyfulness of the tune. And the pace was perfect. Dave quickly found the rhythm.

It had been decided that for the sake of the dress, Jack and Lily should walk ahead of Chelsea, rather than risk having them step on the back of her gown. They were only too delighted to lead the bridal party. Sophie and Izzy would follow behind. Since their dresses had been among those ruined by the fire, they were instead dressed in the matching All Saints numbers they had worn to Chelsea's hen party. Not exactly festive but definitely themselves and they were secretly quite pleased not to have to wear the red velvet Chelsea had chosen for them.

There was a little surprise for the procession. Annabel had been out that morning and bought the two children white wicker baskets that she had filled with white feathers tipped with silver glitter. Father Malcolm had given his permission for the children to throw the feathers as they walked up the aisle, so long as Annabel promised to sweep them up afterwards. The feathers created a wonderful effect. They were like big, fat snowflakes as they floated through the air and drifted to the floor.

Jack and Lily got so involved in the joy of being human snow machines, that at one point they held the procession up and Ronnie had to hiss, 'Come on, you two. Before the music runs out!' from her place on the front pew. Jack and Lily skipped the rest of the way.

The front two pews of the church were filled by Chelsea and Adam's families. Sally and Graham, Adam's parents, gave Chelsea the 'thumbs up' as she passed. Adam's sister Julie beamed and mouthed 'gorgeous' when she saw Chelsea in her dress. On the other side of the aisle, Jacqui had started crying the moment the organist struck up the processional. Even Annabel was dabbing at her eyes. Granddad Bill was tapping his foot to the stately rhythm.

Adam waited for Chelsea at the front of the church with his best man, his younger brother Tim, beside him.

Chelsea couldn't stop the prickling sensation of tears that built in her throat as she drew nearer to the man she loved. 'Sheep May Safely Graze' set a sedate pace for her walk down the aisle but her heart rushed out ahead of her.

Adam looked so handsome in his dark-grey suit. He wore a deep-red rose as a buttonhole. His hair was incongruously neat. She could imagine him in front of the bathroom mirror at Ronnie's, trying to get it just right. She wondered if he was at all nervous. He was jiggling slightly from foot to foot. But when Chelsea was beside him at last, he gave her a confident wink.

'You look beautiful,' he whispered.

Everything was going to be fine.

'Dearly beloved,' Father Malcolm began.

Chapter Seventy-Three

Chelsea and Adam

The service went without a hitch though there were some surprises. It had always been the plan that Annabel would do a reading. What Chelsea didn't expect was that Annabel would share the lectern with Ronnie and they would read together, taking it in turns with each paragraph and smiling down on their little sister between.

Sophie and Izzy also gave readings. Izzy read from St Paul's letter to the Corinthians, which, like 'Sheep May Safely Graze', was a favourite from weddings Chelsea had attended in the past. Meanwhile, Sophie read the suitably festive 'Love and Friendship' by Emily Bronte, with its invocation of holly as the symbol of the enduring friendship at the heart of any good marriage.

Sophie had chosen the poem herself and she read it beautifully. Chelsea was delighted to see that her younger niece had grown so much in confidence over the past eighteen months. It was hard to imagine that she was the same girl who had mooched around Lanzarote in an ugly black T-shirt, carrying some unknowable teenage grudge. Soon she would be leaving school and heading for university. Chelsea had no doubt that Sophie would go far. She winked at her niece as she walked back to her place in the pews.

Next came the vows.

Chelsea and Adam locked eyes as they made their

promises to one another and the rest of the world seemed to melt away. Chelsea had never felt so loved and happy in her life as she did in the moment Adam slipped a ring onto her finger. It seemed impossible that she had ever thought the moment might not come. Now it seemed inevitable that she and Adam should have found each other and be together for the rest of their lives.

When Father Malcolm finally pronounced the newly married couple man and wife, the congregation let out a cheer and Adam folded Chelsea into his arms for a kiss that warmed the whole church. While they signed the register, the church choir performed a medley of carols, including the 'Coventry Carol', of course, but Chelsea and Adam walked out of the church to the joyful and triumphant sound of 'Ding Dong Merrily on High', followed by Lily and Jack, strewing yet more feathers.

It was the perfect day for photographs. It was bright and not too cold, so that people didn't mind having to stand around for a little while, while the photographer arranged them in the myriad permutations a wedding album required.

'Bride's family! Groom's family! Friends! Bridesmaids!'

'And page-boy!' Jack piped up.

Jack and Lily competed to pull the most terrifying face in the picture of Chelsea with her attendants. When Jacqui saw what they were up to, she reminded them that they were supposed to be angels. 'You little devils,' she said.

Sophie and Izzy, meanwhile, insisted on looking at the back of the photographer's camera after almost every click of the shutter, so keen were they to ensure they looked their best.

'No selfie faces!' the photographer shouted in exasperation after discarding ten pictures in a row. 'Chelsea and Adam want you to look like yourselves, not like Kardashians.'

While Sophie and Izzy were laughing at the idea, the photographer quickly fired off a series of frames that were much better than the ones in which they had been posing so self-consciously.

Lily insisted on holding Humfrey for the full bridal party shot. It would be one of Chelsea's favourite photographs. Humfrey was large for his age and his expression was one of surprise as Lily struggled to keep from dropping him. Seconds after the shot was taken, Adam's dad Graham swept in to save Humfrey from the floor.

Later Chelsea and Adam had a special photograph taken with Granddad Bill between them. Bill grasped Chelsea's hand and she was both relieved and thrilled to hear him say, 'Well done, our Chelsea. You did it at last. And Adam's a very lucky man. He's won the bloody lottery, he has.' Bill was having a very good day. Adam and Chelsea were so glad that he was able to be there to celebrate their marriage. To have him be on such good form made them certain that bringing the wedding forward had been the absolute right thing to do.

Even Leander got in on the action. Annabel had decorated his collar with a big red bow that made him look like a furry Christmas gift. Izzy had brushed the dog's coat until it gleamed. He was persuaded to sit nicely at the front of the group shot with the help of one of Granddad Bill's Trebor mints. The Trebor mints were also deployed in persuading Jack and Lily to do just one more pose. Unknown to the bride and groom, Lily and Jack would both appear in the very last frame cross-eyed and doing 'gang' signs.

* * *

After the official photographs were taken, Ronnie and Annabel quickly ushered the guests towards the church hall so that they could warm up with tea and mince pies. Lily and Jack were having the time of their lives, racing round with their cardboard wings flapping and using Granddad Bill in his wheelchair as 'base' in a game of angel tag. Nobody seemed to mind that there was no champagne. Everyone had been left uplifted by the service. They were especially taken with the little angels. And the mince pies were delicious. Ronnie, Jacqui and Sally and Julie Baxter had baked a hundred each. They soon disappeared.

Just an hour into the low-key party, Richard told Chelsea and Adam that their car was ready to take them to the hotel where they would be staying the night. Their guests waved them off enthusiastically, throwing the last of Annabel's feathers in lieu of confetti. As the feathers whirled about them, Chelsea was sure she saw real snowflakes in the air too.

'You are my snow queen,' Adam said, kissing the cold tip of her nose.

'Short but very sweet,' Adam commented when he and Chelsea were alone at last in the back of the car. 'I think all wedding receptions should be like that.'

'I feel bad that so many people came so far for nothing more than a cup of tea and a mince pie,' said Chelsea.

'None of those people were only coming to our wedding for the dinner afterwards,' said Adam. 'They all came because they love us. You especially. Seeing you married was all the incentive they needed.'

Still, Chelsea wished she might have been able to offer them something more. Little did she know.

Chapter Seventy-Four

Ronnie

Once the bridal car had disappeared round the corner, Ronnie and Annabel went into action mode. They handed Jack and Lily their baskets again but this time they were filled with strips of paper rather than feathers.

'Make sure everybody gets one,' said Ronnie.

'OK, everybody!' Annabel addressed the crowd since she had the loudest voice. 'We'll see you all in half an hour, at the address on the piece of paper you've just been given. There's going to be food and plenty of champagne but if anyone wants to stop off at an off-licence on the way, they're more than welcome.'

'Beer would be much appreciated,' Mark piped up. 'Spitfire, if they've got it.'

The guests all headed for their cars and made a procession to Ronnie and Mark's home via the local branch of Threshers.

Chapter Seventy-Five

Chelsea and Adam

After they had been in the car for half an hour, Chelsea began to be suspicious. 'Does Richard know where he's supposed to be going?' she asked. 'I'm sure we've doubled back on ourselves.'

'Of course he knows where he's going,' said Adam.

'He doesn't,' said Chelsea. She leaned forward to tell him. 'Richard, I think we've missed the turn-off.'

'No we haven't,' said Richard.

'What's going on?' Chelsea asked. 'We're supposed to be going to Leamington Spa. You're taking us back towards Coventry, Rich. Leamington's in completely the opposite direction.'

They were within three streets of Ronnie's house now.

'Richard,' said Chelsea. 'You need to put your sat nav on.'

'No he doesn't. We're not going to the hotel. We're going to our wedding reception,' said Adam.

'We're not having a reception,' Chelsea countered.

'Chelsea, did you really think that your sisters and I would allow that to happen?'

Chelsea's mouth dropped open.

'Are you serious? Where are we having it?' she asked after a moment.

'Only the best party venue in town.'

* * *

As soon as she heard that, Chelsea wasn't in the least bit surprised when the wedding car drew up outside Ronnie's house. She was, however, astonished by the number of cars that lined the cul-de-sac and by the transformation that had taken place since Chelsea and Dave drove by when they left for the church less than two hours before.

Cathy Next Door had proved herself to be a very capable set dresser. The outside of the Benson-Edwards' house was always covered in Christmas lights at this time of year but Mark's usual gaudy display had been augmented with lights borrowed from every other house on the street. The front garden was a grotto straight out of Disneyland. Chelsea gawped at the enormous glowing Santa and the full-sized sleigh that had appeared since she last looked.

Jack and Lily, who had been waiting by the front window for what to them seemed like hours, started bouncing up and down when they saw Richard's car. The front door of the house opened and both sets of parents came out to greet the bride and groom. Soon people were pouring out of Ronnie's house onto the street. They made a guard of honour, throwing confetti and feathers into the air as Adam and Chelsea walked up the path. Jack and Lily led a cheer.

Inside, the house was even more magical. With the greenery they had bought from their friend with the farm, Cathy Next Door and her husband had turned Ronnie's hallway into a green cave that smelled of Christmas.

Scott and Cathy Next Door and Dev and Sangita Pandey had been incredibly generous. As well as decorating the house, they were providing extra space for the partygoers. They'd actually taken down a panel from each of their fences so that guests could wander from one house to the next without having to go via the front doors. It wasn't the first time they'd done it. The whole street had thrown a party before for the Queen's Jubilee. The weather on that day in June 2012 was terrible, so they knew exactly what they would need to keep their guests comfortable that grey and cold December afternoon.

Just as had been the case for the Jubilee, each house became a station for a different part of the event. Drinks and canapés were at Ronnie's. Rather than run backwards and forwards through the houses to their van, the caterers had set up a barbecue under a gazebo in Cathy's garden. They were roasting the turkeys on that. The Pandeys were hosting dessert. And the cake – Jacqui and Ronnie's magnificent cake, made with such love and care – had pride of place in Ronnie's sitting room.

Chelsea couldn't help but burst into tears when she saw the effort so many people had made to ensure she had the wedding day of her dreams after all. The love and care that had gone into transforming Ronnie's house and those of her neighbours somehow made the scene even more beautiful than the barn had been in those brief moments before the fire.

'Don't you like it, Auntie Chelsea?' Jack asked when he saw her crying.

'I love it,' she said. 'These are happy tears.' She pulled him close for a cuddle. 'I've got the best family in the world.'

'You don't think it's all a bit over the top?' Ronnie asked her new BFF Serena as they watched Adam and Chelsea posing for photographs with the inflatable reindeer on the front lawn.

'Are you kidding?' said Serena. 'This is spectacular. You should do this for a living.'

'What do you think, Annabel? When the barn's put back together, maybe you and me should go into business.'

'I think that would be a very good idea,' said Annabel.

Chapter Seventy-Six

The Wedding Party

Chelsea soon stopped crying and threw herself into enjoying the party of the year. At the church and in the church hall afterwards, Chelsea had been a little too overwhelmed to properly appreciate just how many of her favourite people had turned up to see her marry. Now, at her wonderful reception, every time she turned her head she saw someone she needed to hug. Not a single person who had RSVPd in the positive for the swanky reception in the barn had been put off by the idea that there would be nothing but mince pies and tea after the ceremony. Everybody had made it. Everyone was having a wonderful time.

Chelsea felt her heart expand a little more with every heartfelt greeting. Her whole life was in her sister's house. Friends from as far back as junior school and as recent as the people she had worked with on *Society*. And all of them were mingling and laughing and making new friends of their own.

The food was delicious. The drinks – served by Mark and Richard – were generous. Jack and Lily provided running entertainment as they treated the guests to songs and dances and *Doctor Who* impressions. Fishy the cat retired to Ronnie's bedroom where she made a nest of Serena's shearling jacket by Alexander McQueen.

Leander ambled from room to room, making doe eyes and gathering titbits. Too many titbits. He would have terrible wind that night.

Talking of terrible wind, Granddad Bill had the party-goers in stitches with a medley of well-belched carols. Seeing that Granddad Bill was drawing an appreciative crowd, Jack and Lily soon joined him, singing along to the choruses and making their own burping sounds.

Adam's mother Sally watched her granddaughter in bemusement. 'I never knew Lily was so musical,' she told Jacqui.

'Watch this, Granny!' Lily called.

Sally had even more cause for astonishment when Lily picked up a pair of spoons and played them against her knee with aplomb.

'Granddad Bill taught me that,' she said proudly. Then she pressed a kiss to the old man's dry cheek to thank him for his expertise.

'He taught me this,' said Jack, sticking his good hand under his armpit to produce a very realistic fart.

'Oh Jack,' said Jacqui. 'Sally, you must think we Bensons are awful.'

'Not in the least,' said Sally. 'Believe me, my Graham could give Bill a run for his money on the flatulence front.'

'Granddad Bill,' Jack cried. 'Let's do "My Old Man's A Dustman"!'

'Yes,' Lily squealed. 'That's my favourite.'

The whole party came to a standstill as the unusual trio performed their much-loved show-stopper. Jack counted them in.

'A-one, a-two, a-three . . .'

Bill kept up the melody while the children danced like dervishes. When they finished, the audience gave three cheers and Jack and Lily smothered their new joint great-grandfather in hugs.

'I love you, Granddad Bill,' said Lily.

'I love you even more,' said Jack.

Then it was time for the speeches.

It was Annabel who drew everyone's attention by tapping a fork against a glass. Her voice rang out loud and clear across the chatter as she called the party to order.

'The Father of the Bride. Come on, Dave Benson. You're up.'

Dave stood near the cake, which seemed to have become the focal point of the room. Jack and Lily joined Annabel in ssshing his audience.

'Honestly,' said Dave, when it was quiet enough for him to begin. 'You wouldn't believe the lengths I went to trying to avoid having to make this speech. But even hiring Mark and Richard to burn the wedding venue down doesn't seem to have worked.'

Richard and Mark toasted each other across the room.

'So, here goes . . .'

Dave pulled a veritable sheaf of paper out of his jacket pocket, then he threw most of it away so that he was left with only one sheet. He began to read.

'Milk, eggs, washing powder . . .'

A ripple of laughter went round the room.

'Wrong list . . .' said Dave. He pulled out one more piece of paper. And his glasses. He cleared his throat.

'Get on with it!' shouted Granddad Bill.

Dave pushed his glasses up his nose and started. 'Chelsea, my youngest daughter, from the day you were born, you've brought your mother and me endless happiness. We're so very proud of the way you've turned out.

You've always been loving and helpful and kind. We knew you were going to be the perfect catch for some lucky man. But we have to admit, we were surprised it was taking so long for someone to catch you, no matter how hard you chased them. Now we know why.

'Adam, the day we met you, we knew you were a good bloke. When you pulled our granddaughter out of the sea in Lanzarote, you didn't just save her life, you became an important part of all our lives. We were chuffed when Chelsea started seeing you. We were over the moon when we heard that you proposed. We're very pleased to welcome you to the family, young man. And Lily too. Who is already showing herself to be a fine upholder of Benson family traditions. Give us a belch, Lily.'

Lily dutifully obliged.

She was given a round of applause.

'I won't go on because I've lost the bit of paper with the end of my speech on,' Dave admitted. 'But I think I've said it all already. Chelsea, we love you. Adam, you take care of my girl. Lily, there's a place for you in the Benson Family Choir. Now I'd just like to raise a toast to my daughter and her new husband. Chelsea and Adam. Man and wife.'

'Chelsea and Adam,' everyone echoed.

Dave slipped out of the spotlight to stand by his wife.

'Did I do OK?' he asked Jacqui.

'You were brilliant,' Jacqui said.

Adam spoke next. Like Dave, he took a spot by the wedding cake. Like Dave, he pulled a sheaf of paper out of his pocket but Adam wasn't going to throw any of it away.

'There are an awful lot of reasons why I love this woman,' he explained.

Chelsea beamed with pride as Adam took the audience back to the day they first met and the holiday in Lanzarote where the newly-weds found themselves going head-to-head in the Kidz Klub, culminating in the Kidz Klub sports day when Chelsea thrashed Adam in the parents' race. And Chelsea was subsequently stripped of her champion's title when Lily accused her of cheating for 'steadying' her potato in the potato and spoon section.

'I've forgiven her for that,' Adam said. 'And I think that may actually have been the moment I fell in love with her, when she showed me who was boss in the swimming pool. Not just because she looks great in a bikini, but because I know Chelsea was only in that race because Jack asked her to be. The love she has for her nephew shone through. And that's the love she gives to Lily and me. Fierce and loyal and full of fun.'

Ronnie and Annabel nodded in agreement.

'Anyone who knows Chelsea for longer than a couple of minutes soon learns what a great woman she is. When I look at her, I know I am the luckiest man on earth. Chelsea, you have brought me back to life. Lily and I can't wait to grow old with you. Thank you for being my wife.'

Chelsea curled into Adam's side as another toast was given.

Then the best man spoke. Tim's speech was short, sweet and surprisingly tasteful. Because he was ten years younger than his big brother, Tim's anecdotes largely related to the naughty tricks Adam had helped him to play on their parents rather than nights of heavy drinking gone horribly wrong. Both Adam and Chelsea were relieved about that. Everybody noticed how Izzy and Sophie blushed when Tim kissed them as he handed them the traditional bridesmaids' gifts. He was a very good-looking young man.

'Now it's time for the cake!' Jack announced, clearly relieved that the speechifying was over. But he was out of luck.

'Hang on a minute,' said Chelsea. 'I know it isn't traditional for the bride to speak, but I'd like to say a few words. There are people in this room who have known me for a very long time. You've seen me at my best and my worst.

'As you all know, today's reception was meant to be held at my sister Annabel's barn in Little Bissingden. I want to thank Annabel and her family for everything they did to create my ideal wedding at their home. Believe me, for the fifteen minutes between the barn being decorated and catching fire, it was quite the most beautiful thing you have ever seen. I was absolutely distraught when I saw the devastation caused by a simple half-ton of unattended fireworks.'

The guests laughed.

'I'm sure it would have been an amazing display,' Chelsea assured her brothers-in-law. 'And I'm sure there will be another occasion to celebrate with fireworks in the future.'

'No way,' said Ronnie and Annabel in unison.

'But the best-laid plans . . . This time yesterday, I didn't think we were going to have a wedding reception. Selfishly, I even thought about calling the wedding off altogether.'

Quite a few people looked to Adam, to see his reaction.

'Only for a second. How could I have missed out on marrying the most wonderful man in the world? But I can tell him how great I think he is every day for the rest of our lives. Right now, I want to thank a few other people. Mum and Dad. My beautiful bridesmaids. My handsome page-boy.'

Jack gave a little bow.

'My brothers-in-law. Cathy and Scott. Dev and Sangita. Granddad Bill for helping us to choose the date. But, most of all, my sisters, Ronnie and Annabel. Annabel and Ronnie. No-one ever had a better pair of siblings.'

Chelsea raised a toast to them. There was much more toasting in return.

'Now,' said Jack, flopping across his grandmother's knee as the toasting tailed away. 'Can we please just have the cake?'

Chapter Seventy-Seven

The Wedding Party

The sitting room became a disco once the cake was served and Adam and Chelsea had their first dance to the song they thought of as their own. 'Mirrorball' by Elbow. It was a little slow and sloppy but it was theirs.

Right afterwards, Lily and Jack commandeered the iPod Mark was using to keep the party dancing and had everyone up on the floor for 'Happy'. Even Granddad Bill danced along in his chair. Well, he submitted to being 'danced' by Lily and Jack, who took one handle of the wheelchair each and jerked him backwards and forwards more or less in time to the beat. Jacqui danced with Adam's father while Dave whizzed Adam's mother Sally around the floor so fast that she actually shrieked. Even Sophie and Izzy got up to boogie. On the proviso that Ronnie would not tag the pictures on Facebook. They kept close to Tim who was a surprisingly funky mover.

Chelsea and Adam danced only with each other for five songs, before Dave cut in to dance with his daughter and Adam was left to the clutches of Cathy Next Door.

'I'll lead,' she said.

Adam was not in the least bit surprised.

The night only got better. The Spitfire beer and champagne flowed. The cake was completely demolished.

There was a brief moment of panic when Jack said that he needed to be sick but, like a Roman at a banquet, having thrown up he was soon back at the buffet table. The incident was merely a means of making room for more cake.

Lily too, was on great form, threatening a small meltdown only when she suddenly thought about the party favours she and Jack had spent so much time making. They'd been left behind at the Great House. Forgotten in the rush to move the wedding party from the barn to Ronnie's house.

'Never mind,' said Izzy. 'It means we'll be able to share them out amongst ourselves later on.'

Lily was happy with that.

The party went on late into the night. So that Jacqui and Dave did not have to miss a moment, Cathy Next Door had made up a bed for Granddad Bill in her dining room. She'd equipped it with an old baby monitor. Jacqui was very grateful that Bill had made it through the day without any significant hiccups. She kissed him on the forehead as she tucked him in for the night.

'Have you had a lovely day?' she asked him.

'It's been like winning the bloody lottery,' Bill replied.

Ronnie need not have worried that Chelsea and Adam's posh London friends would sneer at her efforts. Everyone agreed that it was the most unusual and most fun wedding they had ever attended.

Serena even ended up snogging one of Mark's kitchen-fitting colleagues under Father Malcolm's enormous ball of mistletoe.

Chelsea and Adam would have stayed all night as well until Adam's mother reminded them that etiquette dictated that none of the guests could leave before they did. Only a little reluctantly, the newly-weds announced that it was time for them to go, again.

'This is the craziest, most wonderful, most perfect wedding I could ever have imagined,' said Chelsea, as she hugged her sister Ronnie goodnight.

'It's a proper family wedding,' said Ronnie. 'That's all.'

Chapter Seventy-Eight

Christmas

Adam and Chelsea left their wedding party at around eleven o'clock. Like Ronnie and Mark the previous year, they were going to be spending their wedding night at Mallory Court, the posh hotel in nearby Leamington Spa. While planning the wedding, they'd decided that they would save their proper honeymoon for later. Holidaying around Christmas cost a fortune. Besides, they had both decided that they would like to spend Christmas Day itself back in London. Just the three of them, Chelsea, Adam and Lily, starting their very own traditions. They would be visiting the various grand-parents on Boxing Day and the day after that. They would be back at the Bensons' for New Year's Eve.

Annabel, Richard, Izzy and Humfrey had already planned to spend Christmas Day away from home. They travelled down to Annabel's adoptive mother's house on Christmas Eve and were happy to let Sarah take care of them after all the excitement of the fire and the wedding.

Meanwhile, Ronnie and her gang went to Jacqui and Dave's on 25th December. Jack and Granddad Bill pulled the turkey wishbone. Jack won. He wished for world peace. And the latest version of Minecraft.

Celebrations at the Benson Baxters' began on Christmas

Eve. As children, Adam and his siblings had always sent letters to Father Christmas by 'posting' them up the chimney, with the help of the thermals from the open fire in the sitting room. Unfortunately, there was no working fireplace in the Benson Baxter house so, once Lily had written her letter, she, Chelsea and Adam took it outside and sent it up into the sky attached to a Chinese lantern. After that, they went inside to prepare Santa's midnight snack of two mince pies and a shot of Baileys.

It took a long time to persuade Lily to go to sleep. Once they were sure that she was safely in the Land of Nod, Chelsea and Adam retrieved Lily's Christmas gifts from hiding places all over the house. And from the garden shed. Chelsea had used her sewing skills again to make Lily a personalised stocking. When Lily found it at the end of her bed the following morning, she was over the moon. The stocking was almost a bigger hit than the presents inside it.

Chelsea had made Adam a stocking too and filled it with dozens of little treats including Marmite and a packet of refreshers. Adam responded by gifting Chelsea one of his old socks. She tried to look pleased as she pulled out a satsuma, a walnut and a barbecue fire-lighter (in lieu of a piece of coal). She was genuinely thrilled when she pulled out the pair of silver earrings hidden beneath.

Once all the presents were open, Adam and Chelsea made Christmas lunch together. They had chicken rather than turkey (neither of them really liked turkey) and banoffee pie instead of Christmas pud. Instead of Christmas cake, they ate left-over wedding cake. Lily surprised her parents by telling them that she had decided she liked fruit-cake after all.

'It's what Granddad Bill ate during the war,' she explained.

Granddad Bill had become Lily's favourite. In the afternoon, when Chelsea and Adam rang both their families and put Lily on the phone to deliver her Christmas greetings, she chatted to Bill for quite a while.

Tea time was left-over chicken and more wedding cake in front of the television. They watched the DVD of The Snowman. Lily cried when he melted at the end. But she cheered up in time for a bedtime story. Chelsea made one up on the fly about the 'Christmas dog' that would be waiting for them at Battersea Dogs Home in the New Year. Lily had not forgotten she'd been promised a puppy. She went to sleep holding onto the plush stuffed Labrador which had been a gift from Jack and Sophie.

Chelsea and Adam spent the very last of Christmas Day cuddled up together on the sofa. As she snuggled up against Adam's warm chest, Chelsea wished she might have been able to give Adam the ultimate gift that night but the timing wasn't quite right. Just a few more days, she told herself. Just to be absolutely sure.

'What are you thinking about?' Adam asked her as she gazed at the 'real flame effect' gas fire.

'I'll tell you next year,' Chelsea told him.

Chapter Seventy-Nine

New Year's Eve

On New Year's Eve, Jacqui's house was the party venue. There was no need to go to the cash-and-carry this time though. Chelsea and Adam's wedding guests had been extremely generous. There was still enough sparkling wine and Spitfire stashed in Mark's garage to celebrate for a whole twelve months.

Jack and Lily greeted one another as though they had been apart for weeks rather than days. They had much to show and tell one another. As soon as Lily was in the house, Jack had dragged her off to look at his Christmas presents. Chelsea and Adam took their places with the adults and shared their own Christmas tales.

'Mark has basically been drunk since your wedding,' Ronnie complained to Adam.

'I'm giving up tomorrow,' Mark said in mitigation. 'I'm having a dry January.'

'Dry January,' said Dave. 'There's a bloody stupid idea. January is the worst month of the year. Can't get through it without a drink, personally.'

'Good point,' said Mark. 'Good point. I'll go dry in February. It's three days shorter.'

Listening from the kitchen, Chelsea smiled at her brother-in-law's logic and discreetly swapped the wine he had poured her for an elderflower cordial. Jacqui saw the swap and raised her eyebrows. Chelsea put her finger to her lips but Jacqui tucked her arm through Chelsea's in a conspiratorial way as they headed back into the sitting room.

'Grandma! Mum! Auntie Chelsea! Me and Lily are going to do a New Year's show,' Jack interrupted. 'We need costumes. Can we look in Granddad Bill's wardrobe?'

'Why do you want to look in Granddad Bill's wardrobe?' Ronnie asked.

'It's going to be about the Elizabethan times,' Lily explained.

'I'm not that bloody old,' said Bill.

'Don't say "bloody"!' Jack and Lily chorused.

'Let's have a game of charades,' Jacqui suggested. The adults groaned but Jack and Lily were delighted. Jack mimed three different episodes of *Doctor Who*. Granddad Bill guessed Lily's *Frozen*. Sophie was hugely relieved when Izzy arrived with her family, interrupting the game right before Sophie's turn in the middle of the floor.

Ronnie budged up on the sofa to let Annabel sit between her and Chelsea. Ronnie and Annabel were thick as thieves again. Their hen night falling out was long forgotten.

'My three lovely girls,' Jacqui cooed, when she saw her daughters all sitting together. She insisted on taking a photograph. Then Jack and Lily insisted she take a photograph of the pair of them with Granddad Bill.

'I've won the bloody Lottery,' Bill said as he soon found himself flanked by all his great-grandchildren, with Humfrey on his lap.

Chapter Eighty

Adam and Chelsea

When the New Year had been welcomed in with the traditional shouting and hollering, Adam and Chelsea loaded Lily into the back of the car for the short drive to the Holiday Inn where they would be staying that night.

It took a while to persuade Lily to go to sleep. She was still full of energy after an evening with Jack. But at last her eyelids began to droop. Her questions became quieter and more disjointed. And then she was out for the count, silent but for the whiffly sound of her breathing. She was coming down with a cold.

Adam and Chelsea lay silent for a while, not wanting to break the spell. When Lily rolled over onto her back and let out a proper snore, they held their breath, wondering if she would have woken herself up. She didn't. She was in a deep sleep. It was safe to talk at last.

'I've got something important to tell you,' said Chelsea.

Adam tilted his head to one side. 'What is it, Mrs Baxter?'

'I'm pregnant.'

Adam sat bolt upright.

'You're what?'

'I'm pregnant. We're having a baby.'

'Yes!' Adam exclaimed. He punched the air. 'Yes! Oh, Chelsea. Oh, darling. This is the best news of all.'

He wrapped his arms around her and cuddled her hard. He pressed his face into the warm curve of her neck. She quickly realised he was crying.

'Adam,' Chelsea whispered. 'Adam, what's wrong?'

'Nothing,' he assured her. 'I just never thought I could be this happy again.'

'It's only going to get better with every day that passes,' Chelsea promised.

'What are you talking about?'

They had woken Lily up.

Adam and Chelsea made room in their double bed for Lily to climb between them.

'We've got some good news,' said Adam. 'Chelsea is having a baby.'

'You're going to have a little brother or sister,' Chelsea clarified.

Lily frowned for a moment. 'Does this mean I won't be getting a dog?'

Chapter Eighty-One

Granddad Bill

While Chelsea and Adam were quietly celebrating their good news in the Holiday Inn, at Jacqui and Dave's house, everyone was tucked up in bed.

It had been a good New Year's Eve party. It was wonderful to have been able to gather the whole family together again so soon after the wedding. Everyone seemed on great form. There were no arguments. Not between the children or the adults. Even Granddad Bill had been in fine fettle. At midnight, he led the whole family in a chorus of 'Auld Lang Syne' complete with a chorus of belching. Lily was the star of that show.

The party didn't last much longer after that, though. Chelsea, Adam and Lily had an early start ahead of them. Annabel and Richard left soon afterwards, as did Ronnie and her gang. By half past one, Bill was in his bed and fast asleep.

Granddad Bill dreamed he was back in the house he'd grown up in. Though it wasn't the summer, his brother Eddie was throwing a cricket ball. Bill, standing at the other end of the garden with a bat Eddie had bought for him, managed to hit it back, one in every three times.

'Come on, Billy-boy,' said Eddie. 'You can do better than that. Watch the ball. Watch the ball. Don't take your eyes off it until it makes contact with the bat.'

Eddie bowled another. This time Bill hit it out of the garden, right over the fence. It bounced on the turfed roof of next door's Anderson shelter.

'That'd be a six!' said Eddie. 'We'll make a cricketer of you yet.'

Eddie checked his watch. He was working the night watch in the centre of town.

'I better go and get ready.'

'Will you bowl for me again tomorrow?' Bill asked.

'You bet I will,' he said.

Then the air raid warning sounded. It had become such a familiar sound, Bill didn't panic to hear it any more. Still . . .

'Better get a move on, Billy,' Eddie told him.

Bill picked up his precious bat to take it into the shelter. Eddie would not be following Bill down there. He had work to do. He gently cuffed his little brother around the ear. It was the closest thing to affection they ever showed each other, those Benson lads, but Bill knew his brother loved him.

'I'll be back for you later,' Eddie said.

And that night, Eddie did come back for his little brother. When the all clear finally sounded, Bill climbed out of the Anderson shelter into the dusty air and found his big brother waiting there for him there in the garden. He was smiling his big friendly grin.

'I told you I'd come back for you, didn't I?' said Eddie. 'You ready now?'

'I think I am,' said Bill.

The two brothers joined hands and at last Bill followed Eddie into the light.

Chapter Eighty-Two

Bill

Bill passed away in the early hours of New Year's Day. It was Jacqui who found him when she went in to take him his morning tea. When he arrived, the emergency doctor assured her and Dave that Bill had left this life peacefully. Bill certainly looked at ease as he lay on the pillows. The lines seemed to have dropped from his face, leaving him looking twenty years younger than his age. There was a slight smile on his lips. He looked happy.

Everyone agreed it was the best way to go. In his sleep. In his own bed. There was no pain. Hours earlier, he'd been celebrating the end of the old year with his family: a year in which he'd seen his youngest granddaughter married. He'd lived his whole life surrounded by love and the very last of it was no exception. They would all miss him terribly. Especially the children. Dave kissed his father's forehead. Jacqui squeezed the old man's cold hands.

'We love you, Bill,' she said. 'Always will.'

In light of what had happened, Chelsea and Adam waited a couple of days to share their good news with the rest of the family. Chelsea wished she'd been able to share it with her granddad but, since that moment had passed, it seemed best to let people have a little while to properly mourn Bill before giving them something else to digest. There was too much high emotion floating around.

Indeed, when Jacqui heard the news, she immediately burst into tears. Then laughter. Ronnie, who was there in Jacqui's kitchen when Chelsea made the announcement, gave her little sister a big bear hug.

'I knew it!' she said. 'I knew it when you didn't want to go clubbing on your hen night.'

'And I knew it when you swapped your wine for elderflower on New Year's Eve. Oh, Chelsea,' said Jacqui. 'This is the best news in the whole wide world.'

Chelsea smoothed the knitted dress she was wearing over her bump so that Jacqui and Ronnie could admire her progress.

Jack was slightly nonplussed.

'You will always be a little brother,' Lily told Jack. 'But I am going to be somebody's *big* sister.'

Annabel had, of course, let Jack know that he was in no way responsible for the broken china dog but in the New Year, when Lily came to visit, she and Jack did look through the films they had made in the hope of making some money on the big computer screen in Sophie's room. Sophie helped them to pick out the ones that might actually be worth sending in to *You've Been Framed* after all. On the surface of it, the clips were all fairly similar. Jack making his grand introductions, Lily counting 'a-one, a-two, a-three' followed by a blur of Jack flying across the room to bounce on Annabel's sofa.

What Jack and Lily didn't notice, but Sophie did, was what went on in the background of one of the shots. While Jack made an extra-long introduction, Leander came into the room behind him, silent as the cats he hated, and snaffled two mince pies from the plate on the coffee table. It was the way in which the Labrador went about his mission with such quiet efficiency that was especially funny. When Sophie zoomed in on that part of the frame that showed the dog, it was easy to see how he snuck a glance at Lily from the corner of his eye before attempting the grand theft.

'That's the one,' said Sophie.

'But my somersault is rubbish in that one,' Jack protested.

'I know. It's not the somersault that makes it funny.'

Sophie was right. A few months later, the clip was featured on *You've Been Framed*. The children shared the spoils between them, saving just a little to buy Leander a squeaky toy. He would rather have had another mince pie.

Chapter Eighty-Three

Chelsea

Seven months later, Chelsea was standing in the kitchen, watching Lily play in the garden with Hector, the puppy they'd promised her the previous bonfire night. Chelsea sipped a cup of herbal tea and considered how lucky she was.

Granddad Bill had left each of his grandchildren a surprisingly large amount of money. It had enabled Chelsea and Adam to keep going while Adam had turned down the job offer from Jarvis and Jones and instead made a go of starting his own practice. It was going well.

Chelsea's pregnancy too had been easy. She had expected all sorts of horrors – thanks largely to the things she had heard from Ronnie over the years – but none of them had come to pass. And now she was at forty weeks, the baby could come any day.

She and Adam had decided not to know the sex of the baby before it arrived. Ronnie was sure that Chelsea was carrying a girl. So was Annabel.

'You could name her after one of your sisters,' said Ronnie. 'And I think you know which one of your sisters I mean.'

Adam's mother and Jacqui were of a different opinion.

'It's a boy,' said Jacqui. 'You're carrying exactly the same as Ronnie did with Jack.'

'And as I did with Adam,' said Mrs Baxter.

'Whether it's a boy or a girl, it will be perfect,' said Adam.

'I want a little brother,' said Lily. 'Like Humfrey.'

Chelsea hoped Lily wouldn't be too disappointed if she got a sister instead.

Lily threw the ball into the air and Hector leaped to catch it before it hit the ground. He missed. The sound of Lily's laughter as she watched the puppy bounce just out of time with the rebounding ball made Chelsea's heart soar.

And then she felt a twinge. More than a twinge. An almighty squeeze deep inside. It was unmistakable. Not a Braxton Hicks but a real contraction. Baby Baxter Benson was coming.

Adam was just a couple of streets away, discussing a quote for the conversion of a house full of flats back into a single dwelling. He quickly made his apologies when he got Chelsea's text.

'Now!' was all it said.

As Adam headed home, he called his mother, who immediately got into her car and drove over to take care of Lily and Hector. Chelsea did her best to carry on through the cramps. Her overnight bag was already prepared. While she and Adam waited for Sally to arrive, Chelsea walked around the garden, panting and puffing and holding her back. Lily walked alongside her, panting in time.

At last, Sally rang the doorbell. There was barely time to say 'hello'. Chelsea's contractions seemed to be coming alarmingly fast. She squeezed her mother-in-law's hand and thanked her for taking over.

'You're doing great,' Sally assured her. 'Just try not to have it in the car!'

Chelsea wasn't sure she could promise that, though Adam broke numerous speed restrictions on the way to the hospital.

'You're going to get hundreds of tickets,' Chelsea warned him.

'It will be worth it,' Adam said.

Chapter Eighty-Four

Bill

Though Chelsea had been convinced that the baby's arrival was imminent, she was in labour for another four hours. It was enough time for Jacqui to get on a train from Coventry and come to London. She arrived at the maternity ward just in time for the birth of her third grandson.

Yes. Baby Benson Baxter was a boy. Just as Jacqui and Sally had predicted and Lily had wished for. He weighed in at seven pounds eight ounces. He was perfect. Chelsea could only gaze in slightly dazed awe as the maternity nurse placed him in her arms. Adam sat beside her. His eyes were glittering with happy tears. He touched each of his new son's tiny fingers and counted his ten little toes. The baby already had a wisp of dark hair, which curled into a miniature quiff.

When Dave first saw his new grandson later that very same day, he nicknamed him Elvis, as a result of the hairdo. Lily declared that she wanted him to be called George, after the prince she still intended to marry some day. Sally thought the baby looked like an Edward. Jacqui suggested James. But really, there was only one possible name for him. Adam and Chelsea had discussed the possibilities throughout her pregnancy but they kept coming back to just one name should the baby be a boy.

William, which would, of course, be shortened to Bill.

Two months later, Adam and Chelsea took their new addition to be christened in the church where they had married. Father Malcolm was delighted to do the honours. And as if to confirm that he was happy with his new moniker, as the christening ceremony ended, Baby Bill let out a tremendous burp.

ACKNOWLEDGMENTS

Well, here I am at the end of my twentieth Manby novel, marking two decades with the fabulous team at Hodder and Stoughton! Hooray!

This time, special thanks are due to not one but *two* editors: Francesca Best and Emily Kitchin. Thank you both for your kind words and insightful notes. Thanks also to Lucy Upton, Eleni Lawrence and Jenni Leech for all their hard work in promoting the 'Proper Family' series. And to copy-editor Nicky Jeanes for catching my spelling mistakes.

Thanks as ever to Antony Harwood and James Macdonald Lockhart for taking care of the business side. I'm also very grateful to Anna Jarota for brokering the Benson family translation into French. *Je suis* delighted.

Thank you, Victoria Routledge, Alex Potter, Michele Gorman, Bernie Strachan, Lauren Henderson and Serena Mackesy for the writerly advice and the occasional kick up the arse.

Thanks Mum and Dad and Kate and Lee for your endless support and encouragement. Thank you especially to my nephews Lukas and Harrison for giving me some of Jack's best lines. And, last but not least, thank you once again to Mark, who inspires all my best romantic heroes . . . I couldn't have done this without you.

If you liked *A Wedding at Christmas*, catch up with the first three hilarious instalments following the lives of the Benson family and their friends:

Chrissie Manby

A PROPER FAMILY HOLIDAY

Could you survive a week-long holiday with your entire family? Newly single magazine journalist Chelsea Benson can't think of anything worse.

Your grubby small nephew torpedoing any chance of romance with the dishy guy you met on the plane . . .

Your eighty-five-year-old granddad chatting up ladies at the hotel bar . . .

Getting nothing but sarcastic comments from your older sister, who's always been the family favourite . . .

And all this is before your parents drop their bombshell.

Is a week enough time for the Bensons to put their differences aside and have some fun? Or is this their last ever proper family holiday?

Out now in paperback and ebook.

Chrissie Manby

A PROPER FAMILY CHRISTMAS

Take one Queen Bee: Annabel Buchanan, with a perfect house in the country, a rich husband and a beautiful daughter, Izzy . . .

. . . and one large, loud family: the Bensons.

What happens when their worlds collide?

When Izzy suddenly falls dangerously ill, adoptee Annabel has to track down her biological family to see if they can help her daughter. But can she see past the Bensons' brash exteriors to the warm, loving people they are at heart?

With December just around the corner, is it too much to hope that the Bensons and the Buchanans can have a proper family Christmas?

Out now in paperback and ebook.

Chrissie Manby

A PROPER FAMILY ADVENTURE

Could you spend two weeks at sea with your family?

Thanks to an unexpected windfall, the Bensons are treating themselves to a luxury cruise. With stop-offs in Barcelona, Rome and Marseilles, plus constant entertainment onboard, it's a dream come true . . . Or is it? Last time Chelsea Benson went on holiday with this lot she nearly went crazy.

Her mum and sister are convinced Chelsea's boyfriend Adam will propose on the ship. Chelsea's sure he won't, but she can't help feeling butterflies as they set sail. Is Adam going to pop the question, or will the only thing to pop be Chelsea's ego?

Out now in paperback and ebook.